Praise

"Wow!! Finished this book in a day it was so good I absolutely could not put it down. There were so many beautifully written characters and the story was amazing. This one had my heart from the beginning and had me rooting for the characters. This book is an absolute must read and I am so excited to read more from this author ♥"~ Mary M., Goodreads

"Really well written - the ultimate later life love story with more." ~ P., Goodreads

"Sweet & funny. I enjoyed the banter & the feel good moments. Family both blood & non portrayed beautifully. Entertaining indeed!" ~ Bec, Goodreads

"The song references are spot on throughout this page turner. John is a perfect mixture of a tough military man with a big heart and a soft side. ... This is a must read and leaves you feeling so good about people and proud of our military." ~ Carol H., Goodreads (Faking it with the Green Beret)

"Faking it with the Green Beret provides feels, enlightens, entertains and is good for the soul." ~ Cheryl, Goodreads (Faking it with the Green Beret)

"In this touching, at times heartbreaking as well as heartwarming story, the reader gets a chance to see these two seemingly opposites, be perfect for each other." ~ Yvonne C, Goodreads (Faking it with the Green Beret)

Not Faking it with the Colonel

A Sweet Faking It Romantic Comedy

Tracy Brody

Not Faking it with the Colonel

ISBN: 978-1-952187-13-1

First Edition

Also available as an ebook

ISBN: 978-1-952187-12-4

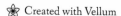 Created with Vellum

In memory of Betty Link and Bethann Standiford

Important note to readers

Dear Reader,

This is a sweet-with-some-heat book with no detailed sex scenes on the pages. I've heard from readers saying they've read enough sex scenes to last a lifetime. However, I know many readers can take the heat and would feel cheated *not* to see what happens. I get that! So, I'm giving **you** the option to read the tastefully steamy love scene if you'd like. It's free and accessible at Https://BookHip.com/LNWFQXR It's time to read it when you see **Open the bedroom door** at the end of Chapter 18.

I love that this later-in-life couple enjoys a mutually satisfying relationship in bed (and other places) but the choice to read the details is yours. And if you choose not to, you can use your imagination. 🌑

Chapter One

"Do you have an explanation I can give the general?" Colonel Graham Holmstrom addressed Captain John Bryson.

"I do. But you aren't going to like it." Bryson lowered his oversized frame into the chair across from Graham's desk.

"I didn't expect I would. Does it involve Mateo?"

Bryson nodded. "It hasn't been a seamless transition. He's openly questioning the reason you moved him to my team and made comments that border on insubordination. That's what led to today's altercation with Cruz during our lunch break."

It wasn't uncommon for Graham's Green Berets to occasionally butt heads with their teammates, but it took place on the training compound. General McKittrick witnessed it. Not a good look.

"Elaborate," he ordered.

Bryson shifted his gaze and rested his forearms on his thighs before resuming eye contact. "Mateo thinks you moved him so he'd deploy earlier—because you're interested in his wife."

"What?" That was absurd. Or *should* be. However, with the history of the unit's prior two commanders, trust issues still lingered in 3rd Group. Graham had picked up on some hostility from Mateo towards him but thought it was due to transferring him to a different team.

"Someone said they'd seen you with Michelle and buying her dinner. Rumors got back to Mateo."

Let no good deed go unpunished. Graham sighed. "I was at the grill on post waiting for my food. She was there with their son and had forgotten her debit card. I recognized her, and, since she didn't have enough cash to pay for her order, I gave her ten dollars to cover it." He would have done the same for the wife of any man under his command. Except Michelle wasn't *any* wife. On Mateo's last deployment, she'd been sleeping with Colonel Thomsen, the commander of 3rd Group, whom Graham had replaced.

It didn't matter if Mateo confronted his wife about this rumor. He wasn't likely to believe it was an innocent encounter. And Graham trying to explain would only make them both look guilty.

"Cruz told him he had it all wrong, but with the situation being what it is and Cruz being single, it didn't carry much weight," Bryson continued. "Mateo claimed there are others in the unit who are concerned there could be a three-peat of conduct unbecoming."

"With *me* this time." This was worse than Graham feared. Men under his command needed to trust their leader had their backs. "Any thoughts on what would set their minds at ease?"

"Maybe if you got remarried," Bryson cracked—except, for once, he wasn't grinning.

Graham waited for the punch line. "Are you serious?"

Bryson shrugged. "Traditionally, the Army expects their officers to be married. I used to get that Why-aren't-you-married-yet-Bryson? question all the time. Especially from McKittrick."

Graham had gotten some of those remarks from the general recently as well. Not quite as direct, but the general had dropped hints regarding his wife pulling double duty with the unit's Family Readiness Group after Bethann's passing. And in discussing plans for the unit's upcoming military ball, McKittrick mentioned Graham needing a date, not once, but twice.

"Send Mateo and Cruz to see me."

By addressing both, maybe he could squelch any rumors and doubts about his leadership.

"The captain said you wanted to see us, sir." Cruz stood in Graham's doorway, projecting a calm demeanor despite being ordered to report to his commanding officer. In comparison, Mateo's expression resembled a man awaiting sentencing.

"I'd like an explanation of what happened between you two today," Graham ordered.

"I said something out of line and provoked him," Cruz immediately offered up. "We're all good now."

The way Mateo's eyes flicked in Cruz's direction told Graham that his teammate just covered for him, or at least he had his back. That was a good thing. "Is that all that happened?" He focused on Mateo.

"Yes, sir. We're good." A hint of hostility lingered in Mateo's tone.

"Your team deploys in seven months. I need you all to operate like a cohesive machine well before then. Is that understood?"

"Yes, sir!" The pair said in unison.

"Cruz, you're dismissed."

Cruz cut his gaze toward Mateo ever so slightly. "It won't happen again, sir."

Mateo's posture stiffened. He stared past Graham as Cruz departed.

"My understanding from Captain Bryson is there's a rumor about your wife that prompted today's altercation."

Mateo didn't speak, but his jaw shifted. He shot Graham a cold, dark glance.

"Whatever your issues are with your wife, they cannot affect the team. If you can't resolve them, you need to make a decision. If you need a permanent change of station, where you can get a fresh start, that can be arranged. Have you thought about 7th Group?" Graham offered the young soldier an out.

Mateo sucked in a breath. "We bought a house after I made it through selection and was assigned here at Liberty. Michelle's sister takes care of our son while we work. It's the best childcare option we have. Her sister has three kids and depends on that income."

That explained their reasons for staying. Word of what happened between his wife and Colonel Thomsen at the military ball had likely spread through the tight-knit Special Ops community. Even though nearly two years had passed, it could impede getting a fresh start in units at other bases.

"I can appreciate your dedication to family." It was Graham's top priority too. "However—"

"I don't need interference from you when it comes to my family, *sir*."

"Noted. However, from what I observed at the grill the night she didn't have the means to pay for her order, your wife may be struggling to feel part of the unit. Unfortunately, my wife isn't alive to support her through this, but I could help out yours by giving her the cash she was short. Regardless of whatever rumors you may have heard, I moved you to Bryson's team to help you—and her. Bryson's fiancée is already plugging in with the Family Readiness Group. A new FRG might be beneficial support."

Mateo's demeanor relaxed a notch, and his gaze darted around Graham's office as he contemplated this information.

"What I can't have is discord among my men. You need to trust one another. And you all need to trust me."

"Understood. But . . ."

Graham cringed inwardly at the word and Mateo's hesitation. "Yes?"

"Considering what happened with Boatman and Thomsen, I'm not the only one on the teams concerned about their wives with you being alone now. We know guys have needs, and our wives do too. We're gone a lot and . . ."

"You do not need to be concerned about me repeating their actions." Having his integrity and character questioned made bile rise in Graham's throat, but he understood where these men were coming from, especially in light of former command. He needed to prove they could trust him. But how?

After dismissing Mateo, Graham tried to wrap his brain around the situation and evaluate his options. There weren't any good ones. He'd been brought in to rebuild trust between the boots-on-the-ground men and command. Not an easy assignment when everyone in the unit knew *both* colonels proceeding him had slept with wives of men under their command.

Mateo had given his wife a second chance. After Graham accepted the new command and moved here, Bethann had tried to get Michelle to reengage with the Family Readiness Group. But the other women in the unit hadn't been as forgiving as Mateo. With Bethann's sudden death, General McKittrick's wife had taken over Bethann's role with the FRG. It didn't surprise Graham that the general's wife hadn't gone out of her way to support a woman whose actions raised a red flag about the general's leadership.

Not only had Graham's world been turned upside down by losing his wife, but now it looked like the headway they'd made together those first few months here had been wiped out. Even taken a leap backward.

McKittrick motioned for Graham to enter his office. "Did you talk to Bryson?"

"I did. I also spoke with Cruz and Mateo."

"Did Mateo initiate the scuffle?"

"He did." Graham expected this might be Mateo's last strike with McKittrick rather than wait for a third.

"Is everything resolved?"

"Not exactly."

"Is Mateo not integrating onto Bryson's team?"

"That wasn't the issue. Cruz actually had his back. Mateo heard a rumor about his wife."

"Don't tell me she's cheating on him again." The General pressed two fingers to his temple.

"No," Graham started.

"You can't be sure of that."

"In this case, I am. Because the rumor involved *me*." Better to put it out there since he had nothing to hide.

"You?"

"There's absolutely no truth to it. We happened to be at the grill on post at the same time and spoke to each other."

"Even if it's false rumors, Mateo clearly doesn't trust his wife. He has to make a choice."

"Even though 7th Group would be a fresh start, he wants to stay here for family reasons."

"I can't have him deploy if his focus is here rather than on the mission."

"I agree. But I'd like to see how things shake out before we make a decision that can't be undone."

"I understand you wanting to give him another chance, but it's not just your neck on the line if this goes south. I'm responsible for what happens under my command." McKittrick remained silent for several seconds, then sighed long and loud. "And it goes beyond this incident with Mateo. With what happened previously in the unit, all eyes are on you. There could be more rumors—now that you're single. And sympathetic."

The general's tone turned Graham's blood cold. "Sir?"

"We'd discussed plans to keep you here beyond your initial assignment for continuity, but we need to look at posting options for you."

Graham had made plenty of moves throughout his career. While he'd never minded it, the idea of leaving Fort Liberty and starting over again on his own dredged up a fresh wave of grief. He'd always had Bethann at his side. And for years, the kids.

When Graham was offered command of the elite Green Beret unit, it had been a no-brainer decision to return to Fort Bragg, now renamed Fort Liberty. His daughter and her husband were already here and would be long-term since his son-in-law served in 3rd Group. Then, his son chose the 82nd Airborne, also based here at Liberty. Having the family all based at the same post had been a miracle and a blessing.

He also loved this posting. In large part because of the

caliber of men he commanded. "What other alternatives are there?" Graham asked.

"Where would you like to go? Vincenza? South Korea? Back to Fort Lewis?"

No. No! And no. His son had just returned from his first overseas deployment. Graham didn't want to be across the country, much less an ocean, while they were still trying to find a new normal without Bethann. Outside of an opportunity with USSOCOM at MacDill in Florida, he wanted to stay with his family here at Fort Liberty. Joint Special Ops Command was here and a good fit. He also hoped to utilize his decades of experience by teaching and developing the next generation of problem solvers through the JFK Special Warfare Center and School eventually. That both were here at Liberty and he wouldn't have to relocate, other than down the street, made it worth a shot. "JSOC or Swick."

"Don't we all. Those slots tend to be invitation only."

"What options keep me here? In my current position."

McKittrick drummed his fingers on his desk. "Have you thought about getting remarried?"

"I, uh, haven't even thought about dating." First, Bryson, and now the general with the same outlandish suggestion? He needed to get Mateo and any other men in his unit with doubts to trust him. Would marriage lessen their concerns when both the prior commanders were married and still messed around with the wives of men under their command?

"I understand the first year's the hardest, but it's been over a year and a half since Bethann died," McKittrick said.

"It's not like you hit a period of time and things magically get better." The first six months had been crushing. It was getting better, but the grief still came in waves, like with each milestone. First birthdays—his, hers, the kids. Their anniversary. Every holiday. He'd made a brief appearance at last year's military ball—alone. That had been harder than he expected.

"I hand-picked you to replace Thomsen because, with your wife at your side, I knew you had the integrity to restore trust between command and the men carrying out the mission. This garrison needs not only a strong man at the helm but one with an equally strong wife at his side. And that's no longer you. This whole situation isn't fair, but a pretty new wife could alleviate concerns. Let the men focus on their missions rather than worry about their wives back on post with their widowed commander, who's younger and considered more attractive than your predecessors," McKittrick smiled like a salesman about to close a deal. "I can't make it an order. However, for the good of the unit, it's worth considering."

"I don't think anybody will buy it if I suddenly turn up married. It could make things worse." Like he was covering up something. Not to mention how his kids would react.

"Of course not. Though, people would see you together while dating. A proposal at this year's ball would be a nice switch from the drama of the past."

"The ball is in less than four months." Graham hadn't even come to grips with the idea of dating, and the general had him publicly proposing marriage 'for the good of the unit?'

"And Bryson's team deploys in seven. You want to give Mateo a chance to stay? This is *your* chance."

For a man to make it through the grueling selection process to become a Green Beret, getting bounced from the team because of his wife's actions could be as hard a blow as her infidelity. It could well end the marriage they were trying to save.

Recalling the innocent face of Mateo's preschool-age son,

Graham didn't want to play even a small part in the boy growing up without his father regularly in his life. However, Graham's options seemed limited to finding a new wife or bouncing Mateo. Neither of which he was ready to do. Especially since transferring Mateo might be like putting a Band-Aid on a gunshot wound.

Chapter Two

AFTER THE DING from the incoming message tone assigned to her daughter, Piper, Erin picked up the phone to see the reply to her earlier text.

ETA 5 minutes.

"You two be nice to Piper. She'll want to pet you," Erin said as if the two cats understood her. As long-term pet-sitting gigs went, this was an easy one. Feed them and change their litter boxes and the cats typically ignored her, except for the occasional rub against her leg or foot.

A few minutes later, headlights slowly approached. Piper parked her SUV out front.

Erin stepped outside. "Hey, sweetie." She embraced her youngest daughter.

Piper hugged her back longer than usual. "I've missed you."

The tightness in Piper's smile pulled at Erin's heart. "Can I help you carry anything in?"

"I've just got the one bag." Piper studied the parked cars

and exterior of the older condos as the hatch lifted, and she grabbed her duffle bag.

Erin led her inside, making sure neither cat snuck out.

"Oh," Piper crooned, setting down the duffle. She dropped to her knees and held out a hand to the cats.

"The yellow tabby is Tink." The larger cat studied Piper for a long moment before edging close enough for Piper to scratch behind her ears.

"Like an Army tank?"

"Tink. Short for Tinkerbell. She even has a green collar with bells on it. I switched it out because it gets annoying when she and Smokey engage in a game of chase at seven in the morning."

"Maybe they're on Army time instead of our night owl clock." Piper sat cross-legged on the floor and coaxed Tink closer. "Were their owners able to get you any connections with Special Forces guys?"

"No. They're in a medical unit. They said there's a bar called Jumpy's that's known for being a hangout for the Spec Ops guys. Can you see me hanging out at a bar at my age, offering to buy drinks for guys in their twenties and thirties? 'Hi, handsome. Can I pick your brain, or will you invite me to shadow you for a few days of training for research for the TV series I'm writing?'" That hadn't been picked up by a studio yet. Which meant she had zero credibility.

Smokey ventured closer to Piper. It'd taken three days after Erin moved in before Smokey didn't run from the room every time she got near. Piper was clearly the cat whisperer in the family.

"It could happen. You have a way of connecting with people."

"I'm hoping I'll make a connection at the USO on base. I volunteered at a homecoming for the 82nd Airborne two weeks ago. One of the wives I talked with seemed receptive to introducing me to her husband, but I want to give him a few weeks home before I reach out. I have five more months here, though I hope it won't take that long. My former student, Ian, says his boss is already talking to some actors to gauge interest. If we can get a big name attached, it would increase the chances of HBO, Netflix, Showtime, or Amazon picking up the series."

"That's all great." Piper stroked Tink's fur, not meeting Erin's gaze.

"Are you nervous about your year abroad?" It was a big step.

"No. Well, a little. Dad and Madison have been texting about you all coming over for Christmas and traveling around Spain."

"All? As in together?" Their divorce was amicable, as divorces go, but not *that* amicable.

"Yeah. Madison brought up how her friend's parents got back together after spending time doing stuff for her wedding. She wanted me to bring up the idea of a joint trip."

Erin patted the space beside her on the sofa and waited for Piper to join her. "Madison hasn't been home for longer than a two-week stretch between school and moving to Austin after graduation. She hadn't seen how bad it'd gotten before we separated. He's your dad, and it's not your place to tell her. She still thinks the car accident was because a deer ran out in front of him."

"What? You never told her?"

"He asked me not to and said *he* would 'handle it.'" There may have been a deer, but that wasn't the sole factor, and the police officer knew it. Why would Madison suspect her father of being over the legal alcohol limit for driving at one-thirty on a Sunday afternoon?

"She thought maybe you could try counseling again."

"Honey, you know I went. He came once." And got all defensive. "The next week, he had business meetings scheduled and couldn't make it." AKA wouldn't go. "And the same too-busy scenario played out the next week." She'd continued to go and was in a better place thanks to over a year of therapy.

"Maybe he'd go now."

"It could be beneficial if he went, but as for us doing joint counseling, that's not going to happen."

Piper nodded, though a few tears still escaped. "If I had—"

"No. It's not your or Madison's fault." And not entirely Phil's either. Erin accepted her share of the blame.

"But if he stopped drinking?"

"There was a lot more to our problems." She also doubted he'd stopped.

"The financial stuff?" Piper's voice dropped.

"I wasn't happy that he liquified our savings without telling me when the business deal stalled. But we had other problems and suppressed a lot of things rather than communicate and work them out. For years, I didn't stand up for what I wanted and wasn't helping the situation with my attitude. After the car accident, I couldn't pretend or be complicit by being silent anymore. Next time, he might seriously hurt himself—or some innocent person. I'm working on me, and I like myself better now. I can't go back to the way things were."

"But you're having to live in somebody else's little condo—"

"That's my choice. It works well with being here since it's temporary. I'm tutoring seven students for finals and the SAT. I'll teach the summer session at Fayetteville Tech, then online this fall semester while I'm at the beach writing scripts."

Even if Phil found a buyer for the commercial property he acquired right before COVID hit, the carrying costs while it sat undeveloped had drained all their assets. He'd used the home equity line to pay his employees, and since he had no net income on paper, she got no alimony. Fortunately, money for Piper's college was in a 529 Plan, since it looked like Phil's commercial development project might never come to fruition.

"Are you going to move to California if the TV series gets picked up?"

"If that's what I have to do, I will. I may not need to be where the studio films. They may even shoot here in North Carolina or in Georgia."

"That's good." Piper managed a weak smile.

"And if Dad comes to Spain for Christmas, I can come over Thanksgiving or spring break. His plans may change."

Piper rolled her eyes and nodded. "Yeah, he'll probably have some deal at work come up."

Erin didn't mention he probably didn't have the funds to travel overseas. At least pet sitting for the deployed soldiers cut her rent to half of what she'd be paying for an apartment. If her series did get picked up by a studio, and she got to write for it, it would go a long way toward rebuilding some retirement savings. "I only need a few weeks' notice to get a ticket if he can't come."

"He keeps saying, 'Mom is going to marry some widowed two-star general or divorced Special Forces guy now that she left me.'"

Erin laughed, despite the question in Piper's voice. "Right. Eventually, I may date, but right now, the idea of getting married again is not a consideration. The only widowed generals I know are the fake friend requests on social media. Half the time, they don't use the right first name of the real military officer they're pretending to be, or they spell it wrong. And it only takes a minute to find a picture of the real general with his wife. Then there's the 'I'm an honest man looking for a kind-hearted woman' in their bio. Or commenting on some old post, saying they enjoyed what I shared and sent me a friend request, but it didn't go through. Would I add them? Seriously?"

"I can't believe anyone falls for those scammers."

"You'd think everyone would be suspicious of those random requests by now," Erin agreed. However, her friend Cyndi had spent weeks messaging with a man who'd sent a random friend request. After he sent Cyndi a gift, she'd reciprocated with a more extravagant one. Once her kids found out about her online boyfriend, they ran a search using his profile picture and found it was from a stock photo site. Her friend had been so embarrassed at falling for it. Erin knew better. "People get lonely and want to believe it's real."

"What about you? Aren't you lonely?"

"I don't have a network of friends here like I did in Charlotte, but with teaching, tutoring, writing, and volunteering, I keep busy and interact with a lot of people. I like the freedom and independence to make decisions without having to get approval." And didn't need another man giving her orders. "I'm going to live at the beach for four months."

"In the winter."

"Still, it's the beach. I finally have a real shot at screenwriting for this series. It's what I've dreamed about for over a decade and want more than teaching creative writing or how to write a fabulous essay for the SATs. Now's the time to pursue my dream—before I'm chasing grandbabies."

"Don't look at me for that. I haven't had a date in six months."

"Maybe you'll meet some special guy in Spain." She tried

to sound excited, though her chest ached at the idea of her daughter and potential future grandchildren living overseas where she'd rarely see them. Madison had only been home once in the past year, partly due to the awkwardness of the divorce. "I thought we'd watch a movie tonight, and tomorrow we can go shopping for anything you need for your trip. And you're helping me volunteer at the USO's bowling night."

"Are you trying to set me up with a soldier?"

"I just thought it would be fun for you to see what I do." Piper had a way better shot at meeting a single soldier her age than Erin did. Though she wasn't looking for a romantic hookup, just the right person to get her access to a Special Ops team for a day or two.

Chapter Three

GRAHAM TOOK a breath before exiting his car at his daughter and son-in-law's house on post Sunday night. McKittrick couldn't order Graham to date or marry, but he could most definitely get him transferred to a new post. And he had not figured out an alternative around the general's ultimatum.

His daughter, Megan, and son Jace's wife, Alex, divided Bethann's jewelry and helped him pack Bethann's clothes to donate months ago. The past two days, he'd walked around the house, taking in Bethann's lingering presence. Her decorative touches made any standard Army base housing into a home. Shelves filled with family photo albums and books she loved to read. A kitchen stocked with the gourmet cookware they'd bought when they were based in Vincenza, Italy.

He carried the box of china and the store-bought chocolate cake to the door. It wasn't the same as Bethann's famous Texas sheet cake. With his hands full, he rang the bell with a knuckle.

Reece opened the door. "Let me take that for you." His son-in-law took the heavy cardboard box.

Graham inhaled the aroma of freshly baked yeast rolls. A

pleasant rush of emotion gripped him, walking into the small kitchen filled with the people he loved most.

"What's this?" Megan asked when Reece set the large cardboard box on the kitchen table.

"Six place settings of our wedding china. I thought we'd use it for our family dinner tonight. Mom would want you to have it." He swallowed the lump in his throat.

"Thanks, Dad." Emotion choked Megan's voice.

"There are copies of her favorite recipes for you and Alex."

Megan put away the plates on the counter and began unwrapping the china. Reece set a platter laden with pork tenderloin and vegetables on the table, along with a basket of yeast rolls. It was like old times, except for the vacant seat.

Graham finished a second helping. "That was every bit as good as your mom's."

"Not quite. She had the magic touch. You and Jace both look like you've lost weight," Megan added.

"Maybe." These days, Graham usually picked up a sandwich or salad. Rather than an evening walk with Bethann, he'd added a run to his routine to fill the quiet evenings.

"You weren't kidding about eating chicken at least three times a week while deployed. Better than an MRE, but not by much." Jace slathered honey butter on another yeast roll.

"With Jace home, I was thinking we could resume regular family dinners," Megan said.

"I'd be happy to take turns hosting," Alex offered.

Less than two years apart in age, Megan and Jace had always been close, supporting each other and Bethann through their many moves and Graham's five deployments. He'd missed so much time with them early in his career that when they moved here, Bethann had instituted family dinner nights. They'd stopped after her death.

"I'm in. It would make your mother happy if we continued the tradition. I'll even take a turn hosting. Grill some steaks or ribs. Not chicken—for a while." Graham grinned at Jace.

"Back to doing them every other week, or is that too much?" Megan cleared dishes from the table.

"I'm certainly free." Which may be why Megan suggested it. She'd invited him to dinner several times while Jace was deployed, but he didn't want to infringe on her and Reece. But now . . . "Actually, there's something I need to tell you. There's a strong possibility that I will be transferred after my initial assignment here ends."

"I thought General McKittrick planned to keep you in command." The I-don't-like-the-sound-of-this in Megan's tone was just like her mother.

"Well, some things have changed with your mother's death."

"You don't want to be here without her?" Megan asked softly.

"I want to be here *more* than ever. To be near you all. But I may not have a choice. I don't know how much you know about Colonel Thomsen, who had command before me."

Reece snorted as he carried dishes to the sink. "Everybody in 3rd Group knows."

"What?" Alex asked wide-eyed.

"At our military ball two years ago," Reece launched into storyteller mode, "a guy on one of the teams just back from deployment noticed his wife had gone MIA and went looking for her. He found her and Thomsen in an empty conference room. They'd been screwing around while Mateo was deployed and decided to have a quickie at the ball. Only they weren't quick enough. Understandably, Mateo went a little nuts and pulled Thomsen off of his wife, decked him, then hauled him into the ballroom before he could get his pants up."

"You're kidding." Alex's mouth hung open.

"Trust me, I'm not." Reece met Graham's probably equally astonished gaze. "Mateo's wife rushed in, trying to pull him away from Thomsen. Next thing you know, Kiser's wife screamed 'You cheating son of a bitch'—at Thomsen—and gets a kick in."

"Kiser's wife was the one who also fooled around with Colonel Boatman, Thomsen's predecessor," Megan rolled her eyes and shook her head.

"They managed to keep the Boatman thing fairly quiet, but that was not happening with a few hundred witnesses," Reece went on. "Thomsen and his wife were off the base by noon on Monday. No way to keep him in command after losing the respect of every man in 3rd Group. Kiser was also out, and he filed for divorce this time. That was a military ball no one will forget or top."

Graham knew the gist of it, but . . . wow. No wonder McKittrick hadn't shared all the details.

"It certainly ruined the night." Megan loaded the last of the dishes into the washer.

"You were mad because the whole bru-ha-ha went down while the DJ played JT's 'Can't Stop the Feeling.'"

"It was the one song I requested. But what does Thomsen have to do with you transferring?" Megan asked.

"I got called into General McKittrick's office Friday."

"Is that like getting called into the principal's office?" Alex asked.

"Worse. Way worse," Jace answered before Graham.

"I hope you don't know from experience," Graham studied Jace.

"No. I've heard, though."

21

"General McKittrick witnessed an altercation between two men on Captain Bryson's team. I already knew that because of Boatman and Thomsen there's a trust issue between the teams and command, but apparently, there's a rumor floating around that had to do with Mateo's wife —and me."

Reece's mouth puckered as he took his place back at the table.

"There's no truth to it," Graham assured his family. "However, with me being single, McKittrick's afraid the teams could be distracted from their mission if they're worried about things back home."

"Do they not know you? You'd never sleep with someone else's wife, much less someone under your command," Megan went on the defensive.

"They were told they could trust Thomsen too. Instead, they're seeing a pattern of bad behavior." Rather than take it personally, Graham tried to view things from the men's perspective.

"Reece, can't you say something?" Megan pleaded.

"Honey, they might think I'm biased since your dad would never sleep with *my* wife. And it wouldn't be a good look for either of us," Reece said. "This is McKittrick covering his own six. If something remotely similar happened under his command again, he'd be out too. Mateo gave his wife a second chance, but he'll be watching her, especially since Kiser's wife screwed around with *both* prior commanders."

"I'm guessing they wouldn't transfer you to the 82nd or SOCOM," Jace said.

"They don't have a reason to bump Ayers from the 82nd. McKittrick pretty much laughed when I brought up SOCOM, JSOC, and Swick. He mentioned Vincenza and South Korea. Maybe back to Fort Lewis."

"They can't do that. We're planning to start a family soon. With Mom gone, I want you here." Tears glistened in Megan's eyes.

The idea of grandchildren, something he and Bethann had looked forward to, tugged at his gut. "I won't be gone permanently," he promised his daughter.

"We need to figure out what it would take to convince them to let you keep your command." Megan shifted to strategy mode.

"Probably castration," Reece cracked.

"No," Graham chuckled. Though that might be an easier option. "He did say if I were to get married, but that's—"

"Excuse me?" Megan collapsed against the back of her chair.

"If I were to get married before Bryson's team deploys in seven months, he'd keep me in my position here."

"Remarried? You're kidding." Megan stared at him in disbelief.

"I wish I were."

"Guess you just need to go to the post exchange and shop in the Army-issued wives department," Jace joked.

"Right." That'd be easier than dating again after nearly three decades. Except, finding a partner to share your life with didn't work that way.

"That doesn't make any sense," Reece said. "Being married didn't stop Boatman and Thomsen."

"Have you thought about the possibility of dating or getting remarried?" Megan's flat tone and blank expression revealed nothing of what was going through her head.

"Until this came up, I hadn't thought about dating, much less marriage." He'd anticipated encountering heavy resistance from both kids if he considered the idea so soon after losing their mother. And he couldn't blame them. "Maybe

23

eventually. When I'm ready, versus being ordered 'for the good of the team' and to cover a general's backside." He missed Bethann and the companionship. He wasn't opposed to dating and possibly marrying again—after they all had more time to grieve and accept the loss.

"I remember how you used to tell Mom that if anything happened to you, you wanted her to move on. Find someone who made her happy," Jace commented.

"That's different. *I* was the one deploying to danger zones." His gaze flicked over the scar on his left forearm. "Nothing was supposed to happen to her." His voice cracked, and the ache that had dulled, but not abated, since her death mushroomed in his chest.

It still seemed surreal. Bethann had a headache that morning. That wasn't unusual; she'd had migraines since he'd known her. But she'd collapsed while having lunch with friends. When Dianne Mahinis called to say they were taking Bethann to the hospital, he'd gone straight there.

The doctor told him the scan showed a major brain aneurysm had ruptured. He'd called it a silent killer.

Graham had been in a state of shock when he'd called Megan and Jace. They'd rushed to the hospital, where he'd broken the news to them. They'd barely had a chance to say their goodbyes before she'd died four hours later with Graham holding her hand.

"Mom would have told you the same thing if she'd had any idea. She wouldn't want you to transfer away from us and a job you love just to honor her memory. You've got half your life ahead of you. She'd want you happy," Jace stated with authority.

"Jace is right," Megan backed up her brother. "You should think about it."

Were they worried about his well-being? He was doing

okay. Other than his weekly golf round, he didn't get out much, but he wasn't totally a hermit. In his grief group, they gave repeated warnings to have realistic expectations and said particularly the first romantic connections after losing a spouse rarely lasted and could compound and lengthen the grief cycle. He wanted to avoid that mistake for himself, but there were worse mistakes he could make that could alienate his kids.

"What are the chances I'd find someone I'd want to share my life with and marry in a few months?"

"Zero—if you don't try," Jace challenged.

"He can't really expect you to be married in that short a time," Reese said. "If the teams saw you in a serious relationship, that *could* suppress concerns."

"I wouldn't even know where to start. I haven't dated anyone other than your mother in nearly three decades."

"I remember you saying you knew Mom was the one by your third date." Megan gave a dreamy sigh.

"We were nineteen. Now, I'm old and set in my ways."

"You aren't old-old." Jace grinned.

"You could join one of those dating sites for mature adults," Reece said.

"Don't you have to be over fifty for those?" Graham was close but not there yet.

"You could check out the older singles groups at church. Take ballroom dance lessons or join a bowling league. Or pickleball! That's big for people your age." Even Alex jumped on the bandwagon.

"What about your grief support group?" Jace asked. "Wasn't there some woman you knew who put out the interested vibes?"

"That was Major Jepson's widow. She invited me to have coffee after a meeting is all."

"Oh, she was interested," Megan said. "Though she might be engaged or married since she was dating five months after her husband was killed in action."

"Five months? Sounds a little desperate," Reece said. "I'd wait at least a year if anything happened to you."

"Thanks, honey," Megan said with false sweetness. "But it was way too soon after Mom died to be inviting you out then."

"I haven't seen her in a while." It would seem random to reach out now. Maribel Jepson was attractive. Having been married to a Special Ops soldier, she knew the life's hardships, even if Graham was no longer kicking in doors. However, she had come off as over-eager.

Maybe that wasn't a bad thing *should* he consider dating. He had not expected his kids to encourage him to date. The idea of a grandbaby gave him another big reason to stay here. But the timeline was unrealistic, even if he had known he wanted to marry Bethann in much less time than that.

"I'll think on it," he conceded. "And I promise I won't elope and then introduce you to my wife like Grandpa Warren did."

"Your dad and Linda eloped before you met her?" Alex asked.

"No. My dad and his *second* wife."

"He's been married three times?" Alex looked from Graham to Jace.

Graham held up a hand with four fingers extended.

"Four? You never told me that," Alex said to Jace.

"I wanted you to see my parents' long, loving relationship as my role model," Jace explained.

"Good call." Alex shook her head. "Your grandpa Warren seemed so charming and normal."

"He can be charming all right," Graham gave a wry laugh. "But he's not good at being alone. He and my mother split after my tenth birthday. For my eleventh birthday, he sent a card signed by him and his new wife. They'd only been dating a few months, and no one in the family had met her before they eloped."

"Wow. That *is* fast," Alex agreed.

"Too fast. Once the excitement waned, he discovered she was a little off. That marriage didn't even last a year. After that divorce, Dad came around again. My brother and I thought he and Mom might get back together. But Mom wasn't having any part of that after he bailed on her once already. He married wife number three about a year and a half later. Unfortunately, wife number three didn't want anything to do with Dad's past—including my brother and me. When we went to visit the summer after they were married, she put us in a day camp for one week. Then she sent Dad and us on a camping trip for a week."

"And she didn't come?" Megan asked.

"No. She went on a cruise with her parents and sister's family." Graham had never shared that with his kids.

Megan frowned. "She didn't want to be a mom?"

"She was at least ten years younger than him, but they never had kids." Graham hadn't witnessed her having any maternal traits. Not that his father exhibited a lot of paternal interest either.

His limited contact with his dad dwindled further after the visitation agreement ended when Graham turned eighteen. Other than attending Graham's West Point graduation and wedding and a few family funerals, they'd only seen each other a handful of times during that twenty-year marriage. Graham usually originated their occasional phone calls. "Once they split, he reached out and wanted to rebuild our relationship."

"He came before Christmas when I was nine or ten," Jace

said. "He brought gifts and told us all these wild stories. But it was like, *who are you?*"

His dad may have blamed his third ex-wife for his lack of involvement in his children's lives, but he'd made the choices based on his wants years before marrying her. That drove Graham to be a different kind of father. However, he hadn't anticipated when he'd enrolled at West Point that 9/11 would happen. Or how many times he'd be deployed or away for training.

Graham had done all he could to stay plugged in with his family—cards, letters, vacations together. Megan and Jace would never doubt how important they were to him. Even if he dated or eventually remarried, it wouldn't be to the detriment of his relationship with his kids.

"Dad's made an effort since then. Fortunately, Linda isn't like wife number three." While his dad was in Graham's life more the past decade, due to the missed years, trust issues, and complicated feelings toward his father kept them from having a close relationship.

"Weren't he and Linda together over four years before she agreed to marry him?" Megan asked.

Graham nodded. "I think he'd been asking her for a while and eventually wore her down." They'd passed the honeymoon stage of their relationship by that point and been through some tests, like Linda's bout with breast cancer. "At their ages, maybe this one won't end in divorce. And I can guarantee I won't get married to stay here." His father had married so he wouldn't be alone, which only brought him more heartache. Graham was smart enough not to repeat that mistake, nor would he repeat his predecessors' indiscretions.

Chapter Four

ERIN'S STUDENT waved to a camouflage-clad man making his way through the busy café.

"You did a great job implementing what we discussed last week," she said. "For next week's essay prompt, focus on eliminating word repetition. Find a synonym or other way to say it and combine sentences. It's better to keep it shorter and engaging than to say the same thing over and over."

"Thanks, Mrs. Downey." Garrick closed his laptop, and his father stepped over.

She tried to make out the unit patch, but his right shoulder was angled away from her.

"My wife said he's learned more from you in three weeks than this past semester in class."

"With tutoring, he's getting individual attention over trying to teach general concepts to thirty-five students at a time."

"You're seriously undercharging for your services and expertise."

"It's my way of supporting our military kids. I'm too old to enlist and go through basic training," she joked and summoned her nerve. "What unit are you with?"

"Sixteenth MP Brigade." He turned his shoulder so she could make out the patch on his sleeve. "You help Garrick get his scores up enough to get a college scholarship, and I'll let you off with a warning for any parking or speeding violations on base." He grinned as he spoke.

"Hopefully, I won't have to take you up on that. But can you connect me with any Special Forces units for some writing research I need to do?"

"Probably not. The Army keeps those guys hidden pretty well."

That was an understatement. "It was worth asking. I'll see you next week, Garrick. We'll be back at the library at our usual time. Thanks for meeting me here this afternoon."

After occupying a table for two hours, Erin went to the counter and ordered dinner.

When she returned to her seat, one of the two teen girls at the table next to her asked, "Do you tutor in math too?"

"You wouldn't want me to tutor you in anything beyond multiplication and division. I was no help to my daughters when they took geometry and calculus."

"I'm in calculus and barely have a B," the girl wearing an NC State T-shirt said.

"Bs are great. You can't get As in everything."

"Tell that to my parents."

Dining out alone was one of the more challenging adjustments of divorce. Usually, she took food home, or, like most solo diners, she read on her Kindle, checked email, or browsed through what her friends had posted on social media. Tonight, she people-watched as she ate, largely ignored by the high schoolers occupying most of the tables.

With the grill being on base, she scanned the soldiers in

uniform. Though it wasn't like she'd have the nerve to walk up and introduce herself if she recognized someone's Special Forces patch. She was far more likely to connect with someone at the USO facility. Volunteering at the center at different times and days and by working events, she hoped to connect with the right person to get her foot in the door. Observing a day or two of training would be ideal, but, if she could get a real-life operator to review the scripts, it could add authenticity. She had five more months to complete her mission: get an inside look at a Spec Ops team's dynamics. She needed to prove she could write credible military characters as a civilian—and a woman.

She studied the profile of a man in civilian attire as he filled his cup at the drink dispenser. There was something vaguely familiar about him, and, when he turned around, she immediately recognized him.

While she hadn't met or interacted with him at the 82nd Airborne's homecoming, she'd certainly noticed him. He'd been in uniform and too far away from the USO table she'd manned to make out his name or rank. This man had the muscled physique and confident posture she associated with the image of a Special Forces soldier, and the 82nd Airborne was just a rung under Special Forces. She guessed he was in his mid-forties, which could easily make him a first sergeant—the perfect rank to get her access.

She diverted her gaze when he turned and wandered in her direction carrying a food tray. It would be too obvious if she quickly cleared the trays the girls had left on the table, so she waited for him to move closer, then made eye contact. "I'm pretty sure they aren't coming back." Erin pointed to the table next to her before he could walk away. "They packed up their computers a few minutes ago."

"Thanks. I didn't realize it'd be this crowded on a

Thursday night." He set his food down, then cleared the trays left behind before he took the seat on the bench versus looking at the wall. Typical Spec Ops positioning.

"High school finals start next week, and the SAT is coming up. The grill has free Wi-Fi and good fries."

"Ah." He nodded, taking in the tables of teens before angling his body toward her a bit.

He had some gray at his temples and faint lines at the corner of his light blue eyes. The smile he gave her made her pulse race a bit faster. She'd always preferred the clean-shaven, short-hair look, and she'd cast him in her Special Ops series in a heartbeat.

"You look familiar."

Her pulse jumped another notch despite the gold band on his left ring finger. "Maybe I've tutored one of your kids."

"Mine are both out of college."

"Have you been in the USO recently? I volunteer there." She knew he hadn't been in the center when she was there because she would remember him coming in, but she decided to play it low-key.

"You were at the homecoming for the 82nd Airborne two weeks ago. I remember seeing you make sure soldiers got a proper welcome-home hug, even if they didn't have family there. Thank you for volunteering."

Heat crept up Erin's chest. He'd noticed her? "Is that your unit?" *Please say yes. Please say yes.*

"My son's unit. Jace is a first lieutenant. It was his first deployment."

She managed not to groan aloud at having her hopes shot down—again. It was a long shot, but maybe he could connect her with his son.

Pride showed on his handsome face. He also didn't tell her what unit *he* was in, but that didn't necessarily mean anything. However, there was a distinctive ring on his right hand.

"Is that a West Point class ring?" she asked.

"Yes." He turned it her way briefly. "I played baseball for the academy, though that was a few decades ago."

Attending West Point meant he was definitely not enlisted.

"How long have you volunteered at the USO?" he asked before taking a bite of his burger.

"Here? Only the past month. But I've volunteered at the Charlotte Center at the airport for over ten years."

"That's dedication. Thank you. What brought you to Fort Liberty then?"

"Work." And divorce.

"What kind of work do you do?"

"It's classified." She didn't expect the pleasant laugh he gave.

He wiped his mouth with a napkin. "That's supposed to be *my* line."

That was telling—and probably all he'd say. And she wouldn't ask since doing so could land her on a watch list or get her banned from base. That'd be the worst thing that could happen. "I teach creative writing, and I tutor."

"You had me going there for a minute." He gave her another kick-up-the-heartbeat smile. "Is your husband or other family in the service?"

"My ex is in real estate development, but my dad did ten years in the Army. He volunteers at the USO in Charlotte too. Before he started volunteering, I thought the USO only put on entertainment shows, which, trust me, no one will come for my singing and dancing. That's what I do to clear out the center at closing time."

He laughed again. "I doubt that would work."

The way he said that and smiled sent a rush of warmth through her. "You haven't heard me sing. I need to head out for a USO family function tonight. Maybe I'll see you at the USO or an event sometime."

"Thanks again for volunteering. It means a lot. I'm Graham." He held out a hand.

"Erin." She put her hand in his tanned one, probably staring into his eyes a little too long. Get a grip. He was fine-looking. He was also married. She didn't need some jealous military wife misinterpreting her intentions. She'd save that drama for the television series. With over fifty thousand troops based here, seeing him twice was a fluke. She probably wouldn't see him again in the next five months if she launched an all-out search mission.

Chapter Five

GRAHAM ARRIVED at Jace and Alex's for the Sunday night dinner somewhat more hopeful than two weeks ago. That his kids and their spouses wanted him to stay at Liberty meant a lot. There'd been no hiccups with Bryson's team, though it would take a lot more than merely smooth sailing for the general to change his mind and keep Graham in command beyond this initial assignment.

He made a point of interacting even more with the teams. Let the men get to know him personally to trust him as a leader and a man. He'd tackle this like any other mission— with thorough planning and accounting for multiple contingencies. While he hadn't ruled out dating, to find a woman and get to the point where the men and the general were comfortable before Bryson's team deployed in approximately six and a half months? He didn't see that happening.

Voices carried to him, so he opened the screen door. "Hello," he called out, noting the halt in conversation before Megan whispered something.

"Hey, Dad." Megan gave him a falsely bright smile, as did Alex, who took the potato salad and coleslaw from him.

"I'll put the burgers and dogs on." Jace picked up the platter of meat from the kitchen island.

"I'll join you." Graham sensed his dilemma would be the topic of conversation at some point tonight, but he didn't want it to be the sole focus.

The sizzle of meat soon accompanied the scent of applewood charcoal briquettes. While cooking, Jace shared some details and stories from his deployment with Graham and Reece.

Reece smoothly transitioned the conversation to baseball when Megan and Alex carried food and utensils to the patio table. A pattern both men learned from Graham. Their wives knew enough about the dangers of their jobs; they didn't need to hear specifics or about close calls.

They'd nearly finished eating as Alex passed the tea pitcher for a refill. Megan fixed her gaze on Graham from across the table.

"So, Dad, did you make any dating decisions?" She made an effort to sound casual.

"I'm still considering the possibility." After what Reece said, Graham wondered if merely dating someone might be sufficient to quell the concerns or provide some leeway in the deadline McKittrick mentioned. The general was fairly reasonable, and his wife had been Bethann's friend. Any romantic relationship would have to be visible to convince the men in the unit and General McKittrick there wouldn't be a threepeat of conduct unbecoming. "When I was picking up dinner at the grill on post, I decided I'd eat there rather than do carry-out. I did meet someone."

"You met someone?" Megan eyed him warily. "What does that mean?

"I recognized a USO volunteer from Jace's homecoming

reception. I had a conversation with her. It wasn't as hard as I feared it might be."

"That's a—start." His son smirked.

"And she's single?" Megan asked.

"I think so. She mentioned an ex and wasn't wearing a wedding ring." After his dad's multiple divorces, he hoped he heard right that it was *an* ex, not exes.

"Did you ask her out?" Jace grinned.

"She had to go work a USO event before things got very far. I didn't get her contact information or last name. I realized later that I was still wearing my wedding band. She may have noticed because she commented on my West Point ring."

"Ah, rookie mistake." Reece nodded his head.

"I ate dinner at the grill a couple of times the past week in case she was there tutoring a student again." He'd taken his wedding ring off Monday before going. For something that he'd rarely given a second thought to for decades, he was keenly aware of the ring's absence now. "No luck, and I think finals wrapped up."

"Was she attractive?" Megan asked.

"I thought so. She also had a nice smile and sense of humor." He smiled, recalling her 'it's classified' comment. "She seemed outgoing. I noticed her hugging and talking to the single guys in your unit at the welcome home reception."

"I remember her," Alex said. "She was about your age, had shoulder-length, reddish-brown hair, and wearing a red USO polo shirt?"

"That's her. I, uh, checked out a few dating sites. I had no idea there were so many. I haven't signed up or anything." He hadn't found Erin on any of them. While he'd guessed Erin was close to his age, if she was over fifty, she might be on one of the dating sites he hadn't checked—or not looking to date.

"You know she volunteers at the USO. You could look for her there," Jace suggested.

"What are the chances she'd be working? It's not like I have a reason to keep showing up there. It could look like I'm stalking her."

"Just ask the center director when she's working or for her contact information. You're a colonel. They'll probably tell you. Sounds easier than trying to find her tutoring with the school year ending."

Leave it to Jace to make it sound simple.

"Whatever you do, don't set up social media accounts saying you're a widowed colonel and start friending or following or messaging women you don't know." Megan rolled her eyes.

"Amen to that," Alex added.

"Why's that?" Besides needing to keep a low profile in the Special Ops community, he had better things to spend his time on than social media.

"Because scammers set up fake accounts claiming to be some divorced or widowed military man, often with kids. They'll download pictures from soldiers' social media accounts, Wikipedia, and even the official Army profiles," Megan explained.

"I'm always *so tempted* to accept when they post pictures of flowers or a stuffed teddy bear. Not. Seriously, do you know any military guy who would do that?" Alex asked.

"Not even the Chair Force," Jace concurred.

"What do they get out of setting up fake accounts?" It seemed like a waste of time to Graham.

"I guess to convince some woman they're romantically interested enough for them to send money and gifts. The FRG constantly sends warnings. Though, if we're married to military hunks, we aren't the right target audience." Megan ran a hand over Reece's arm. "Single women thirty to eighty though . . ."

"Do any of them fall for it?" Sending care packages to deployed soldiers was one thing, but Graham would discipline any of his soldiers who scammed people for money.

"Apparently. If scammers contact one to two hundred people a week and get even five to fall for it, it can be a big payday in some poverty-stricken countries," Reece pointed out.

"Where do they find that many people?" Graham asked.

Alex smiled subtly. "They mine your contacts. Kind of like networking, but in a less personal way."

"This is a whole new world for me."

"Don't settle for the first woman you meet. And remember, you promised no eloping before we meet her." Megan laughed, but her eyes held a warning.

"I won't," he promised. He knew firsthand how that could alienate his kids.

AFTER THIS MORNING'S BRIEFING, General McKittrick had made a point of asking Graham how things were going in his personal life. A not-so-subtle reminder that the clock was ticking and every day mattered.

Graham left his office for a late lunch and headed to the USO. He hoped to arrive just before the shift change, which could double his remote chance of finding Erin there. Two volunteers were at the desk when he walked in just before thirteen hundred hours. That neither were Erin dampened his mood, even though he hadn't expected her to be there. Still, it would have been confirmation or a sign.

"Welcome, Colonel." The cheerful, balding volunteer greeted him.

"Is the director in?"

"He is. I'll get him for you." The volunteer rounded the desk and disappeared around the corner.

The director walked to the front a minute later. "Hello, Colonel. How can we help you today?"

"I wanted to pass along a compliment. My son is in the 82nd and just returned from deployment a few weeks ago. The USO had a strong presence at the homecoming. I appreciate all your volunteers did to make sure those without family present were welcomed home." Graham swallowed. "There was a volunteer there. I think her name was Erin."

"That'd be Erin Downey. She's a new volunteer here but has volunteered at the Charlotte Center for years. She's jumped right in working in the center and events. It's a shame she's only here for a few months."

Downey. Downey. He locked the name into his memory, only to have hope sucked out of him. "Oh. Why's that?"

"She's here temporarily doing research for a writing project."

"Do you know when she's scheduled to work? I didn't get to thank her personally that night." That wasn't quite a lie, even though he'd thanked her at the grill.

"She doesn't have a set schedule. She's been filling in when we're short-staffed—so a lot."

"Do you have her contact information?"

"I can't give that out, but if you want to write a note, we can leave it at the desk for her," the director offered.

"That's okay." He had no clue what he'd say, and he might waste a week or two waiting with no guarantee she'd get the note.

"She's really good about sharing our USO posts. You might try connecting with her on social media."

"I'm not on social media, but thanks again for all you do." While he now knew her last name, he left the USO feeling like he'd taken three swings and hadn't even hit a foul ball.

~

"KEARNS, YOU HAVE SOCIAL MEDIA ACCOUNTS?" Graham asked his unit's adjunct officer before shutting down for the day. He wasn't going to ask Megan about this after her warning.

"Yeah," Kearns answered, a question in his voice.

"Can you pull up the account for the USO here?"

"On which platform?"

Graham didn't know the difference. "Platform? Facebook, maybe."

"What is it you're looking for?"

"Is there a way to see who shared a post?" Isn't that what the director said?

"Sounds like Facebook." In seconds, Kearns had it pulled up and found the USO page. "Which post?"

"I don't know." Graham's chest and ears heated. "One shared by a woman named Erin Downey."

Kearns dropped his gaze, but not in time to hide the amused look on his face. He tapped on the tablet's screen. "Here you go." He handed Graham the tablet.

He squinted at the tiny picture next to the name. That was her. "How would I contact her?"

"Click on her picture. Just tap where it says 'message.'" The screen changed. "Only I don't think you want to do that from *my* account."

"Does she have an email listed?" That would be way easier.

"Let me see." He took back the tablet and scrolled through the information listed below her picture. "Not that I can see since we aren't friends."

Graham caught a glimpse of Work and Education titles. "Thanks. That'll be all."

"Yes, sir." Kearns closed the app, still grinning but not asking questions. Wise man.

AFTER EATING dinner at the grill again with no sign of Erin, Graham drove home, debating his options. What did he have to lose worse than his command here? According to stats shared in his grief support group, the first relationship after losing a spouse rarely lasted anyway. Asking her out could be a practice run to overcome the awkwardness of figuring out how to act on a first date again. And, if she said yes, he could brush up on his conversational skills.

Going through the initial steps to set up a Facebook account seemed simple enough—until he came to the daunting decision about adding a picture. Other than his Army headshot, he didn't have many pictures of just him. Cropping an image of him with Bethann didn't feel right, and when the kids did group selfies, he never knew where to look and typically ended up staring anywhere but the right place.

It was probably easier to add a picture later than take it off, so he added a few details before finding the Army and USO's pages.

Here goes nothing.

He clicked on Erin's picture next to her comment on a USO post. Her picture looked fairly recent, and in it, she had the same engaging smile he'd been drawn to when he'd seen her at the homecoming and the grill.

He'd heard the term Facebook stalking and wondered if he was crossing lines looking at the information she had listed. Work, education, and places she'd lived were innocuous enough. She didn't list her relationship status. He'd put widowed. She'd probably noticed his wedding ring, but he could explain. He sighed.

He clicked the message button, then read the notification that because they weren't "friends," the message could be delivered to her "other" box. What did that even mean? Probably like spam emails where she might not see it for a while—or ever.

It would be easier if Erin had an online dating profile, but he was not signing up for half-a-dozen sites to look for her. Why was dating today so complicated?

He tapped the screen to add Erin as a friend. *Request sent.* Now what? Rather than stare at the screen, he clicked on the TV to watch the Nationals game. It could be minutes, hours, or days—or longer—before he heard anything. Or maybe never.

Chapter Six

Erin spent a rainy Tuesday morning in the condo reviewing her students' practice SAT essays before tomorrow's sessions. After she finished, she opened her browser and went to the USO's online schedule. She signed up for a shift on Thursday, checked emails, then went to Facebook.

The notification of a friend request from *Graham* Holmstrom made her breath hitch in her lungs. It wasn't a common name, but what were the chances it'd be *the* Graham she'd met at the grill?

Slim to none.

She clicked anyway.

There was no profile picture. The account intro listed the US Army and West Point Military Academy, and for "Lives in" it said Fayetteville, NC instead of Damascus, Syria, which, for some reason, the accounts claiming to be military officers loved to list. It also said he was widowed. The Graham she'd met wore a wedding ring.

Things were spelled correctly, and there were no grammatical errors. However, there were also no posts and no friends she could see. Just another fake account. Maybe using a real Army officer's name.

The least they could have done was find a picture of the Graham she met to use for her viewing pleasure. A picture of him would attract gullible women. She did a web search for Graham Holmstrom which didn't result in a single hit.

The numerous friend requests and follows from accounts claiming to be military members she'd never met typically earned an immediate block, and she reported any account using the profile picture of a general—not that it typically did any good. She'd happily volunteer an hour a week if Facebook or Instagram would allow her to shut down the fake accounts, though the scammers would just set up another. And another. And yet another. Frustrating. Still, she left this request pending for now—just a day or two.

She had connected on social media with men in the aviation unit she'd supported, ones who were now sources for the aviation component of the proposed TV series. Occasionally, she'd been friended by someone she met while volunteering at the USO, though it was usually the wife of a soldier or a retiree, not a married officer. Of the real generals and command sergeant majors she'd met, not one had ever said "hit me up on my social media accounts." While she suspected some had accounts, they kept them private like the Special Forces guys did to protect their families.

She replied to a friend's comment on a post and sent happy birthday wishes to two friends from the notifications before clicking on the friend request again.

The Graham Holmstrom account had liked and followed the US Army and USO page. Of course, that could be where the account owner found her and could be sending friend requests to thousands of people. The timing was quite a coincidence, though.

Graham had mentioned kids. Wouldn't they show up as friends? Maybe not.

This was ridiculous. She knew better than to fall for a scam or waste time messaging some faker saying he liked her smile or eyes. She wasn't looking for love—just someone to help her get an inside look and feel for the life of a Special Ops soldier. Though she wasn't opposed to a little companionship with someone who was a better conversationalist than Tink or Smokey.

~

AFTER TALKING to Ian about some story ideas, she spent several hours working on her script. Then, Erin fed the cats before fixing a tuna melt sandwich for dinner.

"No, you already ate." She nudged Smokey off the table, then worked the Sudoku while eating. She lasted through cleaning the kitchen before checking Facebook.

The Graham Holmstrom account had replied to her comment on a week-old USO post. If it was one of those "I saw your beautiful smile and want to get to know you" comments, she was one hundred percent blocking the account.

Instead it said *Sent you a message.*

There was nothing in her inbox, but she navigated to Message Requests and found several in the spam folder from weeks ago. Half of those accounts were already deleted. Another from a Willaim Mark in Dubai simply said, "hi Erin!" Madison said bots sent a lot of these messages. But whoever set up the account didn't even spell William right. Delete.

In the *You May Know* folder were three messages. Two were several weeks old. Don't know you. Delete.

Delete. But the one from Graham Holmstrom she opened.

> Hi, Erin

She rolled her eyes, but the messages below made her pause before hitting delete.

> I enjoyed chatting with you last week.

> Graham unsent a message

> Graham unsent a message

> Sorry. I'm new to this and clearly have figured it ouy.

> Meant to say haven't figured this ouy

> Graham unsent a message

> out

> Maybe I should quit now.

This was too funny not to be real. But, she needed proof. She accepted the friend request to see if it gave her access to see more on his page since she could always block it.

Still no picture, no friends, and no posts. That was slightly better than a picture of him leaning against a Maserati, a selfie in the car, or a bunch of reposts and cheesy-saying memes.

> I enjoyed meeting you too. What was the name of the place where we had dinner?

She messaged back. The real Graham would know, but a

scammer either wouldn't answer, knowing he was busted, or claim he didn't remember.

Her phone chimed with an incoming message less than ten minutes later. Her giddy anticipation crashed to earth when she saw the message from Madison.

> Dad says he's coming here for Thanksgiving.
> We planned to go to NC. ugh!

Erin hit the call button rather than continue this via text.

"This is so complicated now," Madison moaned in greeting.

"Thanksgiving is five months away. You'll work it out."

"It won't be the same."

"No, it won't." Erin sighed.

"I thought we could all do Thanksgiving with the whole Downey clan."

"I'm sure your grandparents would love that."

"And you'd come?"

"Me? I don't think I'd be invited." It would be awkward for her former in-laws. They were still cool toward her since she was the one who initiated the divorce. *So, he drinks a little. What's the big deal?* If only it had been a little, it wouldn't have been a big deal. She no longer had to pretend it wasn't a problem. And it wasn't her problem anymore.

"We could ask."

"Let's wait on that." While she and Phil were on decent terms and Thanksgiving was only one day, with the divorce and Piper in Spain, it was time for new traditions. She'd be living at the beach but could come back to volunteer at the USO, serving dinner to the single soldiers. She'd never served on holidays before since volunteering there was *her* thing, and Phil had never been interested in helping or wanted her to work on weekends or nights.

What was it going to take for Madison to accept the divorce? Her dating? Not like that was happening. Either the friend request and messages were from a scammer or a married man. Either way—not good, and she needed to remember that. Maybe Phil would start dating.

"When does Connor start his new position?" She went for the redirect.

"He goes to Dallas for two weeks of training starting next week. I'll drive up and spend the weekend with him so we don't have to be apart for two weeks."

Ah, young love. Erin said a silent prayer that would never change as Madison told her about their plans to see a rodeo in Fort Worth. They ended the conversation on a good note, with Erin saying she'd send pictures of Tink and Smokey. As she tried to get the uncooperative felines to look at the camera for another picture, a chat notification popped up.

Not only did the message say the grill's name, but Graham—yes, the real Graham Holmstrom—even told her what they'd both been eating.

> Believe it's really me now? 😉

> Yes.

But why was he messaging her? If he had a question about the USO, he could call there. He hadn't come off as the kind of man who would initiate a relationship with a single woman, yet here he was messaging her after listing widowed as his relationship status.

Sorry, you'll have to try Tinder if that's what you want. No matter how handsome he was, or how bad his marriage might be, she would never be the other woman. She was probably wildly off-base with thinking he was interested in her anyway.

49

It's not like she'd been putting lonely, horny divorcee vibes out into the universe—yet.

> You've convinced me, so I don't have to block and report the account like I've done to all the divorced and widowed generals wanting to friend me.

Would he pick up on the hint?
His reply was almost immediate.

> Would you give me your phone number so I can call?

From what she knew, scammers usually made excuses about why they *couldn't* talk on the phone, and definitely not video chat, but she wasn't going to ask him to video chat to prove his identity. Still, she wasn't giving her number until she knew what he wanted.

> Not yet.

Dots showed he was typing. They disappeared, then started again, but nothing came through.

> Your profile says widowed, but you wore a gold wedding band.

Send.
She held her breath as the dots showed up again.

> My wife passed away a year and a half ago. I hadn't taken the ring off.

A jumble of emotions waged battle in Erin's head and mind. Sympathy offset the giddiness he inspired as she typed her phone number and hit send.

Her phone rang almost immediately with a 253-area code. "Hello."

"It's Graham."

She recognized the voice. "I'm sorry about your wife."

"Thanks."

"I'm also sorry about . . ."

"Making me prove I really am me?"

She pictured a grin on his face to match what she heard in his voice. "Well, not really."

"No worries. My daughter warned me against setting up social media accounts and contacting women. I went by the USO. You weren't working and the director said he couldn't give me your schedule or contact information; however, he did mention you were active on their social media. It seemed to be the only way I could find you."

That he had not only gone by the USO but set up the account to connect sent electricity buzzing through her. All of her.

"And now that we're 'friends,' I wanted to see if you would go to dinner with me."

How could she say no? "I'd like that." It was hard not to sound over-eager, considering this was the first time someone other than Phil had asked her out in nearly three decades. Unless she counted the much older, lonely divorcé two doors down from the apartment she rented when she had moved out.

"When are you free?"

"I'm volunteering at the USO on Thursday. I can meet you at the grill sometime after five."

"I was thinking some place more upscale than the grill." Graham drew out the words.

"Well, I'm just going to put it out there that you don't need to impress me by going to a fancy restaurant." Even though he asked her out, from things she'd heard about dating these days, he might expect her to pay for her meal. A forty- or fifty-dollar meal would bust her budget. "Having the wait staff hover over us isn't conducive to being ourselves."

"Good point. But, uh ..." he hesitated again. "I might have eaten at the grill a few times last week, hoping to run into you tutoring again."

Oh. Lordy. She fanned herself. "I'm flattered." That he admitted trying to connect with her made Erin feel desirable in a way she hadn't in longer than she could remember.

"If you like Italian food, the place we went for my son-in-law's birthday a few weeks ago had great food and pizza."

"Sounds perfect."

"Do you want to wait until Thursday or . . .?"

"I'm free tomorrow or Friday if either works better for you." It was a good thing they weren't video chatting so he couldn't see her silly smile, though she sure wouldn't mind seeing his face.

"Tomorrow is better. What time would you like for me to pick you up?"

"How about we meet there?"

"Okay," he said after a brief pause. "I'll text you the name and address. Say eighteen hundred hours?"

"I'll see you there then. Will you be in uniform?" Did she really ask him that?

"I'll come by the house and change first."

"I'll see you tomorrow night."

"I'm looking forward to it, Erin."

A date. She'd just accepted her first date in nearly three decades, and it was with an Army colonel. A very handsome, real-life, widowed colonel. *Take that Facebook scammers.*

Still, it was better to proceed cautiously and meet him there. She wasn't looking for a relationship, and definitely not marriage, but having someone to talk to over dinner would be nice.

Except she didn't know the rules or lingo for dating in today's day and age. Her friends had shared stories, though. Like inviting someone back for a drink or coffee meant you wanted to sleep with them. Or that after three dates, you were *expected* to have sex with someone. Three dates? She'd dated Phil for eight months before losing her virginity. Not that she wanted to wait *that* long now. She wasn't a virgin anymore.

However, she needed to chill rather than get worked up. This was one date. She was not going to be having sex with him. Just dinner. And maybe a kiss. That thought made her fan her face again. Only that wasn't the only part of her all heated up.

Chapter Seven

After arriving even earlier than he'd planned at DiLorenzo's, Graham debated whether to get a table or wait near the entrance until Erin arrived. What was the proper dating protocol these days? He wouldn't have to figure this out if she had let him pick her up. He went with being seated and ordered a glass of wine to take the edge off his nerves, then texted Erin so she would know he was here.

When she entered the restaurant, he got to his feet and smiled as she made her way to the table. "You look stunning." He stood there awkwardly. It was too soon to press a kiss of greeting to her cheek, wasn't it? Her turquoise blue dress highlighted her curves and made her eyes look even bluer. Tonight, her hair had soft waves, for a casual, and attractive, tousled look.

"Thank you." She gave him a shy smile. "I haven't had an excuse to get dressed up in a while, so I thought I'd take advantage of this opportunity." She slid into the empty chair across from him.

Okay, no kiss. No handshake. Got it. He sat. Under the table, he wiped his palms on his pants.

The server was at their table within seconds. "Would you care for a glass of wine or something to drink while you look over the menu?"

"I'll just have a glass of ice water, please. It smells amazing in here." Erin picked up her menu, then laid it back on the table and placed her hands over it. "Look, I appreciate you inviting me out, but I'm just going to lay this out there and say that I'm beyond nervous. I haven't gone on a first date in nearly thirty years."

Whew. "Me either. Everything's different these days, and I don't know if I'm doing things right."

"It's been so long, I'm not sure I remember what's right." She gave a nervous laugh.

"Agreed. This is really your first date since your divorce?" Was that good or bad? "How long ago since that was final?"

"Five months. We separated more than a year before that." Erin dropped her gaze to the menu underneath her hands.

Her divorce being so recent threw him a little off balance. "Sounds like you were married a long time."

"Nearly twenty-five years."

"Do you have kids?" It seemed a safe conversation starter.

"Two daughters. Madison graduated from college last year. She and her husband live in Austin, Texas. Piper is studying international business with a minor in Spanish and leaves next week to spend her junior year in Spain."

"That'll be a great learning experience. I spent two years based in Vincenza, Italy. My Italian isn't exactly fluent anymore, but it's passable."

"She had four years of Spanish in high school and two in college but wants the immersion experience. I think it's also her way of dealing with the divorce. It's been hard on them too."

"I imagine it's not easy, regardless of their age."

"What about you?"

"Bethann and I met the summer before my junior year at West Point and married two months after graduation. I also have two kids. Megan is a nurse and works for an internal medicine group. She and her husband, Reece, were already based here. My son, Jace, was finishing his training when I was offered my current position. Jace's wife, Alex, was hoping for the 173rd in Vincenza, Italy, where he was born, but he picked the 82nd Airborne. We were thrilled to have everybody together. With everything going on in the Middle East for the past two decades, I missed a lot of time with my kids due to deployments. Bethann encouraged Jace to come here as much or more for me than for herself. I'm glad she did."

"Considering the possibilities with the Army, you're fortunate to all be together. Is your son-in-law in the 82nd as well?"

"No, Reece is in a different unit."

"Is that a *special* one where its members typically stay at Bragg, I mean Liberty?"

He picked up on the way she said special. Asking without coming right out and asking. "I was based here for almost a decade earlier in my career. I haven't adjusted to the name change either." He dodged answering.

Erin checked out the pizza their server delivered to the couple at the next table. "Any interest in splitting a pizza?"

"Sounds great. What would you like? The Margherita, barbecue chicken, meat lovers?" he read the specials from the menu.

"Those all sound good."

The server set down a water glass for Erin. "Are you ready to order yet?"

"We're still deciding. Any recommendation on the pizzas?" Graham asked.

"My favorite is the barbecue chicken pizza. Though I add pineapple," the young woman serving them said.

"That sounds good to me," Erin said agreeably.

"With pineapple?" Graham couldn't help but ask.

"We can do half and half if you're one of those people who thinks putting pineapple on pizza is breaking some kind of regulation about toppings."

"No," he laughed, already liking Erin's sense of humor and how she put him at ease. "I just hadn't thought of it on barbecue chicken pizza. We'll give it a try."

"Would you care for an appetizer, salad, or garlic knots?" the server asked.

"I was thinking about the mixed greens salad, but that pizza looks like a lot.

"We can split the salad too," Graham suggested.

"Perfect," Erin agreed.

"When I stopped in the USO to do some reconnaissance" —Graham grinned at outing himself—"they mentioned you're only here for a short time. Something to do with writing research. Is that something you're writing for the USO?"

Erin immediately looked down and away, and her tight-lipped smile reminded him of Megan when she got caught sneaking cookies for her and Jace before dinner.

"They told you that, huh?" She swallowed, still not quite meeting his gaze. "No, it's not for the USO. It's a personal project."

"And it's classified?" he quipped.

"Yes," she answered with a relieved sigh.

"I was joking."

"Oh."

That her cheeks turned pink made Graham all the more curious.

She sighed again, and her lips disappeared momentarily

as she glanced at the nearby tables of diners. "For years, I taught high school English, but over a decade ago, I came up with an idea for a screenplay. After writing the first draft, I read books on writing for film and TV, attended classes, and eventually queried agents. But, in Hollywood, it's all about who you know."

"I've heard that."

"I couldn't exactly leave my husband and daughters in North Carolina to go try to make connections, so it didn't go anywhere. However, after learning from many different resources, I created a curriculum for a screenwriting class. The private school where I taught didn't think it had a broad enough appeal for a student body our size. So, I taught it as an after-school, not for credit class. The first class only had seven students, but they were connected with others interested in filmmaking, and interest grew. Some of those kids went on to study film in college, and a few have managed to get a foothold in the industry."

From the way Erin's eyes lit up when she explained, Graham saw her passion.

"A few months ago, one of those students got married. She'd worked on a reality dating show, and several others from her film class were at the wedding. Ian started as a reader at HBO and now works as the assistant to a producer who's done series with Netflix and Amazon, so everyone in the group was pitching him their ideas." Erin gave a shy smile.

"Did you pitch an idea too?"

"I did. After seeing *Top Gun: Maverick*, I spun up a new story idea. It's an Army version with a female lead. I'm partial to the Army and their aircraft since my dad was an aviation mechanic and worked on Black Hawks."

Even knowing she volunteered at the USO, that her idea

involved the military made the hair on the back of Graham's neck and arms stand at attention.

"When Ian returned to California, he pitched the idea to his boss, who loved it. But as a kickoff for a TV series instead of a movie. They asked me to write a treatment."

"What's a treatment?" All of this was new to Graham.

"It's a synopsis for the movie or TV season. A list of characters, the scenes, and the major beats to see if the story holds together. Only we hit a snag when Ian's boss found out I was Erin, E-R-I-N, not A-A-R-O-N. As in a female, and I had no military experience. He decided I didn't have the qualifications to write this idea, but they'd pay me $10,000 to sell them the rights to the story."

"While they stand to make millions."

"Possibly. Or they could *lose* millions. At my age, this is very likely my *one* shot at seeing one of my ideas make it to the screen. The timing with my girls being adults and my divorce," she added with a pained hesitancy, "I'm in a position where I can do the research and go out to LA So, I said I wouldn't sell them the rights unless they gave me a crack at writing the scripts."

"That makes sense since it's your idea." She might not have military experience, but it's not like Hollywood typically got things even remotely right in portraying the military.

"I already have a network of Army pilots through my support over the years, but the story includes a Special Ops team as part of the overall mission and story. Other than a friend from the USO who served in the Green Berets two decades ago, I have no connections there."

At her mention of Special Ops and her Green Beret friend, his heart raced like someone had tossed a grenade in his lap.

"I went skydiving for the experience, hoping my tandem partner would be former Spec Ops. Sadly, he wasn't even former military."

"*You* went skydiving?" He tried to picture that. It had been a hell-no for Bethann.

"I did. It wasn't the same as doing it alone, much less doing a HALO or HAHO jump as I envision in one of my scenes, but I can say I've jumped."

That she knew high-altitude low-opening and high-opening jumps versus calling those skydiving showed Erin had done her research.

"I hoped that by working at the USO here, I might connect with somebody who would allow me a glimpse into their world. I want to give a realistic portrayal of their life at home, training, and on mission. I'm too old for hitting the bars, but I'll make barbecue if someone invites me to a team get-together," she said with a smile.

Graham's guard went higher and higher as Erin came clean about seeking out a Special Ops team for her research. He needed to put the pin back in the grenade now. "Do you know what I do in the Army?"

Her eyes widened at his tone, which sounded harsh, even to his ears. Her posture stiffened, making him keenly aware he'd shifted into battle mode.

"No. That you went to West Point means my initial thought that you were a first or master sergeant was wrong. I'm guessing a lieutenant colonel. I ruled out the 82nd Airborne, but I don't know what unit you're with. Maybe PSYOPs." She eyed him warily.

With writing scripts, had this been an elaborate setup to connect with him? Could she have known he'd be at the homecoming? She could have done research and known about his family. That set him on edge even more. If she'd introduced herself and explained what she needed, there was an extremely high probability he would have turned down her request, but he wouldn't be doubting her motives now.

But she would have had no way of knowing he'd be at the grill. And she wouldn't have scooted off without making it a hell of a lot easier to contact her. He needed to give her the benefit of the doubt. "Close. I'm a colonel."

Erin's lips pursed in a tight smile, and she nodded in acknowledgment.

"I'm commander of 3rd Group." He didn't need to elaborate it was 3rd *Special Forces* Group. She knew.

"If you had your own Wikipedia page, I might have known that." Her chest and cheeks flushed, and she couldn't maintain eye contact. "It's probably too late to cancel our food order, but I understand if you want to beat a hasty retreat."

"And why is that?" Would she admit she played him?

"That's what tends to happen when I mention my writing about Spec Ops guys. The few leads I've had all ghosted me after an email or two. The brigadier general in the National Guard, who boasted that he could get me time with a Spec Ops team, handed me off to his first sergeant in charge of training. He replied to one, maybe two, emails. Then nothing. At a USO fundraising luncheon, I met a captain who was a recruiter in Charlotte. I commented about his Airborne patch, and he said he could get me in touch with the right people. I never heard back from two or three emails to him. When I met the Command Sergeant Major of 7th Group at the Charlotte USO and told him I was a writer, he wouldn't even tell me his name."

"How'd you know who he was then?"

"I recognized the Special Forces logo on the challenge

coin he gave me for the USO's collection. The back said Command Sergeant Major USSOCOM. But I didn't have the nerve to press him since he did an about-face after I mentioned the proposed series."

A gruff chuckle escaped. That sounded about right. Graham was seeing a pattern, and the way Erin explained had a disarming effect.

"He did assure me that my name isn't on a military watch list. Not the terrorist suspect kind, but a don't-talk-to-her-she-might-splash-military-secrets-all-over Netflix list."

"Have you tried going through official channels?"

"You mean Public Affairs?"

Graham nodded despite her yeah-right expression.

"Yes, when I started writing years ago, and they even had a Public Affairs department for media requests, and again when I started on this TV series. A Special Forces medic I met at the Charlotte USO a few months ago referred me to his Public Affairs Officer. He said SOCOM turned down my research request."

The server set plates in front of them. "I had the kitchen split the salad for you."

Erin didn't touch her utensils.

"Would you like another glass of wine?" the server asked.

"Yes, please," Graham said.

"You are staying to eat with me?" she asked once the server left.

"It wouldn't be gentlemanly to leave now." He'd stay but proceed with caution as he tried to assess the truth.

"I appreciate that. Eating alone has been one of the harder things about being divorced and here."

"Did you move to Fayetteville to put distance between you and your ex?" He went with her changing the subject.

"No. Nothing like that. As divorces go, ours has been amicable. My ex is a good father and provider. But when COVID hit, it sidelined a huge commercial real estate deal he was brokering. Interest rates went up, and potential buyers pulled out. He used our savings and investments to keep the property afloat without consulting me, thinking everything would get back on track soon. Of course, no one expected the pandemic to last as long as it did or that with the move to working at home, there would be a glut of available office space. Working from home himself, he'd started drinking, and he changed."

"Oh." Graham looked at his wine glass.

"I don't have a problem with somebody having a drink or two. In college, we both drank. But not to excess."

"But he had a drinking problem?"

"We had a difference of opinion on that. I thought that drinking wine before nine in the morning was a red flag as well as the binge drinking when I'd leave the house. And things like drinking wine out of a coffee mug and hiding empty bottles and cans under things in the recycle bin like I wasn't smart enough to know what he was doing." Pain and sadness flicked across her face.

"Those do sound like red flags."

"A major problem was I didn't like who *I* had become. I was angry and suspicious all the time, which made things worse. I started attending Al-Anon and seeing a counselor. That helped me some."

"Did he go to meetings?"

"No. After he had a car accident and was arrested for being under the influence, I begged him to enter an alcohol treatment program. He said he didn't need a program, that he could stop or cut back. And he did—for three days."

"Did you give him an ultimatum?"

"No. He had to want to quit drinking, or at least get a handle on it, for himself. But I had to do what was best for me and told him I wanted a separation. The first week, I stayed at a friend's house pet sitting her dog while she was on a trip."

"Your moving out didn't motivate him to get help?" That said a lot about her ex's addiction.

She shook her head, her mouth in a tight, straight line. "I thought it might be a wake-up call. Except I checked the recycle bin at our house, and no." She gave a light sigh. "I rented an apartment and told the family I'd moved out. That was scarier than jumping out of a plane. Especially since no one other than our younger daughter knew he drank like that. I can't make him want to change, but I could change myself."

"That's a healthy outlook." Though he still wished she hadn't gone through that.

"That's why I'm being fairly direct with you. Trying to be the new, more confident me. The one who says she wants pineapple on her pizza. Though I've now broken the cardinal rule about not talking about your ex, especially disparagingly, on a first date." She tentatively met his gaze.

"You haven't broken any rules. I appreciate your honesty about what you've been through. What if he got sober now? Any chance you'd get back together?" He had to ask.

"I don't see that happening. We married right out of college, and I never had a chance to be independent. I like only having to answer to myself. I'm working on discovering who I am—or who I want to be. I wasn't even planning to date. However, when a handsome officer hangs out at the grill, goes to the USO for reconnaissance, *and* sets up a Facebook account to get in touch, I wasn't going to say no to a dinner out." She finally smiled again.

Graham smiled back. "Thanks for taking pity on me."

"It's not pity. Though, I'm not looking for a serious relationship. My ex didn't see how I could be a wife and mother and pursue screenwriting, so he was never on board with it. I'm finally getting my shot at that dream, and I'm unwilling to give it up."

He didn't know what to say to that since a serious relationship was exactly what he needed for McKittrick to keep him here. Rather than succumbing to disappointment that Erin wasn't the right woman for him based on her reason for being here, he needed to keep his goal in mind. He hadn't expected this process to be easy.

"Though, if I find out you put my name on a banned-from-the-base list because I'm a writer, I am going to unfriend you."

"We don't ban access for that." There were other reasons, mainly security and safety, but Erin wanting to learn more about how a Special Forces team operated didn't exactly pose a security threat. She'd obviously done a lot of research and gone above the call of duty in supporting troops through the USO. Maybe she couldn't help him with *his* dilemma, but that didn't mean he couldn't help her. He wasn't going to make promises yet, though.

~

IF ERIN HAD any clue about Graham being the commander of 3rd Special Forces Group *before* coming on a date with him, she would have handled things differently. Talk about blowing an opportunity. It was like the universe kept extending her a silver platter holding what she needed to achieve her dreams, and every time she got close, it got yanked away, and someone yelled, "Psych!"

She wanted to cry, but no way was she doing that in front

of him. Instead, she switched the conversation to baseball and managed to avoid more landmine topics as they ate. Graham never totally let his guard back down, though. What did she expect? She'd only been half joking about not putting her name on a list blocking her access to Special Operations teams or even the base.

Why hadn't she deleted the friend request? She was not looking for a relationship. Now, she'd blown any opportunity to observe a Green Beret team and likely anyone in the 82nd Airborne. All in one night.

"The pizza was delicious, and I enjoyed the company," Erin settled for the only thing she could think of to say when he waved off her offer to split the bill. It's not like he was going to ask her out again.

"It's nice not eating alone." He didn't say *Sayonara* at the door but walked her to her car.

"Putting yourself back out there after such a major life change is hard, but we both survived our first attempt." Narrowly, since she'd ruined things by dropping the bomb about her screenwriting project. "Hopefully, it will get easier."

He hesitated before saying, "Good night."

"Good night," she repeated, probably too brightly. She opened her car door so she wouldn't be the one to make the mistake of saying *call me* or *you have my number*. Or start to cry. There was no benefit to making him more uncomfortable.

The tightness in her chest made it hard to breathe. She hadn't come close to getting a kiss and might have just kissed her shot at writing for the TV series that was *her* idea good-bye. If she weren't obligated to pet sit for the next four months, she'd pack up and leave for Fort Benning, or whatever it was called now. She might still have a remote shot at observing a Ranger team. Instead, she'd write syllabi and grade papers until she was seventy and could afford to retire.

She cast another glance Graham's way as he got in a black Lexus sedan. *Goodbye, Graham.* Like so much in her life, she wished things could have been different.

Chapter Eight

Graham arrived at Reece and Megan's on Sunday night, knowing he would face an interrogation. Based on Megan's message about missing him at home several nights in the past two weeks, she knew something was up. He joined the family in the kitchen, where food bowls already lined the counter.

"Wow. Looks like you've gone all out." He handed Megan the bag with a carton of ice cream, whipped cream, and syrup.

"Everything's ready. You can do chicken, beef, or pork tacos. You go first." She handed him a plate.

He waited to eat until everyone was seated at the table.

"How have you been? Any updates?" Jace tried sounding casual, though a slight smile tugged at his mouth.

Alex and Reece did a poor job of camouflaging their smiles by biting into their tacos.

"It was busy. I went on a few dates."

"Multiple dates?" Megan's pitch was higher than usual. "That's why you weren't home or answering my texts."

"Yes. I went by the USO, and they told me how to get in touch with Erin." He didn't go into details about setting up the Facebook account. "I took her to dinner."

"How did that go?" Megan leaned closer.

"She was easy to talk to, and we had a nice time. However, her divorce just became final a few months ago, and she is not interested in a serious relationship anytime soon." He skipped the part about her screenwriting and interest in Special Ops.

"Oh." Megan's shoulders relaxed, and she leaned back in her chair. "We said it wouldn't be the first one."

"Better to know that upfront with such limited time," Jace said.

"That's what I figured." Though it was still unfortunate. "I activated my profile on the online dating site I picked. I started getting wink and heart notifications within five minutes."

"You still have hair and all your teeth. Not bad for a guy your age," Jace joked.

"Thanks, son. I messaged some women whose profiles I liked to see who'd respond."

"How many?" Now Reece was grinning.

"I started with five, thinking I wouldn't hear from half of them. I also responded to about another five who contacted me first." He'd stayed up way too late responding to messages and quickly realized this mission could become a full-time job. "There was one who stood out. Mid-thirties, divorced." And made him feel attractive and interesting right off the bat. "She suggested we meet in person after exchanging a couple of messages. She was booked over the weekend but was free Thursday and suggested dinner at this nice restaurant."

"Booked?" Megan repeated.

"I thought she meant other dates from the app." That should have been his first clue. "She was on time and dressed to impress. Even looked like her picture."

"That's not always the case," Jace said. "Though my wife was prettier than her picture."

"Nice save." Alex accepted a kiss on the cheek from Jace.

"She ordered a cocktail before I even looked at the wine menu and immediately started asking what I wanted out of this relationship."

"Relationship? On the first date? Red flag," Reece stated.

"Remember, I'm new to all this. I told her I'm looking for a relationship that could eventually lead to marriage." He hadn't wanted to scare her off, but after Erin, he wanted to know upfront. "She asked how many nights a week I'd want her to block out for me and how long until we'd be exclusive. That's when she started dictating terms and telling me how much it would cost me for her to be exclusive."

"Dad! What site were you using?" Megan's eyes were huge. "Please tell me it wasn't Sugar Babies."

"It was a regular dating site, although she explained she was looking to date men who provide financial benefits in exchange for her company. She said she used keywords in her profile that I was supposed to pick up on."

"If she's in her thirties, she's a little old for Sugar Babies. Most of those women are in their twenties or younger—from what I hear," Alex clarified.

"How did dinner go?" Megan asked.

"I didn't stay. I told her that's not what I was looking for and left. I wasn't risking being seen with her by anybody I knew."

"Good move," Megan concurred.

When he got home, he'd checked her profile to see what words were supposed to clue him in that she was looking for a sugar daddy. He wasn't making that mistake again. "I wish I could say it got better from there. The next woman spent half our date talking about her ex cheating on her. She's convinced that every man cheats, particularly military men. What do you say to that?"

"Nothing," Reece advised.

"I thought I'd have to take a lie detector test if I wanted to take her on a second date." Which he didn't. "Next, I asked out a widow, thinking we have that in common. She was nice, but there was no chemistry." At all. He could tell she was lonely but passed on her invitation to go back to her place. He couldn't even fake romantic interest. "Side out. Game over."

"Don't tell me you're giving up already. That's only an inning. There are nine innings in a ball game," Jace challenged.

"I hope you're not suggesting I go out with twenty-seven women." Keeping the women he'd chatted with straight was a challenge. "I don't have time for that. I also don't want to get married just to get married and end up hurt or hurting someone else."

"You know, being a serial dater might raise more concerns than being serious with someone—anyone," Reece countered Jace's suggestion. "If you were putting your energy into a serious relationship, there'd be no need or time to mess around with someone else's wife."

"True," Megan agreed. "Neither Boatman nor Thomsen were single, so ordering you to marry doesn't make sense either."

"What would take for the general to back off his order? It's not like the team would go to him and say, 'Colonel Holmstrom's got a girlfriend. I'm not worried about him seducing my wife anymore,'" Jace used a deep, theatrical voice.

"No, they aren't going to do that," Reece admitted.

"You can't give up after four dates. Do you know any generals who gave up the war because they lost an early battle?" Jace reasoned.

"I'm glad I didn't give up after my first dozen or so online

71

matches," Alex chimed in. "I was about to close my account after being contacted by cpleaser 97."

"Eww," Megan groaned.

"Yeah. I wasn't sure if that was the year he was born or the number of women he, uh . . . I didn't respond to ask him."

Graham shook his head. He'd come across some interesting screen names, but nothing like that.

"Fortunately, there was a message sent a few hours earlier, and even though the picture was a car selfie"—Alex eyed Jace—"his smile caught my eye enough that I clicked on his profile and agreed to go on a date."

"After meeting me, she didn't need or want to date anyone else." Jace wore a corny grin as he leaned closer to Alex.

"Anything was better than the other," Megan said.

"I don't know if I'm picky or just not ready yet." Graham wasn't going to repeat his father's mistakes of settling for good enough to keep from being alone—even to stay here.

Megan studied him through narrowed eyes, her mouth puckered. "Did you look forward to going out and spending time with someone, or did that stress you out?"

"I was nervous making the dates, but I looked forward to dinner and some company. I had a good conversation with Erin. Until she disclosed she had no plans to marry, which threw me a curveball. Even though it was only one date, I compared the other women to her, and none measured up."

"Remember the animal matching game Jace and I had as kids?" Megan asked.

"Of course, he does. He always threw the game." Jace laughed. "He'd made sure you got to match the bunny and the kitten since they were your favorites, and I got to match the tiger and dog," he explained to Alex and Reece.

Graham shrugged. A good dad didn't decimate his kids in games.

"Dating is like that matching game. There are a lot of women looking to get married, but not many of them are matches. You've got to keep guessing and remember what qualities you want to find again. Eventually, you'll find a match. It might even be the kitten or bunny or tiger you want to find."

"Just stay away from the vipers, chameleons, and black widows," Reece teased.

"Those weren't in the game." Megan swatted her husband's hand.

"But they're out there," Reece warned.

Chapter Nine

"ARE YOU HAPPY TO SEE ME?" Erin asked Tink and Smokey, who came and circled her legs.

Smokey gave a plaintiff *meow* and pranced to the kitchen with her tail held high.

Right. They wanted moist food. Erin put her bag in the bedroom before heading to the kitchen. This time, the drive back from Charlotte felt longer than two hours.

Spending time with Phil before Piper left for Spain had gone about as she anticipated. There'd been some awkwardness—like when he questioned why Erin was spending the night at Lanie's instead of in Madison's old room. *Because we're divorced* seemed like the obvious answer, but she'd made an excuse about needing to work out details for the upcoming bridal shower she and friends were hosting.

His micromanaging Piper about packing and safety had Piper stressed and asking if she could stay with Lanie as well. A little distance from her dad could be good for her. She could make her own decisions, good or bad, and grow from them. Erin wished she'd had that opportunity at Piper's age. Better to learn that independence later than never.

After feeding the cats, she rummaged in the fridge for something appealing for a late dinner. When her phone dinged with an incoming message, she glanced at the microwave's clock. Phil had started a new family chat group for Piper to post updates and pictures. Though Piper's flight didn't land in Barcelona for another hour, Erin expected Phil had already sent a reminder for Piper to text when she arrived at the hotel for the start of her organized tour.

Instead, it was a message from Graham Holmstrom.

Erin's heart beat faster seeing his name. She hadn't expected to hear from him after their dinner date, considering his reaction to learning her main purpose of moving to Fayetteville was to hang out with operators. Men under his command. She couldn't blame him for thinking their meeting was a setup. Not that she could have managed that.

Twice, she read the message asking if she was free for dinner this week. It had been twelve days. Why was he reaching out now? Had he typed it earlier and forgotten to hit send? Or had he sent it to the wrong person? That would be embarrassing—for both of them. If not, what did it mean that he'd texted instead of calling? Was that just how dating was done these days?

Or was there some remote chance he was considering letting her observe a Special Ops team? Maybe it was a good thing he hadn't called since she couldn't put two words together, and her mouth went completely dry over that prospect.

I'd love to, she typed. No. Love was not the right word. *Sounds good?* No. *I'd enjoy that?* Better. She typed that.

Should she wait for him to reply again in case he sent an *Oops. I sent it to the wrong number message?* No. Be the confident Erin.

> I've been craving Mexican food. Know of a good place? I have plans on Thursday.

She added the last part hoping she wouldn't sound pathetic or desperate sitting here every night.

> If Monday at 1800 works, I like Mi Casita. I can pick you up, or we can meet there.

That he replied right back and chose tomorrow rather than pushing it out later in the week made her feel like a schoolgirl.

> Meet you tomorrow at 6.

He texted back with an address and smiley face emoji.

A smiley face? She hadn't expected that from a West Pointer. Or the commander of 3rd Special Forces Group.

She knew better than to get her hopes up, but she couldn't stop smiling or dispel the giddy feeling about seeing Graham tomorrow night. With him knowing about the TV series, it couldn't go worse than last time, right?

Chapter Ten

GRAHAM SAT on the bench next to the Mi Casita hostess stand, waiting for Erin. Even though he'd had tacos last night at Megan's, he didn't have a problem eating Mexican food two nights in a row. Not when it was with Erin. If that connection he'd experienced on their last date was still there, his plan could work and get them both what they needed.

Graham tapped his phone's screen. 1805. There wasn't a text, and she wasn't *too* late. When the door opened, his head jerked up. A couple in their twenties entered, and Graham went back to waiting. He'd been on many a mission that involved days of waiting. Somehow this seemed harder.

When the restaurant door opened again, Erin entered.

Graham surged to his feet.

"Hi." Her smile had an electrifying effect on him. "Sorry that I'm late. I'm still learning my way around here and didn't realize until I put the address in the GPS that I was thinking of the wrong location."

"No worries." He debated if he should hug Erin.

"Are you ready to be seated?" The hostess interrupted the moment.

"After you." He motioned for Erin to follow the hostess.

Once seated and the hostess departed, Graham thanked Erin for coming.

"You had good timing. I went to Charlotte over the weekend to see Piper off to Spain and can use the distraction."

"It's hard to have them that far away. You said she's going to be there a year?"

"Almost. She's doing a four-week tour of Europe first. Then, she'll take one class in their summer session before going full-time this fall. I try not to be a helicopter parent, but she suffers from anxiety, so this is making *me* anxious about having her that far away for so long. With school out and the class I'm teaching not starting for a few more weeks, I've got too much free time to worry about how she's doing. Her father got us both worked up with his repeated warnings about safety and everything that could happen."

"Good to be smart and safe, but I can see how that would make you both anxious. Is this the time I'm supposed to tell you that if anything happens, you know someone with certain skills . . ."

"I have seen the *Taken* movies. My original movie idea involves the rescue of girls taken hostage by a group like Boko Haram, so my mind has already gone there more than once. Let's talk about something different."

Since she didn't mention that nearly two weeks had passed, he refrained from explaining why he hadn't contacted her earlier. Better to make sure this date went well and not risk scaring her off by bringing up his proposition too soon. He steered clear of asking about screenwriting for now too. "Where all is she going in Europe?"

"They start in England, then Belgium, Germany, Czech Republic, Austria, Italy, France. There might be one or two more countries."

"Wow, that's a lot."

"They'll spend a few days in each country. We figured if she was over there, why not see as much as she can while she's young and can enjoy it? Once you have a job and kids, it's harder to travel. I thought about doing the tour, too, but I wanted her to have fun with people her age."

"She'll have a great time. When I was based in Italy, we did a lot of short trips but still didn't get to hit all the countries we wanted to visit. Though we fell in love with the Amalfi coast and went there several times."

"I'm jealous. I've wanted to visit Italy for decades."

"You should go. I've never heard of anyone hating it."

"I plan to visit Piper at Christmas and travel with her, but I'm waiting until she finishes this trip to see where she wants to go. And plans may change depending on my ex, who is now talking about going to see her then."

"Wouldn't that be a good time for you to go with a semester break from teaching classes?"

"He says that's the best time for him to be out of work too. Despite the time difference, he thinks it won't be a big deal for me to teach online from there."

Neither had looked at their menus when the server brought chips, salsa, and water to their table. Unlike his other dates, conversation with Erin flowed easily through dinner. Though he mentioned Bethann in reference to their travels, that didn't seem to bother Erin, nor did she talk more about her ex. When the server cleared their plates and asked if they wanted dessert, he was ready to put everything on the line. He gave the server his credit card and waited for her to leave.

"There's something I need to come clean on. The last time we had dinner, you kind of threw me for a loop."

"Right after I told you my hopes of hanging out with a Special Ops team? I picked up on that."

"Partially. It was more the not looking for a relationship part."

"O-kay." Erin's mouth curved into a cautious smile.

"I have a proposition for you."

"A—proposition?"

"Wrong word." He rubbed the back of his head. Heat crept up his face.

"Good. Because you should know I vowed not to sleep with anyone to get my big break in Hollywood."

He laughed. Fortunately, she seemed amused rather than offended. He looked around to make sure nobody was listening in on their conversation, then leaned forward and lowered his voice. "What I'm about to tell you is confidential."

"How confidential?" She mirrored his posture, leaning toward him with her arms crossed on the table. "You won't have to kill me afterward, will you? That would really make me regret accepting your Facebook friend request."

Her sense of humor made him hope even more that she'd agree. "No, however, it would look bad for my unit if this got out."

Her smile disappeared, and her eyes widened slightly. "I can keep a confidence."

"Good." That was a necessary trait for a woman involved with a Special Forces operator. "We had incidents of Conduct Unbecoming an Officer with prior commanders of my unit."

"I'm not following you."

"Inappropriate relationships with wives of men under their command."

"Ohhh." She drew out the word. "That's not good. Plural? Really?"

He nodded. "It's created trust issues within the unit. With my wife passing away, it's been suggested that I get married for the good of the unit. Otherwise, I'll be transferred to a new post."

"Oh." Erin's pitch rose, her eyes were bug-eyed wide, and her chatty demeanor was replaced with one-word responses.

"We could help each other get what we need."

Erin's head cocked to the side as she studied him. Her mouth opened slightly as she wordlessly contemplated what he was suggesting.

The server placed the folder with his credit card and receipt on the table.

"Thank you." Graham added a generous tip and signed his name. "You said you wanted to observe a team for research. I can get you full access. I could also review your scripts to give feedback on action and dialogue."

"And all I have to do is date and *marry* you?" She gave a nervous laugh. "I'm flattered, and while that sounds tempting, your plan has fatal flaws. For one, I'm only here house and pet sitting for another four months before I move. That's not enough time for a relationship to reach the marriage stage. I also have absolutely *no* plans to get married anytime soon. Not even a marriage in name only."

"I realize that. That's why I went out with several other women last week."

"Oh. And none of them were interested in your proposition?"

He probably shouldn't have brought that up. "I didn't ask any of them. And won't. I pretty much concluded I'm not ready for that either. But, not only do I love my current position, with both my kids and their spouses here, I don't want to leave Fort Liberty."

"I understand, but . . ."

"But," he picked up, "I don't think we'd *have* to get married. If I were in an exclusive, rather public, romantic relationship, that could take the pressure off. At least buy me more time."

"But you don't know for sure that would suffice."

"True, there's no way to ask General McKittrick without tipping my hand."

She leaned back in her seat and sighed. "This is kind of a huge ask—and risk. I don't want this to backfire and you to get jammed up because you wasted your time faking it with me."

"It's a risk I'm willing to take." And preferable over marrying someone for anything other than love.

"I can't commit to this right now."

"I know this is a lot to process. Take some time to think it over. Then reach out, and we can talk." Even though she looked like she wanted to run, at least she hadn't said *hell no*. Not yet.

She slipped her purse strap over her shoulder.

He got to his feet and took a last drink of water, which did little to counter his parched mouth. He still hadn't figured out what to say to increase his chances of her agreeing.

She spun abruptly when they got to her car. "If we do decide to do this, we'll have to be seen together a good bit."

"I can work around your schedule and cover all expenses."

"That's not where I was going." She dropped her head, and her gaze flitted left, then right. She licked her lips. "Even though we aren't getting married, we have to be convincing as a couple. I don't know about you, but I haven't kissed a man, other than my husband, in a quarter of a century."

"Me either. My wife, I mean." The ache of missing Bethann intensified. When he imagined kissing Erin, a twinge of betrayal blocked him before he thought beyond that. "You're saying we should try for research?"

"At some point. I mean, if you don't want to now—"

"I do want to." It was one kiss to make sure they could pull this off. Bethann was gone and would want him to move on.

He moved closer. It's not like he didn't know what to do, though it had been a long time, and he'd never had this much riding on a single kiss. He rested a hand on Erin's hip. Her face tilted up, and her eyes closed just before his mouth connected with hers.

He hadn't expected the warm sensation now spreading through his chest. He pressed another kiss more firmly to her silky lips. When his lips parted, her mouth opened to welcome a brush of his tongue against hers. Her delicate murmur of pleasure encouraged him to probe deeper for one more kiss.

She gave a satisfied sigh, then put a few inches between them and smiled at him. "I'm a writer, not an actor, but I think I'll be able to pull that off."

"I think we can be convincing," he agreed. He hadn't wanted to kiss the other women he had been out with, but it was an entirely different story with Erin. Except when he leaned in for round two, she put a hand on his chest.

"That was enough to answer my question. I need to stay clear-headed so I can make a rational decision, not one based on . . ."

"I understand." Though he kept his hand on her hip and sure liked the feel of her hand lingering on his chest.

For the first time since the general told him marriage was his chance to keep his position, Graham had hope this could work out. It might not be totally above board, but it also wasn't fair to relieve him of this command because of the bad conduct of his predecessors. Everyone knew the saying *All's fair in love and war*. Well, he loved his family and would do everything he could to stay, even fight a little dirty.

Would dating Erin be enough?

Chapter Eleven

Inside her car, Erin took several deep breaths. There was a lot to like about Graham. Tall, fit, and handsome, with a great smile. All the elements were there for strong physical attraction. When was the last time a kiss made her heart race so fast that it stole her breath and triggered lustful desires? Too damn long.

Between perimenopause and stress over her crumbling marriage, her sex drive had driven into the dry and dusty desert to die a slow death. Those few kisses with Graham were enough to breathe life back into her libido.

While she had said she wouldn't sleep with anyone to get her break, and she was at least a decade too old to appeal to the Hollywood producer type anyway, sleeping with Graham could do more than get her access to a team for research. It could be valuable for research of a whole other kind.

And there was more to her attraction to Graham than physical. The freedom to spread her wings and choose her path was better than the cohabitation with Phil for the past few years. Graham engaged in conversation, listened, and remembered what she had told him. It was a nice change, but marriage? *That* was out of the question.

Could the Army really transfer him because he wasn't married? From stories she'd heard over the past decade, probably. Clearly, he had loved his wife. It showed in his smile and tone when he mentioned her name. While he wasn't ready for marriage yet either, with both of his children here, it was understandable he would want to stay enough to make this risky proposition.

She hadn't been looking to date but wasn't opposed to it either. Could a dating relationship be enough to ease the concerns of the general and the men under Graham's command? Graham arranging for her to observe a Special Ops team could be a win-win situation. It seemed too good to be true—which meant it probably was. She'd always been the optimist, and Phil had been the one to plan for worst-case scenarios. This was not a situation to rush into without considering the possible outcomes to Graham's career.

ERIN REVIEWED the growing list of questions she'd started after dinner with Graham two nights ago. One of the questions she'd scribbled down at three in the morning the first night made no sense in the light of day. The question about when she'd spend time with a team was on the list twice—a clear indicator of her interests.

For years, she'd put others before her needs. Phil. The girls. Her students. She was conditioned to that, but her counselor made her see that asking for what she wanted was fine. She had a deadline, and if Graham expected her to wait until he was in the clear before arranging access to observe a team, that would be too late for her.

If she were braver, she would call. Instead, she texted him and asked if he was available to meet. Less than a minute later, her phone rang with his name on the display.

"I was just thinking of you," he greeted her. "I'd be happy to get together to talk. If you're free tonight, I can take you to the place that serves the best Pad Thai in town."

"That sounds wonderful." And nice not to have to decide since she was on decision overload. "Text me the name and address," she said before he could offer to pick her up since there was no telling how this dinner would go after their last two. This could well be their last date.

GRAHAM BEAT her to the restaurant even though she arrived two minutes early this time. He stood in front of the entrance talking on his phone. The smile he gave her as she approached set her nerves aflutter.

"My date's here. I've got to go. I'll see you Saturday." He ended the call. "Hi."

Graham leaned in, placing a hand on her waist and kissing her as if it were the most natural thing in the world. Though it was just one brief kiss, it was a nice way to start the evening. Who was he talking to that he had mentioned a date? At least he hadn't jumped ahead to refer to her as his girlfriend.

"You could have finished your conversation." She'd gotten used to Phil taking calls even when they were out for dinner.

"We were done. Colonel Mahinis called to say he found a fourth for golf on Saturday." Graham opened the restaurant door. "Two for dinner, please," he said to the hostess who led them to a booth. "Do you play golf?" he asked Erin.

"I don't think you could call it that."

Graham chuckled. "Why's that?"

"I took it as a PE class in college, but unless you count mini-golf, I haven't picked up a club in twenty years. Even then, I was a fair-weather golfer. Too hot? Pass. Too cold or rainy? Pass." Phil losing his temper and hurling his club? Hard pass. Maybe she should offer to go along and drive the cart to see how Graham behaved on the course. How competitive was he? "What's your handicap?"

"Currently, an eleven. I was nine at my best. That was a few years ago. Colonel Lundy is the best player in our usual foursome. I think Mahinis and I have beat him twice in the past year."

"You still play with him though?"

"I'd rather lose to a better player than beat someone adding strokes to kiss up to a senior officer."

"What units are your golf buddies with?"

"Lundy is over the aviation unit here at Liberty. Mahinis is over an elite unit that I can't even get access to. Yang is with Intelligence. Ayers is with the 82nd Airborne and is our usual floater when one of us can't play."

The server placed glasses of water on the table. Her gaze darted over Erin. "I'll let you look over the menus and be back in a few minutes." She gave Erin another once-over before walking away.

"Bethann and I used to come here often," he explained. "After you mentioned wanting some good Asian food the other day, I figured it was time to return."

That he'd bring her to a favorite spot he shared with his wife seemed like a good sign he was moving forward.

"You didn't come to hear about my golf game," he transitioned after they ordered.

"No." But it was insightful to know he had hobbies and friends. "Your proposition came out of left field."

"Yeah. There are no Army standard operating procedures on something like that."

"I hope not."

"And I should have used a better word than 'proposition.'"

"That did throw me a little considering how things work in Hollywood, at least in the past, but I trust you didn't mean it *that* way. I have some questions." She pulled the list and a pen from her purse.

Graham's eyes widened. "Okay. Shoot."

"To start, I was wondering what type of time commitment you want. Are you talking about dinner or other activities once or a couple of times a week?"

"I think we need to spend more time together than dinner once a week to be convincing. And I'd like to spend more time than that with you."

He held her gaze and directed a smile at her that would make nearly any woman swoon. She wouldn't have a problem spending several evenings a week with him.

"We need to do more outings, not just dinners. I'm happy to cover all costs," he added.

"That's not why I was asking. I understand if you don't want to be exclusive right away and keep your options open to find somebody who is looking for the same things you are in the way of a long-term commitment—"

"I plan to keep it exclusive if that's okay with you."

"It's not like I was planning on dating anyone else. I hadn't even planned on dating at all, but your messages made you sound so—"

"Desperate? Clueless about social media?"

She laughed. "I was going to say relatable."

"That does sound better."

Graham didn't come off like the alpha warrior she expected from the man in charge of one of the most elite military units in the world. His people and leadership skills likely got him where he was more than his ability to kick in a door—not that she'd mind seeing him in action. "I just don't want this to backfire if you find out that dating will not cut it. Did the general give you a deadline?"

"Not a set date, but he did mention six months. That was almost a month ago."

"*Six months!* He expected you to meet, date, and *marry*—in six months? FYI, I'm past the shot-gun wedding-because-I'm-pregnant stage of life." Not that her father had resorted to forcing Phil to marry her.

"Good, because I'm looking forward to traveling and spoiling grandchildren, but not having to raise more kids. The timing is before the team he's most worried about deploys. If we had to announce our 'engagement' just before then, that should suffice."

"But there's no way to know for sure? And I need to be clear that I am not getting married in six months. Not even a pretend marriage," she said at the exact moment the server brought their meals.

"Enjoy your food." Based on her wide eyes, she overheard that.

"I understand," Graham said.

Erin took a bite of the shrimp Pad Thai to let the awkwardness fade. "This is delicious." She took another bite and glanced at her list of questions. "Would you tell your children this is 'an arrangement,' or do you plan to let them think it's real?"

"I told them about the general planning to transfer me and the alternative. Both encouraged me to try and meet someone. As for telling them about *this*, I hadn't thought that through yet. Would you tell your girls?"

"It could come up at some point that I'm *dating* somebody. There's no reason to tell them more with them not here. That's something you can think on, and let me know once you decide so that we're on the same page *if* we pursue this."

"I will. I'll need you to go as my date to the military ball."

Something resonated in her chest at the idea of him in a dress uniform. "I would be honored to attend a military ball with you." She hoped his interest didn't wane the better he got to know her.

"Good." His smile drew her in. "That's not for a few months. I'd start by setting you up to observe a team. I would take you out there so they'd see us together."

"You're saying I'd get access to observe a team when?" Her heart beat a little faster.

"Shouldn't take more than a week or two to get that set up. Would that work for you?"

"Definitely."

"And I'd be available as a technical advisor for dialogue and action scenes—to a point," he cautioned.

"I understand you can't discuss actual missions, but any brainstorming would be fantastic." She was getting more than she'd dared to hope for. "You're not worried I'll dump you after I get what I need?"

"I hope you won't, but I'm not drawing up a contract or anything. If, for any reason, this isn't working out, say the word, and we walk away."

That made her feel better. She hadn't seen red flags, though, over time, people and things change. "That goes both ways. I'm not ready to make a decision quite yet. You also need to think about the impact this could have on your family and your career if this blows up."

"I have thought about it."

"Humor me and think about it some more."

"Fair enough. Though I should warn you, I don't typically admit defeat."

"I'll remember that." One particular mission she'd like to assign him made her body temperature soar to dangerous levels.

"I thought about what you said the other night about only being here a few more months. That could work for us. If we had to, we could announce our engagement. Then say doing the relationship long-distance showed us we rushed things and decided we needed more time before getting married. That could buy me enough time for any concerns to die out and my papers for another three-year term to be finalized. This command has been a dream assignment—until this. Megan and Reece are talking about starting their family. If my only options are across the country or overseas, then I'd consider retiring. I missed a lot of time with my kids in the past nearly two decades. They're adults now, but without Bethann here holding things together . . . I've done my time. I need to put them first."

Erin wanted to help him get what he wanted—which wasn't a promotion or material things but the ability to stay connected with his children. His priorities amplified the feelings she already had for him.

After their dinner, Graham was unusually quiet as he walked her to her car. His mouth scrunched in a disgruntled manner. "This is the part I don't like."

The part where he kissed her goodnight? "Why is that?" She took a half step backward.

"An hour together over dinner isn't long enough. I'm not ready to say goodnight and watch you drive off."

"Oh." She swooned at his declaration but managed to stay on her feet.

"Did you think I would say I didn't want to kiss you?

That's not the case. Though being in a public parking lot isn't exactly romantic."

"I don't have a problem with a little PDA." Her upturned face was enough of an invitation for Graham's mouth to claim hers—without hesitation this time. His hand slid to her lower back, urging her close enough for her to feel the effect she had on his body. Her lips parted to welcome his tongue. Her bones began to melt, and she swayed into him. The increased contact elicited a blissful murmur.

He broke the kiss seconds later and did a quick surveillance glance around the parking lot. "Rather than say goodnight, we can get ice cream, go for a walk, or back to my house for a glass of wine on the patio."

"Counteroffer. How about we go bowling? That way, we can talk, and I can see how competitive you are." And she didn't have to stress that this was technically their third date and he might expect her to have sex with him. Not that the idea of sleeping with him hadn't crossed her mind. It had—a few times a day since they met and several times in the past hour. But they needed to figure out what they were doing going forward. Sex now could influence their decision-making, and it could go either way. If they agreed to this arrangement, they could address that component of the relationship later. When they were both ready.

Hopefully, she wouldn't be disappointed or disappoint him—at least not long-term. Rather than keep silent to avoid bruising his ego, she'd be honest and upfront from the beginning to ask for what she needed for sex to be mutually satisfying. She deserved that. Graham was used to being given orders, right?

Chapter Twelve

Bowling with Erin had been fun and capped off a near-perfect night together. Like any battle, there were risks if they went down this road. Risks he was willing to take.

She'd made good points about the need to plan this through. Military strategy was his specialty, but this fell under unconventional warfare, and she wasn't one of his soldiers he could give orders to.

After kissing her goodnight in the bowling alley parking lot, he'd thought about her questions, and once he got home, he started his list of responses and expectations for the relationship. It was pretty much all he'd thought about since last night. He wanted to get details ironed out and move forward.

He pulled out his cell to call Erin after Kearns left for lunch.

"Hi. I was just thinking about you," she answered.

"I like hearing that." Her cheerful greeting and statement released the kind of endorphin rush that would be a good addiction. Though his marriage with Bethann had still been strong and loving after three decades, there was something exciting about a new relationship. At least one like this. He hadn't clicked with any other women he'd gone out with, but everything felt easy with Erin.

With her, Graham certainly wouldn't have to fake attraction. He could make a strong case that marriage didn't make him less inclined to cheat than in a committed dating relationship. Not that he wanted to battle that out with the general. But if McKittrick saw it for himself, maybe he'd ease up. However, based on what Mateo said, he and the general weren't the only ones he needed to convince.

"I've been thinking over the different ways this could go, good and bad, as you asked," he told her. "You mentioned having plans for tonight, but I wanted to see when you're free."

"I'm working the USO's table outside the Woodpecker's game tonight. If you're willing to help us out, I'll treat you to a hot dog dinner and the game."

"I'd love that. Can I pick you up?" That would allow them to talk privately.

"I planned to ride over with Tommy and Nicky to set up. But you can give me a ride back to the USO to get my car after the game."

"I can work with that. What time should I be there?"

"We're going to be there about six fifteen to set up. Why don't you come around six thirty? Oh, I need you to be in uniform. Unless you have a USO shirt," she clarified.

"I don't." Not that he knew why that mattered.

"We'll be set up near the entrance. We should be easy to find."

"See you there."

Since he didn't need to go home and change out of his uniform, Graham stayed late to finish the report he hadn't been able to concentrate on before talking to Erin.

He parked at the Airborne and Special Ops Museum and crossed the street to the stadium. Near the entrance, he spotted Erin and the center director setting up a shade canopy.

Erin flashed a bright smile. "You're early."

"Thought I'd beat the traffic and see if I could help."

"You've got the height advantage to do this." She stepped aside.

He extended a pole until it clicked into place, and then he and the director, Tommy, moved to the canopy's other side while Erin and a female volunteer in a red shirt set up two folding tables.

Erin's gaze roved over him as Graham helped her flip the table and move it into place. "You wanted to see me in uniform," he surmised.

"Maybe," she said with a guilty grin.

He chuckled. "I hope you don't go for *any* man in uniform." He'd have a lot of competition then.

"No. But I am partial to this pattern. I never loved the digitalized camouflage. I think you've met Tommy, and this is Nicky," she introduced them.

"We appreciate you helping out, Colonel," Tommy said.

"Call me Graham." He shook hands with Tommy and then Nicky.

"I'm glad to see you could connect with Erin," Tommy said. "Sorry that I couldn't give you her information. I'm sure you understand the need for security. We had a situation where a soldier liked one of our volunteers a little too much, and she already had a boyfriend."

"I do understand. I would appreciate you not giving out

even the little you gave me on Erin to anyone else." He winked at Erin as she spread the cloth over the table.

"I don't think you have to worry about anyone else asking since I'm old enough to be the mother of half of the troops that come to our center."

"It's the other half I'd have to worry about."

Erin set a cardboard box on the table and leaned over toward him. "Thank you."

"I'm happy to help."

"I mean for making me feel attractive and desirable," she said softly, looking at him in a way that made him want to take her in his arms and kiss her regardless of who was looking.

"You are." Anyone who didn't see it was blind.

After they set out swag, business cards, and a donation box, Graham stood next to Erin as she and Nicky engaged with people coming for the game.

"Graham. I thought that was you."

Graham startled at Sean McKittrick's booming greeting. "General, Mrs. McKittrick. Nice to see you."

"Still in uniform? Am I making you stay too late in the office?"

"That was my doing." Erin placed a hand above Graham's elbow. "I used the excuse that he doesn't have a USO shirt to make him stay in uniform since that's more of a draw than a middle-aged woman offering someone a logo pen. I also like seeing him in uniform," she added in a low, conspiratorial tone to Sally McKittrick. Then Erin smiled at him, playing the girlfriend role like a pro.

"There is something about a man in uniform," Sally agreed.

"I assume you're familiar with the USO and its mission to support the troops," Erin said.

"We are, and we appreciate what you volunteers do." McKittrick eyed Erin before studying Graham.

"We have a number of family and couples' events coming up. It's always great to have senior officers come out too. You can find information on the USO website." Erin handed Sally a pen. "Enjoy the game."

"I'll be sure to check it out," Sally said.

"I'll drop by to see you tomorrow, Colonel." McKittrick actually smiled.

Sean and Sally headed into the stadium. Graham waited for Erin to finish chatting with a young service member, his wife, and their two children. "You were amazing."

"I heard you say general and recognized the name."

"And you sold it, which means you're committed now."

"He knows you're dating, but you could always say you ditched me for somebody better."

"Not a chance." He winked, charmed at how she smiled back before dipping her head.

A steady stream of people stopped by the tent as it got closer to game time. Though several service members struck up conversations about Special Ops when they saw his uniform patch, Graham steered them to the USO's mission. Mostly, he observed Erin in action, liking how she made each person she came in contact with feel visible and important.

"Hey there, Dad."

Graham choked on the swallow of water he'd just taken and nearly spit it into Megan's face. "Hey there, sweetie." He coughed again. Next to Megan, Reece's lips disappeared as he suppressed a grin. "I didn't know you were coming to the game tonight."

"I didn't know you were coming either." Megan looked past him at Erin.

Busted. "Erin." He touched her forearm. "This is my daughter, Megan, and her husband, Reece."

"It's nice to meet you." Erin's pitch rose an octave as she extended a hand.

"This is Erin and Nicky. They volunteer at the USO." He introduced both, though clearly, his daughter had made the connection. "Erin asked if I'd help out tonight, and we're staying for the game."

"I hope you know some basics of baseball, or you'll get a lesson in Baseball 101," Megan said to Erin but grinned at him. "Where are your seats?"

Erin pulled their tickets from her pocket. "We're in section 115."

"Maybe we'll see you inside. Enjoy the game."

Graham hugged Megan and nodded to Reece before the pair headed into the stadium. "That wasn't how I anticipated introducing you to my daughter." With Erin around, he was dropping the ball when it came to situational awareness.

"It caught me by surprise too. First, the general. Now, your daughter. I'm a little scared of who's next."

"I'll do a better job of watching for Jace and Alex. I should have asked Megan if they were coming tonight."

"Your kids are close, then?"

"Very. Comes with all the moves being military kids. She's only two years older, but she has that mom gene in her." He liked the fact that they were close. If he had to change duty stations, his kids would still have each other. He could find new golf partners at a new post, but without his wife to make social connections and keep him balanced, he'd be very much alone.

∽

AFTER TALKING NEARLY non-stop about the USO the past thirty minutes to people who'd come for the game, Erin took a drink of tepid water. They made it through the last twenty minutes without seeing Graham's son or anyone else he knew. A few stragglers hurried past when Tommy gave the order to start packing up.

"Did you want to head in for the national anthem and the first pitch?" Erin asked Graham.

"I'll stay and help. The game's not why I came." His hand scorched a trail along her lower back to her hip.

Let's skip the game and go someplace private. Like she'd really say that.

They packed up the remaining swag. While she and Nicky folded the tablecloths, Graham helped Tommy take down the canopy and then offered to help return the loaded wagons to the van. "Do you want to go on in?" he asked Erin.

"I'll wait for you."

The way he looked at her added more sparks to the fire he stoked.

"I take it you and the colonel haven't been dating long since you hadn't met his daughter," Nicky said as Tommy and Graham wheeled off the supplies.

"We've been out a few times the past couple of weeks."

"He certainly seems smitten with you, and it looks mutual."

"He is great." With meeting General and Mrs. McKittrick, then Megan and Reece, it was like the universe was sending attention-getting billboards to proceed with this dating arrangement. Maybe it would be enough for Graham to keep his command.

Seeing the smile on his face as he made his way back to her now made her heart pick up its pace. Her reasons for agreeing to this fake relationship had as much to do with how she felt when she was with him as much as getting access to a team for research.

Posing as a couple wasn't going to be the hard part. Staying in her lane to avoid getting on the highway to heartache might be a different story.

Chapter Thirteen

DESPITE THE LOPSIDED GAME, they stayed until the end. Graham took Erin's hand as they exited the stadium with Tommy and Nicky.

"Thank you both for volunteering. I wish it had been a more exciting game," Tommy said.

"No worries. It was fun." Especially with Graham testing Erin's baseball knowledge to tease her.

"Good night," Tommy said. He and Nicky turned to the left.

"I parked at the Special Ops Museum." Graham led Erin to the crosswalk. "I was having second thoughts about fake dating you, but after seeing General McKittrick and his wife tonight, I guess we'll have to give it a go."

"You're a terrible liar." She laughed.

"Which is why it's good I won't have to fake anything since I really like being with you." He walked her to the passenger side of his car and then scanned the parking lot.

"See anyone you know?"

"No, but I have this feeling I'm being watched, which I had the whole game. I'm just not sure if it's Megan or the general. Makes for a tricky balance deciding how thoroughly I should kiss you."

"I just went weak in the knees."

He gave a throaty grumble. "Then this is just for starters."

He kept the kisses respectable, probably in case Megan and her husband were watching from somewhere in the parking lot.

"Since we're officially dating now, we should probably make sure our stories are straight and get to know each other a little better," Erin said as he navigated out of the parking lot.

"I say we leave out the part about the general planning to transfer me and start with the truth about meeting at the grill."

"I'm good with that."

On the short drive back to post, she asked him some basic getting-to-know-you questions. All too soon, he parked next to her car.

Graham glanced at Tommy unloading the USO van.

"When do I get to see you again?"

"When would you like to?" That seemed like a safe answer.

"Would tomorrow be too soon?"

"Not at all."

"What are you up for? We've done Italian, Mexican, and Asian food."

"Instead of going out, I bought some salmon earlier this week that I need to cook."

"A homecooked meal and an evening with you sounds like a double win. If you don't mind cooking at my place, it would set the stage for us dating."

"I can do that." The way he said it, dinner might not be the only thing on his mind. They'd just agreed to date. Was it too soon to be sleeping together? A needy part of her wanted to. Very much so.

She'd shave her legs tomorrow, just in case. Or should she get a Brazilian wax? She'd never gotten one since it hadn't been a thing years ago. Now it seemed like a majority of the women did it. But at her age? It's not like she could tactfully ask Graham if he expected that or would want her to. How bad did it hurt? Would she be too sensitive right afterward for intimacy? There was so much she didn't know about dating and intimate relationships these days.

"I'll text you my address. At some point, you'll have to give me yours."

"I told you I'm house and pet sitting. I don't know how you feel about cats, and it's not my place, but if you give me your address, I guess I can give you mine. After one more date," she added, getting that sexy laugh she'd hoped to hear before kissing him good night. "I'll see you tomorrow." And maybe the next morning.

Chapter Fourteen

When Erin's car slowed and parked in front of his house, Graham turned off the vacuum and stored it in the closet. Years of military service had him trained to keep things orderly, but dusting baseboards had hardly been a priority since Bethann's death. Not that he expected Erin to do a white glove test for dust. He wasn't looking for a woman to cook and clean for him, but he wanted to make a good impression with her coming over.

By the time he got out the front door, his neighbor, Noelle Ayers, and her dog had intercepted Erin.

"Can I help you?" Noelle sounded like she was in interrogation mode.

"I'm here to have dinner with Graham." Erin motioned to him as he strode down the front walk.

"You are?" Noelle's posture stiffened.

"I'm Erin." She shifted the cloth shopping bag and extended her hand. "And you are?"

"Noelle." She didn't take Erin's hand. "My husband is Colonel Ayers."

"Yes. With the 82nd Airborne. I saw you both at the home-coming a few weeks ago."

"Can I help you with that?" Graham took the bag from Erin. "Hello, Noelle."

"Thanks." She smiled at him, then turned her attention back to Noelle. "She's a cutie. Is she a Bichpoo?"

"Abigail's a *Poochon*."

"Hey, girl." Erin stooped and extended her hand to the dog this time.

Abigail sniffed, but Noelle kept a tight hold on the leash, maintaining their distance.

Erin straightened. "Nice to meet you both. I hope to see you around again."

Noelle looked Erin over in a way that made Graham envision *we'll see* in a thought bubble over his neighbor's head before she led the dog away for a walk.

He walked Erin to his house and held the screen door for her.

"Was it just me or was that a chilly reception?" she asked once they were inside.

"It's not you."

"I guess I understand if she was friends with Bethann."

"More like acquaintances. Which was a little strange because everyone loved her." That Erin brought up his late wife put him more at ease as often people weren't comfortable mentioning his wife's name in his presence. He was all too conscious of this being the home they'd shared, even if only for a year as he led Erin to the kitchen where she set the bag on the counter and started unloading the food.

"I need a medium-sized saucepan with a lid."

He opened the cabinet under the island. "Will this work?" He produced a pot.

"Perfect. Measuring cups?"

"Check that drawer." He pointed to the one at her hip.

In minutes, she had the water boiling for the rice pilaf and the oven preheating. She removed the tops from glass containers she'd brought.

"That looks fancy."

"Whipped sweet potatoes and pecan-crusted salmon. It's one of my specialties. I'm not a gourmet cook, but this is something I make to impress people."

He liked that she'd gone to some trouble for him. "Is there anything I can do to help?"

"I already made the glaze. I just need to put these in the oven. We'll need plates and utensils."

"That I can do. The kitchen was Bethann's domain. I make sandwiches and man the grill."

"The USO has a cooking class date night coming up. I volunteered to do registration. Would you like to come as my date?"

"I would love to come as your date." Her inviting him gave him more reasons to hope this arrangement would work.

"Great. There are still some slots if you want to invite anyone. Maybe not Noelle and her husband." She poured the rice and seasoning mix into the pot.

"Noted." Graham laughed. "Pete's a good soldier, and Noelle is a good Army wife—and driven to see him make brigadier general. She wants the prestige and to mingle in the circles of the Pentagon elites."

"What about you? Is that what you want? To make general or spend time at the Pentagon?"

"I did my two years at the Pentagon as a major. We were happy to leave D.C. for Fort Lewis. Brigadier general? I don't know. It involves more politics than I want to deal with."

The oven beeped. She put the dishes in, then set the timer.

"Speaking of the general. He stopped by to see me this morning."

"And . . ."

"I told him we've been going out for a few weeks." He didn't relay to Erin that McKittrick implied he'd expected somebody different. Mainly younger rather than his own age. But he'd seemed happy about the fact Graham was dating. "Then I brought up my plans to have you observe one of the teams. He liked that idea to increase our visibility, so he green-lighted setting that up." Way easier than Graham had expected. "Are you free next week?"

"I can be." She didn't move, but her face lit up. "Which day?"

"I'll start you out on Monday morning. If you pass muster with Captain Bryson, you can continue as long as you need throughout the week." Even though the general was right about it increasing visibility, Graham wouldn't let Erin's presence interfere with the men's operations and training.

"Really?" Her mouth curved into a disbelieving smile.

"I recommend you observe quietly from the sidelines unless invited to participate."

"I can do that. What should I wear? Camouflage so I don't stand out?"

He nearly laughed at her instant enthusiasm, but she might not appreciate that. "Best not to wear camouflage. It'll look like you're trying too hard. Something casual that you can move in to follow the team around would be best."

"No high heels. Got it." She aimed a sassy smile at him.

"Right. They won't take you seriously then. Though I should warn you, Captain Bryson has quite a sense of humor. That part of the post is restricted access, so meet me here at 0700 sharp. I'll take you over and pick you up at the end of the day. That will also allow the team to see us together. Are you good with all that?"

"Definitely. Thank you." She took a step closer. "I can't believe this is really happening. I'm shaking." She held out her hand to show him.

"Just be yourself and follow Bryson's orders. You'll win them over. Just don't ask if they've killed anyone. They will shut you out in a heartbeat." It was a question he didn't want to be asked by anyone, even Erin.

Over dinner, they discussed the types of training that would be most beneficial for her to observe based on her story ideas. One day with Bryson's team couldn't possibly cover it all.

"The meal was amazing, and so was the company. I've missed this." Having Erin in his house stirred up a mix of emotions. Sadness, yet hopefulness. He didn't quite know how to describe the loneliness of losing the person you thought you'd be with forever, but Erin nodded in understanding. "I hope you'll stick around for a while."

"I didn't plan to run off. This may be 'an arrangement,' but I'm not faking that I like you and spending time with you. I wouldn't have agreed to this otherwise." She held eye contact with him.

"Same. Though this could get complicated." He took hold of her hand.

"Not if we stay focused on what we agreed to. And with what everyone says about the first relationship after divorce being . . ." She paused as if afraid to say the word.

"A rebound? They say the same thing in grief support groups."

"I'm staying realistic. No commitment, but that doesn't mean we can't enjoy our time together." She broke eye contact, squeezed his hand before removing hers, and started clearing their plates.

He got up to help. While they loaded the dishwasher, Erin's phone rang. She looked over at it but didn't move right away.

"That's Piper's ringtone." Erin's countenance changed to one of a concerned mother. "It's late there. I better take it." She released a deep breath.

"Use my office." He pointed down the foyer. "You'll have privacy there."

"Thanks." Phone in hand, she greeted her daughter as she entered his office and closed the door behind her.

"I'm sorry about that." Erin returned her phone to her purse. There'd been no way to tell Graham things would take a while once Piper told her what was happening.

"No apologies needed. Is everything okay?"

"I wouldn't say okay, but she's better after we talked. The girl she's rooming with on the trip went out with some others from the group tonight."

"They didn't invite her?"

"I didn't ask. Piper's not much of a party girl. The problem was her roomie coming back to the hotel room drunk with some guy in tow."

"That doesn't sound good."

"No. Not when sharing a small room. It's not like she could pull the covers over her head and ignore them getting busy."

"What did she do?"

"First, she turned on the light. Only that didn't stop things, and they invited her to participate."

"Oh."

"Yeah. That might have been what pushed her over the edge. She didn't want to wake up one of the chaperones in the middle of the night, and she was afraid her roomie might lock her out if she left, so she took refuge in the bathroom and called *me*." And it's not like she could tell Piper that she interrupted when she didn't know Erin was now seeing Graham.

"That's a hard one."

"For sure. We talked through some options. She ended up texting a chaperone who, of course, didn't answer. So, we stayed on the phone until they were done. Then Piper told the guy he had two minutes to get dressed and leave, or she was calling hotel security to throw him out." Erin kneaded the knotted muscles in her neck. "It's a shame because she was getting along with this girl up until this. Now she's afraid she's ruined the friendship, and the rest of the trip will be hell."

"Piper didn't do anything wrong."

That didn't matter. "I told her to talk to her roommate once she's sober and not hungover to say that can't happen again. If things go bad, she can ask the chaperones to change room assignments for the rest of the trip."

"At least she wasn't wanting to get on a plane and come home."

"Oh, she was thinking about it until I pointed out how she'd probably regret that later. Especially if she had to stay home with her father for the semester." Which was playing dirty, but Erin had panicked at what it would mean for Piper to come home now—for both of them. "Doing a year abroad was her decision. She needs to give it a chance. Adulting is hard, but I can only do so much from across the ocean. Hopefully, she can sleep, and things will be better than she expects tomorrow—or she can make a new friend. She usually bounces back pretty quickly. But when she crashes, it can be so far and fast that it's hard to see the light when you're at the bottom of that pit."

"I imagine it's hard on the entire family."

"It is. Neither Phil nor I have experienced severe anxiety or depression. I might get down for a day or two, but I can't relate to what she's feeling. I just do my best to help her get through it and keep from crashing."

"You're her go-to person."

"I'm not a professional, but I try to give sound advice. I am glad she'll tell me what's going on—usually. We have an agreement. If she goes to a dark place, she has to talk to me and then wait forty-eight hours before she can harm herself." Though Piper could break that promise at any time. "I'm sorry to bring the mood down." She rubbed the muscles in her neck and shoulder again.

"No apologies. Your daughter needed you."

"I appreciate your understanding."

"We should sit out on the deck and unwind with a glass of wine. I swung by the Bundt cake store and picked up something for dessert."

"I love those."

"I know. When I was looking for you on the USO's Facebook page, I saw your comment on a post about a fundraiser they did. Since you were bringing dinner, I thought I'd do my part."

"After that phone call, I can use wine *and* dessert."

He poured two glasses. Outside, he lit the citronella candles and set one on the glass-top table beside his wine. "I know something else that might help you relax." He straddled the chaise and patted the space in front of him in invitation.

Once she sat, he began to massage her shoulders and neck.

"That feels divine." She sighed and melted under his touch. Her head lulled as he worked on the knots.

He ran his thumbs along either side of her spinal cord from her scalp to her shoulders. "Let me know if it's too hard."

"It's perfect. You're good at this."

"Two of my groomsmen gave us a couples' massage class as a wedding gift. In part, because one was dating the massage therapist and partly because they thought it'd be kinky."

She laughed. "And was it?"

"The first class was basic massage. Bethann and I took the next two more advanced classes. Those took things up a level, but not in a kinky way. Turned out to be the best wedding gift ever." He gently kneaded his way down her arms.

With that lead-in, and the fact she didn't have to look him in the face, this seemed like the opportunity she needed for them to address an aspect of this arrangement they hadn't discussed. Sex could well come into play if they dated for months. "Remember how I told you I hadn't been out with anyone or kissed anybody but my ex in several decades?"

"I do. Same here."

"Well, I haven't been intimate with anyone in a long time. Like over two years."

"I see."

Now, she wished she could see his face to try and gauge his reaction. "You don't have to worry about STDs or pregnancy. But there's something else that I should tell you." Her mouth had gone parched, and her heart beat against her chest so hard he could probably feel her body shaking. "My experience is rather limited." Understatement. "Okay, really limited. Phil is the only man I've ever been with." She took a sip of her wine to fortify her courage, trying to be the new, empowered Erin and shake off the shackles of her past to go after what she wanted in a relationship.

"That's, um, admirable," Graham said.

"We were both brought up in the church and met through a campus ministry group in college, so we were both waiting for marriage. We dated for a year and a half before we got engaged. Being engaged, we justified *it* was okay not to wait any longer. Except, I got pregnant. Instead of having the church wedding we were planning, we had a small ceremony for family and a handful of friends on the beach."

"Nothing wrong with that."

Graham's nonjudgmental attitude made her fall a little harder for him. "Rather than teach why it's best to abstain, the churches I grew up in hammered home the message 'Don't do it. It's bad. It's dirty.' Then all of a sudden, you're married, and it's like, *Okay, its fine now*."

"Are you saying, you plan to wait until you're married before—"

"No. I'm not saying that." At all. "It's just that between the church, the stigma in our social circles around getting pregnant outside of wedlock, and having a baby right away, we never had an exciting sex life. I don't want to disappoint you when, or if, we . . ."

"You don't have to worry about disappointing me. I can't see that happening."

She so hoped that was true. How did she say this tactfully? What did she have to lose by confessing this now? Not as much as she'd lost by never speaking up in her marriage. She took a breath. "I don't know if it was physical or mental for me, but I rarely had an orgasm when we made love. But I want that. I'm telling you this because I have high expectations. And, if I don't have an orgasm, I'm going to be really, really disappointed, especially since I'm having mini-ones every time I merely think about having sex with you."

"That's flattering," he said through amused laughter.

"I'm not saying that I want things—kinky," she referred back to what he had said, "but something more, uh, mind-blowing than missionary position in a dark bedroom." Which didn't cut it for her, and from what she'd read, that wasn't uncommon. She didn't see it doing it for an alpha military man, either. "I feel like I've missed out." On a lot.

"It shouldn't be that way," he assured her.

"I know that now. Early in our marriage, I made the mistake of telling him something in front of my mother and sister that he took as criticism. He blew up at me later for disrespecting him in front of others."

"Did he hurt you?" Graham's voice sounded ominous, and his hands stilled.

"No. He never got violent or physical."

"Good." He resumed his tender massage.

"But, after that, I did whatever I could to avoid conflict. And did my best never to criticize him aloud. Which is why I never felt like I could tell him that our lovemaking left me unsatisfied." And frustrated. And like a horrible person for fantasizing about more—with other men. The 'harmless' kind of fantasies about celebrity crushes she'd never meet.

Had they played a part in the failure of her marriage? Would things have turned out differently if, rather than settle, she had found a way to tell Phil that he wasn't meeting her needs and *she* felt like a failure in the bedroom? Or would she have hurt his pride, insulted his manhood, and made things worse?

Between the church and Phil, sex was a four-letter word and only 'making love' was acceptable and biblical. But she didn't know better then. Now she was a mature woman, not a scared virgin. This time, she'd do things differently. Be more confident and adventurous. She had nothing to lose with

114

Graham. She took another gulp of wine. "This week I bought a book . . ."

"You bought a book?" The amusement in his voice almost made her pause.

"Not the Karma Sutra, but a pocket guide to sex."

"Oh. Maybe I should read this book too." He pressed a kiss behind her ear. "Because, when we're ready, I will make it my mission to ensure you aren't disappointed."

His hot breath rekindled the fire inside her as his hands slid down her arms, over her hips to her thighs.

"Abigail!" Noelle called as she descended her deck steps. "Oh. Sorry to interrupt." Her attempt to sound casual was nearly comical as she peered over the hedges dividing the two yards.

Graham moved his hands to cover Erin's as Noelle's eyes widened as if they were doing something far more illicit than sitting fully clothed on a chaise.

"There you are." Noelle ducked out of sight, reappearing with Abigail in her arms. "Have a nice night." She stared at them briefly before carrying the dog back inside.

"She was peeking through the blinds a few minutes ago." Erin had noticed them move.

"Abigail was probably at her feet the whole time. I might let those hedges grow higher."

Erin chuckled. "She hasn't seen anything gossip-worthy —yet."

"But she is friends with Sally McKittrick, so anything she sees may get reported back. I don't have a problem with that. In fact . . ." He pressed kisses to the side of Erin's neck.

"You should keep doing that for her benefit."

"Just hers?"

"I admit I'm enjoying every second of this pampering. I've missed this kind of touch."

"I know what you mean. On deployments, we go months without meaningful touch. We used to joke about designating Tuesday as Hugs Day—and we weren't entirely kidding." He wrapped his arms around her.

She reclined against his chest and ran her fingers over his forearms. Her thumb brushed over the four to five-inch raised scar she'd noticed on the underside of his forearm. That his muscles twitched served as a warning not to ask how he'd gotten it.

"Did you want to go in and have dessert?"

"While I appreciate you getting the cake, I told Piper to check in with me in the morning. With the time difference, I'll probably hear from her at like five a.m. I should head home soon and try to get some sleep. Can I get a rain check?" She angled her face to kiss his jawline.

"Of course. Tomorrow, we can have a nice dinner and come back here for dessert."

"I like that plan. Along with a couple more minutes of this."

"Is that an order?"

"I don't think you have to take orders from me."

"Just remember, I'm conditioned to follow them, especially if the person issuing them has a certain objective in mind."

His deep timbre and implied promise drew out a low, breathy laugh as she imagined his hands moving to other parts of her body.

Chapter Fifteen

When Graham returned home from golfing and lunch on Saturday and saw Megan's car in his driveway, his gut tightened. It wasn't unusual for Megan to drop by, but her running into him at the game on Thursday gave him a good idea of why she popped in.

"I'm back here, Dad," she called out to him.

He did a double take, seeing her wearing Bethann's gardening gloves and pruning the rose bushes. She looked so much like her mother. "You don't have to do that." He motioned to the yard waste can next to her, half filled with clippings.

"It gave me something to do while waiting for you to get back. How was your golf game?"

"Not my best." It'd probably been one of the worst since he started playing again after Bethann's death. Today, he'd been distracted thinking about Erin. Hopefully, she'd heard from Piper that she was doing better. "Do you want to come inside and get something to drink?"

"Sure." She pulled off the gardening gloves and followed

him inside. "It was good to see you getting out, and I hope you enjoyed the game." She started in while he poured them glasses of iced tea. "So, Erin? I thought she didn't want to get married."

"She doesn't, but we enjoy each other's company. A lot. I got to thinking about what Reece said about how if I were in a serious relationship, that could suffice, especially considering both Boatman and Thomsen were married."

"*Might* suffice. There's no way to know. If General McKittrick insists you follow through with getting married, what happens? Do you think she'll change her mind?"

"That's doubtful. But I did explain the situation. If we have to, we'll announce an engagement and see how long we can string that out."

"She's willing to go along with this?"

He was going to have to come clean. "It's a mutually bene-ficial arrangement. See, Erin is writing a TV series that involves the military. I've set things up for her to observe a Special Ops team."

Megan cocked her head, and her eyebrows rose. "What's to keep her from bailing on her end of this *arrangement* after she gets what she needs?"

"Nothing other than her character. Well, and she does like me. She did not seek me out. I pursued her. I would rather see how this turns out than try to fake it with someone I don't enjoy being with as much as Erin."

"But this could backfire, Dad. It's not like you can fake a marriage. You'd have to produce a marriage certificate to get her a spousal ID."

"We won't take things that far." Erin had made that clear. "If only marriage will suffice, we can break the engagement, and I'll deal with whatever comes my way, even if it's a permanent change of station until I retire. I can always come back here as a civilian contractor."

Megan sighed. "I don't want you to leave, but I don't want to see you get hurt, either."

"Sweetheart, nothing will hurt me as much as losing your mother. I understand seeing me with someone new might be hard for you."

"It looked like you were having a good time with her at the game," she conceded.

"Were you watching us?" He looked at her over his glass of tea.

"Maybe."

"In the stadium, or were you parked at the Special Ops Museum?"

"We passed your car going in. That's how I knew to look for you at the game," she told him without coming right out and answering.

"General McKittrick and his wife were also there and met Erin."

"I guess that's a good thing."

"It is. The general gave his approval for Erin to shadow Bryson's team this week as research for a writing project."

Megan's surprised look quickly morphed into one of understanding. "And Mateo's on that team, right?"

"Yes. He's under Bryson's command now."

"It'll be a good thing if he sees you two together. Maybe that will take care of any crazy talk and keep him from planting ideas in anyone else's head." Megan paused, her mouth shifting. "Why don't you invite Erin to the family dinner next Sunday?"

"I will," he said despite the hesitation in her tone. "You'll like her. She's a lot like your mom."

Based on the look Megan shot him, that wasn't the best thing to say. "Give her a chance."

"I will." Megan relented. "But warn her I've learned things being your daughter and married to a Green Beret myself. And she better not hurt you."

"I can take care of myself." It was the general he needed to worry about.

Chapter Sixteen

When Erin's phone played the "American Soldier" ringtone she had given to Graham's number, it was like getting a shot of adrenaline or ecstasy or whatever drug made a person instantly feel great. "Hi. How was your golf game?"

"Uh, it wasn't my best round. I hate to do this, but I have to cancel dinner tonight. Something came up at work, and I'm going in now."

"I understand. Do what you need to do." She didn't tell him she'd shaved her legs again—just in case.

"I don't know how long this will go on. It could easily be an all-nighter. Maybe longer. It may impact Monday too. I'll call you when I can," he promised before ending the call.

"I guess you two are going to have to put up with me tonight," she said to Smokey and Tink, who both lounged on the other end of the sofa. Tink raised her head for a second as if giving a bored acknowledgment. "Trust me, it's not what I wanted to be doing tonight either."

Several friends had warned her not to share Piper's mental health struggles with anyone she dated. With Graham, did it matter since this was a short-term arrangement, and she wasn't looking for a long-term commitment? He had been so supportive last night, but what if he had second thoughts? She refused to give in to the sinking feeling in her gut.

She'd worked most of the afternoon on a list of questions and things she hoped to observe with the Green Beret team this coming week. If things ended, she would definitely be disappointed. Maybe as much over not seeing Graham as not spending time with a Special Ops team. What did that mean?

~

SUNDAY AFTERNOON, Erin talked to Madison and heard about her trip to Dallas. She'd been tempted to tell her about observing the Special Ops team this week, but since she hadn't heard from Graham, and Madison didn't ask what was new with her, Erin decided to wait until something definite had happened.

Then Piper called again. Hearing things had gone "pretty good" the past two days was better than getting a "not so great." After debating it, Erin decided not to call Phil to tell him what had gone down with Piper, knowing he'd ask her a dozen questions she didn't have the answers to, and he'd reiterate how he'd known Piper going abroad wasn't a good idea. If Piper wanted him to know, she was an adult and could tell him herself.

Erin ate dinner alone again Sunday night. Afterward, Tink settled on her outstretched legs, and Smokey perched on the back of the couch as she read—or tried to. It was hard to focus.

Patience wasn't her strong suit, but she wouldn't get anxious that Graham hadn't so much as texted her after canceling dinner yesterday afternoon. If it was work, it took precedence over her. The weight of responsibility he had to feel for the men under his command made her view him in a new light. It also made her see why having a partner made him a more trusted leader.

When her phone played "American Soldier," she grabbed for it. Tink meowed her displeasure. *Take a breath. Don't ask for details he can't give.* "Hey there."

"Hope I'm not waking you."

"You can call me until midnight. Just not before nine in the morning."

"Should I tell Captain Bryson you won't be there until lunchtime?"

"No! I will get up for that. *If* we're still on."

"We are. I'm headed home now. I need to get some sleep myself. I'm getting too old for all-nighters. Is everything okay with Piper?"

A warmth spread through her that he'd ask about her daughter despite everything else on his mind. "She sucked it up rather than confront her roommate who apologized and promised it wouldn't happen again. Fingers crossed on that."

"Hopefully not. Bringing strangers back to their hotel room is dangerous."

"I agree. I've learned I can't make her stand up for herself. Unfortunately, she gets the conflict-avoidance gene from me." Which is why it took so long for her to leave her marriage despite it sucking the joy from her life. While she didn't seek out conflict, she wouldn't run from it anymore.

"See you here in the morning. Come a few minutes early if you can. I could use a good long hug."

"I will." She hung up feeling wrapped in a hug just from talking with him, as well as relieved and looking forward to tomorrow.

Chapter Seventeen

Erin's heart skipped a beat as she hurried up Graham's walk.

He opened the door, barely waiting for her to get inside before he wrapped her in a hug. "Good morning. This is a nice way to start the day."

"I agree." She lifted her face and got a coffee-flavored kiss from him. "Is what I'm wearing all right?" She'd gone with a pair of gray leggings, a sage-green t-shirt, and a gray ball cap with the USO patch on it. "You said not to wear camouflage, but I thought I'd try to be inconspicuous."

"Inconspicuous and quiet are good, but they're going to know you're there."

"I wanted to see if it would be okay to take some pictures and video along with written notes—strictly for research purposes."

"As long as I have your word that you don't share them with anyone or post them anywhere. The men on my teams have to keep a low profile."

"I totally understand. That's why I had so much trouble getting what I needed. You have my promise."

He slid a hand lower on her back and kissed her again. "I trust you won't dump me for one of these young operators."

"I'm excited to watch them in action for research, but I prefer someone closer to my age for dating." And she liked how things were going with Graham way too much to mess that up.

Despite the guard at the gate recognizing Graham, he still had to stop and hand over Erin's ID to get her a visitor's badge, allowing her on their part of the base. She took a sip from her water bottle since her mouth had gone completely dry, and she had the same nausea as when she'd been pregnant. This was really about to happen.

Graham parked in a small lot near a cinderblock building. She slipped her backpack's strap over her shoulder and walked alongside him to a clearing where a metal tower stood at least fifty feet high.

When the men saw Graham headed toward them, they assembled to meet him.

"Good morning. I want to introduce you to Erin Downey. She's a longtime USO volunteer and troop supporter. She's going to observe your team today for writing research purposes."

"Thank you, Colonel. I appreciate you all letting me observe. The project I'm working on is for a television series that involves joint missions with a Special Forces team. As you can probably tell, I never served in Special Ops." Several of the men chuckled. That was a good sign. "Which is why I need to observe what you do on a day-to-day basis. See how you interact with one another to develop believable, engaging characters. If I can't do that, they'll assign the writing to someone else. Very possibly a former Navy SEAL, and the Army gets cut out." The men appeared unfazed.

"Or perhaps somebody in the Air Force," she tried again.

"Oh, no. No. No." The protests began.

"I agree. DEV-GRU is one thing, but Chair Force?" Now, the men laughed. "I don't want that to happen. Ignore me and be yourselves. Don't worry about watching your language. I taught high school English, so nothing you say will shock me. Be nice to me, and if this series gets picked up, you may inspire a character. And if you're not nice to me, you may inspire a character you may not like because he'll lose his girl to some hipster with a man bun."

Next to her, Graham laughed loudest. "You know how to motivate these guys. Erin, this is Captain John Bryson. He's the one whose orders you need to follow out here today."

While Graham was around six foot one, the captain towered several inches over him and the rest of the team. "Nice to meet you. You look familiar. Have you been in the USO recently?"

"No time recently," the captain said. "But I get that a lot."

He was memorable with his size, but she couldn't place where she might have seen him if not the USO.

"I'll leave you all to get to it." Graham nodded and then departed.

"I didn't want today to be too boring for you, so we're going to start with running urban insertion drills," Bryson said. "You'll see us breach a residence and do run-throughs in the shooting house. After lunch, we'll do climbing and rappelling practice here on the tower, followed by hand-to-hand combat exercises."

"Do you normally do all that in a day?"

"It depends. I want to make sure you get a good overview. Let's get started."

❧

FOR HER FIRST THREE HOURS, Erin listened and observed as the men ran through drills. She couldn't shake the feeling that the men were overly cognizant of her presence and not being their true selves like she'd hoped. It was still progress, especially with Captain Bryson explaining to her what the men were doing.

"Have you ever worn night vision goggles?" he asked.

"I did when I went to the 5th Ranger Open House in Dahlonega, Georgia. You guys use the newer thermal imaging version to detect heat signatures, right?"

"We do use ENVGs." He nodded as if impressed. "You want to do a run-through using them with the team in a blackout scenario?"

"Hell, yes," Erin replied automatically.

The captain chuckled. "Before we break for lunch here shortly, I'll put you in for Gabler." Bryson strolled over to join the team. "Gabler, it's your turn to get the MREs for lunch."

"MREs? What are you talking about?" the soldier with a long, narrow face asked.

"MRE Monday," Bryson said authoritatively.

"That's not a thing, Captain," another man said.

Their confused gazes shifted from Bryson to Erin. It dawned on them at the same time as Graham's warning about Bryson's sense of humor replayed in her head. "I hear most are pretty decent, so if you think that making me eat an MRE for lunch is going to scare me off, that won't work."

"True. They're probably better than my cooking. Just wanted to give you the full Green Beret experience," Bryson drawled, breaking into a big grin. "We typically send someone to pick up food."

Bryson opened an app on his phone and handed it to Gabler, who typed, then passed it to a teammate.

"The USO is hosting a cooking class for couples in a few

weeks. It's free and will be a fun date night." It would also be an incredible opportunity for her to meet their wives, see the men outside of training, *and* for all of them to see her with Graham.

"Sign me up," Bryson said. "My bride-to-be might appreciate me expanding my repertoire beyond grilling and cooking eggs and bacon."

"Couples means you're out, Cruz, unless you want to bring your roommate," Gabler said.

"He and I are not a couple," Cruz protested. "And I could bring a date to a cooking class, but I'll leave that to you old married couples."

Erin had already picked up that the outgoing soldier and shortest team member was the target of much of the good-natured ribbing.

"My wife would love for me to take her to something like that, especially if it's cooking something fancier than mac and cheese or spaghetti. Put me down," another of the men said.

She'd overheard Bryson using some of the men's names in snippets of conversation. But, with the men wearing combat shirts or brown t-shirts instead of uniform tops with name patches, she hadn't matched up the names she'd heard with who everyone was. "If you want me to sign you up, I'll need your names, and they like to get your email and phone number to send a confirmation and reminder. If you prefer not to give that to me, you can go to the USO website yourself."

"The colonel trusts you to be here, so I do too. I'm Louie Atkinson," the man readily supplied his name.

"Louie, Louie. Oh, oh," Bryson sang. "That never gets old."

Atkinson groaned and rolled his eyes. "For you, maybe."

"You need a name like mine. There are no songs for Gregory."

"I will come up with a song for you eventually," Bryson promised, waving a finger at his teammate.

"You've been saying that for a year, and the best you got was trying to incorporate Nishiyama into 'Mama Mia.'"

"That was bad," Bryson admitted.

Nishiyama nodded in agreement. "Cindy and I could use a date night. We can never come up with a restaurant because we don't like the same foods. Put us down."

"Great." She input his information while two others promised to check with their wives.

Bryson requested Gabler's night vision goggles before he headed to the parking lot. "Put in whatever you want," he said when the phone reached Erin.

"What do I owe you for lunch?" she asked.

"You just arranged to feed half my team *and* score us points with our ladies. I got you." He handed her the ENVGs. "We're gonna let"—he snuck a glance at her left hand—"Miz Downey here do a run-through or two in the shooting house until Gabler gets back with the food." He removed his handgun from the holster, emptied the magazine, and checked the chamber before handing it to her. "We're not using live ammo today, but we don't need you firing blanks at close range either."

"Understood." Even without the magazine, the weapon was heavy in her hand. Checking the side confirmed her guess that Bryson carried a Sig Sauer.

"I am going to want that back." Bryson motioned for three men to head into the shooting house before giving orders to the rest of the team and putting Erin third in the line for breaching the residence. He showed her the settings on the ENVGs and helped her situate them over her head and face.

When she turned them on, instead of the eerie green glow she'd seen on videos, much clearer images outlined in a glowing white light allowed her to distinguish the men in front of her and their weapons.

Nishiyama signaled and led the team through the house. She didn't know what the hand signals meant but followed on Cruz's heels. After the team located the men acting as tangos, they invaded the room, spreading to the perimeter with weapons aimed. Before she could process what was happening, it was over. She would have been shot dead three times over since all three "tangoes" in the room aimed at her.

"Wow. Thanks for the indoctrination, guys." She laughed.

"Let's run through it again and not target our guest this time," Bryson ordered.

Erin felt more prepared on the second run. The men performed flawlessly as a unit, sweeping through the house to locate the "targets" dispersed in different rooms this time including a mock hostage—a life-sized female doll wearing a brightly colored dress and head scarf.

"A blow-up doll?" Erin raised an eyebrow at the men.

Bryson shrugged. "She appeared one day. No one took credit. Each team blames the others. It's good training. More dimension than a flat cutout. The first time I saw her, it threw me. That's the point. Expect the unexpected. With what we do, you never know what you'll face. Gabler will be back any minute, so let's break for lunch." Bryson moved them to the shooting house's kitchen and passed everyone water bottles from the fridge.

"Tell us about this writing project," Cruz requested.

All eyes turned to Erin. "I originally pitched this story as a movie that was inspired by *Top Gun: Maverick*. The main character is a third-generation Army helicopter pilot. Her grandfather flew in Vietnam—"

"A female pilot?" Cruz contemplated that with a narrow-eyed expression.

"Now she's selected as one of the best to test a top-secret aircraft her grandfather helped design. The heroine's fiancé is a Special Forces soldier—"

"Is this a love story?" Cruz interrupted, his interest clearly waning.

"There's a romance subplot, but it was about the aircraft and the missions. The operator thinks it's all too risky since he lost a leg in combat and is trying to figure out his future. The movie version was about her going anyway and them being reunited on a mission using the aircraft to rescue girls kidnapped by a group like Boko Haram."

Several men nodded and appeared interested now, so she continued. "However, the studios are interested in making it a television series focusing on the Special Ops team over the aircraft. That means I have to develop the entire cast of characters, not just the two leads. Their back stories, their goals, and motivations to make them real so viewers connect with them. I've been plotting more mission ideas and an overarching storyline that carries through a season. Start the series with the mission where the hero loses his leg, the pair at Walter Reed doing his recovery, then work in the movie storyline and end the first season with the mission that brings them back together."

"Are you expecting to get mission stories from us?" Bryson asked.

Erin noted his reserved tone. "If you have any you can share, I'd be very interested in hearing them—after you revive me."

"Revive you?" he repeated.

"If you agreed to tell me any, I'd likely faint or expect you to BS me with some storyline from a movie."

Bryson laughed. "Glad you understand we won't talk about missions."

"I adopted an aviation unit after I began writing years ago. The only stories I got from them were things like saving the chips and salsa, and Hooch crunching away while hiding under the bunks when they were being mortared. Or the time a pigeon crashed through the Kiowa's chin bubble and sat bleeding on the pilot's boot until they tossed it. Fortunately, I have an overactive imagination. But if you have any fictitious story ideas, I'm open to your input."

"For the most part, fly boys aren't gonna have great stories. They fly around way up in the sky, looking for things to shoot. You know those guys are required to get at least eight hours of sleep a night?" Cruz quipped.

"I've heard that. But they were easier to find than you guys."

"Boots on the ground missions must be cheaper to film than anything with aircraft. Though they retired the Kiowas. The studio could probably get one cheap," Atkinson added.

"That won't work since you can't extract a Special Ops team in a Kiowa."

"That's for sure. Did the Navy letting them use their aircraft for 'Maverick' have anything to do with you getting green-lighted to observe us?" Bryson asked innocently.

"Not directly. I knew from previous attempts that it would be hard to research the Spec Ops angle, but this story required them to be from a top-tier unit. A fellow volunteer at the USO in Charlotte was a Green Beret, but he's been out of the service for nearly thirty years. A lot has changed since then. I figured I'd have a better chance of encountering someone at the USO here who would invite me to a team barbecue so I can see how you guys interact with each other.

I'll even bring the barbeque." She gave a cheesy smile despite her offer being for real.

"That'd be easier to arrange than getting this approved. So, how'd we get so lucky to have you here?" Bryson delivered a subtle smile along with his interrogation.

"I, uh, volunteered at the homecoming for the 82nd Airborne."

"The 82nd Airborne?" Cruz scoffed.

"At the homecoming, I met a few wives, and one gave me her contact information. I also noticed a soldier I thought might be a First or Master Sergeant in the 82nd. I didn't meet him that night, however, I did run into him at the grill on post after I finished tutoring a student a few weeks ago. I noticed his West Point ring while we talked and knew I was slightly off about his rank."

"Yup," someone said, and a few heads bobbed in agreement.

"So, Colonel Ayers . . .? *He* set this up?" Bryson hadn't made the connection.

"No, I met Colonel *Holmstrom*, and in talking about my volunteering with the USO and me moving here to do research for the series, Graham agreed to help me." She left out everything in between.

"You didn't know who he was?" Atkinson questioned her.

"I'm a little embarrassed to say I did not. I thought Colonel Thomsen was still in command."

"They did keep that change of command rather quiet." Bryson didn't elaborate further. "The colonel must like your storyline to arrange for you to be out here."

"Graham cleared it with General McKittrick. It was definitely a case of meeting the right person at the right time."

"The colonel's a busy man. If you need someone to look at the scripts or act out scenarios to make sure they work, I'd be happy to help. We hate it when they don't even try to get things right." Cruz leaned in as he spoke. "You know, adding a real-life Green Beret to the cast could give you that authenticity you're looking for. Let me give you my contact information."

"Dial it back a notch, Cruz. You just re-upped for another three years," Bryson said.

Erin chuckled. "I'll mention that *if* the series gets picked up." Having these men interested enough to help could make all the difference. "We made it past the first stage, and they've ordered a pilot script, but that doesn't guarantee anything since networks only order five to ten series each year, and the majority don't last a full season."

"And yet, they put out some crap programs and tons of reality shows," Atkinson said.

"The only reason I even got my idea presented is that I have a former student working as an assistant for a studio exec. Being a female and over forty are two strikes against me. That's why I need to nail this pilot episode and have at least a treatment, which is basically a synopsis, for the rest of the season."

"It sounds like breaking into the business is tougher than what we do," Bryson remarked. "And like you need to observe more than just today."

"I would like to observe longer. Graham said that would be your call." He could put her with another team, and it would benefit him to have more men see them together, though for her purposes, staying with the same team would help her get to know the men and develop her characters.

"We'll see how this afternoon goes. Tomorrow, we're supposed to do some jumps. That would be a lot of standing around on the ground bored unless you wanted to jump with us." Bryson looked serious, but Erin didn't buy that.

"I'd love to. But could I get earplugs if we do HALO jumps? I didn't expect it to be so loud when I went skydiving before."

"No way. You've jumped?" Bryson asked. "Jumping out of a plane is a hard pass for my fiancée."

"It was research. However, doing a tandem jump isn't the same as doing a free fall. And watching videos isn't the same as doing an actual run-through in the shooting house."

"Don't be telling everybody you did that. The majority of research requests get denied. I'm surprised that one conversation with the colonel at the grill was enough to get you authorized." The captain was clearly fishing for information.

"It took more than one conversation," Erin admitted since he'd given her an opportunity to convince these men she and Graham were romantically involved.

Chapter Eighteen

GRAHAM HEADED over to the training compound shortly before the end of the workday. It took a few seconds to spot Erin observing the men engaged in hand-to-hand combat in the sawdust-covered area at the base of the climbing tower. He stopped next to Captain Bryson, who whistled, then signaled for the men to assemble.

"Came to see what she was up to?" Bryson asked.

"I drove Ms. Downey through security. She'll need a ride back to her car." Graham downplayed it despite Bryson's grin.

"Ms. Downey, huh?" Bryson said.

Erin beamed as she made her way toward them in the midst of the men like she was one of the team.

"Did you have a productive day?" Graham asked.

"Oh, yeah. They let me use the ENVGs and do run-throughs in the shooting house. And I fired the squad automatic weapon and an M-4 rifle."

He raised an eyebrow at her, not that it surprised him that she'd charmed her way into the team's good graces.

"She didn't hamper any training," Bryson assured him.

"After she told us more about the series over lunch, I offered to let her do more hands-on with the team."

"And they all know we're dating," Erin said.

"They do?" That explained the amused grin that hadn't left Bryson's face. He'd been the first to suggest Graham consider a relationship, though he'd specifically mentioned marriage. Graham would give it a little more time before asking the captain how Mateo had reacted to this news.

"I kept calling you Graham instead of Colonel. They're pretty smart and picked up on that. I figured it was better not to try and hide it."

"I didn't want to say anything that would make you feel obligated to assist with her research." Though the men learning they were involved was the number two reason Erin was here.

"She knows more about Ranger training and Special Ops missions than ninety percent of the regular Army. It's obvious she wasn't hanging out with us just for fun and games," Bryson said. "Do you know she's been skydiving?"

"She's mentioned that."

"I tried to punk her, saying she could do a freefall from a Black Hawk. You may have to line that up."

"Really?" Graham looked at Erin, whose smile got even bigger.

"We're good with her coming back out as much as she needs this week. I'll let you two discuss whether she gets to jump out of the Black Hawk." Bryson's grin ratcheted up another notch.

"Sounds like it was a good day," Graham said to Erin.

"I'm having the time of my life," she said.

"Oh, no." One of the team said as Bryson broke into song.

"That's where I know you from!" Erin waved a finger at

Bryson. "You were the groomsman at Cecilia Ryan and Nate Crenshaw's wedding who said you were going to sing 'I've Had the Time of My Life' while they danced."

"You were there?" Bryson's eyes narrowed as he looked at Erin. "How do you know them?"

"Cecilia was a student in one of the first screenwriting classes I taught. We had a mini-reunion at the rehearsal dinner after-party. That's where I pitched this idea to one of my former students who works for the producer in LA. What a small world."

"Nate's the best man in my upcoming wedding. I'll send the colonel an invitation and you can come as his date."

"Congratulations," Erin said rather than stating she'd be there. "Are you and your future wife doing that dance at your wedding?"

"Probably not *that* dance." Bryson laughed again. "But it will be a party." He checked his watch. "We've got a little time left. Anything else you want to see today?"

"I'd like to see the colonel in action." She eyed Graham, wearing a not-so-innocent smile.

"I bet you would." Cruz gave a lusty chuckle.

"Anything in particular you want to see him do?" Bryson asked.

"Fast rope out of a Black Hawk," Erin said without hesitation.

Graham laughed and shook his head. "I can't just make a phone call and have a Black Hawk arrive like a taxi."

"You can't?" Erin batted her lashes at him,

"*You* want to ride in a Black Hawk, don't you?"

"Yes. I also think fast roping is sexy." She stared into his face and ignored the other men.

She was doing a great job selling them as a couple. Maybe

too good as heat rushed up his neck to his face—and down to his groin. He broke eye contact and cleared his throat.

"How about climbing and rappelling from the tower then?" she suggested. "What do they call it when they tie knots around the rope to help climb using their feet?"

"The Prusik climb?" Graham had excelled at that—a decade ago. "With everyone watching me?"

"Told you she's done her research," Bryson said. "We can do a pairs event. Who wants to go up against the colonel and me?"

"I will," Cruz volunteered. "We win, you make me a character in your series. I get to audition for the role too."

"I'll put in a good word for you." It was the best she could do since writers—especially ones with no track record—had zero sway over casting.

"Come on, Mateo. We got this." Cruz led the way to the tower.

Gabler handed out harnesses, gloves, and rope to the four men.

"It's been a while since I've done this." Graham stepped into the harness and began tightening the straps.

"Need a refresher on how to tie a Prusik knot, Colonel?" Cruz asked.

"I might. At least he didn't say the winner gets dinner with you since they have a definite age advantage." He winked at Erin.

"I don't care who wins—as long as I get to watch you."

Even if she was playing things up for Bryson's team, the impact of her innuendo had him ready to scale a tower—and a whole lot more.

❡

SPENDING the day observing Bryson's team had been informative and, if she was honest, a turn-on. Not that she was thinking about *them* that way. But when Graham strode into sight minutes ago in camouflage with his commanding posture *that* had one hundred percent worked for her.

Her body tingled as Graham and Bryson took up position on the left side of the tower.

When Gabler gave the signal, the men began tying knots in the ropes. From where she stood, Graham knew what he was doing. He and Captain Bryson ignored Cruz and Mateo, talking smack about Bryson having a height advantage.

Cruz worked faster as Graham started his way up the rope.

Her eyes stayed glued to him. *Please don't let him get hurt.* Watching Graham climb sent her lust level rising as well.

When he paused halfway up, she saw Mateo gaining on him. Graham continued and hauled himself onto the platform seconds before Mateo.

Bryson immediately began climbing. His extended reach gave him an advantage, but Cruz worked the rope hard and fast and both men disappeared onto the platform nearly simultaneously.

The ropes for rappelling undulated from the opposite sides of the tower to the ground. Graham's camouflage-clad figure backed to the edge of the platform. He stepped off, swinging out halfway down to slow his descent, and landed solidly on his feet. The fall only took three seconds, but it was enough to make her insides quiver.

As soon as Graham was clear, Bryson followed, barely beating Cruz to the team's cheers. Graham walked over, stopping mere inches from her and removing his gloves.

"That was impressive," she said.

"I think they let us win."

"I feel like I'm the one who won." She raised on tiptoes to kiss him.

"Rematch, or does anybody else want to challenge the winners?" Cruz asked.

"That was my workout for today," Graham said.

Bryson leaned closer to Erin. "You keep sweet-talking him, and you might be able to get that Black Hawk ride."

"I wouldn't want to get anyone in trouble, but if the opportunity presents itself, I would love a ride."

"Good night, gentlemen. We'll see you tomorrow," Graham said in a sexy, authoritative tone and steered her away from the training field to the parking lot. He took hold of her hand. "What was your favorite part of today?"

"Seeing you climb and then rappel down that tower." She'd already been fantasizing about him before that.

"Have I told you you're good for my ego?"

"I vaguely recall that."

"Other than that, what did you enjoy?"

"All of it. I've been to a shooting range but never fired anything other than a handgun. I thought there'd be more recoil. I wanted to participate in the hand-to-hand combat, but they were afraid of what you might do if I got hurt."

"I'm guessing you worked up quite an appetite for dinner. Anything in particular you're in the mood for?" He opened the car door for her.

"*Dinner* is not what I'm in the mood for." She trailed her hand across his solid chest, circling his raised nipple with her fingertips.

He met her gaze head-on, his smile broadening. "Okay, then. My place or yours?"

"We can go to my condo, though there are two cats. You're not allergic, are you?"

"No, and unless I were fatally allergic, I'd risk it."

141

"Then you get to see my temporary quarters." And Tink and Smokey might just get a show. At least they wouldn't tell anyone.

Open the bedroom door.

Chapter Nineteen

Waking up in Erin's bed, with the morning sun peeking through the shades, made Graham instantly happy. And hard.

Deployments meant going long periods without sex. Coming home to Bethann after being apart for so long had kept things interesting, even adventurous. Making love with Erin last night had been different but in a good way.

The look on her face when she'd been about to come and during the orgasm was something he wanted to make happen again and again. There'd been no faking it then or the next time either.

His feelings for her were real, too, and growing stronger and stronger. He hadn't expected to feel this way about anyone after Bethann, but with another forty to fifty years left to live, he didn't want to spend them alone. These past few weeks with Erin made him see he'd been surviving but not fully living.

If she weren't leaving Fayetteville in a few months, he could see things working out between them, despite what he'd been told repeatedly in his grief group about first relationships after a loss rarely working out. However, he was a traditionalist and believed in marriage and commitment, whereas Erin had been adamant she wasn't ready for those things anytime soon. He shouldn't even be thinking long-term. That wasn't part of their agreement and could lead to another heartache. For now, he was willing to take what she could give him and hoped it was enough to keep him at Fort Liberty.

He didn't see a clock, and his phone was probably still in the kitchen, so he didn't know how much time they had. They'd gone to bed early but hadn't gone right to sleep. He kissed her bare shoulder. She stirred and gave a dreamy murmur.

"Good morning." This time, he kissed the side of her neck.

"It's morning already?" She pressed her body into his. "What time is it?"

"I'm guessing it's a little after six. I didn't want to wake you, but I don't want you to be late for your second day with Bryson's team."

Erin yawned and turned to face him. "You're right. We're doing orienteering today, which is research I need for the series. We can't stay in bed all day, but we might have time for a little something." She trailed a finger down his chest.

With only two minutes to spare, Graham parked in view of Bryson's congregated team outside 3rd Group's command post. The team looked in their direction, and Bryson held up his left arm and tapped his watch.

Graham escorted Erin over. "Don't lose her in the woods or make her do anything dangerous," he said.

"She's the one who wants to jump or helocast out of a Black Hawk," Bryson retorted. "If you set that up, we won't make her wear a sixty-pound rucksack."

"Thank you," Graham said. Erin batted her lashes at him. "I'll think on it. No promises." He waggled a finger at Erin. It wasn't all that dangerous, but he didn't want anything to happen to her.

"If you want to come show off for me again, I like watching you." She leaned in for a kiss.

He obliged her. Might as well with Mateo and the rest of Bryson's team watching. "I'll be back to pick you up by 1600 hours. Maybe earlier." Probably earlier.

Graham headed to his office. He was still studying the updates on happenings in Central Africa when General McKittrick entered his office unannounced and closed the door behind him.

"Your lady friend spent the day with Bryson's team yesterday?"

"Yes, sir."

"How did that go?"

"Really well. She got good information for her writing research."

"That's good, but I was referring to whether the team knows that you two are romantically involved."

Graham nodded. "They figured it out by lunchtime."

"Good, good. And has Bryson said how things are going with Mateo?"

"No further incidents, and he's integrating well."

"That's good too. Maybe she can observe another team later this week."

"She's with Bryson's team again today doing land navigation exercises. And they want me to set up jumps from a Black Hawk."

"Seriously?" The general's eyebrows rose.

"She's done a jump with a civilian outfit before. I'd rather she jump from a bird than do a high-altitude jump."

"You've got a live wire there. But we don't want anything happening to her to derail your plans."

Now seemed a good time to feel the general out. "Speaking of those plans, Bryson's team deploys in six months. It isn't doable for us to date, get engaged, and plan a wedding before then."

"Why would you need to plan a wedding? Just go to the justice of the peace or have a simple ceremony at the chapel. That can be set up in a week."

"That's not exactly romantic." Graham wasn't going to wave the white flag yet.

"You've been married before. Say you want to be together without the stress of planning a wedding. Take her on a romantic honeymoon to Aruba or Italy. Anywhere she wants. You've got a little time to decide."

"Boatman and Thomsen were married and still fooled around with team wives. Me getting remarried isn't going to automatically negate any concerns the teams may have about *their* spouses' fidelity."

"True. We are all human and fallible, so there's never a way to entirely alleviate the potential for bad behavior. Your relationship with your wife and the fact your daughter and son-in-law were here made you the obvious choice at the time. Under your command, morale has improved. But rebuilding trust takes time, and, unfortunately, Bethann's untimely death changed your situation. I feel for you. I truly do. But I have to consider what's best for the unit."

And cover his own backside.

"Getting married again gives you less opportunity and less incentive to mess around with someone else's wife than if you were single. I don't know any other way to assure the men and keep the unit operational ready."

Graham was getting nowhere. He needed another

approach. "It goes beyond who's in command. We need to fortify the foundation of our family units. We train our men for battle, but we need to equip them and their spouses with skills to successfully reintegrate after deployments."

"I agree that would be beneficial and, as head of the Family Readiness Group, your new wife could be instrumental in setting up programs and date events, especially with her ties to the USO."

"We've only been dating a few weeks. Let's not scare her off by referring to her as my wife yet."

"She'll be lucky to have you, but I see your point. You've still got a few months. And I still think you can be the right man to continue to lead 3rd Group."

On the condition he got married. That meant a fake engagement could be their only play—and *if* that bought them a reprieve, how long could he draw that out?

~

GRAHAM MADE it to a little past fifteen hundred hours before he texted Erin.

> Should I arrive around 15:30 to pick you up?

> That works. Find us in the field by the village used for urban insertion training.

She responded nearly five minutes later.

When he arrived at the designated spot, no one was in sight. Were they still somewhere in the mock village? It made sense to incorporate some urban insertion exercises rather than do land navigation all day. He listened for Erin's telltale chatter to carry from inside the seemingly abandoned village and heard nothing.

He reread the text. *Find us.* Yup. Between Bryson with his sense of humor and what Erin had told him about her story, it fit. It also said the field, not the village. This felt like a challenge. The team would be in camouflage, but he should be able to spot Erin, even wearing muted tones of black and gray.

He surveyed the rolling hills surrounding the village. Tall grass provided cover for anyone on the ground. If he had a military working dog, drone, or thermal imaging goggles, he'd have no trouble finding them in seconds. However, his teams didn't always have access to those tools. He would have to go old school and hope they weren't stationed in the village laughing at him as he strode to high ground. Grass rustled in the slight breeze as he looked for movement amongst the swells. If this were a real situation, the team could take him out with one long-distance shot, but they wouldn't want to alert a village to their presence prematurely, either.

He expected Erin to give herself away with her clothing, movement, or inability to remain silent. However, he hadn't spotted her, even after he picked out three of the team because he knew what to look for. Walking the route, he tapped out those he'd spotted. He came across another who popped up quickly.

"I'm relieved you found me." Cruz urgently brushed his left sleeve with his right hand, then pointed to a fire ant mound a foot from where he'd lain.

"Where's Erin?" Graham asked under his breath.

"You'll never get that information from me, sir." Cruz grinned.

Graham chuckled. "All right. I give up. You win. You can come out." No one else popped up. "Guess I won't have to worry about setting up the ride in a Black Hawk then."

"What?"

He turned in the direction from where the muffled word

had emanated to see Erin struggle to her feet, still covered by the ghillie blanket she shared with Bryson. Though camo paint covered her face and hands, she managed to look adorable and fierce at the same time. "I see you're going for the full-on experience."

"It helps me get in the mindset. And you were right about the fear of discovery," she said to Bryson. "My mouth was dry, and my heart was pounding even though this wasn't a life-or-death situation. You did well figuring out the clue." She smiled at Graham, her teeth gleaming against the camouflage paint.

"It took me a minute." Thankfully, he had figured it out. "Do you have some mineral oil and wipes for her to get that paint off?"

"You don't want me to wear it to dinner?" she teased.

"I guess it depends on where we're going."

Her throaty chuckle made him think delivery two nights in a row wouldn't be a bad thing.

"We'll help you get cleaned up back at the command center." Bryson's sly grin indicated he picked up on the innuendo between them.

It took scrubbing for a good five minutes to remove the visible traces of camouflage paint from Erin's skin.

"We'll see you tomorrow," Bryson said.

"I'm looking forward to it," she confirmed.

"It sounds like you had another fun day," Graham commented as he escorted Erin to his car.

"I'm not sure I would use the term 'fun.' Bryson used the phrase 'embrace the suck.' That's a pretty good descriptor. It was informative and helped me figure out scenes I've struggled to write. I need to jot down some notes on the drive so I don't forget. I didn't get to make notes last night." Her pitch dropped.

"Did you want to go out for dinner now or later?"

"I stink, and I still have camo paint in my hair. I need a shower first."

"Did you want me to take you to your place?"

"My car is still at your house. If you don't mind me using your shower, I brought an overnight bag and left the cats plenty of food this morning." Her sexy smile telegraphed her thoughts.

"You are more than welcome to use my shower." And if he read her right, she'd just invited him to shower with her.

Chapter Twenty

THE GENTLE KISS Graham pressed to Erin's bare shoulder woke her for the second morning in a row. After another mind-blowing night. She could get used to this. Though she'd never been a fan of morning sex, Graham was changing that too. She rolled onto her back and smiled up at him as she ran a finger along his bare shoulder and down his muscular arm.

"Good morning," he said seductively.

"That it is."

"Are we calling in sick and staying in bed today?" he teased.

"It's tempting." Very tempting. "However, I might need a doctor's note to prove I wasn't just playing hooky. How much time do we have?"

"If we don't shower again, we've got"—he angled his head to see the bedside clock—"thirty minutes before we have to be out the door. Though I need to shave this morning. I'm pretty sure the general noticed I hadn't yesterday."

Graham had shaved last night after they'd showered, though she already had beard burn on her neck and cheeks by then. She'd been thankful he had shaved when they went in for round two in the kitchen and then round three in the bedroom.

Three times! And each one resulting in a definite orgasm.

She couldn't recall a time when she'd had sex three times in a week other than maybe her honeymoon. She owed Phil an apology for not speaking up to make things better in the bedroom. Missing out for over two decades led her to conclude that a lifetime of monogamy was overrated—at least in her case.

"Thirty minutes," she repeated. "I'm not opposed to a quickie."

"Then I know just the thing to make that happen." He kissed her shoulder before working his way lower, his hot mouth igniting the fire as his tongue traced circles around one breast tip and then the other, while his right hand slipped between her legs to stroke and tease her to begin his mission objective.

~

"I'll start the coffee." Graham playfully patted her butt as she pulled her hair into a ponytail. He grabbed his electric shaver and tucked it in his pants side pocket.

So much for him having time to shave before they left. She turned her face up and got another kiss before he hustled downstairs.

She put in her contact lenses then joined him as he divided the first cup of coffee between two travel mugs and started a second pod.

"I've got a dinner meeting tonight. I may not have time to pick you up, so it would be best if you drove separately today," he said as she spooned sugar into her mug. "Just follow me, and I'll get you through security. I don't know how late it will run. Do you want to come back here this afternoon?"

"I'd better go home to write notes and care for the cats."

"I guess you can't abandon your post entirely. If you're tired of me and need time alone, just say so."

"Hardly. Though I do need sleep."

"Maybe you can take a nap." He winked at her. "This Sunday is our standing family dinner. I'd love for you to come. I thought I'd offer to host."

"Are we ready for that?" Erin's voice squeaked, and Graham looked up from pouring the second cup of coffee between the two mugs.

"You've already met Megan and Reece. This would be a good opportunity for you to get to know them and meet Jace and Alex."

Convincing the general and the teams they were a couple was one thing, but spending an evening with his family, who knew about their arrangement, was another. "I'll check my schedule." She needed to think this through.

"Okay. I'll call you when we're finished tonight so you can tell me about your day." Graham's voice held an edge of guardedness as he headed to the door.

Great. The invite had surprised her, and she hadn't handled it well. She'd explain tonight after she had time to process her feelings.

Abigail's yippee bark startled Erin as she neared the end of the driveway. Noelle clutched the leash, looking from Erin to her car, which had been parked on the street the past two days.

"Doing the walk of shame?" Noelle's gaze shifted to the bag in Erin's hand.

Did she really just say that? "Are you referring to me spending the night?"

"If you don't want people to know what you're doing, you should at least close the windows so people don't hear."

She was definitely talking about sex. "Graham and I are consenting adults in a relationship. We don't have anything to be ashamed of. And I'm pretty sure the windows were closed." The sex was just *that good*.

Noelle's face turned pinker than Abigail's collar. Erin flashed another smile and got in her car, closing the door harder than necessary.

Noelle stood there staring, her mouth open as Graham pulled out and waited for Erin to follow. So, what if they weren't married? These days, nobody expected previously married adults to wait until they were married to have sex. And that was a good thing because, even if she was falling hard for Graham, neither were ready to get remarried. She was not letting Noelle ruin a good thing.

Chapter Twenty-One

NORMALLY, Graham enjoyed these dinner meetings with arms manufacturer reps showing off their newest technology or weapon improvements, hoping to supply his teams. Tonight, he struggled to focus. Erin had texted him twice during the day. Both just quick updates on what she was doing with Bryson's team.

He didn't understand her hesitation about coming to the family dinner since they would be dating for the next few months—or longer. Unless they weren't. She promised she wouldn't bail after spending time with the team. That they were sleeping together felt like a genuine relationship, not just an arrangement. While he had told her she could walk away at any time, he sure as hell did not want that to happen, not with how strongly he already felt about her.

When Graham's phone chimed in his pocket, he discreetly slipped it out and angled back to see the screen under the table. Seeing Erin's name, he swiped his screen to open the text.

> What can I bring for dinner on Sunday?

The tension locked in his neck all day released.

"Does that smile mean you've already got approval to order?" the rep asked as Graham pocketed his phone.

"Not yet. I'll have a team give them a test run and let them make the call before I run it past the general."

~

ONCE GRAHAM EXTRACTED himself from the dinner, he headed to Erin's rather than call or text. With light illuminating the front room, he rapped on the door.

She peeked through the sidelight before opening the door. "Did I miss a text?" She motioned him in.

"I thought I'd swing by and see if you were still up."

"I'm catching up on *Say Yes to the Rose*. It's a guilty pleasure."

"Sorry for not giving you warning and catching you in your jammies."

She gave a bashful grin despite him having seen her in far less. In addition to wearing the floral print short set, her face was scrubbed free of any makeup, and she tasted like mint toothpaste when he kissed her.

The yellow tabby ceded her spot when Erin waved her off the couch to take a seat. "I had to shower when I got home after Bryson's team tried to punk you."

"Punk *me*? How's that?"

"We did the obstacle course this afternoon, including crawling through the mud. Captain Bryson picked up on their plan to send your mud-covered girlfriend home in your nice car and busted them."

Graham shook his head. "I'm so sorry. I'll order them to detail your car."

"Not necessary. Bryson had a poncho liner in his truck

that he let me borrow. He told them if they tried something like that again, *they'd* drive home without showering first. That I didn't fuss earned me some street cred. I'm seeing their true personalities, which is a good thing."

"I'll let it slide then." It sounded like she'd handled it better than he would have. "You can always tell them no to anything you don't want to do—or could be dangerous."

"Like helocasting out of a Black Hawk?"

"About that, I heard back from Colonel Lundy. He's out of town, so no riding in a Black Hawk this week."

"I appreciate you trying. It doesn't have to be this week."

She smiled and laughed at the same time, and he chuckled at her spunk. The way Bryson and his team accepted Erin affirmed he had made a wise, though still risky, choice. He had a lot on the line and more than his career. "And if you aren't ready to come to a Holmstrom family dinner, we can wait on that."

She sighed. The mood shifted as she rested a hand on his thigh. "About this morning, your invite caught me by surprise. I freaked out a little because I thought it might be awkward with your kids knowing about our 'arrangement.'"

"This is more than 'an arrangement.' I like spending time with you." Even if the general had changed his mind and said today all was good and Graham would keep his command, he'd keep seeing her.

"I like being with you too. A lot."

"Good. If it makes you feel better, Megan suggested I invite you."

"So, if I don't come, it'll look like I'm scared or dumped you. Which I have no intention of doing."

He was relieved to hear that. "With as much time as we're spending together, you'll have to face them sooner or later."

"I know."

"Don't worry. They'll see you're good for me."

"Ditto. I talked to Piper earlier—"

"Everything okay with her?"

"Yes. She called this afternoon, and I told her I couldn't talk because I was about to do the obstacle course with a Green Beret team. She wanted all the details of how that came about. On the way home, I told her the short version *and* that we're dating."

Erin telling her daughter about them was unexpected and good news. "How'd she react to that?"

"She asked if I was dating you as a way to get to observe a team."

"Did you tell her you were?"

"I explained I went out with you before I knew who you were because I liked you and how you make me feel. She took it pretty well, considering I told her before she left for Spain that I didn't plan to date. Madison will be the harder one to tell. I'm not doing that tonight, though. Since you're here, do you want to stay?"

"I'm not in uniform and didn't bring a Go Bag. I don't want to wake you too early, but we could go to my place."

"Are you willing to risk your neighbors seeing me sneak in wearing my PJs?"

"It's not like you're in a slinky negligee." Though he wouldn't mind seeing her in one. "Wait, by neighbors, do you mean Noelle? Did she say something this morning?" She had been near Erin's car with the dog when they left.

Erin made a sound and waggled her head.

Damn, Noelle. "I'm sorry."

"You said she's friends with Sally McKittrick?"

"More like a sycophant than friends. Noelle tries to work her way into circles with wives of higher-ranking officers."

"Well, if Noelle is the gossipy type—"

"She is." At least from everything he knew of her.

"Then Sally will know that we're sleeping together, which is good in the scheme of things."

"Today has been rough for you, and it seems to be my fault. If you ride with me, she probably won't see you, and I'll make it up to you."

Erin eyed him. "Who cares what she thinks or sees? Give me a minute to pack clothes for tomorrow and leave food for the cats. And if it's not too hot out, we'll open the bedroom window."

"What?" he asked as she flashed an impish smile and headed to the kitchen.

Chapter Twenty-Two

Friday afternoon, Bryson gathered the team together shortly after Graham arrived to pick Erin up. The week had been packed with seeing what the men did on a daily basis in non-combat situations and gave her insights for planning some mission storylines for the series.

She'd witnessed the bond and trust between the men. The past two days, she'd gotten past the façade most of the soldiers first presented and gotten to know them as people. She learned what motivated some to serve, like Bryson wanting to belong in the kind of tight-knit family the team formed. And Gabler having followed in his father's footsteps. Though they sometimes butted heads, they were a unique kind of family.

This all helped her create unique characters instead of writing stereotypical, alpha warriors. Getting to meet their wives, or, in Bryson's case, his fiancée, at the upcoming cooking date night would provide even more depth to her characters. Dating Graham had her curious about the unit wives. She knew it took a special woman to support these men and what they did. Would she fit in with them? Not that it mattered in the long run.

"You may not be an official part of the team," Bryson started, "but we got you a little something to remember us by." He pulled a black plastic bag from his pant leg pocket.

"Trust me, I won't forget any of you. I've had the time of my life." She winked at the captain. "Even if I didn't get to ride in a Black Hawk—yet," she finished before he could sing, which he tended to do whenever he thought of a song to fit the situation.

The men laughed, and everyone's gaze shifted to Graham.

"It could still happen. I'll ask Lundy next time we play golf. I hope that's not camo paint." He pointed to the bag in Bryson's hand.

"She could be totally camouflaged, but I give it half an hour max before she'd say something and give away her position," Gabler, the king of keeping a low profile, cracked.

"Thirty? Maybe if she were asleep, she'd be quiet that long. Or does she talk in her sleep?" Mateo joined in the ribbing, his gaze fixed on Graham, who didn't respond other than the instinctive upturn of his mouth.

Erin reached into the bag, which weighed nearly nothing, and drew out a patch the size of a credit card. The inverted dome shape had yellow, red, black, and white blocks with arrows crossed over a sword and *De Oppresso Liber* written on a black ribbon background.

"That's the unit flash for 3rd Group," Captain Bryson explained. "I wore that one on my uniform on my last deployment."

"I can't take this." A brand new one was one thing, but one he'd worn took things up several levels.

"I've got more. Some guys get flags that they give away to supporters. I did patches."

"Thank you. This is . . ."

"There's something else." Cruz pointed to the bag, his face beaming like a kid on Christmas. "It was my idea."

She pulled out a name patch with Downey embroidered on it. "You guys are going to make me cry." Her vision clouded a bit as she looked from the men to Graham. "Thank you all for letting me spend the week with you and making me feel part of your special family with these." She sniffed back tears.

"I've got something that's for both of you." Bryson pulled a slightly bent envelope from the pocket on the other pant leg. "It's the wedding invite. I hope you both will be able to make it. But don't say anything to Cecilia about coming."

"Why not?" Erin asked.

"It's classified," He gave a playful smile and winked at her.

"All right. Is the wedding formal with you guys in dress uniforms?" Erin would love to see Graham in his.

"We're keeping it casual. It's outdoors at my fiancée's property."

"Darn."

Graham shook his head. "Guess you'll have to wait until the unit ball to see us in Dress Blues."

"I look forward to it. And I look forward to seeing some of you next week at the cooking class and other USO events. Thank you for everything."

"If you need anything else for research or want to run through dialog to keep it authentic, I'm happy to help," Cruz offered. "I won't be available much after we deploy. When do they, uh, start filming?"

"Don't answer that. I need him on this deployment. Army owns you for three more years," Bryson reminded him.

"Yeah, yeah. Can't blame me for wanting to get paid big money to have fake bullets fired at me."

"Leaving your steady Army paycheck for an acting career is probably riskier than getting shot at. If it gets picked up and I am hired to write, I still won't have a lot of pull, but I'll do what I can to get any of you an audition." She had a lot riding on this series getting picked up, but, even if nothing came of it, she wouldn't regret pursuing her dream. She could continue to teach, and this journey had brought Graham into her life—at least for a while.

She exchanged fist bumps with the men, getting the explosion effect from Atkinson, who'd mentioned his kids several times this week.

"You're not planning to enlist, right?" Graham asked, walking her to his car.

"Hardly. I'm too old and not cut out for this. I could barely keep up with them, and I wasn't doing daily PT or a third of the training they do in a day. I need to soak in a tub, get a massage, and sleep for twelve hours. Not necessarily in that order."

"Since we've been doing take-out this week, I was going to treat you to a nice dinner and a proper date."

"In case you haven't noticed, I haven't minded staying in with you." It truly had been the best week of her life, not just because of observing the team. "If it's all right with you, can we postpone that? I'd love a quiet dinner in before I collapse into bed—with you."

"We can do that," he said agreeably, his hand resting on the door frame. "Wish I had a hot tub for you to soak in, but how about I give you a massage?"

"You know how to sweet talk a lady." She leaned in, tilting her face up. He kissed her in a way that made her feel desirable despite her being sweaty and dirty.

"My place?" He opened the door for her. "I've got an

early tee time, but I'll try not to wake you, and you can stay and work at my house."

In the seconds it took for him to come around and get in the car, she mulled over the idea of being alone in his house. "I don't have my computer, and I'd probably be more productive at my place. You're welcome to stay with me—unless you need a break."

"I don't need, or want, a break." He started the engine. "I'm spoiled after spending every night with you this week. Is this about Noelle walking her dog as a way to stick her nose in our business?"

"Maybe a little." Or his daughter might stop by. There'd also be the temptation to cross boundaries and snoop around his house. He might not appreciate her looking through the scrapbooks on the bookshelves in the family room without his permission, even if her motivation was to know him better. "I should stay and work at the condo since I've been gone so much this week. I don't want to get fired for failing to be a responsible pet sitter."

"I don't think they'd fire you unless you abandon the cats for a week or so. Don't worry about Noelle. The more people who know I'm involved with you, the better—unless you're worried about your reputation. I doubt she'd say anything that could bring blowback on Pete's career. We'll just keep out of her line of fire."

"Roger that." Erin wouldn't risk the possibility of Noelle learning about her arrangement with Graham and outing that to General McKittrick in some way. The last thing Erin wanted was for this to tank Graham's career and separate him from his family.

Chapter Twenty-Three

THE CAR DOOR closing just outside Graham's kitchen sent the butterflies in Erin's stomach aflutter again.

"It's going to be fine. They're going to adore you." Graham placed a hand on her lower back and kissed her temple.

"I still can't believe we're doing ribs." She'd suggested steaks, chicken, even burgers. What impression would she make picking up ribs and licking her fingers?

"I promise they'll fall right off the bone, and they're Jace's favorite. That, with the banana pudding you brought, and you're a shoo-in," he promised.

The young woman who entered first smiled at Erin in a manner that helped set her at ease. The man that followed was a younger version of Graham with the same blue eyes and a similar athletic build. The smile and hug the men exchanged spoke of the bond between them.

"Good to see you both. This is Erin," Graham made the introductions.

"I've been looking forward to meeting you. Your dad is quite proud of you." Erin shook hands with Jace.

"I'm just getting started. He set a high bar to follow." Jace motioned to his dad.

"And I hear you work for a non-profit," Erin addressed Alex.

"I'm their chief graphic designer." No sooner had Alex set a baking dish on the counter than the door opened to Megan and Reece.

"Thanks for offering to host, Dad." Megan's gaze drifted over them as she placed an insulated tote bag on the counter and removed containers. "We're glad you could make it tonight, Erin."

That Megan's smile seemed somewhat forced was what Erin had feared. "Nice to see you again. Thanks for including me."

"I hear you had quite a week with Bryson's team." Reece grinned at Erin.

"How did you hear?" Had Graham told him?

"Cruz's roommate is on my team and gave him a daily report about the colonel's girlfriend training with the team. Is it true you've been skydiving?"

Girlfriend? Reece said it without blinking; however, Megan's mouth tightened, and her gaze again shifted between her dad and Erin.

"Just one time." Erin pulled up pictures on her phone. "But I'd go again. Especially out of a Black Hawk." She watched as Graham rolled his eyes.

"No way." Alex stared wide-eyed at the photographic proof. "You're braver than I am."

"It wasn't as scary as driving on Interstate 85 in Charlotte. And I-95 here is as bad."

The men all laughed.

"See? I told you." Jace wrapped an arm around his wife's neck in a mock headlock and kissed the side of her head.

"Not happening. I'll leave that to you guys. And you're welcome to go, Erin. Tell me about it *afterward*," Alex said.

"I didn't tell my parents until after I went." And she hadn't told them about this past week or dating Graham yet, either.

Jace leaned forward and spoke lowly. "I don't tell her half of what I do. I learned that from Dad."

"*My* wife learned too much from him," Reece said. "At least she knows not to ask questions she doesn't want to know the answers to. Which is a lot."

"What kind of things did you get to see and do?" Jace asked.

"Almost everything. Hand-to-hand combat, orienteering, camouflage."

Graham laughed. "You should have seen her. They had her face and hands camouflaged and covered her in a Ghillie net. I had to find them in the field outside the mock village."

"Your dad also did the Prusik climb up the tower and rappelled down." Her skin heated at the memory of that and what followed, but she wasn't going to tell his kids about *that*. "I fired weapons and did a run-through in the shooting house using night vision goggles. And Bryson arranged with one of his Delta buddies to set up a defensive driving exercise for me to observe."

"Based on my husband's driving, that could be terrifying," Megan said.

"Babe, I know what I'm doing."

"Yeah, scaring the bejesus out of me." Megan scowled.

"What is it with men thinking they'll impress us by driving fast and taking risks?" Alex turned her gaze to Jace.

"I have no clue," Megan said. "Dad never drove like that."

"Not with you or Mom in the car." Jace exchanged a conspiratorial look with Graham.

"I did give you both some defensive driving lessons," Graham said.

"Not the same," Jace said out of the side of his mouth.

"Did you get to drive?" Reece asked Erin.

"No," Graham answered for her.

"I didn't *drive*." Erin drew out the word.

"You were supposed to observe." Graham's voice held an accusatory tone.

"When a Delta guy invited me to go for a ride through the course with him, I wasn't going to say no. I may never get that opportunity again. I'd watched him do it, so I knew what I was getting into. It was scarier than jumping out of a plane, though," Erin admitted.

"I'm glad my soldiers do a better job following orders than you." Graham cut his gaze at her, one side of his mouth turning up.

"I don't remember it being an order," Erin countered what she hoped was teasing. "More of a suggestion."

Reece snickered. "She's got spunk."

"You don't have to tell me. I'm going to check the ribs." Graham touched the middle of her back and winked on his way out.

After the door closed behind her dad, Megan began uncovering the containers. "Did you get everything you needed by observing the team this past week?"

"I got a lot of great information. As I'm writing, I'm sure I'll have questions that your dad or one of the team can answer."

"How did you end up writing a series about the military?" Reece asked.

"My dad was in an Army aviation unit. I also had some extended family who served. Mainly, it's me having an overactive imagination and coming up with a story where I decided the male had to be in the military. I did a lot of research and wrote a movie script. That project also led to sending care packages and volunteering at the USO."

"Those packages mean a lot," Jace nodded appreciatively as Graham reentered the kitchen. "We gave out stuffed animals and candy to local kids, which created lots of goodwill."

"I supported a platoon of helicopter pilots over several deployments. I wrote a script featuring a female pilot and based the other pilot characters on the guys I'd gotten to know."

"I'm starting to worry you have a thing for fly boys," Graham said.

"You *should* be worried. They were sweet and good communicators," she teased. "They were also easier to find than you *Special* Ops guys."

"We're called the *quiet professionals* for a reason." Graham motioned to his family members.

"I can see a woman writing convincing aviators, but operators are a whole different mindset." Reece's voice held an edge of caution.

"Exactly. And I don't want my operators coming off looking like sissies or alpha holes. That's why I needed to see the team training and how the guys interact. I may still have a rather romanticized view." She batted her eyes at Graham.

"Did anything happen with those movie scripts?" Alex asked.

"Unfortunately, not having any connections in Hollywood, I didn't have any success pitching those. I switched gears and began teaching screenwriting classes. I hadn't written much in the past ten years. However, the movie *Top Gun: Maverick* started an idea spinning that came together perfectly. So, I wrote out all the highlights and the backstory for the heroine so I wouldn't forget and put it out of my mind. Until we had a reunion of some of my students. A few started pitching ideas to one who works as an assistant to a network exec in LA. They pressured me to pitch. I finally did, and Ian loved the idea. He returned to LA and told his boss, and now here I am. Still facing overwhelming odds for anything to come of it, but I'm giving it a shot."

"I hear Hollywood is notorious for stealing ideas. What's to stop them from launching something based on your idea?" Reece eyed her as he poured a glass of tea.

"Very little. I did register the treatment with the Writer's Guild, but I wouldn't be surprised if they have staff writers working on an outline of what they view for the series and sample scripts. That means I have to do it better."

"If it goes forward, will you move to LA?" Megan asked.

"I'm hoping not. I'm sure I'd have to spend some time there, but I can write from anywhere. The cost of living and the lifestyle there is just not me."

"I'm glad it's not. I'm going to grab the ribs." Graham stepped back outside.

GRAHAM BRUSHED a second layer of glaze on the ribs and let them cook for another minute. The dinner wasn't off to as smooth a start as he had hoped. Erin was holding her own, but Megan was not her usual cheerful self. And, even though he had asked her to give Erin a chance, his daughter's questions were coming off not quite hostile but like she was digging for dirt or treating Erin as a potential combatant. Maybe Megan was missing her mother and having second thoughts about him dating. That didn't justify her taking it out on Erin.

He turned off the grill, put the ribs in a pan, and hustled back inside.

Jace licked his lips. "That's a lot of ribs."

"Save room. Erin brought banana pudding for dessert. Ladies first." Graham tried unsuccessfully to get Megan to make eye contact with him.

"Go ahead, Erin. You're company. Dig in." Megan handed her a plate.

After Erin filled her plate with some of everything, she moved to the table and discreetly pointed to the seat next to Graham's usual place at the head of the table. He nodded.

Megan's expression softened a bit when she turned around and saw Erin in Reece's usual spot rather than where her mother had sat at the other end of the table.

"You *can* come back for seconds," Graham said to Jace and Reece.

"I will." Jace ate one of the deviled eggs Alex had brought rather than try to make room on his overflowing plate.

So much for eating like civilized people in front of Erin. And she'd been worried about gnawing on ribs like a cavewoman.

Once they all sat down for dinner, Erin tactfully shifted the conversation by asking his kids and their spouses how they met, claiming she needed ideas for her characters. He wasn't sure that was her main purpose, but the vibe relaxed a bit.

"Nothing exactly exciting," Alex started. "We met through online dating."

"And Megan pegged me for Special Forces and started flirting with me the night we met."

"I did not," Megan protested.

"Really?" Reece raised an eyebrow.

"Okay, it wasn't hard to guess you were in the Ranger

Battalion with the high and tight haircut and the fact that the groom was also a Ranger, but I wasn't flirting. Much."

Graham couldn't help but snicker. Subtle had never been Megan's M.O.

"She wanted the bride to switch things so *I'd* walk her down the aisle after the ceremony." Reece aimed a cocky grin at Megan, who gave a casual shrug and smiled back at him.

"And did she?" Erin asked.

"No. She'd become a bridezilla, and we had to go in the order of the program, which paired me with her younger brother because I was the shortest bridesmaid. Like it mattered since, in the heels she made us wear, he only came up to my chin."

Erin laughed. "Did you know who her dad was?" she asked Reece.

"Not until the wedding reception the next day when I saw her tent card with her name at the wedding party's table. I was in the Second Ranger Battalion, and he was the lieutenant colonel. Holmstrom's not exactly a common name."

"I'm glad that didn't scare him off. I liked him better than any of her other boyfriends," Graham said lowly to Erin. With Megan's independent nature, she needed a strong-minded man. Growing up exposed to the Special Forces community also made her an ideal match for an operator because she knew the hardships that life entailed, and many marriages didn't survive them. It was partly why he was in this predicament. He could see Erin as the kind of woman who'd fit into this life with the responsibilities that came with it. Be a role model for the younger wives in the unit—if only she were open to marriage.

∼

"ARE we having dessert before or after we play games?" Jace asked after finishing two plates of ribs and sides.

"After. Even I can't eat anything else right now." Reece pushed his chair away and started clearing plates.

While the family used to play games after dinner, they hadn't since Bethann had died. Graham considered it a good sign that Jace wanted to revive the tradition and include Erin. "Do you play games?" Graham asked her.

"Yes, to card and board games. I stink at video games. They tried to teach me how to play *Call of Duty* at a USO game night. Half the time, I was dead before I figured out which button did what. And if my video game driving skills carried over to real life, it would result in death or at least losing my license."

Jace laughed. "You ever play a card game called Generic?"

"No," Erin answered.

"No one seems to know it. The Withams taught us while we were at Fort Lewis, and our family got addicted," Graham explained to Erin. "It's similar to a game called Hand and Foot."

"A quarter of the 82nd Airborne knows how to play after our deployment. There were only so many video games to go around. I'll get the cards." Jace got up.

"Let us clean up first." Exasperation crept into Megan's voice.

"I'll help." Erin stacked Graham's plate with hers.

"We've got this. You're company." Megan quickly claimed the plates. "Jace can explain how to play."

Graham cringed inwardly at how the word *company* sounded like a reminder to Erin. Maybe this was moving too fast for Megan with dinner and games, but he hadn't expected Jace to suddenly resume game night. "You need the same number of players on each team, so we haven't played in a while. We should do two teams of three while she's learning." The game would go faster too.

"We should probably put you two on the same team so you don't throw the game," Jace suggested.

"I wouldn't do that," Graham said.

"I do want to see how competitive you are and if you're a good sport." Erin eyed him.

"He's typically a good sport. With his years of military service, he's also a master strategist," Reece added.

"But you can't control the cards you draw," Graham countered. That proved to be the case, with them losing after less than an hour of play.

"Sorry," Erin said.

"No apologies needed. We just didn't get the cards," Graham said. She'd quickly picked up on the game and been a good sport and fun to play with.

"How about some banana pudding as a consolation prize?" she offered.

"Definitely." Jace continued to shuffle cards.

When they finished dessert, Erin loaded her bowl into the dishwasher. "I'll leave the banana pudding for you all."

"You're not leaving already, are you? We need a rematch." Jace motioned to the cards he'd stacked in the center of the table.

Graham hadn't expected her to beat a hasty retreat either.

"I'm still wiped after the week I've had. This was fun, and I hope to see you again soon." She picked up her purse.

The family said good night, and Graham walked her out. "I'd hoped you'd stay longer."

"I thought it'd be better if I left before they did so they don't . . ."

Ah. "I think they suspect we're sleeping together."

"Suspecting is different than making it obvious. Better to give them time to adjust to us dating first."

"True." Considering Megan's reservedness tonight, Erin made a good point. "I'll call you after they leave." He stroked his thumb down her cheek. While it wouldn't surprise him if either his kids or Noelle were peeping out a window, he pressed a light kiss to her lips.

Watching her drive away rather than stay delivered a punch to his gut. The past week, he'd begun to believe that while he could never replace Bethann and didn't want to, he could find love again. It'd be different, but he was different now too. His guilt about moving on had lessened considerably, except it had climbed back up a notch tonight. Hopefully, Megan would come around to accept his relationship with Erin. He didn't want to choose between his daughter and a woman he already cared a great deal about but who wouldn't commit to a future with him.

He took a deep breath before walking back inside and to what his family had to say after spending the evening with Erin.

Jace had put away the cards. Megan and Alex were loading their serving dishes and leftover containers into cloth bags.

"No more games?" Graham tried to keep the mood light.

"Can't play Generic with five, and there's something I found out this week that I need to tell you." The seriousness of Megan's voice sent a chill through Graham's body.

Chapter Twenty-Four

SMOKEY'S TAIL wrapped around Erin's calf affectionately as she refilled the bowls with fresh water.

"Thanks," she said to Smokey for her version of a hug. Most of Graham's family seemed fine with her presence. Only Megan hadn't been warm and overly welcoming.

She understood there was a special kind of bond between a girl and her mother. Besides, Madison would likely give Graham an even less enthusiastic welcome if the situation were reversed.

Graham called before her brain had settled enough to try to sleep. "Hey there." She forced lightness into her voice. "Did they already leave?"

"We called it quits on the games after you left. Megan found out something this week she needed to tell me about."

Something she didn't want to do in Erin's presence.

"I know you're tired, but can I stop by to talk?"

She'd never heard this much raw emotion from Graham, even when he discussed his late wife. "Sure," she said despite the tightening in her chest.

"I'm on my way." He hung up before she could respond.

Had Megan heard something from one of the wives in 3rd Group that would impact Graham's position? That could explain things. Would it affect their relationship? She wanted to continue seeing him, but she'd walk away to protect his career and his family.

She mulled over the possibilities, unable to come up with any positive scenarios. By the time Graham knocked on the door, she couldn't draw a full breath.

Her gaze flicked to his hand, hoping she had read him wrong and he'd brought an overnight bag. His hands were empty. Instead of his usual smile, his eyes were narrow, and his lips pinched as if in pain.

"Sorry if I got you out of bed." He touched her arm but didn't kiss her. "I wouldn't be able to sleep until I'd talked with you. Can we sit?"

She nodded and took a seat on the sofa. Tears already burned her eyes and throat.

He sat down, not looking at her as he wrung his hands.

"When Megan went in for her OB-GYN visit, Bethann's death came up as part of her family history. She told him Bethann's grandmother also died of a stroke at an early age."

Erin sat back a bit. Maybe this wasn't about them.

"Apparently, aneurysms can be genetic. With Megan and Reece planning to start a family, the doctor advised her to get an MRI because pregnancy can elevate the risk."

"I can certainly understand her being stressed, but until she has the MRI—"

"She already did." Tears shimmered in Graham's eyes when he looked at Erin. "This past Thursday. And they found she does have an aneurysm."

"What does that mean? It's treatable, right?" That this didn't have to do with her and Graham should have helped Erin breathe easier. Instead, it had the opposite effect.

"Determining what to do is the next step. With her age and overall health, they don't consider her high-risk, but they still want to refer her to a specialist. However, with the shortage of medical staff, including neurosurgeons, TRICARE has a long wait list to get an appointment anywhere. Here, it's even longer."

"What about seeing a civilian doctor?" Erin didn't know how that worked.

"She's looking into that. Even with a referral, seeing someone could take three or more months. Meanwhile, the stress of knowing there's a ticking bomb in her head is sending her blood pressure skyrocketing."

"I can imagine."

"Being a nurse, she's gone down the research rabbit hole. She's questioning if she should even have children because she could pass the likelihood of having an aneurysm to a child. Having kids is the thing she wants most in life." His voice broke.

Erin laid a hand on his arm, and he covered it with his other hand.

"All I've ever wanted is to protect my family. Then something like this . . ."

"As a parent, you wish it were you instead of your child." She felt that way about Piper's anxiety and depression.

"Exactly."

"I was afraid you coming over now had something to do with us. I wish it were instead."

He squeezed her hand. "You saying that means a lot. I didn't mean to scare you. I'm just reeling. She asked me to apologize for not being herself. She didn't want to cancel or ruin the dinner but knew she'd cry and be a mess if she said anything. That's why she waited until you'd left to tell us."

"She's okay with you telling me, though?"

"Yeah. The jury might still be out on our plan, but *you* passed muster, and she knows I like you."

Erin snuggled against his side. "It's mutual."

He kissed the top of her head, then wrapped his arm around her. She listened to his heartbeat as they reclined against the sofa back.

"This is what I needed. Can I stay a few more minutes?"

"Stay as long as you want."

"I wasn't thinking about spending the night when I left, so I didn't bring anything. I just"—he tightened his hold and sighed—"needed to be with you."

Instead of shutting her out, he'd turned to her. Even though this was supposed to be an arrangement, it felt more real every day. And, tonight, he'd made her fall even harder for him.

~

Graham woke Erin with a light kiss on her forehead. "I need to run home and get ready for work. Thanks for last night."

"I didn't do anything," she said sleepily.

"Yes, you did. You were here for me. I had to stay strong and hold it together for Megan, but I needed someone to help restore my balance. You did that by listening. It hit me last night how much I've missed having that someone. You came into my life at the right time."

Just like he'd come into hers. Giving her the access to a team she needed and so much more.

Chapter Twenty-Five

"WE'RE HERE," Megan called up the stairs while Graham changed out of his uniform Wednesday night.

He joined her and Reece in the kitchen. "You got here fast." He kissed Megan's cheek. She looked better than when she'd left here Sunday night, but the sparkle was still missing from his daughter's eyes.

"I texted you we were at the PX and on our way."

"I didn't see it." He picked up his phone from the counter. "Erin should be here any minute."

"Did she say what she wanted us here for?"

"No, and Kearns was in my office, so I didn't ask in front of him." But she'd been excited about something.

While they waited, Megan gave him an update, which, unfortunately, was that she had an appointment scheduled—in October. Before he could finish counting how many weeks away that was, Erin tapped on the side door's window. She entered wearing the kind of beaming smile he needed.

She stopped halfway to him, pivoted, and set her purse on the counter. Turning to face them, she squeezed Megan's hand. "I can't imagine what you're going through, but I have

180

some news," she said breathlessly. "On Monday, I was talking with Ian, my contact in Hollywood."

Graham hoped Erin didn't plan to incorporate this into her story idea, but he'd let her continue rather than assume the wrong thing.

"In Hollywood, the adage that it's not *what* you know, but *who* you know is one-hundred percent true. But I started thinking how it applies everywhere. Ed, the husband of my professor friend with the beach condo I'll be renting, always talks about his best friend, a big wig at Duke University's School of Medicine. He's not a doctor but in administration. I figured it wouldn't hurt to ask Ed to reach out. I hope I didn't overstep in giving them some medical history, but I thought maybe his friend could recommend a neurosurgeon or more."

Her smile grew as she dug in her purse, produced a piece of paper, and extended it to Megan.

"Ed's friend said this is the neurosurgeon he would want operating on his brain. Mention Ed's friend's name when you call the surgeon's PA. That's his direct number. They're expecting your call. I can't promise this will go anywhere. I'm used to people saying they will help you make connections and then not follow through, but if you don't ask, the answer is always no. And sometimes you get lucky and make the right connection."

She smiled at Graham, and it took every bit of willpower he had to keep from scooping her up and declaring his love for this amazing woman right now.

"Thank you. I'll—I'll call tomorrow." Megan wiped a tear from the corner of her eye. "We've got frozen groceries in the car and don't want to postpone your plans." She swallowed whatever emotions were choking her. "I'll let you know what happens."

An awkward silence settled in before Megan gave Erin a

semi-hug. Next, Graham wrapped his daughter in a tight embrace. He wanted to tell her it would be all right, but he wouldn't make promises about things over which he had no control. "Talk to you soon."

"Thank you." Reece gave Erin an appreciative nod. He wrapped an arm around Megan's shoulders and pressed a tender kiss to her temple.

They were so young to be facing this kind of challenge. Seeing his daughter's anxiety tore at Graham's gut. He'd spent deployments knowing every day could be his last. He did not wish that for his daughter.

How different would their lives be if they had known about Bethann's aneurysm beforehand? She'd probably be alive today and here to support their daughter.

He let out a long breath once he and Erin were alone. "You didn't say anything about this earlier."

"Because I didn't know if anything would come of it. I made a call, but Ed had to call his friend, who doesn't know me and might not feel obligated to help. Which is why I may have played the Green Beret card."

"You what?" He placed a hand on either side of her body, trapping her against the counter.

"I know *you guys* don't strut around saying you're Special Ops." She trailed her index finger down his chest. "But I thought it might garner some favor. So, I may have mentioned what her husband does—and how important it is that he can focus on his mission rather than be distracted by things back home."

She made him see it from a less personal perspective. She was also darn cute in the way she looked at him, wearing a guilty grin, and spouted the same reason Sean McKittrick gave him when telling him to get married again.

"Under the circumstances, I'll let that slide. It's not like we need to keep that top secret for mission safety."

"Good. I wasn't even sure it would carry weight or get relayed from Ed's friend to a surgeon. When I saw Duke Medical on my caller ID this afternoon, I was hopeful. Ed wasn't kidding about his friend being way up there because the PA started asking me about getting medical records and scans for the surgeon to review."

"That sounds better than you let on to Megan."

"I know what it's like to get your hopes up and nothing to come of it. I'd rather under-promise and over-deliver than be the reason she's disappointed—especially about something this important."

"You are one brilliant woman. And I'm feeling lucky that those other guys under-delivered on promises to help with your research, and you ended up in *my* sights." He closed the distance between them.

Erin draped her arms over his shoulders and interlocked her fingers behind his neck. "And I got lucky that you never fail to under-deliver on your promises." She pulled his face to hers.

The kisses got deeper and hotter, with her body pressing harder against his aroused one. "You didn't bring an overnight bag?" he asked between kisses.

"Since Megan and Reece beat me here, I left it in the car."

"Get it now or later?"

"Later." She tugged his shirt upward, giving him that sexy smile that conveyed what she had in mind.

"Here?" He smiled down at her. She nodded, smiling even bigger when he lifted her to the counter.

Chapter Twenty-Six

"Hey, sweetheart," Graham answered his daughter's call.

"We wanted to see if you were home and it was okay to stop by," Megan said.

"Of course, it's fine." Though it was unusual for his daughter to request permission versus dropping in.

"Is Erin there?"

"She should be here anytime." His guard went up higher.

"I'll see you soon." She ended the call before he could ask if everything was okay.

Erin arrived first.

"You look extremely nice." He admired her in a skirt that showed off her slender legs and a purple top that flattered her figure. "Megan is going to stop by any time now. She didn't say why, but I'm hoping she's got an update about contacting the doctor at Duke."

"Will you run this upstairs while I put away the groceries?" She handed him her overnight bag.

"Sure, but I don't have a problem with my kids knowing we spend the nights together. If you want to leave some things here, I've got empty drawers upstairs." He'd been keeping his

Go Bag in the car, but he wouldn't mind leaving a uniform and change of clothes at her place either.

"I'll think about it."

She didn't commit, but he gave her a kiss to think about too.

A few minutes later, Megan rapped on the door. She waited for him to open it rather than walk in as she'd typically done in the past.

He couldn't decipher her expression, but she extended a bouquet of yellow, pink, purple, and white flowers to Erin. "These are for you."

"You didn't need to do that." Erin accepted the bouquet.

"I wasn't as welcoming as I should have been last weekend."

"You had a lot on your mind."

"They're also a thank you for reaching out to your friend with a connection at Duke."

"Did you find out anything?" Graham couldn't wait to ask.

"I spoke with Dr. Verner's assistant yesterday. He sent me a detailed family history form to complete. I sent them my medical records today, but can you get Mom's records so I can send those as well?"

"Sure. I'll log in and access them or have them released to you or his office."

"If I can get everything to them by Monday or Tuesday at the latest, he'll see me next Thursday."

"Is that good or bad?"

"They called to schedule the appointment after Dr. Verner looked at my MRI. They didn't give details, but I take it to mean what he saw concerned him. I called and talked to Aunt Sharon to get information on Mom's side of the family. I need some medical information from you on your side too."

Reece held up some papers.

"And I should warn you," Megan continued, "Aunt Sharon is coming to visit."

Graham's groan drew Erin's attention. "Did she say when or where she was staying?"

"She didn't, and I didn't ask. Or offer. She already has me stressed out, going worst-case scenario, talking about great grandma, and there might be other female relatives who died young. She's freaking out and going to schedule an MRI herself."

"You don't need that right now. Have you, uh, told her I'm dating Erin?"

"I was not going to get into that with her because I'm sure she would have something to say."

"Sharon is Bethann's oldest sister," he explained to Erin. "She's the one who instigates ninety percent of the family drama."

"More than ninety," Megan muttered lowly.

"When Bethann was alive, Sharon stayed with us when she visited, but it might be awkward now."

"Because she's not married? I've noticed she's kind of bitter about that." Reece nailed it with that observation.

"That's part of it. See, I spent a summer with Tyler, my best friend from West Point. His sister was friends with Sharon."

"And Sharon developed a crush after meeting you." Erin hitched a brow at him.

"How'd you know?"

"I have sisters too."

"Well, I didn't know." He'd been oblivious, especially with Sharon being a few years older than him. "Sharon and Tyler's sister tagged along with us to a movie, which I didn't think of as a date in any way. A couple of days later, Tyler and

I went to a party thrown by his high school friend. I immediately noticed Bethann. I didn't know she and Sharon were related until I picked her up for our second date. Years later, Sharon had too much to drink at a family get-together. Something triggered her, and she started in on how Bethann stole me from her. Which was ridiculous since we were never together."

"She wouldn't make a play for her late sister's husband, right?" Erin asked.

"There's no telling with Aunt Sharon," Megan said. "She still talks about her old boyfriends, all two of them, like they dated a year or two ago instead of two decades ago. When she turned fifty, she bemoaned that she would never have children, but she hadn't given up on getting married and being a stepmother, or at least a grandmother, someday. She kept saying she felt bad that I didn't have my mother here to support me, but I could count on her." Megan cleared her throat.

"Should I be worried?" Erin asked Graham with a hint of a smile.

"No!" He never had been, or would be, interested in Sharon romantically. But Erin even asking was a good sign. He hadn't thought he was ready to date, much less marry, but Erin had slipped into his life so smoothly that he didn't like thinking of his future without her in it.

"Not entirely true. Sharon comes off friendly, but you don't want to get on her bad side. She holds a grudge, and sorry is not in her vocabulary." Megan worded it more diplomatically than he could. "She does have a lot of good points."

"Duly noted." Erin chuckled.

"Maybe I'll offer to pay for her to stay in a hotel if she insists on coming." It seemed like a reasonable solution—and worth the cost for his and Megan's peace of mind.

"You do that once, and she'll expect it going forward. She might even come more often," Megan added. "I've told her to wait until we know more. No guarantees." She held up both hands in a surrender motion.

"Would you two like to stay for dinner?" Erin offered.

"We don't want to intrude. I just wanted to update you and drop off the history forms."

"You're hardly intruding. You're family. We're having Hawaiian shrimp tacos, and there's enough for four. You can work on the forms together while I fix dinner."

"Tacos?" Reece repeated.

Megan sighed. "My husband has never met a taco he didn't like."

Graham's heart swelled. No doubt he was falling hard and deep for this incredible woman. "Let's see if we can pull up Mom's records."

"Anything I can do to help?" Reece asked.

"You can help Erin with dinner," Megan said.

"Especially if you're willing to take the tails off the shrimp."

"I will for tacos."

"Thanks." Graham kissed Erin's cheek before heading to his study with Megan.

ERIN FILLED the kitchen sink with water. "It'll only take a few minutes to defrost the shrimp. I'll start making the marinade." While Reece opened the bag of shrimp, Erin began measuring the ingredients. "How's Megan dealing with the news?"

"Up and down. Getting a little better most days. She was hoping the doctor would take a look at her scan and say there was nothing to worry about, so this was a step backward. But she's forging ahead with what needs to be done."

"You're doing good as a calming influence. I didn't pick up that anything was off with you on Sunday."

"I'm trying. Can't have both of us falling apart. We appreciate you reaching out to get her in with the specialist. Army neurologists mostly deal with traumatic brain injuries. Meeting with a surgeon who specializes in aneurysms to determine what we're dealing with is half the battle. Then we'll know how to plan an attack."

"She's got strong allies." Erin couldn't resist throwing in a military analogy too.

"Having positive people in her corner assuring her she can win this fight is key. Along with setting up boundaries to keep out anyone who isn't positive."

Erin needed to make sure she didn't cross those boundaries. She was Graham's not exactly fake girlfriend, but she was not Megan's stepmother.

"Here you go." Reece handed her the colander filled with peeled shrimp. "Thank you again for the invite. I thought it would be good for you and Megan to get to know each other better since she wasn't her usual self on Sunday—and the jury is still out on your relationship with her dad," he said with a grin. "It's obvious he likes you, and you're good for him. But it's been a tough year and a half. She doesn't want to see him get hurt with this arrangement you two have."

"I understand. The last thing I want is to hurt Graham or any of your family," she assured him as she started the rice.

"Good. We'd hate to have to kill you."

Erin couldn't help but laugh. "Death doesn't scare me."

"Torture?"

"I worked with middle schoolers at church and taught high school."

"You might make it through SERE training." Reece chuckled.

"That smells delicious," Graham said as he and Megan rejoined them in the kitchen a short while later.

Reece looked up. "Done already?"

"It didn't take long to get in the system and request Mom's records be sent to Dr. Verner at Duke. Dad called Nana and left her a message. But no red flags on his side so far. Suddenly, I am starving." Megan eyed the food.

"I just need to heat the tortillas. Everything else is ready."

The conversation started somewhat stilted as they fixed their tacos, but Graham and Reece steered it into an easy pattern over dinner and ended on a high note, with Megan asking Erin to send the recipe before they headed home.

"How are you doing?" Erin asked as they cleaned up. Graham's features still seemed strained, and he hadn't eaten as much as usual, even though there'd been plenty for everyone.

"Pulling up Bethann's medical records made reality hit hard. Like you said, you wish you could take this on yourself so your child wouldn't have to deal with it. Megan's too young to be thinking about dying. And she's still questioning if she should have kids because of the elevated risk of passing it on. I told her that if we had known her mom had an aneurysm and decided not to have kids, we would have missed the blessing of having her and Jace. An elevated risk doesn't mean she'll pass it along. And it doesn't have to be fatal, especially since they can check and either monitor it or do intervention if needed."

"You're right, and there are worse things she could pass along. Even if you're perfectly healthy, there are no guarantees." She didn't say how she would trade Piper's anxiety and depression for a more treatable condition.

"I appreciate you inviting them to dinner. Her asking you to send the recipe and giving you both her email and cell number is a positive step. Though I'm glad you didn't bring up becoming Facebook friends. I was afraid she might find my account."

"You still have it up?"

"I do, but I haven't logged in since you gave me your number. I guess I should shut it down."

"You can always set your profile to private, then people can't find you. Or we use it to your advantage. Add your picture to the account and post some pictures of us together to sell us being a couple. Though you may want to change your relationship status from widowed or other women might start contacting you."

"I thought the problem was accounts claiming to be military men contacting women and trying to scam them."

"Typically, but I don't need real women thinking you're available and sending you messages or even naked pictures."

"They wouldn't."

"Oh, they might. They also might not be pictures of them. They could be computer-generated or stock photos from some site. They chat you up trying to get you to think you're in a relationship and ask you to send them money or get you to send naughty pictures back that they can use to blackmail you."

"There's a reason I was never on social media." He shook his head. "I've got you. I don't need to chat with other women. Is there a way to remove the comment to you on the USO page so my daughter doesn't stumble across it in the meantime?"

"I can show you how to do that."

"Thanks. I'd like you to stay, though I may not be the best company tonight."

"Would you be up for reading the series' pilot episode and giving me your thoughts?"

"Definitely. I didn't know you'd finished it."

"Finished is a relative term. This is the third draft. I'll do another after getting your feedback. Do you prefer digital or a hard copy?"

"Print."

"Be right back." She went upstairs and got the bound copy and the pen she preferred for notes from her bag. She took a deep breath, then rejoined him in the kitchen and handed over her manuscript.

"Do you want me to make comments on it or is it better to use a notepad?"

"On the page will be fine. Use this pen. Purple is friendlier than seeing a lot of red. But don't be afraid to mark up anything confusing or wrong. I may take some artistic liberties, but I don't want your guys banging on my door telling me what all I got wrong."

"Yes, ma'am."

"And feel free to include a smiley face if you like something or LOL if it makes you laugh. Writers need some affirmation too. I'm going to be in another room while you read. Otherwise, I'll be interrupting every time you sigh, or laugh, or cough, or roll your eyes, or make a note, wanting to know where you're at and what you think."

Graham chuckled. "I'll go to my office, and you can watch television or take a walk. How long will this take?"

"That depends on how many notes you make—forty-five minutes to hours. Don't go easy or think you'll hurt my feelings."

After explaining some of the terms in the headings, she got a kiss to fortify her, then went into the family room and picked a show to watch while she tried not to think about

Graham reading her script. Except her stomach twisted in knots, and her mind drifted to her storyline and second-guessed her choices. When he appeared holding the script in his hand, her lungs froze. "You're already finished?" Or had he hated it so much he couldn't read it?

"It didn't take long. I only made two or three comments. I got so caught up in the story I may have missed some things. I'll read through it again tomorrow and add more smiley faces." He winked and moved closer.

"You liked it?"

"You drew me in with the opening scene. I immediately connected with Sunny and Travis and felt I knew who they were and what they wanted. The characterization was spot on for them and Travis's team. I could visualize everything. And when you fade to black at the end and left me hanging with my heart pounding in my throat . . . I have to know what happens next."

Erin barely refrained from bouncing on the couch. "Really? You're not just saying that?"

"I wouldn't lie to you." He handed the script back and sat next to her. "For Hollywood to be interested, I knew you had to be good, but you blew me away. And I can say you're *my* girlfriend." His tone dropped. "I wasn't in the mood to fool around after Megan's news, but, well, you took my mind to a different place."

"Are you saying that my script got you worked up?"

He gave a bashful smile. "When Sunny and Travis were at the bakery for the cake tasting, and she sucked the icing off his thumb, was that intentional?"

"Maybe." Definitely.

"Subtle, but effective." Graham grinned. "I checked to see if I still had one of those little Bundt cakes left to bring in, but I thought that might be obvious."

"We can try that another time. But . . ." She shifted to straddle him and looped her arms around the back of his neck.

He let out a cross between a happy moan and a sigh.

She took his left hand from her hip and raised it to her mouth while staring into his eyes. His thumb toyed with her lower lip. Her tongue swirled and stroked. Then she lightly clamped his thumb with her teeth. His pupils dilated, and his breathing deepened. His other hand covered her breast. When he pinched her nipple, a needy moan escaped, and she pressed against his erection. Having this effect on him was empowering.

She released his thumb and kissed his mouth. Had she ever been this aroused? Only a month ago, she wouldn't have wagered on ever having sex again. Now, here she was, initiating it and practically begging him to make love to her. It's a good thing he never made her beg—for anything.

Chapter Twenty-Seven

GRAHAM SLOWLY OPENED the sliding barn door between the bedroom and bath. Erin was still asleep. Rather than wake her, he slipped downstairs.

While the coffee brewed, he wrote a note inviting her to stay if she wanted and left a spare house key with the note. Then he snagged a protein bar and hurried to the golf course.

"I overslept." He stowed his clubs on the back of the golf cart.

"You're not *officially* late." Ed Lundy checked his aviator watch and cracked a grin. As usual, he wore a golf shirt and hat with embroidered helicopters. Maybe Graham could get an extra hat from Lundy's unit's golf tournament for Erin.

Graham sat next to John Mahinis, the serious commander of the elite Delta unit.

"Late night? Good night?" Mahinis asked dryly.

"Both."

Mahinis stroked his chin as a subtle way of telling Graham he noticed that he hadn't shaved.

"It's the weekend." Graham tried to downplay it.

"Earlier this week, Dianne and I were out walking and

ran into—or were ambushed by—Noelle walking her dog. She claimed she'd just been thinking how we should go out for dinner together and how our dinner group had been so much fun."

"The dinner group we stopped having because of her?"

"Exactly. It was just an excuse for her to bring up how she's surprised you're dating already. She asked Dianne if she'd noticed your friend's car being parked at your house or yours being MIA all night. Dianne claimed she hadn't noticed. She had."

"Does Noelle not have anything better to do than gossip about me?"

"She was expecting support from Dianne since she and Bethann were so close. Dianne did ask if I knew how you two met."

"Erin volunteers with the USO." Graham left it at that.

Mahinis stopped the cart at the first tee box. "Wait. USO? Is this the same Erin that was observing one of your teams?"

"How do you know about that?"

"My guys did that defensive driving course with one of your teams. They mentioned she was there and something about research for a television series she's writing. They wondered how she got approved for that. Guess I know now." Mahinis grinned.

"McKittrick signed off on her observing the team."

"He did? What's in it for him?"

Graham laughed, got out of the cart, and pulled his driver from his bag rather than answer. Though he trusted his friend, Graham wouldn't get into his dilemma even if Mahinis didn't report to McKittrick.

"What do you know about the TV series?" Mahinis asked while they waited for the foursome ahead to move on.

"What series?" Lundy asked.

"The woman I'm seeing is writing scripts for a series she pitched as being an Army version of *Top Gun: Maverick* with a female lead."

"Is that why you tried to line up training flights with a Black Hawk last week?"

"Guilty. Think you can at least get her in a simulator?"

"That's easy enough." Lundy agreed as he teed up his ball.

Erin was going to love that. Conversation halted as they took turns teeing off. As usual, Lundy outdrove them all. As they headed down the fairway, he contemplated Noelle's motive in bringing his love life up to the Mahinises. He couldn't think of any reason for Noelle to talk about him and Erin to people, but if gossiping about them to the McKittricks helped him keep his command, maybe he would invite the Ayers to dinner.

"THAT'S MADISON," Erin said as her phone played "Under the Sea" while Graham drove them to meet the Mahinises at DiLorenzo's for dinner Saturday evening.

"Hey, sweetheart. How's everything?"

"If my boss doesn't ease up, I will change roles or quit. I told him about needing time off for Mackinnley's shower and wedding back in March. Except my co-worker is on vacation the whole week before the shower, and he won't even let me take Friday off."

"I'm sure Mackinnley will understand, especially since it's a long way to come from Texas for the shower."

"If I'd bought a plane ticket, I'd quit or call in sick and let him flounder."

"No, you wouldn't. At least without another job lined up,"

Connor piped in from the background as the calming influence and voice of reason to counter Madison's impulsive nature.

"You can communicate your needs to your boss and work out a better work situation or look at making a change rather than stay in a job that's making you miserable." Like Erin had done staying in her marriage.

"I may start looking. But I wanted to let you know about the shower since you're helping with it."

"I wish you could come. Maybe I can come to Texas sometime between now and October." She glanced at Graham.

"That might work better since you don't have a jerk boss dictating your schedule and can come whenever."

"I have a few things on my calendar." A helicopter roared overhead.

"I couldn't hear you. Where are you?"

"We're near the airfield. Graham and I are on our way to dinner with one of his golfing buddies and his wife."

"Who is Graham?"

"The colonel who set it up for me to observe the Green Beret team."

"Hello, Madison," he said.

Silence engulfed the car.

"And the colonel we're having dinner with is over an elite unit. Graham hasn't said which, so I'm presuming it's Delta."

"Which I will neither confirm nor deny." He winked at Erin.

"Oh, so this is research. Cool. Don't let her do anything crazy, like jump out of a Black Hawk helicopter.

"We're still negotiating that. I'm getting her time in a simulator."

"You are? I am? When?" This was the first Erin had heard of this.

"I let Lundy beat me in golf again, then I asked for you."

"Stick with the simulator. That's safe. She will probably ask you a hundred questions and hit you up to attend some team or family event. You've been warned. Have fun. Bye."

"Bye, honey." Erin barely got the words out before Madison ended the call. "I'm getting to pretend I'm flying a Black Hawk?"

"Lundy said getting you time in a simulator wouldn't be a problem. Madison didn't know we're dating?"

She should have known he'd pick up on that. Little got by Graham. "I thought Piper may have mentioned it, but I haven't come right out and told Madison. Her standard M.O. is to ignore anything she'd rather not hear." Like her father's drinking or their marital problems. Her refusal to acknowledge it didn't mean it wasn't true. "I love her, but she is a little wrapped up in herself."

"It's an age thing. Partly generational too. Ease her into it however you think is best. That was our agreement."

An agreement that she tended to forget now with so many real feelings involved. "I'm trying to address conflict myself, but it's hard when it's your kid. I'm already in the doghouse with her because of the divorce."

"I understand."

"Thanks, and I will not ask Colonel Mahinis a hundred questions or even what unit he's with."

"Good plan. He may bring it up, but don't count on it—at least not tonight. Dianne is a good ally to have. She's well respected and tight with Sally McKittrick. She was also close with Bethann, so you may have to pass muster, which I'm confident you can do. Just be yourself."

Chapter Twenty-Eight

"Do you need help with anything?" Graham offered when Erin exited the condo with the box of supplies for the USO's cooking date night.

"It's just this box of swag and the video release forms. All the food for the class is provided." She set the box on the back seat of Graham's car.

He leaned over to kiss her once she got in. "What happened to your wrist?" He pointed to the parallel pair of scratches. "That didn't happen this morning when we . . ."

"No." Her face heated, and pleasant tingles started at the memory. "This was Smokey's doing. I had an urgent message from her owner, Mareena, this morning that she'd forgotten about Smokey's vet appointment. Then she added, 'Oh, and she doesn't like to be put in the cat carrier.' She suggested I try to lure her in with some treats and allow ample time.' As soon as Smokey saw the cat carrier, she took off and hid. I got this lovely scratch when I tried to get her out from under the bed."

"Ouch. Did you get her to the vet?"

"I did. I put away the carrier and put a cardboard box with some treats next to the bed, hoping to lure her out."

"Smart." Graham navigated out of the complex.

"I thought so. Except Tinkerbell jumped in and ate those treats. So, I went dumpster diving and got a second box."

"You didn't." Graham chuckled.

"I didn't have to *climb* in. I just leaned in really far. It was worth it because Smokey finally came out from under the bed and got in the box. But before I could close it up, Tink jumped in with her. That lasted about three seconds before Smokey jumped out."

"What's that saying about herding cats?" Graham full-on laughed with her now.

She shook her head. "Using the last of the treats, I got her in the original box and closed that sucker up. I made it to the vet's two minutes before the appointment and waited for thirty-seven minutes."

"Sounds like you went over and above in your cat-sitting duties today. Are you going to finish your assignment, or are you looking for an opportunity to transfer?"

"I won't abandon my post—since I don't have to take her again or force her to take pills." If Graham was referring to her moving in with him, that was still taking this too far—even if they had spent almost every night together the past two and a half weeks.

She savored the time with him—trying not to think of how it would end in a few short months unless they could figure out a way to draw out a fake engagement—indefinitely. Or if they ended a fake engagement, who's to say they couldn't get back together and start dating again? Couples broke up and got back together all the time. Though he might decide he was ready to marry. And meet someone and . . .

No. She would not ruin tonight by letting an uncertain future steal her joy. "I didn't get lunch, so I am looking forward to this class."

"Do you have a list of who's coming?" Graham asked as he pulled into the shopping center parking lot.

"It's in the box."

"Are Sean and Sally McKittrick on it?"

"They're not."

"I didn't think so, but I brought it up yesterday when he asked about you, and he said he'd run it past Sally. I didn't think he was serious."

"The class filled up not long after I told Bryson's team about it. Half of the class is his team."

"Good. It would have been nice if the general were coming, but having the wives meet you and see us together is a positive."

Graham carried the box of supplies into the brightly lit space where a woman about her age wiped down the front row of workstations.

"Hi. We're here for the USO class. I'm Erin, tonight's volunteer coordinator. Where would you like us to set up for registration?"

"I'm the owner, Mikie. That back table is fine."

Graham set the box down. Erin hadn't even finished laying out the name tags before the door opened.

"Hey, Captain. Good to see you again," Erin greeted John Bryson.

"This is my fiancée, Elizabeth." John smiled at Elizabeth like a man totally in love. He picked up their printed name tags.

"Nice to meet you after hearing him talk about you," Erin greeted her.

"He talked about you spending time with the team too. You're a brave woman to hang with these guys for a week."

"They went easy on me and kept it fun. Especially him."

Erin pointed to John. "Graham and I are looking forward to the wedding. Thank you for the invite."

"We're glad you're coming."

Atkinson entered with his wife and exchanged a fist bump with John.

"Are you going to sing tonight?" Atkinson's wife narrowed her eyes at John.

"Is he going to breathe?" Atkinson answered before John could.

"I told him he could only do one song." Elizabeth gave John the side-eye.

"One? I thought we compromised on two song references."

"One is enough," Mrs. Atkinson rolled her eyes. "Especially since you cannot carry a tune if your life depended on it. Which doesn't stop you from singing like you're in some Disney musical."

"It's one of my more endearing qualities. Maybe we'll be cooking 'Cheeseburgers in Paradise,'" John broke into song.

"That was your one." Elizabeth held up her index finger.

Erin laughed as John continued the banter, then she greeted the Nishiyamas. "Cindy, Greg said you're a professor at the university here."

"I'm a neurobiologist and teach in the psychology department. He mentioned you teach English and are writing for a TV series. That's so exciting."

"I'm writing. We'll see if it gets made as a series." She tried to temper people's expectations—including her own. It had been a good week of writing, though.

"Greg wouldn't give me any details, other than saying he was impressed with your research. Good luck."

Cindy's compliment and the proud look on Graham's face gave Erin another boost of confidence.

The door opened again, and Graham did a double take. She looked that way quickly.

"General, Mrs. McKittrick, it's nice to see you." Erin's mind raced with how to handle this.

"Please, call me Sally." She gave a genuine smile.

"Graham told me the USO was doing this cooking demonstration, and since you had invited us to an event, we thought we'd come." The general returned a mock two-fingered salute to Captain Bryson.

Sally eyed the name tags. "Except it looks like we needed to RSVP. Is there room for us?" she asked sweetly.

"We have a full house; however, we often have no-shows. Please, stick around. If everyone does come, you can have our slot."

"Oh, we couldn't take your spot," Sally said.

"It's no problem. Since I was coming to coordinate, I signed Graham and me up. But it's supposed to be a date night for the troops. We've been on several dates already the past week." She smiled adoringly at Graham.

"Erin's already quite the chef," Graham added as reinforcement. "Last week, she made us salmon and whipped sweet potatoes that was fabulous."

"I've got extra name tags." Since Erin wasn't sure what the general would want on his, she handed Sally the blank name tags and a marker. "Claim any empty workstation."

"All right then." The general overrode any further objections his wife might have and took his name tag.

"Thanks for that," Graham whispered near Erin's ear after the McKittricks claimed a spot in the center of the room.

"Absolutely." She could go hungry a while longer to sell her and Graham being a couple for the general and the team members here.

Erin greeted three more couples, including Sergeant

Mateo and his wife. Michelle scanned the room. Rather than pick a station next to other members of Mateo's teammates, she led her husband to one in the back corner.

Erin checked the time on her phone. The class was supposed to start in five minutes, and three couples still weren't there. As she went down the list of contact numbers, the door opened.

Noelle Ayers entered with her husband, and Erin groaned inwardly.

"Pete, have you met Erin?"

"Not yet." Pete smiled and extended his hand as Graham made introductions.

"Nice to meet you, Colonel. Hello, Mrs. Ayers."

"Sally said they were doing a cooking demonstration for the troops here tonight." Noelle's usual frosty tone softened a bit in her husband's presence, and she made a point of waving to the general and Sally.

"It's a cooking *class*. I don't recall seeing your names on the registration list, though." She was one hundred percent certain they were not.

"Sally didn't mention registration. Wait, class? *Doing* the cooking?" Her pitch rose with each word.

"Doing it ourselves might be even better. You could learn something new, dear." Colonel Ayers's suggestion and encouraging smile garnered a tight-lipped, totally forced smile from his wife.

"Unfortunately, I don't have any spots available unless two of the three remaining couples don't make it."

"Well, we are here before them." Noelle motioned to the unclaimed name tags.

"However, they registered. And here's one of them now." Thank goodness.

AJ Rozanski, one of the Delta operators who had done the

defensive driving class, slipped up to the table to grab his name tag. "My girlfriend got held up at the hospital, but she'll be here in a few minutes."

"No problem at all."

AJ set the cloth bag he'd carried in on a station at the back next to John and Elizabeth.

"I'm sure my husband outranks anyone you're waiting on," Noelle persisted.

"Honey," Pete started.

"At the USO, we treat all military members equally regardless of gender, race, religion, *or rank.*" Noelle was not pulling rank with Erin in charge. "I'll try to get in touch with the other two couples to verify if they're coming." Erin smiled, though, behind closed lips, her teeth clenched.

"We appreciate that. If there's no room, we understand," Pete said for him and Noelle. "We'll know to register next time." He placed a hand near his wife's elbow. "Let's say hello to the general." He stepped in that direction, still gripping his wife's arm to lead her.

Erin immediately called one of the two couples still MIA. *Please let them come.* Her call went to voicemail, and she left a message. She also sent a text in case they'd screened the call. She copied the message and texted the other couple before calling. The woman who answered apologized and said their sitter had canceled and they wouldn't make it.

A pretty redhead wearing hospital scrubs hurried in. "You can start without me. After ten hours in scrubs, I need to freshen up for my date." She picked up her name tag.

"We still have a few minutes. Take your time," Erin assured her.

The woman gave AJ a brief kiss, picked up the bag he had brought, and disappeared into the bathroom.

Erin rechecked her phone. Still no response from the

other couple. She tried calling one last time but didn't leave another message. She sighed and looked up at Graham. "I'm going to go tell them there are slots for both of them."

"Sorry. I had no idea that they'd show up."

"No worries," Erin said, though Noelle could have picked a better time to schmooze with the McKittricks.

"It's going to be interesting since Noelle doesn't cook. At all."

"Really?"

"Her family was based overseas and had servants when she was growing up. They pick up food or eat out."

"She has to have some good qualities." Erin just hadn't seen what they were yet.

"She loves animals and volunteers at the shelter. Oh, and she's patriotic. You saw how she decorated for the Fourth of July? She does that for Memorial and Veteran's Day too." Graham stretched for nice things to say.

"I do like when someone's patriotic." She went to inform them they could stay.

Noelle kept talking to Sally as if she didn't see Erin waiting rather than interrupting. Finally, Erin tapped Colonel Ayers on the arm. "We did have a cancellation and a no-show, so we have space for you to join us. I believe there's an empty station in the front and one in the back. We'll get started in a minute."

Noelle paused and looked at the groups on either side of the McKittrick's work area. "Would you mind switching places so we can be next to our friends?" she said to the Nishiyamas.

Erin caught the way Pete cringed. She bit her tongue as Greg agreed, and Cindy reached for her purse. Had Noelle always been this way, or had her husband's rank gone to her head? Noelle should take a lesson from Sally McKittrick, who didn't treat the enlisted troops like plebians. Erin had decades of experience not saying the first thing that came to her mind, but Noelle was someone Erin needed to steer clear of rather than risk saying something that would reflect poorly on Graham, especially in front of the general.

Graham had taken up a post in the back with Mateo and Michelle on one side and John and Elizabeth on the other.

"Hello, everyone. I'm Mikie, and this stud muffin is my husband, Scott. He does the couples classes with me because he takes credit for the suggestion. See, we had gone from the 'everything was all fun and romantic in the kitchen' stage to where his tombstone was going to say, 'He wouldn't stay out of the kitchen when she was cooking.'" People laughed when she held up a large chef's knife. "Some of you who have been married for a while know what I'm talking about. Show of hands if the kitchen is *your* domain, and you don't want your significant other in there. Don't be shy."

Graham looked at Erin's semi-raised hand. "I wouldn't have guessed that."

"We're in that early stage. As long as you don't start snacking while I'm cooking and get in the way, we should be good. Oh, and don't rearrange the dishes I loaded in the washer because your way is better or is the *right* way." Or wipe down the counters after she cleaned them. More things in her marriage that she tried to let slide because she feared telling Phil how that made her feel.

"Got it." Graham couldn't hold back a smile. "If I slip up, remind me."

"I will," she promised. She'd trust Graham could handle her expressing her feelings without receiving it as criticism or that she viewed him as inadequate. Through counseling, she'd learned effective ways to express herself. She couldn't change the past, but she could do things differently in the future.

"Tonight, we're going to teach you cooking techniques and put a little sizzle back in the kitchen. I don't just mean food." Mikie exchanged a heated smile with Scott. "For our first 'recipe' tonight, I want you all to turn to your partner."

With looks of confusion, the couples slowly faced each other.

"Get closer," Mikie ordered. "Now, y'all stare into each other's eyes for ten seconds. No talking. It's okay to blink. Start."

The utter silence lasted a few seconds.

"Is someone counting?" Noelle blurted out.

"Five. Six," Greg called.

The internal heat built as Erin continued gazing into Graham's blue eyes. They leaned even closer to each other.

"All you couples in the back row got it going on," Mikie said. "If this were a competition, one of you would win."

"Competition? You didn't mention that. Can we do this again?" Atkinson asked.

"Sure. When you get home. That was just a warm-up. We don't want it to get *too* hot in the kitchen." Mikie gave a good-natured laugh as Scott rolled a cart down the center aisle, passing out containers filled with the food items. "Tonight, we are making sweet and spicy pork meatballs with ponzu glaze, green beans, roasted carrots, and dulce de leche lava cakes for dessert." Mikie began walking everyone through the prep.

"If you've got this part, I'm going to take pictures of all the couples for the USO website," Erin said as Graham placed the ground pork in the bowl to mix with the panko and seasoning.

"You're abandoning me to do KP duty?" he teased.

"I'm sure you can handle this. I'll be back to help." Erin got shots of Mateo and Michelle, then moved to the middle row.

"You don't want to overwork the meat," Mikie said, watching a couple in the front row.

"Yeah, save that for when we get home, honey," Louie Atkinson cracked.

"You wish," his wife replied as Noelle shot a shocked look Louie's way.

After taking pictures of each couple, Erin returned to their workstation. Graham had nearly finished forming all the meatballs. "Great job, honey," she said loud enough for the general to hear. "We should get a picture of us together."

"I'll take one for you." John extended his hand for her phone.

"For the USO website or Facebook?" Graham's eyes narrowed.

"For me. I didn't have any pictures of us together when Piper asked." Regardless of how things ended with Graham in the next few months, she wanted to remember her time with him and the woman she'd become due in part to his help. Would any man she met in the future measure up after Graham?

Erin watched several couples walk out holding hands after the class. "Have you gotten a wedding gift for John and Elizabeth?" she asked Graham.

"Not yet."

"A gift certificate for a cooking class would be more appropriate than a couples' massage class, considering you're his commanding officer."

"Agreed. Great idea. I'll take care of it."

"I'll split it with you. I wanted to do something to thank

Mikie and Scott for tonight. They gave the USO a great deal on the rates."

"We can settle up later." He raised his eyebrows and gave a suggestive grin.

Sean and Sally McKittrick strolled over before heading out. Noelle and Pete lingered a few steps away.

"Thanks for inviting us. It's been a long time since we did anything like this." The general smiled at his wife. "And you know what you said about supporting our family units, Graham? This kind of event is perfect." He fixed his gaze on Erin. "I'd love to see you set some things up like this when you plug in with the FRG."

"Honey, you might be rushing things a little," Sally stated. "But since he did bring up the FRG, next weekend we're doing a brunch for Gold Star widows of the unit. Graham is one of this year's speakers. With your involvement with the USO, I'd love for you to come."

"I would love to, except I'll be in Charlotte helping friends host a bridal shower. If you need help with setup and decorations, I'm available Friday morning, or I can provide food items. I love to bake."

"I'm sorry you won't be able to attend since the wives find you relatable, but we never turn down baked goods or casseroles."

"I can pick up some donuts or pastries," Noelle chimed in. "And I would be happy to help serve, especially since I already know many of the women in the unit." She cut her gaze Erin's way.

"Thank you, Noelle. I hope to see you soon, Erin," Sally bid them goodnight.

"Sorry about the general putting you on the spot that way," Graham said as they exited. "At least it shows they're buying us as a couple, and they both like you."

That was better than the death glare Noelle had shot her. "I probably should have let it slide when Noelle commented Pete about outranking others coming. But with my dad having been an NCO, I don't take kindly to officers, or their wives, who act like rank automatically makes them more important than enlisted personnel."

"There's still a clear line of division between enlisted and officers in the Army. Noelle's father was a high-ranking officer, so she doesn't come from the same perspective as you do. She once asked Bethann how we could let Megan marry a non-commissioned officer."

"She didn't."

"She tried to roll it back, but Bethann knew what she was implying. I'm sure it never occurred to Noelle to marry anyone less than a captain. She doesn't appreciate the caliber of highly intelligent and hard-working men who make up Special Forces—many of whom earn college degrees. That's one of the things that makes Bryson such a good leader. He served before getting his degree. I'll take a man who's served in combat over one who partied through college and still came out with bars on his collar over stripes on his sleeve. It's about character over rank. I'm in this position now because of the shortfall of ethics and character in officers."

No one who knew Graham's character could seriously think he'd repeat the actions of his predecessors. He simply wouldn't do that to his family or the men he commanded and lose their respect. And Erin would do everything in her power to keep his reputation from being blemished.

Chapter Twenty-Nine

THE LUMP in Graham's gut expanded on the drive to Jace and Alex's for the family dinner. Erin had kept him distracted enough to refrain from calling Megan or Reece to get an update on their consultation with the neurosurgeon. Until he heard the doctor's conclusion, Graham could hold on to hope that his daughter would be given a clean bill of health or at least a reprieve.

"Have you talked to Meg yet?" Jace asked as they joined Alex in the kitchen.

Erin set the salad and bruschetta on the counter.

"No. I'm trying to respect her saying she'd tell us tonight." It hadn't been easy, but based on the tone of her text, Graham wasn't sure she'd answer.

"Same," Jace said. "I can't believe it's only been two weeks, and she's already seen a neurosurgeon."

"They're here," Alex said seconds before the front door opened. "You didn't have to bring something." She reached for the glass baking dish Megan carried in.

"I'm not an invalid," Megan stated.

"But you were away. I—"

"It gave me something to do."

"What did the surgeon say?" Graham asked the question on everyone's mind.

Megan sighed. "I was hoping to wait until after we ate, but I might as well get it over with." She sighed again, and Reece placed a hand on her back. She motioned for them to sit at the table, but she remained standing.

Even though it went against his instincts, Graham followed her orders. Erin sat next to him and covered his hand with hers.

"Dr. Verner was super nice and reassuring. The size and location of the aneurysm are why he wanted to see me. Because of my age and overall health, I'm not in the high-risk category, but, with the family history, he suggested I consider surgery at some point." She paused. "I want to do it before we start a family—just in case. It's not like there's ever a good time, but I'd much rather do it while Reece is here and not deployed. There were two options, and we both agreed with Dr. Verner's recommendation of the less invasive coiling procedure over surgery to go in and clamp or cut out the aneurysm."

"What does that entail?" Graham asked.

"They insert tiny metal coils into the weakened artery to block blood flow. It's still brain surgery, but it's less risky. It only requires a night or two in the hospital and about a week for recovery."

"They're not going to cut open your brain? Darn. I guess that means they can't cut out the part that makes you so bossy. Though I guess that wouldn't leave a lot," Jace joked.

Alex elbowed him in the ribs.

"No." Megan stepped close enough to swat Jace on the

shoulder. "But you're going to have to be nice to me until the surgery and at least six months afterward."

"You're making that up," Jace scoffed.

"I can get a doctor's note. The surgery is scheduled for two months from now. There's a possibility I could get rescheduled if something gets canceled because we can get there on short notice. And, for the record, *if* something goes wrong, Reece has to wait eighteen months before dating, or I'm going to come back and haunt him."

The laughter broke the tension.

"Nothing's going to happen. We just have to treat you like a delicate princess for a little while." Reece pressed a kiss to her temple.

"That's nothing new. She dressed up like a princess *every* Halloween." Jace rolled his eyes.

"Not every one. I went as Hermione Granger my last year trick-or-treating."

"When you were fifteen. She was in love with Daniel Radcliffe as Harry Potter," Jace told Reece.

"I'm over him. I got my happily-ever-after." Megan batted her lashes at Reece.

"That all sounds encouraging." Graham got up and embraced Megan, holding her for several long seconds.

Then Jace hugged his sister. "Enough mushy stuff. Let's eat."

Alex took a turn hugging Megan. "We are doing make your own pizza. You get to go first." She set out baking sheets with pizza dough.

"I'll be back in a minute," Graham excused himself. After stepping out into the solace of the front porch, he released a deep breath and said a silent prayer of thanks. Even with his eyes closed, he sensed movement. When he raised his bowed head and opened his eyes, he wasn't surprised to find Erin standing within arm's reach.

"You okay?" She placed a hand on his lower back.

"I am now. I feel like I've dropped a ninety-pound rucksack I've been carrying around since she told us about the aneurysm. I didn't know there was an option where they wouldn't have to cut into my daughter's brain. I can't thank you enough."

"All I did was make a call."

"You did more than that. You cared enough about my daughter, whom you barely know, to think of how you could help. That call moved mountains. You also stood by me these past two weeks when I needed you and your positivity." He pulled her into his arms and kissed her lips lightly before resting his forehead against hers.

He wanted to tell her he loved her because that was the only word that accurately summed up his feelings. But love wasn't part of their arrangement. How would she take it? Things were going smoothly in their relationship, but would a declaration of love make her run or bail now that she'd gotten access to one of his teams for research?

He swallowed the words. It could be some of the emotion of Megan's situation. Better to wait. However, if she said it first, he wouldn't have to think twice about telling her how he felt.

"Hey, are you two going to come in and fix your pizzas? Because if you're going to keep making out, I'm going next," Jace interrupted the moment.

Graham chuckled. "We're coming. Sorry. We tried to teach him manners." He pressed a quick kiss to Erin's cheek before leading her back inside.

The vibe over dinner and two hours of games this week was much more relaxed. Erin participated in the conversation like she was family. That realization hit Graham like a round in the gut.

He hadn't thought he was ready for a relationship. Their connection may have started as a way to help each other so he could stay here, but he'd never anticipated the way she'd slide right into his life. Would she glide out of it as easily?

Chapter Thirty

GRAHAM LOOKED IN THE REFRIGERATOR, trying to figure out what to do for dinner. It was only the second night without Erin while she was in Charlotte for the shower, but somehow, it felt longer. If being apart only two days was this hard, he didn't want to think about what it would be like when she left for the beach. Why did it have to be Kiawah Island, four and a half hours away, instead of Myrtle Beach or Wilmington where it would be possible to meet up for dinner or an easy commute for a weekend?

The unexpected knock at the side door came before deciding what to eat. He closed the fridge and turned to see Pete Ayers standing on the stoop.

"Hope I'm not interrupting. Noelle sent me to invite you for a drink and dinner if you're free. Maribelle Jepson is over and said she'd loved to see you."

He'd spotted Maribelle in the audience when he spoke to the Gold Star group this morning. However, he left immediately after speaking to meet Pete, Mahinis, and Lundy for golf. "How's she doing?"

"Come over and ask her yourself." Pete stayed the course

like a man on a mission and didn't leave him a graceful way to decline without potentially hurting the widow's feelings. It's not like he had other plans tonight. "Should I bring a bottle of wine?"

"We're good. Noelle picked up food and wine."

They joined Noelle and Maribelle on the Ayers's back deck.

"Graham! It's been too long." Maribelle got to her feet to embrace him in a full-body contact hug that lasted several seconds longer than it should have.

"How are you doing?" He settled into the chair next to hers.

"You understand better than most when I say it's still hard."

"Help yourself to some hors d'oeuvres." Noelle pushed the charcuterie board his way. "Would you like red or white?" She picked up an empty wine glass and gestured to the two bottles.

"White, please."

Noelle filled his glass with a generous pour.

Maribelle took a drink of her wine and held her glass out for Noelle to refill. "My youngest just got his driver's permit, but riding with him is about to give me a nervous breakdown. When Daniel was learning, Kurt took him out and let him drive at the training course on post. I can't do that and don't have near the restraint, so we've had a battle or two." She gave a light laugh. "And Daniel's been looking at colleges. He'd planned to do ROTC and join the military, but after losing his father, he's having second thoughts about that."

"That's understandable. Though plenty of specialties aren't dangerous or don't even deploy. He could talk to somebody in HR. That's one of those positions."

"I wish he had someone to talk to about that besides me.

It's hard making all the decisions on my own. I'm sure you can relate."

"It's a change being on your own."

"Yes. I figured you're in stage three. First is shock, then there's grief. Then you have lots of support from family and friends. That's so important, but that wanes as people move forward. You're no longer part of a married couple, so you don't know exactly where you fit in." The whole time she spoke, she stared into his eyes with her beseeching gaze. Now, she leaned in and placed a hand over his. "I know exactly what you're going through. Feel free to reach out if I can help in any way. Even to have someone to talk to or share a meal with so you're not alone."

"I appreciate that." He turned his hand and gave hers a light squeeze before extracting his and taking a sip of his wine.

"Put my number in your contacts and text me so I can add you and that way I'll answer."

"I don't have my phone on me."

"Then I'll put you in mine." She typed in his name and handed him her phone to enter his number.

Mentioning that he was dating Erin now would make things awkward. Maribelle was sweet, intelligent, and attractive and came off as looking to settle down again; however, he hadn't thought about her after meeting Erin. Maybe she was offering support as a friend rather than trying to clear all obstacles in her path for him to ask her out. Regardless, he wouldn't risk things with Erin, even if marriage was off the table with her.

"Should we go inside and fix a plate?" Pete asked when the conversation stalled.

Graham pushed to his feet. It didn't surprise him that Noelle had picked up a sandwich tray and sides from the PX rather than cook.

They had barely sat back down outside when Maribelle tapped Graham's arm, then rested her hand there. "I was thinking about what you said regarding other specialties. Daniel thought he needed to follow Kurt into Special Ops. He might be more receptive if *you* encouraged him to consider other areas over some recruiter. I could have you over for dinner. You probably haven't been getting a whole lot of home-cooked meals lately." She smiled hopefully at him.

"Actually, the woman I'm dating is a great cook. I've put on a pound or two already." He patted his stomach.

"Oh." She drew out the word into two syllables, then cleared her throat.

"I can meet up with Daniel at a coffee shop. I don't want to be an imposition." Though Maribelle left Graham no choice but to bring Erin up now, he glossed over the semi-veiled invitation in hopes of sparing her feelings.

"It wouldn't be an imposition since I have to feed two boys already, but I'll see what he's comfortable doing."

Noelle picked up the bottle of wine and moved to refill Maribelle's glass.

Maribelle waved off the refill. "I need to slow down a bit since I'm driving home tonight."

"I'm good too," Graham said when Noelle pointed to his glass. This sudden invitation to dinner smacked of being a setup. Maybe Noelle was trying to sabotage his relationship with Erin. But why? Just because Erin fraternized with enlisted military?

At dinner with the Mahinises, Erin had fit right in, hitting it off with Dianne. He felt like they were a couple in every way. And the longer they were together, the more he wanted them to have a real future.

"I hope you saved room for dessert." Noelle gathered the

empty plates. "You two stay put. We'll take these plates in and be back out with the cookie assortment."

Noelle motioned to Pete, who carried the potato salad and condiments into the house.

"It's nice to see you, Graham," Maribelle said once they were alone. "I didn't know you were ready to start dating. I thought you might need more time. If I'd known . . ."

"I wasn't looking to date. Then I met Erin, and everything changed." Not quite in that order, though he wasn't going to explain.

"How long have you two been *dating*?" She said the word almost as if it were profanity.

"Around two months."

"*Hmm*. Then, if you aren't exclusive—"

"We are at that point in our relationship," he cut her off.

"Oh. Well, you know what they say in the grief support group about that first relationship after losing a spouse typically being a rebound one that doesn't last. If things don't work out, I'd love to be the one you call when you're ready to try again."

"I'm, uh, flattered. Have Daniel text me if he wants to get together to discuss different MOS options." He broke eye contact rather than send the wrong signals. *Please come out with the cookies now.* Not that he wanted a cookie. It could be that the wine allowed Maribelle to speak her mind more freely, in which case it was good that she'd stopped drinking. However, he was prepared to pull an escape and evade maneuver if she or Noelle tried to make him the designated driver. That could go wrong in so many ways.

Chapter Thirty-One

Erin hadn't even changed the litter box before Graham knocked on the front door.

"Couldn't get here sooner?" She teased before offering him a kiss.

"I didn't want to look too desperate by camping in the parking lot. I also didn't resort to tracking your phone or task a drone to search for your car."

"You couldn't do that." Could he?

He shrugged. "I wouldn't want to get in trouble for misappropriating government resources, so I'm glad you called. How was your weekend?" He followed her into the bedroom and set his overnight bag on the bed.

"The shower for Mackinnley went well despite a hiccup. When I got there Friday, Lori was panicked because her puppy, Zeus, had gotten into a container of bacon-wrapped cracker appetizers and knocked a tray of cupcakes onto the floor in the process."

"Sounds like the puppy needed to be put in time out."

"He did, but he's too cute to stay mad at him." She pulled dirty clothes from her suitcase and dropped them in the laundry basket. "We had to fix more in addition to decorating for the shower. Katy and Lori commented how I was glowing and asked how things were here in Fayetteville. It came up that I was seeing somebody. But one of my other friends tends to be judgy."

"That you're dating?" Graham took a seat on the corner of the bed.

"I was trying to be cute about how you contacted me from your Facebook page. But Monica immediately started in about how she knows some woman who was scammed by someone claiming to be a military officer. After messaging for weeks, he asked for her help paying his daughter's college tuition because he couldn't access his bank accounts while deployed overseas. Said he'd fly her to some resort for them to meet and pay her back when he got home from Syria in a few weeks." Erin rolled her eyes. "Of course, she never heard from him again after sending thousands of dollars."

"That's ridiculous. I can't believe people fall for that."

"I assured her I had seen you in camouflage on base and met you and your kids in real life. I told Monica and my friends you arranged for me to spend an entire week with a Special Forces team and showed them the picture of us from the cooking class. My other friends were supportive. However, Monica's marriage is, well, complicated. She seems determined to stick it out for better or for worse. I told them I'm happier than ever, but I behaved myself and didn't come right out and say we're having mind-blowing sex." That might have sent Monica over the edge.

Graham sputtered and blushed as she hung the dress she'd worn for the shower in the closet. "Then don't put her with Noelle. She might tell her."

She didn't tell him how Monica got under her skin talking about relationships after divorce rarely lasting and spouting statistics on the failure of second marriages. Erin hadn't come into this relationship with unrealistic expectations. She was the one who said marriage wasn't an option and knew there was a deadline. That didn't mean she couldn't enjoy every second with Graham.

"Speaking of Noelle, she had Pete invite me for dinner last night."

"Dinner? Did Noelle cook?"

"No. Picked up food at the PX. Maribelle Jepson, one of the .widows from the Gold Star brunch, was there. Her husband served in 3rd Group. Kurt was killed in action shortly after Bethann and I arrived at Fort Liberty. As head of the FRG, Bethann helped Maribelle with things after his death."

The responsibility Bethann carried as Graham's wife hit Erin. Not only was the trust of the men under his command an issue, but there were aspects of his job that fell to his partner. That was likely why Sally had invited Erin to the brunch. Graham might be able to put General McKittrick off temporarily, but there were other reasons why he wanted Graham married. In his current position, Graham needed more than a girlfriend. He needed a fully committed wife.

"Her oldest son will be a senior in high school in the fall," he continued. "Daniel had hoped to follow his father into Special Forces. She wants me to talk to him about other, safer specialties. She invited me over for dinner to talk to him."

"Like she's interested in more than you talking to her son?" Erin's radar pinged. She zipped the empty suitcase and stowed it in the small walk-in closet.

"Don't worry. I told her I was dating you, and we were exclusive."

"Do you think Noelle instigated this dinner or did Maribelle?" Noelle knew Erin would be out of town this weekend.

"I'm not sure. And maybe I'm imagining her interest, but I

wanted to tell you because Maribelle's got my number since I offered to meet with Daniel, *and* she's already texted me."

"As long as she didn't kiss you or pat your butt, I'll keep the claws put away."

He reached for her hand and pulled her closer. "Since it did feel like a setup, I don't want Noelle bringing it up to make you think I was keeping things from you."

"Since we're doing full disclosure, I went by the house and saw Phil this afternoon."

Graham's eyebrows hitched up, and he released his hold on her hand.

She leaned against the dresser. "I still have things stored at the house, including some furniture. He's trying to line up painters and wanted it moved out to make things easier for them."

"Can't they just cover it with drop cloths?"

"I thought about telling him that but decided I'd rather cut those ties."

"Does he know about us?"

"Not yet. And he may not take it well, which is another reason to get some sentimental things, like the scrapbooks with pictures of the girls and my grandmother's cedar chest and quilts. I said I'd line up a storage place and come get it moved since it doesn't make sense to move it here and then to the beach condo." She stepped closer and rested her arms over his shoulders. "I'm just glad to be back here. With you."

"What do you need to reset? A walk? Ice cream? Cake? Bed?"

"I'm not ready to go to sleep." She lowered her forehead to his. "But bed is sounding good. I missed you."

"Not as much as I missed you."

"I don't know about that."

"I don't want our first fight to be over who missed who

more. Why don't we concede to a draw where we both win." He gripped her hips and kissed her in a way that made her weak in the knees.

This was the kind of win she needed to banish all her tension.

Chapter Thirty-Two

"Do you need me to drive? Erin asked as Graham put the overnight bags in the trunk of his car.

"I'm fine," he said, despite the fact they'd both had trouble sleeping after Megan called last night with the news her surgery had been moved up.

He had offered to make a hotel reservation for Megan and Reece so they could hit the road to be there for the early morning procedure. Before he called them back with the hotel information, he'd asked Erin if she would go to the hospital with him today. She was touched that he'd want her there but insisted he ask Megan and Reece if that was all right first. That they also wanted her to come made it a no-brainer to go with him.

The traffic was light on the early morning drive to Durham. After finding a place to park at the hospital, he texted Reece to find out where to meet him.

Reece pushed to his feet when they joined him in the waiting room. He shook Graham's hand and hugged Erin. "They just took her back to prep her for surgery ten minutes ago. The nurse said the procedure should last around an hour and a half. Two hours max."

"How's she doing?" Graham asked.

"A little anxious, but she's ready to get this over with. When they called to say a patient had canceled, she immediately took the slot." Reece sounded remarkably calm for a man whose wife was about to have brain surgery, but Erin figured it came from years of training to keep calm in every situation.

They took seats together in the waiting room where several other families huddled, awaiting news of their loved ones.

"Here, I brought something to distract you." Erin handed Graham her bound script. "It's the next episode."

"What about me?" Reece asked.

"If you want to read the first episode, I've made some changes based on Graham's suggestions. I haven't printed it but have the file on my tablet. You can make notes in the file or on a pad of paper."

"I'd love to read it."

"Okay. Now is the time to fix anything before I send it to Ian out in LA, so be honest," she stressed, opening the document and handing him her tablet. "With both of you reading my scripts, I'm going to walk around for a bit so I'm not staring at both of your expressions trying to gauge what you think. I've also got a scene I need to figure out. Let me know if you guys want me to bring you coffee or anything."

"I could go for a coffee," Graham said.

Reece also gave Erin his coffee order.

She exited the hospital, went to the Duke Gardens, and walked the trail around the fishpond. A few minutes into her walk, inspiration struck. She dictated a note into her phone to run her idea past Graham when she returned. She walked for another twenty minutes fleshing out the scene before returning and picking up three coffees.

"There you are." Reece got up and headed toward her.

"Is everything okay?" She shouldn't have been gone so long.

"You tell me. What happens to Travis?" Reece gestured to the tablet.

"You're already finished?"

"Yes, and he won't let me start reading the next episode yet." He waved a hand toward Graham, still reading his paper copy.

That Reece was desperate to know what happened to her fictional character sent a rush of energy through her. She handed the men their coffees with hands that shook noticeably. "I can't tell you until I know what you think of the story."

"I don't normally watch shows or movies about the military. *This* I would. I started making notes on a couple of terms we would use until I realized you had to make it understandable for civilians."

Erin did an internal squeal. "Exactly. Believe it or not, not everyone even knows that in military terms a klick is a kilometer or that 'got your six' means I've got your back." She turned to Graham. "And what about the second episode?"

"I'm almost done. I only noted two or three minor points." He pointed a finger at Erin. "You made me teary."

"Is that good or bad?"

"Very good. Your characters are going to resonate with people. They aren't perfect, but they're likable and relatable."

"Yeah, Megan hates it when the media portray military guys as alpha holes," Reece agreed. "Hurry up and finish. I like to binge-watch shows rather than wait a week or two for more. I want the third episode by the end of the day."

"If only." Erin laughed. "But I do have the second episode on that tablet."

Once the men were both reading, she put in her earbuds to drown out the voices on the TV and began typing on her laptop. She didn't know how much time passed until Reece stood and stepped toward the man in blue scrubs who approached. Graham got up too.

"The surgery went just how we hoped," the doctor started. "We put coils in both the main aneurysm and the smaller one to be safe."

"Two?" Graham said in a tone so low it was barely audible.

"She's in recovery now. Her sensory reflexes are as expected," the doctor continued. "In about an hour, she'll be moved to her room. She will be groggy and may have some speech or memory issues when she first wakes up, but that's normal. I'll check on her tonight and again in the morning. It's possible she could go home tomorrow as long as someone is with her at all times."

"I'll be there," Reece promised.

"I can help if needed too," Erin volunteered.

"I'll have a better idea once I check on her tonight. Again, thank you for your service," Dr. Verner said to Reece and nodded to Graham before departing.

"*Two* aneurysms?" Graham eyed Reece.

"The doctor wasn't worried about the smaller one, so she didn't want to make you worry more than you already were. Need to know basis," Reece explained.

Graham returned a semi-amused grin and let out a deep breath. "Thank you." He kissed Erin's temple.

They took seats and let the good news seep in.

～

GRAHAM FINISHED READING Erin's script and gave her his notes. The second episode was every bit as engaging as the first. Now, Reece was flying through the pages.

Erin ran some questions past them for the scene she was working on, which helped pass the time while they waited. It was well over an hour before a recovery nurse called Reece's name, then escorted them to Megan's room.

Reece stroked Megan's cheek as she slept. Relief and sadness choked Graham. If they'd only known about Bethann's aneurysm before it ruptured. But Megan should be able to move forward to live a full and long life and Erin was here. He counted his blessings rather than focus on regrets since they couldn't change the past.

When the nurse came to check on Megan later that afternoon, she woke up for a few minutes. Her speech was slurred, but she was able to respond to the nurse's questions, which further assured Graham that Megan would be okay. He and Erin went to the cafeteria to eat, then returned to cover so Reece could grab food too.

"Has she woken yet?" Reece asked when he returned with a tray of food.

"She stirred a little, but the nurse said it'll probably be another hour or more before the sedatives wear off," Graham relayed.

Reece settled into the recliner next to the bed. When the door opened next, it was Bethann's sister, Sharon, who entered. Graham immediately removed his hand from Erin's knee.

"Sharon, I didn't know you were coming." Reece hesitated, then got to his feet.

Graham followed suit.

"Of course, I came. I couldn't get here faster since I didn't get the text about the surgery being today until this morning."

"We didn't know until last night ourselves," Reece said.

"I replied to her text but didn't hear anything back."

"I turned off Megan's phone once they prepped her for surgery." Reece sounded unfazed by Sharon's accusatory tone.

Sharon's gaze landed on Erin, still seated on the sleeper sofa, and studied her for a few seconds. "Who are you?" She paused between each word.

"This is Erin. The woman I'm seeing," Graham introduced her.

Erin got up. "Hi. It's—"

"Seeing? Like dating? Megan didn't mention that. Does she know that you're dating already?" Sharon talked over Erin before she got out more than two words.

"Yes." Graham kept his voice even. Why else would Erin be here?

"It'll take a few minutes for me to process that."

"Take all the time you need." Graham kept his cool despite his sister-in-law's tone.

"It was Jace and Megan who encouraged him to start dating. And Erin is the one who connected us with the surgeon here. Without her, we'd be waiting a few more months to *see* a neurosurgeon. The surgery went well." Reece smoothly shifted Sharon's focus to the reason she was here.

"That is a relief." Sharon scanned the room.

"You can take my seat. I'm going to stretch my legs for a bit," Erin offered. "Would anyone like a coffee or snack?"

Graham started to say he needed to walk around, too, before Erin's likely strategy dawned on him. Bethann's family would all know he was dating by the end of the week—if not tonight—and he needed to make Sharon an ally rather than have her sabotage his relationship with his in-laws.

Erin returned armed with snacks for everyone and

promptly began winning Sharon over by asking her about her work, travels, and interest in genealogy. Graham admired how Erin skillfully handled Sharon's inquiry about how they'd met, sticking mostly to the truth though leaving out a few details.

"Did I survive?" Megan's eyes flickered open.

Reece surged to his feet and took hold of her hand. "You most definitely did." He kissed her forehead.

"Hey, honey." Graham moved in and squeezed her hand.

"Did they shave my head?" she mumbled.

"Just the one side," Reece deadpanned.

"Noooo." Megan touched the hair on her right side.

"Don't tease her like that," Sharon scolded and went to the side of the bed. "They didn't shave your hair off."

"Aunt Sharon? You're here?" Megan's face scrunched.

"Of course, I am."

"Oh. Where's Erin?" Megan tried to look around the room, but her head fell back into the pillow.

"I'm right here." Erin edged up to Graham's side.

"We have to shop for our dresses for the military ball." She gave a loopy smile. "You can't dress slutty when you're an officer's wife. Or his date," Megan amended.

"So, no thigh-high slits or plunging necklines." Erin winked at Graham, clearly not offended by inferences made while Megan was drugged up on painkillers.

"I can show some cleavage." Megan dropped her head to stare at her breasts. "But, since I'm his daughter"—she waved a finger in his direction—"I have to keep it pretty classy."

"You always do, babe." Reece couldn't quite keep from laughing.

"I always loved buying you cute outfits. I'll help you find the perfect dress," Sharon offered.

A minute later, Reece had Jace and Alex on a video call.

"Her surgery went fine. She's awake, and I guarantee they didn't cut the bossy part out of her brain. She's already giving orders."

"I am not," she protested, drawing the words out in a whine. "You all have to be nice to me."

"Yes, your majesty," Jace answered.

Megan stuck her tongue out at the screen.

They ended the call when Dr. Verner entered the room dressed in his white doctor's coat. With him was a man who had a hospital employee ID on his lanyard but wore a navy suit jacket, striped dress shirt, and tie. Dr. Verner introduced Dean Hodgkins, the friend of Erin's friend.

Erin and Graham spoke with the dean while Dr. Verner examined Megan.

"She's doing great, though she probably won't remember much of this evening," Dr. Verner promised them. "I'll check on her in the morning. If she's doing as well as I expect, she may be discharged early afternoon."

The tension knotting Graham's neck and shoulders abated as the family thanked both men.

The staff caught wind of Dean Hodgkins's involvement with Megan's case based on the VIP treatment stepping up another notch after the men left. A friendly nursing student brought in pillows and blankets for Reece only minutes after requesting them.

"Are you sure you don't want me to stay too?" Sharon asked Megan. "You might need someone to help you go to the bathroom."

"Reece will be here. He can sleep anywhere, and he's seen me naked plenty of times," Megan said with a groggy smile.

"That may be our cue that it's time to go." Graham got up,

squeezed Megan's hand, and kissed her cheek. He led the way to the elevator.

"I didn't book a hotel since I planned to stay overnight in the hospital with her," Sharon commented. "I'm not officially her godmother, but I'm the one who kept her while Bethann was in the hospital after Jace's birth, and I came to help out during times while you were deployed."

"That's thoughtful, but I can understand her wanting her husband with her." Graham didn't point out Sharon had invited or inserted herself some of those times rather than Bethann asking for her help.

"Do you have one hotel room or two?"

A cold draft seeped under Graham's collar and inched down his spine. "We're sharing a room."

"I guess I'll get my own then. I thought it'd be nice to get to know each other better," she said to Erin.

Whatever Sharon's real motivation for asking, he wouldn't let what she, or any of Bethann's family, thought about his relationship with Erin ruin what they had. Not when it was clear that his daughter wanted Erin here over her aunt.

Chapter Thirty-Three

"It's pretty." Megan did a turn in front of the full-length mirror in her bedroom, wearing a coral, A-line dress with full tulle skirt.

"But too matronly?" Erin finished for her.

"Yes. It was one of Aunt Sharon's picks. I ordered it to humor her. Take a picture for me to send her." She smiled for the picture, then picked up the next dress and stepped into the bathroom.

Sharon had stayed with Megan and Reece for the weekend, not that she'd given them a choice. Reece invited Erin and Graham, along with Jace and Alex, for dinner both nights since wives from his team had brought over meals and to give Megan some breathing room from Sharon's well-intentioned but smothering care. After dinner, the women surfed websites for dresses while the men watched baseball on TV.

It had been a few years since Erin went prom dress shopping with her daughters or had to try on fancy dresses herself, and both went a bit overboard ordering numerous dresses. After opening the packages with the dresses that had arrived today, the two were having a fun fashion show.

Next, Megan emerged wearing a jade green, off-the-shoulder mermaid gown. "This is the one Alex picked. What do you think?"

"That fit is perfect, and so is the color with your hair and skin tone."

Megan smiled and did a slow turn. "I love it. Of course, it's the most expensive one."

"Reece isn't going to complain. Especially with how amazing you look." Erin took a video to send to Sharon and Alex.

"Your turn," Megan declared and picked up the top dress from Erin's pile. "The color is fabulous with your eyes, but it's not fancy enough for the ball."

"But it's not slutty." Erin waggled a finger and laughed.

Megan hid her face behind a hand. "I can't believe I said that. For the record, I've never seen you in anything remotely slutty."

"You were on painkillers. And this dress is for John and Elizabeth's wedding." She set the dress aside.

Megan held up two of the other dresses. "You should look so fabulous that when General McKittrick and the men on the teams see you together, they'll know they don't need to worry about Dad. Try this one."

Alone in the bathroom, Erin mulled over Megan's comment as she changed into the dress. Going to the ball was about appearances. She needed to remember not to get swept into a Cinderella fairytale because the magic would end. Maybe not when the clock struck midnight on the night of the ball, but before her royal colonel slipped a wedding ring on her finger.

The first dress she tried on lacked the wow factor.

"I love the color," Megan said when she came out in the second.

"Except the sizing's off." Erin turned around to show her.

"Want me to try to zip you up?"

"It's not going to work, and I'm past the age of fasting for weeks in hopes of fitting in a dress. Next."

The sequins on the third dress were eye-catching, but they made it heavy and scratchy, and the train wasn't practical for dancing.

"Hopefully, I saved the best for last. Can you unzip me?" Erin picked up the fourth dress. Typically, she preferred a sweetheart or V-neckline, but she'd come back to this dress with a boat neck time and again online. She loved the cascading ruffle and modestly daring, offset slit. The V in the back showed some skin but was tasteful. Now she prayed it looked half as good on her as the model in the ads.

Her phone rang as she stepped into the cobalt dress.

"It's Ian Stewart," Megan called.

Erin hustled out, her heart already racing.

Megan's arched brows slowed Erin for a second.

"He's the assistant to the Hollywood producer," Erin explained before answering the call. "Hey there, Ian."

"I read your manuscript and treatment the other night. I gave it to my boss, Levi, yesterday."

That had to be good. "How long do you think it'll take him to read it?" Weeks? Months? Waiting would be torture.

"He already did. It didn't knock his socks off."

Her hopes crashed. Tears burned her eyes as she sank onto the side of the bed. The fabric of the unzipped dress sagged off her shoulder. She sniffed hard to keep from crying on the dress. After all the work she'd put into it, and Graham and Reece's praise, she'd been so hopeful.

"That's only because Levi's trendy and doesn't wear socks," Ian continued.

"What?"

"Your story and writing blew him away."

"Really?" Why couldn't he have led with that? She could breathe again.

"He could not believe a middle-aged woman with no military experience wrote it. I told him you spent time with a Green Beret team and had a network of resources. He read our in-house writers' version afterward and agreed with me that it wasn't nearly as compelling as yours."

She'd take that as a compliment—and a warning.

"He wants the next two episodes and asked that you come to LA to meet."

This was really happening. Her mouth was parched, and her heart pounded. Next to her, Megan bounced on the bed.

"When?" She prayed it didn't conflict with the wedding or the ball.

"He's headed to Catalina today for the weekend. He'd like you here early next week."

"Let me check my calendar and get back to you." She tried to play it cool.

"Be quick. Levi's already brainstorming who he'd like to see film the pilot and mentioned Chris Remington for the lead. They worked together on a series before Remington hit the big time. That's all good, but this is Hollywood, where shiny new things are daily distractions. The political climate is positive for the military today, but it could change tomorrow. All it takes is a whiff of scandal to shelve a project rather than risk backlash and losing millions in ad revenue."

"I'll get back to you today," Erin promised before Ian ended the call. "I can hardly breathe," she told Megan.

"I'm not surprised. I knew as much as Dad and Reece loved the scripts, it had to be fabulous."

"Will you be okay if I'm gone next week?" With Reece at work, Erin had spent the past few days with Megan. Although her headache and fatigue had abated, she still had to limit her physical activity.

"Yes! If needed, Alex can help, or Reece can take off work. Heck, I'd have Aunt Sharon come before I'd let you miss this opportunity because of me." Megan hugged her awkwardly from her position beside Erin on the bed. "Now stand so I can see this dress on you to decide if you're wearing it for the ball or the Academy Awards."

～

RATHER THAN TELL Graham the news over the phone, Erin headed to his house to wait for him. Of course, Noelle came out to walk her dog the second Erin pulled into Graham's driveway. It was like the woman had a radar lock on Erin or an Intel unit tracking her car, but she was in too good a mood to take evasive action.

"Colonel Holmstrom's not home yet," Noelle stated as if Erin couldn't see that his car wasn't there.

She used the key Graham had given her to unlock the door but decided not to even joke that Noelle didn't need to call the MPs about somebody breaking into his house. Better not to give her any ideas.

"Did everything go well with Megan today?" Graham asked when he arrived home.

"Yes, the headache's completely gone. And we had fun trying on the dresses that arrived. She's picked hers for the ball, and I think I have too." The bright blue dress made her feel beautiful, and it was now her lucky dress since she had been wearing it when Ian called.

"And do I get to see you in it before then?" Graham raised his eyebrows in a way that made her heart race and her skin heat.

"No, I'd rather wait for the big reveal."

"Really?"

"Yes."

"Fine. Let me change into something cooler. Did you get any writing done?"

She followed him upstairs. "A little this morning before we tried on dresses. However, Ian called." She proceeded to fill him in on the phone call. "It's still not a sure thing, but getting the pilot ordered would be huge. That Levi wants to see more scripts from *me* means there's a good shot at becoming one of the primary writers for the series."

"That's fantastic." He wrapped her in a hug. "Congratulations. I know you've worked hard for this. Based on what I've read, they'd be fools not to bring you on as a writer and advisor."

"I know this is short notice, but is there any way you could go to California with me next week?"

The grimace on his face told her his answer before he even spoke.

"While I'd love to make the trip with you, I should have clarified earlier that I don't have free reign. I'd have to run it past public affairs before I could talk with producers, even unofficially. It would also require bringing a public affairs or Pentagon movie liaison officer along."

She'd known how hard it was to get access to the team, and that the use of military vehicles required approval, but she hadn't known all that.

"In addition to things I have scheduled next week, we couldn't get approval that quickly."

"I knew it was a long shot. I thought it might hold some sway if I showed up with my sexy Special Ops boyfriend." She kept it light, eyeing him as he removed his uniform.

"I don't think I will have the same effect on them as I do on you." He broke into that endearingly bashful grin.

That was probably true. And thinking it through, if Ian and his boss knew she was in a romantic relationship that would end soon, it might hurt her case rather than make it stronger.

"Thanks for understanding. It's not that I don't want to support you. The Army just has lots of rules and regulations when it comes to dealing with the media. But I certainly would like to take you out to celebrate."

She closed the distance between them. "How about we celebrate *before* we do dinner?"

Chapter Thirty-Four

Graham knocked before entering the code to unlock the condo door.

"You're early." Erin remained on the couch with Smokey on her lap.

"I was afraid I'd have to wake you from a nap."

"I didn't think the three-hour time difference would be so bad, but they kept me up late in LA, and I cannot sleep on a plane if my life depended on it."

He leaned over to brush a kiss on her forehead. Smokey gave a possessive meow at being disturbed. "The cats missed you. Not as much as I did." He sat and stroked Smokey's fur. Even though they'd talked the three days Erin had been gone, he'd missed her even more than he'd expected.

"I was able to go back to sleep after you left to play golf, but I still took a short nap. I wanted to be refreshed for the wedding. Let me change." She lifted Smokey off her lap, then stepped over Tink, who'd made her way to sit near Graham's feet. "Be back in a minute."

She'd been so animated last night telling him all about her meetings with Levi and the other writers. He was proud of her talent and bravery in pursuing her dream. That they didn't expect her to live in LA full-time was the best part of her news for him.

She came back in a few minutes later. "Wow." Graham's gaze roved slowly down her body, then back up. "I may be underdressed."

"It's outside and casual, but still a wedding. It's not too much, is it?"

"It's perfect. I like how it shows off your legs."

"They are one of my better features."

"I like your eyes and your smile even better." He slid a hand around her waist and pulled her close enough that he could breathe in her sweet floral scent. "And everything about you," he added lowly. He stared into her eyes for several long seconds, his body reacting to her nearness before finally kissing her. "We'll pick this up later. We've got a wedding to go to, and nothing says a couple is in a serious relationship like attending a wedding together." He steered her toward the door.

She had her professional reasons for attending, and he had his. Though a top-tier officer, Bryson was susceptible to the same fears and distractions about a spouse's fidelity as the men under him. Maybe more so since Bryson had returned from a deployment to find out his girlfriend at the time had reunited with her ex while he was deployed—and hadn't told him. Graham hadn't met that woman, but that Elizabeth had been willing to give up her counseling practice here and move to Florida with John showed her commitment to him. Bryson passed on a promotion to stay with her and his team with Graham's full support. If Bryson hadn't mentioned Graham getting remarried, he might not have met Erin. Funny how that worked. He owed Bryson.

The GPS directed them down a two-lane rural road.

Fields of cotton grew on the left, and neat rows of tall pines in a timber field to their right gave way to a white fence running along the road. A message saying they'd arrived flashed on the navigation screen as they reached an open security gate decorated with oversized pale pink bows and greenery.

"Is that a police car?" Erin drew out the words and stared at the cruiser parked alongside the white clapboard, two-story farmhouse with two inviting rocking chairs and a hanging swing on the porch.

"It is. I don't know if that's a bad thing or a warning." Operators had a reputation for partying hard, but this wasn't the time or place, and they knew it.

As the parking attendant, Cruz motioned to them from a row of cars in the grassy field.

"What's up with the police presence?" Graham asked Cruz.

Cruz laughed. "I wondered the same, especially since Bryson's truck isn't here."

"Did you find out anything?" Erin's grip on Graham's arm tightened.

"One of the bridesmaids is a police officer. And she says she'll arrest anyone who tries to stop the wedding or us guys if we get out of line."

Graham laughed at that. It'd take more than one cop with a weapon concealed under her bridesmaid's gown to deal with one of his teams. "Where's Bryson?"

"They said the captain spent the night at a hotel because Elizabeth wouldn't let him see her in the dress before the wedding. I know for a fact he's not ditching out. The entire Taliban couldn't keep him away."

They headed to the rows of chairs in front of an arbor draped with white fabric and accented with greenery and pink flowers.

Half the seats were already filled. Erin waved to a group of women in the second row. Graham didn't recognize any of them as team wives, but one did a double-take. Her mouth hung open before she motioned them to join her. She got to her feet and hugged Erin. "What are you doing here?"

"John didn't tell you?"

"No. He just mentioned he had a surprise."

"Graham, this is Cecilia Crenshaw, my former student I told you about. Her husband is John's best man. Graham's a colonel in John's unit and arranged for me to observe his team for research purposes."

"Research? For the project you pitched Ian?" Cecilia's eyes lit up. "Has anything come of it?"

"His boss, Levi, loved it but wanted to change it from a movie to a TV series."

"That's still awesome!"

"Initially, they offered to buy the rights. But I told them I wanted a shot at writing."

"Good for you. And you can make more money—if the series makes it past a season."

"Well, Levi backpedaled when he found out I was a female—and my age."

"Typical Hollywood," she said as they sat.

"I wrote a treatment for what I envision for the first season and developed characters. They bought the pilot episode I submitted, and I went to LA this week to meet with Levi. They're currently lining up actors for the pilot."

"Wow! If this were only a year ago, I would be schmoozing you up, begging to be part of your writing team. But I do not miss LA."

"I'm glad I won't need to relocate there."

"Why not?"

"The cost of living. The pace and lifestyle."

"I get that. I mean, don't you *need* to be out there?"

"The writing team can consult over video chat, and I can fly out and spend a few weeks when needed."

"Who told you that?" The edge in Cecilia's tone made the hair on Graham's arms stand up despite the August heat.

"Ian said a lot of writers have left LA, and Levi agreed it wouldn't be a problem."

"That may be the case with established writers who already have connections. I might be somewhat jaded, and you can certainly collaborate online without being in the same room. However, Hollywood is all about who you know. If you're not in their face, pitching ideas, someone else is. You might write the first few episodes, then suddenly, someone is taking your series idea in a whole other direction. You could end up cut out of the series you created. I don't mean to be a downer, but watch your back and take everything they say with a tablespoon of salt."

"Thanks for the warning. How are things with you and Nate?"

Graham noted the warble in Erin's voice and how she quickly shifted the focus, but the warning had already pinged his radar.

"Unbelievably great. We're hoping with this new season of *Say Yes to the Rose*, the paparazzi's focus will shift off us. Nate was one of the builders selected for the Showcase of Homes in the Atlanta area. The interior designer I worked with to stage Nate's entry offered me a position as her assistant, so I'm learning the business. I love the creative aspect."

"I'm glad you're doing well."

"It was an unorthodox journey, but I've never been happier or more fulfilled. And you're doing well?"

"Same." When Erin cut her gaze at him, he smiled and put his hand over hers.

"Tell me about hanging out with a Green Beret team," Cecilia said.

"It was informative and a lot of fun. I got to use some of the gear and fire weapons. Though I did not get to ride in a Black Hawk—yet."

"I did get you in a simulator," Graham interjected. "And after that, you're not flying a real one."

Erin laughed. "I just want a ride, not to fly one. I *crashed* in the simulator. Again and again," she explained to Cecilia. "I did better shooting an M-4 in real life than in video games."

"But I wouldn't give her a weapon with real ammo," Atkinson said from the row behind them.

"Nate had a blast doing some of that stuff that another buddy and John set up for his bachelor party." Cecilia waved to someone behind her. "They're here."

Graham turned to see the groomsmen and Bryson staging for their entrance.

The music that had been playing softly in the background changed. An Army chaplain came down the aisle and turned to face the guests. After the other family members were seated, John took his place with the same confidence he projected in every mission he undertook.

Graham deduced the other groomsman was John's father based on his age and the similarities in their appearance. He hoped the bridesmaid with toned arms was the police officer as the petite blonde bridesmaid wouldn't stand a chance against one of his operators.

"I can't wait to see John's face when he sees Elizabeth in her dress." Cecilia snuck a look over her shoulder and then focused on Bryson.

"Have you seen it?" Erin asked.

"They came to Atlanta right after they got engaged, and I took her shopping at Bridals by Lori. The third dress was perfection. It's so romantic and so Elizabeth."

Shopping for Megan's wedding gown had been an exciting experience for Bethann and Megan. They'd come home exhausted but so excited when she'd found "the one." The sense of loss evoked by the memory was a shadow of what it had been before Erin came into his life. What if she had to move to LA? That kind of distance could mean the end of things. While that had been their agreement, it was something he wasn't ready for.

Instead of turning to see Elizabeth enter, he intently watched John's reaction and easily read his lips when he mouthed *Wow* and broke into a huge smile.

Ripples of laughter made Graham turn to see an oversized dog walking Elizabeth down the aisle. The personalized vows the couple exchanged had the tough operators in attendance laughing but were also very moving.

"Do you need a tissue?" Cindy Nishiyama offered.

"I'm good," Atchinson said as Graham looked over his shoulder in time to see him knuckle away a tear. Graham swallowed the emotion choking him too.

The ceremony was short and sweet. After the chaplain pronounced them Captain and Mrs. John Bryson, John dipped Elizabeth for a long, romantic kiss to cheers from nearly every guest there.

While the wedding party posed for the photographer, appetizers and drinks were served. Guests took tours of the tiny home where John had temporarily lived.

"I've got to see this." Erin pulled Graham by the hand to the row of three tiny homes.

He pictured the six-foot-five-inch soldier commando-crawling into the sleeping loft, which only had about three feet of clearance. Erin laughed when Graham stepped into the tiny shower. "I've lived in tight quarters when deployed, and I could do this if I had to, but I don't know how Bryson did it."

After the guests took seats for dinner, John and Elizabeth made their entrance and danced to a custom medley. Following dinner and toasts, Bryson led Elizabeth to the dance floor. Partway through "Somebody Like You," their family members joined them. Bryson whistled, and the woman in charge of his dog let him loose to romp on the dance floor with the happy couple.

Another pang of nostalgia hit Graham when the song "Look what God Gave Her" played. The last concert he'd attended with Bethann had featured the singer, Thomas Rhett.

He shook his head as Bryson's team quickly got into the action, leading their wives and dates to the floor, performing choreographed moves, and serenading the women. "I heard something about Bryson's team practicing some 'unique training maneuvers.'" He pointed to the dance floor.

"Don't be mad. It's good for morale and relationships."

"That's exactly why I let it slide. It gave me an idea for the ball." He took Erin's hand, and they made their way to the dance floor. The line about having haters made him think of Noelle, who had no valid reason to act like she did toward Erin.

After another song, the bridal couple exited the dance floor and made their way to the table holding the wedding cake. Guests gathered around, and Cecilia brought her husband over and introduced Nate to Graham.

"So, you were the bachelor guy on the dating show I let Bryson go on?"

"Yes, sir. I appreciate you letting him do that."

"So do I." Cecilia hugged Nate's arm and smiled adoringly at him.

Maybe he should thank them, since, indirectly, it led to Erin coming here for research purposes.

Even though it wasn't a military wedding in terms of dress, the Brysons still cut the cake using a sword as all the guests watched.

Elizabeth gave Bryson a look of warning before he fed her cake with a fork—in a loving manner. She reciprocated, then playfully dabbed frosting on his nose. He laughed and kissed her, leaving a smear of icing on her cheek.

Graham and Erin took seats to eat their cake. Cruz slid into the seat on the other side of Erin.

"What's the latest word on your series?" he asked before taking a bite of cake.

"They're casting for the pilot, and we're working on other episodes."

"Wow. If she catches the bouquet, you better catch the garter, Colonel, and lock her down before she goes out to LA and some Hollywood hotshot makes a move on your lady."

Erin shook her head and laughed. "I'm not fighting all these single women for the bouquet. Besides, Graham has a much better shot at getting the garter, and I don't want whoever catches the bouquet to get ideas." She stole some of the frosting from Graham's slice of cake with her finger, then sucked it off while eyeing him.

Blood flooded to Graham's groin as he recalled her straddling him after he'd asked about the wedding cake scene in her script. However, avoiding the bouquet and garter toss could raise questions since they were supposed to be on the fast track to marriage.

Between dancing, Erin chatted with the wives from John's team and several other women guests while Graham stayed with the team guys or couples. He and Erin joined the crowded floor when the DJ played popular line dance songs.

"I'm surprised you know this one, Colonel. I took you as a "Macarena"-era guy," Cruz joked.

"I'm not *that* old," Graham retorted, though he did remember when the Macarena had become popular. With all the weddings and military balls he'd attended over the years, he'd learned many line dances, rather than sit on the sidelines. Bethann always enjoyed dancing—another thing she and Erin had in common.

After a series of line dances running the gamut of musical genres, the DJ slowed things down with a love ballad.

"This has been fun"—she raised her face and spoke near his ear—"but I'm ready to be alone with you."

The kiss she gave him started innocently enough before her lips parted. The kiss deepened and heated to the point he nearly forgot where they were. "We should head out."

As they made a quick round of goodbyes, it was apparent Erin had connected with the women—which wasn't an easy task. Women in the Special Ops community were conditioned to be protective of their men and slow to accept outsiders. The cooking class had been a good start, but this went up a level.

Their agreement needed renegotiating.

"Congratulations again." Cecilia hugged Erin. "That they're filming a pilot and have ordered scripts for more episodes is *huge*! And they better list you as the show co-creator because that gives you executive producer credit. If you need, I can recommend a top-notch entertainment lawyer to look over any contracts."

"I'd love to get their contact information."

"Ian's a good guy, but it's Hollywood. Guys like his boss will steal your idea and pass it off as their own in a New York minute. Or buy the script, have their in-house writers make a few changes, and take writing credit. I'd hate for them to cut you out or screw you on what you're paid and residuals. And I know living out there is not convenient or ideal, but you should consider it. I'll send the lawyer's name and contact info."

Erin didn't say anything as they walked to the car or even turn for a kiss before sliding into the seat. Cecilia's repeated warnings had killed the romantic vibe and verbal foreplay.

"What are you thinking?" he asked after over a minute of silence, a long time for Erin.

"That Cecilia has good insight. I wanted to believe what Levi and Ian said about not needing to be out there, despite what my gut told me."

"Any chance she's saying this because she's envious of you getting this opportunity?"

"Not Cecilia. She's the definition of Ms. Congeniality, always supportive of others. She also knows the business side better than I do." Erin sighed, looking out into the darkness. "I was banking on not going back soon, but I'm going to need to go out there for at least a week or two around the filming of the pilot."

"I understand. We can turn it into a vacation."

She gave him a weak smile.

"What?"

"Traveling together is a sure way to test a relationship."

"I'm up to the challenge."

She broke eye contact after several long seconds. "I know our arrangement is to keep up appearances, then we're going to say we broke up after I left here, but I didn't count on this."

His stomach clenched. He understood the importance of her pursuing this opportunity, but did it have to exclude him?

"Graham, I don't want things between us to end. I love you and—"

"You do?" He braked hard, steered the car off to the shoulder, and shifted to park before fully turning to her. She loved him. She'd said those magic words.

"I know it wasn't part of our arrangement, but you're—"

"In love with you too," he assured her, reveling in the smile on her beautiful face. "I've been wanting to tell you that for a while."

"You should have." She gave a relieved laugh, leaning closer to him.

"I thought it might send you running."

"It wouldn't have—probably."

"Probably?" He laughed as the pressure in his chest dissipated. "See why I didn't?"

"If you'd said 'I love you' before I agreed to your proposition, or even right after, I might have. I would have been okay with it for a while now."

"I'm sorry I didn't say the words sooner. How can I make it up to you?" He leaned across the console.

"I could probably think of some ways." She angled her body toward his but waited for him to close the distance.

They'd been kissing long enough for him to heat up and hands to begin exploring when light penetrated his eyelids. He squinted against the high-beam headlights slowly approaching. The pickup truck crossed the center line, rolled up next to Graham's car, and stopped. The window lowered, and an older man wearing a green John Deere ball cap stared at them. When Graham lowered his window, the driver nodded in a friendly manner.

"You having car trouble?" he asked with a thick Southern drawl.

"Uh, no. I pulled over because I got some life-changing news that I needed to process."

"Guessing it was good based on the fact I thought you were two kids necking."

Erin gave a guilty chuckle.

"Definitely good news, but we'll take it home. Thanks for stopping to check on us." Graham nodded and put up the window.

Erin continued to giggle. "I haven't been caught making out in a car in nearly three decades."

"There is something about being in a car and fearing discovery. But better that farmer to catch us than any of my men. There's putting on a show, and then there's putting on a show. We can wait until we get home, where there's a king-size bed." He put the car back in gear and eased back onto the road.

"True. And, after you saying you love me, tonight should be something special."

"And did you have something particularly *special* in mind?"

"Maybe. There are positions in the little sex book we haven't tried yet, but I'm thinking lots of kissing and tender touches and bodily contact. And then the big O."

"Yes, ma'am. I'm committed to completing that mission."

Chapter Thirty-Five

"THE GENERAL WANTED TO SEE ME," Graham told McKittrick's aide. That the general hadn't said what it was regarding wasn't highly unusual. However, these days, it put him into alert status.

"Send him on in," McKittrick called through the open door. "I got your leave request. Is everything all right with Megan?"

"Yes, sir. She's doing great. They'll have her come in for a follow-up MRI after six months to check that the coils remained in place, but they felt everything went as well as can be expected."

"Good. Good. I just wondered since your leave request is such short notice."

"Erin's going to California for the filming of the pilot episode she wrote for the television show."

"That's moving forward?"

"It is. I've read the script, and I think the series has a real shot at getting picked up."

"You aren't going to be involved in that, correct?" McKittrick interjected. It was more an order than a question.

"No, sir. I plan to join her afterward. We might go to the Bay Area or maybe Tahoe for some R&R."

McKittrick nodded. "Sounds like things are continuing to go well. Vegas isn't far from LA. You could go see some shows, gamble a little, stop by a wedding chapel."

"About that. Things are going well, but I haven't met Erin's daughters yet. One's in Texas, and the other is doing a study abroad in Spain."

"You need to get on that. Though I'm sure they would approve." The general wasn't giving an inch. "And you wouldn't be the first couple to get married without family there."

No. His own father had done that. And Graham would not repeat that mistake. "It wouldn't be the best start, ambushing her girls like that. I'm unwilling to push and ruin a great thing with a woman I love."

The general's eyebrows rose, and he nodded. "I can see your point. If Vegas doesn't work on this trip, maybe you can get her girls here and have a small ceremony over Thanksgiving."

"Bryson's team has seen us together enough to know we're solid and aren't going to be distracted from their mission."

"It was good to see Mateo with his wife at that cooking class. I'd still prefer you and Erin were official before they deployed. Then there are the other teams who haven't seen you two together. The ball is coming up, but that's just one night. And, with your tour here ending in a few months, we need to start looking at other assignments—*if* you're not staying. Aside from a recent opening in the Pacific Theatre, there could be a joint exchange with the SAS. That would look good on your resume to make brigadier general."

"My top choices are staying here or SOCOM."

"Glad to hear it."

"So, you are approving my leave then?" Graham returned to the reason he was here. With things progressing with Erin, marriage could be an option—on their timetable, not because they were forced into it. He wasn't faking his feelings for her, but he wanted any engagement to be real.

❧

"STILL USING the cardboard box carrier method?" Graham smiled wryly as Erin set the box with both cats on the floor in his kitchen.

"Why change what works? No scratches. You two need to be on your best behavior," Erin warned Tink and Smokey. The cats' owners were okay with her bringing them over to Graham's, though she left out the part about him being a colonel since they might have freaked out if they knew a colonel had been spending the night in their condo regularly.

The earlier test run when she'd brought the cats over for an evening had gone well, but leaving them alone while they went out for dinner and spending the night here could be a whole different story. The new arrangement wouldn't work if the cats clawed the furniture or wouldn't use the litter box.

When she opened the box, Smokey jumped out. Tink sniffed the air before joining her to strut around the kitchen with her tail held high.

Graham went out to get the litter box and bag of cat food while Smokey stalked Tink in a game of chase. Erin's phone chimed, and she checked the message.

"Megan texted us, wanting to know if we were here. She said she and Reece were going to stop by." That Megan now included Erin in family texts made her long to get her daughters on board with her and Graham's relationship.

The cats bolted from the room to hide when Reece

opened the side door into the kitchen. Megan followed carrying a flat pastry box.

"We wanted to bring you a little something to say congratulations that they're filming the pilot for the show. Dad said you love these little Bundt cakes." She set the box on the kitchen table. "Hello, Pops."

"That is so sweet. I'm taking your dad to dinner at the Italian place where we had our first date. Come with us. We can come back afterward and have cake."

Megan looked at Reece. "Uh, sure, but why don't we each splurge and have one now." She opened the box of mini treats and handed Erin a chocolate one. "What flavor would you like, Pops?"

Graham gave his daughter a befuddled look. "Any. Surprise me."

Megan's smile grew bigger as she stuck two decorative toppers in the cake she handed Graham.

He pulled out two cake toppers and stared at them for a second. "You called me Pops." His face lit up. "Are you—?"

"Yes!" Megan squealed before he could finish.

Even though they hadn't said the word pregnant, the embrace he engulfed her in said it all. The toppers of pale pink and blue baby onesies in Graham's hands were also a blatant clue.

"Oh my gosh! Congratulations." Erin hugged Reece, then Megan while the men exchanged a man hug.

"You weren't pregnant when you had surgery, were you?" Graham asked the question that had popped into Erin's mind.

"Not *technically*. I went off the birth control pills before the procedure. We didn't use any protection the night before surgery or in the—"

"Got it." Graham held up a hand. "Isn't it too early to tell then?"

"Remember how Mom first knew she was pregnant because her boobs hurt? Well, last night we were—"

"TMI, honey. TMI." Reece avoided eye contact with his father-in-law.

"I did a blood test at work this morning. It's positive."

"Have you told Jace and Alex yet?" Graham asked.

"No, you're the first. I'll wait until I'm about five months along to see if he notices."

"Right." Reece laughed. "She couldn't even wait until Sunday dinner to tell you."

"We can invite them to dinner. My treat," Erin offered.

"Are you a millionaire now?" Reece rubbed his thumb and fingers together.

"Hardly. But what they pay for each script is over half of what I make in a year of teaching. Fingers crossed the series gets picked up and I stay on as part of the writing team. Long-term, it could be more money than a movie." Once she got her first check, it would give her an emergency cushion, but she wasn't quitting teaching until she was on solid financial footing again.

"It will be so exciting to see your story on TV." Megan gave a dreamy sigh as the cats raced past the kitchen. "Was that two cats?" She pointed and looked from Graham to Erin.

"I've been feeling guilty about leaving Tink and Smokey alone, so we're testing how they do on visits here."

"It would be more convenient than you two alternating between here and the condo."

They had never come out and said they were practically living together, but Megan knew and seemed perfectly fine with it. In the week since Bryson's wedding, Erin's relationship with Graham had gotten even better. Everything was coming together, and she'd never been happier.

Graham's phone dinged from an incoming text. "Jace said they already have plans tonight."

"Don't tell him the news in a text," Megan warned him.

"He'll probably hear you're pregnant before dinner Sunday," Reece said.

"No, because I'm not telling anybody but family. It's too early. Let's go to dinner. Is it normal to feel overly hungry this early?" Megan asked Erin.

"Didn't you say you skipped lunch to get the Bundt cakes?" Reece said.

"Oh, yeah. That could be why." She helped herself to two of the cakes.

"She's already glowing," Graham said as they drove home after dinner.

"She's not the only one," Erin teased him. "You haven't stopped smiling the whole night either."

"I didn't think I'd be this excited—at least so early." He was still trying to believe it was true. "I know how much she wants this. It's been a rough year and a half with losing her mom and the aneurysm. Getting pregnant now might not have been intentional, but it beats months of trying."

"True."

"I'm sorry she bombarded you with questions." Though Erin wouldn't replace Bethann as Megan's mother, he liked that his daughter was so accepting of Erin in his life.

"I didn't mind. I'm touched by how your kids have accepted me and made me feel like family. You've met Piper via video chat, but I want you to meet Madison. And not just video chat, though that needs to come first."

"I'd like that," Graham assured her.

"I was thinking you could meet when they come to Charlotte for her friend's wedding, but that's not until October. I don't want to wait that long. Did the general approve your leave?"

"He did. He also suggested we go to Vegas, and . . ."

"And get married?" Erin guessed.

Graham nodded. "I told him that wasn't happening and used the excuse that I haven't met your girls."

"I'm glad he understands."

"I'm not saying that. He mentioned your girls coming here for a Thanksgiving wedding. And where there are openings for potential assignments. Overseas ones." His chest constricted at the likely alternative. While he and Erin loved each other, and she'd wear an engagement ring to keep him here, they wouldn't be tying the knot. At least not in time to make the general change his mind.

McKittrick had never experienced the profound loss of a spouse through death or divorce. Or been to a grief support or divorce care group to hear the warnings about subsequent relationships. Graham had told Erin about his dad rushing into later marriages. Now that she knew about his complicated relationship with his father, she understood his reasons for not agreeing to the general's timeline. And why Graham wouldn't pressure his newly divorced girlfriend to cross the boundary she'd made clear when he'd proposed their arrangement.

"We may need to call in a big-gun reinforcement," Erin said.

Graham eyed her as he waited to pass through the security gate onto the post. "Reinforcements?"

"The McKittrick's have children. Sally would understand. If she were to plead my—or our—case as an ally, that might have some sway with the general and buy you enough time for him to extend your assignment here. It's worth a shot."

"I don't know that she's aware of what he said it would take for me to stay here, but it wouldn't hurt to have her on our side. And for her to mention our plans to visit your girls to him. Do you want Madison and Connor to meet us on our trip? Treat them to a few days in Tahoe or wherever we go?"

She mulled it over for a minute. "If we offered to pay their way, she might see it as a bribe. With the short notice, they might not be able to get off work either. Or use that as an excuse for why they couldn't come. Instead of California, we could meet in Texas and spend a few days there with them."

"Making it easy for them sounds good."

"I'll text her and schedule a video chat tomorrow. Then we can bring up the idea of a visit. And what would you think about going to Europe with me over Christmas?"

"That sounds like the best present I could get." Graham took her hand and brought it to his lips. With Erin telling him she loved him, Megan's news, and now Erin wanting him to meet her girls, things were going better than he could have imagined. All they needed was a reprieve from the general, and if anyone could assist there, Sally McKittrick was the ally to make that happen.

Chapter Thirty-Six

GRAHAM ARRIVED home while Erin pulled clover from the front plant beds. She straightened and dumped a handful of weeds into the yard waste can.

Her heart beat a little faster as Graham walked toward her, wearing that smile that she never got tired of seeing—especially when he aimed it her way. She tapped her earbuds to pause the music.

"I feel guilty that I'm playing golf and you're doing yard work at my house."

"Don't be. I wasn't in a creative mood." She pulled off her glove and leaned in closer, resting a hand on his chest, the fabric damp beneath her fingers. "I didn't trim the hedges." She nodded toward the Ayers's house, making him chuckle before he kissed her ardently. "*Mmm,*" she sighed. Even a salty kiss from a sweaty Graham aroused her. "How was your golf game?"

"I had a great game. I even beat Lundy. Only by one stroke, but it'd been a while. Did you get in touch with Madison?"

"I did. Unfortunately, it didn't go as well as I'd hoped."

"What did she say?"

Erin caught the way his mouth tightened. "She was still clinging to the idea that our relationship is purely for research. When I said I wanted her to meet you and explained that things have gotten serious, she wasn't ready to hear it. Honestly, she was being a brat. So, a video call tonight will not be happening. I'll give her some time to process it before I bring it up again. And I'm not banking on us going to Texas later this month. Hopefully, she'll come around before the wedding in October. She's going to have to accept me moving on sometime."

"Even if it's short notice and just a weekend, we can fly there when she's ready. Are you up for doing dinner with the Mahinises and Lundys tonight?"

"That sounds good. I haven't even thought about dinner yet."

"I'll text them we're a go. Then, I need to grab a shower."

"I'm going to need one too." She wiped the perspiration from her hairline. "You go ahead. I'll finish the rest of this bed."

"I was going to get something to drink first. I can wait for you." The heat in his gaze scorched her as much as the August temperatures.

"I'll join you in a few." She needed a pick-me-up after talking with Madison. She started the music again and admired Graham's muscular legs as he headed inside. No doubt, she was a lucky woman.

A few minutes later, "Under the Sea" interrupted her playlist. She took a deep breath. This could go one of two very different ways. Or it could be Madison butt-dialing her back by accident. That might not be a bad thing, considering their earlier conversation. She tapped her earbud to answer. "Hey, honey."

"Are you there, Mom? The screen's black."

"I didn't realize it was a video call." She pulled the phone from her back pocket.

"Are you out walking? I don't want to disturb you if you're working."

"No, I'm at Graham's house." She wasn't going to try to hide it.

"About earlier," Madison spoke haltingly, "I thought he was just helping with research stuff for your movie. You sprung the dating part on me, and I guess I didn't take it very well."

It wasn't an apology, but at least it was an acknowledgment.

"I talked to Piper. She already knew about you two and said she met him over video chat."

Despite the accusation leeching into Madison's tone, Erin didn't apologize for telling her youngest about her relationship with Graham first. While Piper hadn't been happy about the divorce, at least she had been supportive.

"I'm calling so we can meet like you asked."

She hadn't expected this. The timing wasn't great, but she wouldn't risk Madison changing her mind. "Hang on. Graham just went inside." She went in through the side door. A glass of iced tea sat on the kitchen table, but he was nowhere in sight. "Graham?"

"Be out in a sec," he called.

Erin sat at the table to wait for him to get out of the bathroom.

"What should I say to him?" Madison asked. "I can't exactly start with 'I've heard so much about you.'"

While it was tempting to let her wade through the awkwardness, Erin didn't want to do that to Graham, who also had no time to prep. "Maybe you can thank him for helping with my research or ask about—"

"What were you saying, hun?" Graham came up behind her.

Erin angled just as Graham leaned in and kissed her neck.

"What the hell, Mom? Is he naked?" Madison shrieked.

Erin slammed the phone face down on the table.

Graham reared back.

"I'm talking to Madison."

"I thought that wasn't happening today."

"She changed her mind and called to meet you."

"Video?" He pronounced each syllable as a question, his eyes so wide she saw the whites all the way around.

She nodded. He wasn't naked, but he was shirtless, had shed his shorts, and only wore a pair of boxer briefs.

"I'm sorry. Let me grab my shirt." He ducked back into the laundry room.

Erin picked up the phone, uncertain if Madison had stayed on the line or hung up on her. "Sorry, he didn't know I was on the phone with you."

"*Clearly*. So, are you two, what, sleeping together?"

"We have been dating for a while now."

"Yeah, but . . ."

"But what? I'm old?"

"Yes. And you're my mother."

"I'm not some shriveled-up crone."

"Mother! I don't want to hear about your sex life."

"I wasn't planning to tell you."

"Tell me what?" Graham was back, his face still beet red.

"Hang on." Erin took out the earbuds and put her phone on speaker. "Let's try this again. Madison, this is Graham."

"Hello." His voice warbled a fraction. "I'm sorry about that. I was putting my sweaty clothes in the laundry before we

—I—went up to shower." He caught himself too late, taking things from bad to wickedly awkward.

"We should do this another time," Madison said.

"No. We're all here. It's, um . . . Are things going any better with your job?" Erin stretched for something to ease into conversation about.

"No." Madison didn't elaborate.

"Graham got me time in a Black Hawk simulator."

"Your mother crashed it. She's not a born pilot." Graham attempted to lighten the tension.

"It was fun though. I think I should try flying an Apache. Just in the simulator." She laughed, but Madison only gave a forced smile. "I finished the next two scripts, and I'm going out to California for them to film the pilot episode."

"That's exciting." Madison sounded sincere, but now wasn't the time to bring up a visit to Texas.

"Graham's daughter helped me select my dress for the military ball."

"His daughter? How old is she?"

"Your age."

Madison sighed and dodged eye contact on the screen as she processed that. "Is going to the ball research?"

"Not entirely. But it could generate some ideas for the couples. There was some major drama at the ball two years ago."

Graham cleared his throat. "There won't be a repeat of that this year."

"When is the ball?"

"In three weeks."

"I'm sure you'll have a great time. Send me a picture. Connor and I are going over to some friends, and I need to get some food ready. This was, um . . . Uh, why don't we try this again in a week or two?"

"I'll touch base with you later this week." Erin didn't want to put it off for two weeks. Madison ended the call before Erin could say more. "Well, that could have gone better."

"It couldn't have gone worse." Graham shook his head.

"Oh, it could have. If you'd been totally naked."

"I *almost* was. I thought you were talking to me."

That he didn't hear most of Madison's side of the conversation while she'd had the earbuds in was probably for the best. "If I had a clue you were in the laundry room stripping instead of in the bathroom, I would have warned you. I'm sorry she overreacted. She's not as accepting of us being in a sexual relationship as your kids."

"Mine have a pretty healthy outlook on sex since they got an early education—because they walked in on us. More than once. I figured out that's why Megan now knocks instead of walking into the house."

"That's smart on her part, considering . . ."

"Yeah. Have you changed your mind about the shower?"

She thought about it for a few seconds. "Nope. I won't let Madison steal my joy or make me feel guilty. Let's get that shower."

~

Sunday afternoon, Erin's phone rang as she reviewed her latest changes to a scene in the script. This time it was a video call from Piper—not that she expected Madison to call so soon.

"Hey, Mom. Where's Graham? Getting dressed?" Her daughter could not keep a straight face.

"Ha, ha. He's out mowing the lawn. I take it you talked to Madison again after yesterday's video chat with her."

"Oh, I did. And because *I* told her she should meet him,

she tried to blame me for being traumatized by meeting your boyfriend when he was wearing only his underwear. Madison expected him to be some old, bald guy, not some stud."

"Did you just call my boyfriend a stud?" She agreed but hadn't expected her twenty-year-old to think so.

"Well, I haven't seen him in his underwear—not that I want to—but he's handsome and in shape. I can tell by the arm porn."

"The what?"

"Muscular arms with veins that pop. Arm porn. My roommate wanted to know why Madison was freaking out. Valeria thought the colonel was hot too."

Good grief. Erin didn't need General McKittrick to hear about women her daughter's age calling Graham hot. That might make him find some old, bald colonel to replace Graham with, even if they claimed to be engaged. "Has your father decided yet on coming over at Thanksgiving, Christmas, or another time?"

"No, but I haven't asked either. We don't have a break at Thanksgiving here. We have time between semesters in February."

"Fall classes start when?" Maybe she and Graham could do a quick trip to Spain between California and the ball.

"The second week in September. Valeria and I are going to Portugal between the summer session and the start of fall classes."

"Okay." That killed that possibility. Christmas seemed so long to wait. "I want you to meet Graham."

"I have."

"I mean in person. Look at your calendar and see what might work for a weekend visit."

"You'd come all the way here for a weekend? That sounds

serious. I thought you were just hooking up while you were there."

Heat raced up Erin's chest to her face. "I care about him a lot." Though she wasn't quite ready to tell her daughter she was in love with him. "He and I might add on a few days since I haven't been to Europe. And I was thinking maybe he could come part of the time if I come at Christmas. If you want to visit the Amalfi coast, Graham knows the area. He also speaks Italian. We've got time to decide."

"And you'll tell Dad?'

"Yes. He can work around us." She went into confident Erin mode. She was no longer settling for what others wanted or expected from her.

Chapter Thirty-Seven

GRAHAM PARKED in front of Erin's condo right on time. He took a deep breath before putting his sunglasses in the cupholder. He hadn't been this nervous since he'd broached the arrangement to Erin.

He'd missed her while she was in California for the pilot's filming, but they'd talked daily despite the time difference and shooting schedule. On their trip up the coast, she'd shared how Levi requested significant changes to the storyline. She'd tweaked the end of the pilot. On their trip, she'd run ideas past Graham, since Levi planned for the second episode she'd written to be the opener for the second season instead.

That opened up the conversation about how much time she'd need to spend in Los Angeles. It might be more than either wanted, but he had to accept that and support her. After nearly two decades of long deployments, if anyone understood what it took to make a relationship work long-distance, he did. It wasn't like they wouldn't see each other for months. They could fly across the country for long weekends.

However, he'd have trouble selling that to McKittrick. To alleviate any concerns that Graham might repeat the sins of the officers before him, the general would expect Erin to be here. Visible, not just at events like the ball. There was a lot on the line tonight in terms of convincing the general and not only any skeptical operators, but every man and woman there that Erin was the only woman he was interested in. Fortunately, he would not be faking that.

Erin's insistence on getting ready for the ball at the condo instead of his house and picking her up amused him, considering they spent nearly every night together. Still, the anticipation of seeing her completely made up had his heart racing as he rang the bell. He tugged his jacket down before she opened the door.

"Wow!" She drew out the word and fanned herself.

"That's supposed to be my line."

"I can't help it. The way you look in that uniform makes me weak in the knees—again."

"You look gorgeous." Did she ever. She wore her hair up in a fancy style, showcasing her neck and glittering earrings. The blue of the stylish gown and her makeup made her eyes stand out. She was the definition of classy and elegant. "I am the luckiest man to have you as my date. But something is missing." He looked her up and down.

"What?" she asked as he reached into his coat pocket and removed the black velvet box. Erin's mouth opened, and her eyes widened as they locked on the jewelry case before he opened his hand to show her the size of the box.

"I love you, but it's not a ring." He ignored the sensation spreading through his chest like Kevlar stopping a bullet. Earlier this week, General McKittrick casually mentioned the ball being the perfect opportunity to propose. Only there was no way he would blindside Erin with a public proposal—or even involve her in one for show. Not when he still had a chance of winning this battle. "But I wanted to give you something special." He opened the top to show her the necklace with seven sparkling diamonds forming a V.

"Graham, it's gorgeous."

"Megan helped me pick it out," he said before she could protest. "I hoped you'd wear it tonight."

"Of course. Will you put it on me?" She swallowed, then turned.

He fastened it, then slid his hands down the silky skin of her arms as he pressed a series of kisses to the side of her neck, eliciting a soft murmur as her back pressed against him.

He breathed in the floral scent of her shampoo before putting enough space between them for her to face him. "Take a look." He led her to the mirror in the bedroom.

"It is perfect for this dress."

"And you're perfect for me. Thank you for agreeing to this crazy arrangement because it's worked out better than I ever imagined." It was so much more than an arrangement, even if she wasn't ready to commit.

"Agreed. I'm guessing we shouldn't be late." She met his gaze and trailed a finger over his service medals, down the satin lapel of his jacket to the mess chain.

"No, but we can duck out on the early side."

"After plenty of dancing and a little PDA," she said in her sultry tone before kissing him gently on the mouth.

He added pressure to the kiss. Any traces of lipstick on him sent all the right messages too. "Let's go before I change my mind about being late."

Two women watched them as Graham opened Erin's car door. He gave them a polite nod of acknowledgment, then slid in and smiled at Erin for several long seconds before starting the car. For a man used to staying out of the spotlight, he needed to draw attention tonight. It'd be easy with this beautiful woman on his arm.

~

THE COUNTRY CLUB ballroom buzzed with voices and movement. Erin should have guessed that fashionably late wasn't in an operator's vocabulary, nor would they miss out on cocktail hour.

Graham pointed out Major General Miller and his wife. Standing with them were Sean and Sally McKittrick and, not surprisingly, the Ayers. Graham and Erin joined John and Dianne Mahinis, who waited in line for drinks. They chatted and then split to circulate with guests before dinner. Erin stayed at Graham's side while meeting the wives, making eye contact with them and Graham as often as possible.

Megan and Reece edged up. "You both look fabulous. When Dad said he wanted to get you a piece of jewelry, I knew something like this necklace would put this dress over the top."

"Thank you for helping him pick it out. I love it. And him."

"I know." Megan smiled at them. Erin and Graham exchanged a loving gaze and Megan leaned closer. "Help me," she said softly.

"What?"

Megan lightly pressed Erin's arm lower and discreetly poured some of her wine into Erin's glass. "A few sips won't hurt, but I'm not telling anyone but family until I get past the first trimester. If I'm not drinking, someone will guess why."

"You can leave your glass on a table," Reece suggested.

"Then I'd have to get another. It's got to look like I'm drinking. And he got a beer." She jerked her head at Reece.

"Sorry." He took a swig from the bottle.

"I've got you covered," Erin promised.

"Thank you. See what I meant about some dresses leaving

little to the imagination? Though Mateo's wife dialed it way back from two years ago. They didn't come last year."

Erin glanced at the couple standing with Greg and Cindy Nishiyama and Cruz and his date. "Michelle might be pregnant. There's a glow to her and a gentle rounding of her abdomen that I don't remember noticing at the cooking class."

Megan gave a light gasp. "You might be right. I won't ask, but I will do some reconnaissance and offer her a little moral support." Megan tipped more wine into Erin's glass before tugging Reece's arm and leading him away.

"She doesn't know how lightweight a drinker you are." Graham looked at her full glass.

"I understand her not wanting to tell people yet." Erin had kept her first pregnancy secret as long as she could, though for a different reason. "I don't have to drink it all."

"You're the kind of player I want on my team."

A series of soft chimes sounded. "That's our signal for the receiving line." He offered Erin his arm and led her to where the senior officers lined up.

"This is my date, Erin Downey."

As Graham introduced Major General Miller and his wife, Erin tried not to gawk at the rows of ribbons and medals decorating the general's chest.

"It's nice to meet you in person," Becky Miller said. "I've seen you two walking and heard complimentary things about you from Dianne and Sally. And it's nice to see Colonel Holmstrom smiling like he does when he looks at you. Is this your first military ball?"

"It is. Does it show?" Erin asked.

"Just in the way you keep eyeing Graham. Seeing them in the mess dress uniform doesn't get old." Becky gave a knowing smile. "I hope it won't be your last ball."

"Me either." And she meant that with her whole heart. Whenever she pictured her future, Graham was in it.

Next, Graham introduced her to the guest speaker, retired Colonel Bailey and his wife. After greeting the McKittricks, they took their place in the receiving line. Erin was impressed that Graham knew the name of every man under his command as they shook hands and spoke with hundreds of soldiers for the next half hour. From the time she'd spent with Graham and John Bryson's team, she could pick out the operators by how they stood and presented themselves with their quiet professionalism.

John and Elizabeth Bryson brought up the rear of the line.

"Did you bribe somebody to put us at the colonel's table?" Bryson teased and leaned in for a hug.

"I just asked nicely." Right after Graham informed her that since McKittrick had extended an invitation to the Ayers, and they'd be seated at the same table. With the Mahinises and Brysons there, she could get through dinner at the same table with Noelle. Maybe this would be an opportunity to get to know each other and find things in common to become friends—or at least reach a ceasefire agreement. It could happen. While she didn't have a fairy godmother, this week felt like the culmination of a fairy tale after things had gone so well in California, both with the filming and trip with Graham.

With their formal receiving line duties completed, Erin and Graham followed the Brysons to their table, where the Ayers were already seated. Noelle's gaze flicked up, and she gave a tight-lipped smile.

"How was the honeymoon?" Erin asked the Brysons.

"It was wonderful. We started in Paris, then hit the wine country and Normandy," Elizabeth answered. "After France, we took the train to Italy and toured Rome, then Positano."

"I'd like to take Erin to the Amalfi coast after we go to Spain to see her daughter," Graham said.

"You'll love it," Elizabeth promised. "The scenery was breathtaking, and the food was amazing."

"Pete and Noelle, this is Elizabeth and Captain John Bryson," Graham made introductions.

"Captain?" Noelle's gaze drifted to the name plates as if to point out that the rest of the men at the table were all colonels.

"Yes, ma'am." Bryson appeared unfazed. "My team was the one Erin observed for research for her TV series."

"TV series?" Noelle's voice rose, her interest piqued.

"I got lucky with that," Erin said. "My original request to observe a Special Ops team got turned down." If it had been approved, she likely would have never met Graham.

"That wasn't my doing." Graham eyed Mahinis.

Mahinis gave a nonchalant shrug.

"Any updates on the project?" Elizabeth asked.

Erin hadn't exactly wanted to talk about the series with Noelle, but the Brysons had no way of knowing that. "They filmed the pilot. Now we wait to see if it gets picked up."

"Is this a documentary or series about the USO?" Pete Ayers asked.

"It's fiction. A military action series involving a Special Ops team and aviators."

"Really? Oh." Pete's eyebrows rose, and he looked at Graham.

"What's *your* role?" Noelle asked.

"The series is based on my idea. I wrote the pilot and hope to write for the series."

"You're writing about military men and missions?" Noelle didn't quite hide her amusement with a finger to her lips. "Will you be moving to Hollywood then?"

"I'll be spending some time out there."

"That's exciting. Good luck with that." Noelle's smile bordered on a smirk.

"Thank you." Erin doubted Noelle was sincere, but this wasn't the time or place to let the woman get under her skin.

Conversation halted for the presentation of the flags and the national anthem, after which the senior officers and guests on the dais were served first.

"Noelle, I love the flowers you have in the planters. They look very patriotic," Erin said during a lull in conversation.

"Thank you," Noelle answered cautiously. "When we were at Fort Campbell, we had similar planters at all the officer's houses during the summer. I wish we did something like that here."

"I like that idea. I can do that at Graham's. Dianne, are you interested?"

Elizabeth Bryson jumped into the conversation about flowers too. While the compliment wasn't exactly like a fairy godmother waving a magic wand, it did seem to thaw Noelle's frigid countenance.

Following dinner, General McKittrick spoke briefly, then introduced Colonel Bailey. His relatability had everyone listening intently. He also had the room laughing with a sense of humor rivaling Bryson's.

"If you'll indulge me for a more serious story, I'll tell you about the two bravest things I've ever done." Bailey paused. People leaned forward in anticipation. "I'd been serving about seventeen years, so I'd already seen a lot when things started to feel off. I didn't want to burden my lovely wife with what was going through my head. I definitely didn't want to tell my commanding officer or the men under my command and risk being seen as weak. Then, one morning, I got a call that one of my soldiers had taken his own life."

Silence settled like the last strings of a symphony dying away while Bailey let the discomfort build. "The next day, I made an appointment with a counselor. A move that probably saved my marriage, career, and maybe even my life. That was the *second* bravest thing I've ever done. The first was publicly sharing that decision—with others and you. There's still a stigma around needing help. We're supposed to be strong, so we say we're fine—which stands for freaked out, insecure, neurotic, and evading."

Ripples of light laughter broke some of the tension as men shifted in their seats. Next to Erin, Elizabeth's head moved in agreement with Colonel Bailey's message as he went on to talk about fear only living in darkness and the need to have hope and a purpose and how the two were intertwined.

He closed by encouraging the audience to talk with someone and to find a new purpose once they hung up their weapons and uniforms for good. The Brysons were the first to stand and applaud Colonel Bailey. Graham headed to the dais, shook hands with Bailey, then went to the podium and addressed the guests.

"Thank you, Colonel, for that powerful message. What he didn't tell you is that after retiring, he went back to school and got his master's in counseling. He is a board-certified counselor here in the Fayetteville area. He understands what we've seen, been through, and might be dealing with, and is, *hopefully,* accepting new clients."

Graham looked at Bailey, who nodded.

"At West Point, we're taught to lead from the front. Be an example. When I lost my wife, I lost the person who kept me grounded. It was the hardest thing I'd ever experienced. I didn't know how to process it. I feared I'd lost *my* purpose." Graham's voice cracked, and tears sprung to Erin's eyes. "I didn't have the answers, so I talked to someone and still do, as needed. As your commanding officer, I encourage you to take care of your physical and mental health. Anyone who thinks that makes me weak can see me afterward. And you can wrestle with Captain Bryson."

Laughter erupted. Graham smiled as he scanned the room.

"I knew this would be a bit of a heavy topic, so I asked my captains to come up with ideas to put you in the party mood. The winning idea involved each company participating in a lip sync challenge."

"Had to be Bryson's idea," someone in the back of the room called out.

"Wrong. It was Elauria's idea," Bryson interjected.

"Maybe to keep you from singing, Bryson," the heckler called out.

"The servers are bringing out dessert, and there's a ballot with each for you to vote," Graham went on. "Everyone in the winning company gets a gift card from the assortment donated by local businesses. The winning company will be announced at twenty-one hundred hours, which means you don't have much time to sway or bribe our distinguished guests for their votes."

"Feel free to vote for my team. No pressure," Bryson said to the table with an amiable smile.

"We didn't want our deployed team to miss out on all the fun," Graham continued. "However, there's a slight time difference and men out on mission at any time, so they recorded their entry and are first in tonight's lineup. To keep things fair, our DJ assigned the teams present a random order to perform."

"There goes my master plan of saving the best for last," Bryson cracked. "Though they could all concede after they see our masterpiece."

"They may take their chances, honey." Elizabeth patted her husband's arm.

"Now, live—from an undisclosed location," Graham's voice dropped, "we have Captain Amaya." A soldier wearing a bow tie and his uniform filled the screens on either side of the dais.

"We hate missing out on the ball this year, but thanks for including us, Colonel. Warning: we had limited access to props and had to keep our location under wraps, but making our video was a fun activity in our downtime."

The person filming Captain Amaya panned to show camouflaged men sitting on black couches in a cramped room. An American flag hung on the back wall over a TV livestreaming the ball. Pictures, postcards, and a smaller Canadian flag covered the other walls.

Simultaneously, the men turned to face the camera, all wearing brightly colored bow ties. One donned a cream-colored Panama hat.

Their heads bobbed as they sang the opening Doh-doh-doh's from "Uptown Funk" before the screen cut to their video as Graham returned to sit next to Erin. Amaya's men had dubbed over the song's lyrics to make it fit the deployment theme, substituting combat boots and camouflage, and the men kissing their weapons and calling them pretty, which garnered laughter throughout the ballroom.

"Looks like you're going to have some competition, honey," Elizabeth said to Bryson.

"They haven't seen the suit yet. But it's all good. It's about morale. And a deployment is when you need that boost," Bryson said.

"It was John's idea to include them and do a livestream," Graham said to Elizabeth.

The entry received a standing ovation as Amaya and his men appeared on the screen and took a bow.

"We'll be watching your performances here live, so you guys better make it worthwhile for us to get up at this hour. Have a great time tonight." Amaya signed off, and the DJ called the next team to the dance floor for their performance.

The fun continued for the next half hour.

"Where did he get a white suit jacket in his size?" Graham laughed as Bryson pretended to dodge bullets with the team lip-syncing to "Stayin' Alive" as part of their mashup of songs.

"eBay," Elizabeth answered. "He has the entire suit now. I'm certain he'll find a Halloween party to attend."

Bryson's team seemed like a shoo-in until the Group Support Battalion ended their performance by executing the iconic lift from *Dirty Dancing* to cheers from the room.

John leaned close to Elizabeth. "Told you we should have ended with that and me lifting you."

"This was for the team, not spouses. Besides, it was funnier with the two men performing it. I'll still vote for you," she promised.

"You don't have to. I'm voting for them. They never get the glory, but they make us look good. We couldn't do what we do without them."

Erin noticed Graham give a subtle nod of approval. Bryson and Graham were clearly cut from the same camouflage cloth.

Chapter Thirty-Eight

JOHN AND ELIZABETH walked off hand in hand to turn in their ballots. Less than a minute later, Megan hugged her dad's shoulders and kissed him on the cheek before she and Reece took the Brysons' seats.

"Excellent choice on having Colonel Bailey speak on mental health," Megan confirmed. "And good call on the lip sync challenge. It set the right mood." She motioned to the crowded dance floor and subtly poured wine into Erin's glass. "You two need to get out there and dance, and so do we." Megan held out a hand to Reece.

"We better follow orders." Graham leaned closer to Erin." She thinks she outranks me. Especially now."

Erin didn't doubt that his daughter wouldn't be the only one with Graham wrapped around their little finger in less than nine months.

They danced to several up-tempo songs before a slow song allowed Erin to catch her breath. Graham held her close, and she inhaled the light musk scent of his cologne. "How did I get so lucky?"

His low, sexy laugh stoked the fire in her. "Luck had

nothing to do with it. You have a big heart for supporting the military and a thing for men in uniform. And an amazing talent for storytelling that landed you exactly where I needed you. I'm the lucky one. Blessed, in fact." Everyone around them faded from sight as they stared into each other's eyes.

"Shout" started playing. "I don't normally retreat, but I can't get low like I used to." Graham guided Erin away as young couples swarmed to the dance floor.

The McKittricks homed in on Graham and Erin.

"Erin, you two certainly look good together out there," Sally said as the general pulled Graham aside.

"I don't know who my fairy godmother is, but I feel like Cinderella, and he's my Colonel Charming."

Sally laughed along with her. "You remember the purpose of Cinderella's ball was to find the prince a wife. The necklace is beautiful, though I was hoping we might see a ring."

That Sally clearly meant an engagement ring captured Erin's attention like waving a big red flag. "It's a little soon for that. Graham hasn't even met my daughters in person yet. My oldest is coming to North Carolina for a wedding in early October, and we're planning a trip to Spain, where my youngest is studying this year. Maybe sometime after that." Surely, Sally would understand.

"I'm sure they'd be thrilled for you."

Or not. "I'm not sure about that. Unfortunately, my oldest is still dealing with the divorce and the fact I'm dating." She went for the sympathetic chord.

"They're adults. You need to think about Graham's career. There's an expectation for officers to be married."

"I've heard that," Erin said as a light bulb flicked on. Why hadn't it occurred to her that Sally might know about her husband's plan to replace Graham unless he remarried? Erin took a drink of her wine. "Though I don't see how a ceremony or a piece of paper to make two people legally man and wife is better than two people in a loving and committed relationship."

"The Army may be a little old fashioned that way, but they don't give identification cards and benefits to partners, no matter how significant or committed they are."

"It's a matter of timing," Erin sought to reassure Sally since she was not the ally Erin had hoped for. She took another swallow of wine to counter her growing queasiness.

"Graham has proved to be good for this unit, which is why my husband hopes to extend this assignment."

"I'm certain Graham would be on board with that."

"The timing may never be perfect, but sometimes life is like war, and you simply do what needs to be done. At times, that requires sacrifices you'd prefer not to have to make—for the greater good."

"I'll keep that in mind. If you'll excuse me, I need to cast my ballot before they tally the votes."

"Certainly. Enjoy the ball, dear. I hope it's your first of many."

"So do I." She meant that, though Sally's implied threat cast a shadow over the evening.

Erin placed her and Graham's ballots in the box and then nearly collided with Megan.

"What was that about?" She swapped her full glass of wine for Erin's nearly empty one.

"I hoped to recruit her as an ally to buy your dad more time. Apparently, she knows her husband's plans to transfer your father if he doesn't remarry."

"It would make sense she would want to cover her husband's butt. If anything else happened under his watch, it could cost him his posting and reputation. This moves us to Defcon Three. Dad may have to get a ring on your finger to keep from going to Defcon Two if he wants to be here when his grandbaby is born. We are not going to stress about it tonight. Keep doing what you're doing, and let everyone see what a great couple you are."

Megan mentioned Defcon Two then said not to stress? Right. Erin sighed, then took a generous sip of the wine she was now thankful to have.

She was in love with Graham, but he understood why she needed to focus on writing for the series right now. She also had to consider Madison. Erin couldn't risk long-term damage to her strained relationship with her daughter by getting engaged, much less married, after only a few months of dating. Due to Graham's situation with his father, he felt the same. She'd do whatever she could to keep him here with his family, except jump into marriage.

"Come with me." Megan linked her arm through Erin's and led her to a table where she introduced several of Reece's teammates.

Speaking with the enlisted men and their wives and finishing the glass of wine allowed Erin to relax again. She wanted to be with Graham, however, when she caught his eye as he conversed with the other officers, he discreetly cut his gaze to McKittrick in a manner that she interpreted as meaning he couldn't tactfully escape. The officers' wives clustered nearby, but seeing the Gablers and Nishiyamas, she decided they were a safer option than engaging with Sally and Noelle.

In the middle of Greg telling a story about going through the selection process for Special Forces, Gabler interrupted. "Incoming. Take cover," he said lowly.

It was too late to retreat as Noelle sauntered their way. "Talking about Colonel Bailey's speech? His message was a little off the mark, considering the audience here is the best of the best."

Erin opened her mouth to speak. Gabler beat her to the punch.

"Thanks for the compliment about us being the best of the best, but we're human. His speech resonated with everybody at my table. I agree with him and Colonel Holmstrom that admitting you need help is scarier than facing insurgents. That took cojones. It was also what some of us needed to hear rather than believe the lie that going to counseling is a sign of weakness." Gabler looked Noelle right in the eyes.

"I agree," Nishiyama chimed in. "Did you know Bryson's taking a psychology class? His wife's a therapist, and he may join her in practice after he retires. He'd be exactly the type of counselor team guys could relate to and open up to. If you'll excuse me, ma'am. I'm in the mood to dance. Cindy?" He extended his arm to his wife.

"You have a good one." The Gablers headed to the dance floor as well.

Noelle forced a smile despite being snubbed. She moved closer to Erin. "I know you're new to all of this, so let me give you a tip. You shouldn't waste your time with the enlisted personnel. They can't advance Graham's career."

"I was talking with them because I spent time observing their training, and we're friends. Besides, Graham doesn't need my help advancing his career. He's got that covered all on his own." He didn't need her kissing up on his behalf.

Noelle gave a gruff laugh. "You really are naïve."

"Maybe, but I'm learning." *That I don't want to be like you.* Erin walked past Noelle.

"You know, the only reason Graham's dating you is because he was ordered to get married to keep his command."

Erin froze. Based on the number of heads that swiveled their way, everyone in the vicinity heard that comment.

She pivoted on one heel to face Noelle. "That's not true." Though it was damn close.

"Maybe *you* don't know it, but I have it on good authority that the only way for Graham to stay with 3rd Group is to get remarried. And right after he learned this, he started dating you." Noelle's smug gaze darted to the small crowd raptly listening.

Cruz sent a hand signal to someone.

"When we started dating, Graham did mention he could be transferred." The way Noelle's haughty expression deflated, she'd expected Graham to keep that confidential. "Of course, Graham would like to stay here. Whatever his motivation for asking me out, it worked beautifully for both of us. I got to observe a team for research, and we fell in love." She wouldn't announce marriage wasn't an option and kill Graham's chances of staying here.

"Love?" Noelle laughed. "He's using you to keep his command—and for sex."

Talk about nerve. Erin took a deep breath. She forced a smile onto her face and sweetness into her voice. "I don't know why you have a problem with him being happy. Are you jealous of what we have?"

Noelle shook her head. "That's absurd."

"So, when you knew I was out of town, and you invited him *and* a military widow over to dinner, that wasn't an attempt at a setup?"

Noelle's eyes opened to an oh-shit, wide-eyed stare.

"If you had a clue about Graham's character, you'd know he wouldn't cheat. Besides, he's not using me for sex. It's *totally* consensual," she couldn't resist adding.

"Sorry to keep you waiting." Graham's voice alerted Erin

to his presence before he touched her arm. "Ready to hit the dance floor with me?"

"I'd love to." She smiled at him, her heart hammering and anger coursing through her. "Enjoy the ball," she said to Noelle, who gave a definitively angry *humph* in response.

"Tell me about that in a minute," Graham said under his breath. They joined the crowd doing the "Cupid Shuffle." When she turned, she saw Pete consoling a distraught Noelle. By the time Erin had done another rotation, Noelle had her purse in hand. The look she shot Erin's way before the pair left the ballroom didn't quite have the power to kill or bodies would be dropping.

~

GRAHAM AND ERIN danced to several more songs before he caught Megan pointing to their empty dinner table. He steered Erin off the floor as Megan marched up to their table like a woman on a mission, with Reece only a step behind.

She took a quick surveillance glance around before sitting next to Erin. "Someone from Reece's team just asked if what Noelle said about you being ordered to marry was true. Did she really announce that to the whole ballroom?"

"Not the *whole* ballroom," Erin said.

That didn't matter since word could spread faster than grenade fragments and be as deadly.

"How did Noelle even know?" Megan said.

"Sally. It had to be." Especially after what Sally said earlier. "But if Noelle knows what General McKittrick wants, why would she deliberately work against it?"

"Mom once said Dianne Mahinis told her Noelle had hoped her husband would get command of 3rd Group after the Thomsen debacle. Hell, she may think he could replace McKittrick if he was removed from command."

Graham motioned to Bryson, who had alerted him to something going down and now stood at attention a few steps away. Bryson and Elizabeth took the empty seats. "What have you heard?" Graham asked his trusted captain.

Bryson watched the men on the dance floor rather than make eye contact. "Cruz signaled me after he overheard Mrs. Ayers claim McKittrick *ordered* you to marry to keep your command. You two are the real deal, right?"

"I thought it was crazy when you brought up me getting remarried, but due to the rumors and McKittrick's concerns following Boatman and Thomsen, he felt the only way to reassure the teams and keep me here was for me to remarry. It wasn't an order. More like an ultimatum." Graham placed his hand over Erin's. "But this is real."

"Very," she added.

"However, if this rumor spreads as it having been an order, it's not a good look for me—or McKittrick." It could guarantee Graham getting a new posting. Likely far away from McKittrick—and Graham's family.

"We can try to contain it." Bryson studied the room. "If that's what you want, we need to move. Now."

"And we have to control the narrative by saying the same thing," Reece advised. "That way, if McKittrick's ultimatum gets outed, the damage is limited."

"Agreed." Graham and Bryson said in unison.

"Stick to the truth. Between Bethann's death and a false rumor, McKittrick feared team members were worried about a three-peat of Thomsen and Boatman. With his priority being that you men focus on the mission, he planned for a change of command." Graham strategized on the fly. "That I'm seriously involved with someone may keep me here." Or not be enough.

"I'll get word to Elauria to tell his men to keep a lid on it. He owes me," Bryson added, then sketched out a notification chain to split with Reece.

"Don't forget the women. They gossip more than men," Megan said. "Elizabeth and I will circulate among them. You two put on smiles and hit the dance floor. We've got your six."

While Graham was used to being in command and giving orders, this situation warranted letting his men and bossy daughter lead the containment effort.

As GRAHAM DANCED WITH ERIN, he observed his men work the room. More than a few covert glances came his way, but he also got a few nods and thumbs-up signals. Still, it was impossible to relax. Were they making it worse by potentially spreading the news? It would only take one man or woman with a grudge, or someone having one too many drinks, to ask the general if what Noelle said was true and there went containment.

He managed to dodge the McKittricks until they said their farewells. They never indicated anything was amiss. Graham waited until only a handful of people remained, including Bryson, Reece, Cruz, and Elauria, who had effectively staked out positions near the general to run interference, if necessary.

"What's the word?" Graham asked when they congregated for a sit-rep.

"We appear to have containment thanks to Cruz's quick notification and observing everyone who overheard," Bryson reported.

"No one wants to see you given the boot, Colonel," Cruz said. "Mateo blames himself."

"It's not his fault. Thank you all. I know this isn't how you wanted to spend your time at the ball." And it didn't mean they were in the clear.

"We all enjoy a covert mission, especially when no weapons—other than tongues—are involved," Bryson joked.

After the last partygoers had departed, Graham walked Erin to the car.

"Let's spend the night at my place," she said. "I might be tempted to throw a rock at the Ayers's house. Do you think she'd notice if I named a character in my series after her?"

"Let's not do anything to further invoke her wrath."

"True. I'm pretty sure she regrets opening her mouth. Not that she'll thank you for covering her uptight butt."

"I wanted your first ball to be a magical experience, not have your reputation questioned. Noelle saying I was using you for sex so crossed the line." He opened the car door for her.

"I'm not worried about me. I nearly told everyone you're the best lover I ever had."

"That might not have helped our case," he said with a chuckle.

"True. And I don't want to reflect poorly on you or negatively impact your career." She rested a hand on his arm.

"You haven't. This is the best command I've had, but you're more important."

Chapter Thirty-Nine

DESPITE THE BRIGHT sunlight filling the bedroom Sunday morning when Erin woke, Graham lay in bed with his eyes closed. "Are you awake?" she asked quietly.

"Yeah." He opened his eyes and turned his head toward her. "I didn't want to wake you by getting out of bed."

They'd both laid in bed, barely moving but not sleeping for nearly two hours after getting home from the ball. Finally, she initiated sex. Neither had been in the mood at first. Graham had fallen asleep afterward. She had lain awake for at least another hour before drifting off.

"How about we go hiking at Raven Rock Park or to the beach for the day," he suggested.

"Are you sure the beach isn't too far for a day trip?"

"I've got nothing else on today's agenda. And it might help take our minds off . . . things."

"Beach it is. But we should go by the house and feed the cats since I wasn't planning on us coming here last night." Erin scooted out of bed.

"I can ask Megan to swing by and do that."

"We need to get your swimsuit."

"I'll be fine."

She drew in a breath but simply said, "Okay."

"No. Something's wrong." Graham stayed put, his gaze fixed on her.

She moved to stand in front of him. "I want you to enjoy the beach. Not just *be* there."

"I will." He took her hand.

"If you don't have a suit, you can't go in the water."

"You can still go in."

"Tell me now if you don't like the beach, and we'll go to the park."

"I'm not saying I don't like the beach. I do want to go there with you. Does this have to do with your ex?" he guessed.

"Yeah," she sighed, realizing he was right. It did. "We used to go to the beach and on trips when we were dating and early in our marriage. Then I had the girls. His work got busy, and he'd spend half the vacation on the phone or computer and be grumpy that he was working. It got worse when he started his own company. While we liked the idea of travel, it became too stressful for me because he wanted me to do all the planning. I'd research locations, things to do, places to stay, and then he'd say he couldn't go because work was too unpredictable."

"That would be frustrating, and I can't promise I won't have to cancel plans at times either."

"I understand that. But there's more." The part that had her thinking about a separation even before Phil was charged with driving while impaired. "Going to the same beach all the time may not sound exciting, but it was familiar, easy, fun. Until Phil started bringing a cooler full of beers down with him. He'd sit under the umbrella and make business calls—getting louder and louder as he got more impaired." Ruining the relaxed vibe not only for her but for the people around them. "I went from envisioning us as an old gray-haired couple walking hand-in-hand on the beach and writing our initials in the sand to wishing he wasn't there. I named our daughters after the mermaid in the movie *Splash* and the Sandpipers I love to watch. Instead of the beach being my happy place, I didn't want to go anymore." Her marriage had been crumbling, and Phil sucked the joy from another thing she loved.

"I'm sorry."

"Don't be sorry. You've brought so much joy back into my life. You can do that again today. Hold my hand as we take a walk. Play in the waves. Watch the Sandpipers scurry along the shoreline. If you can have a Black Hawk fly over, you get bonus points." She tried to lighten the mood.

"You know I have no sway over aviation to make that happen, don't you?" he grinned at her.

"Never hurts to ask. You have friends in high places." She leaned over to kiss him.

"I can follow your orders on the other things."

She threw a swimsuit and towels in a beach bag, then packed a cooler with ice, water, and some snacks. Graham made coffee and texted Megan.

"Megan said she'd swing by the house and feed the cats. Which beach are we going to? Kiawah's too far, and you'll be there soon."

"Oak Island is one of the closest to here, and I've wanted to check it out."

"Do you want to eat here or on the way?" Graham handed her a thermal mug of coffee.

"I'm not that hungry. Why don't you grab a protein bar? We can find a place for an early lunch on the beach. And we're stopping somewhere to get you a swimsuit."

"Yes, we are. And we're going to write our names in the

sand. Even though it's Sunday, maybe the Coast Guard will fly over and get you excited." He winked at her.

"You know I'll wave to them."

"I do." Graham's hearty chuckle helped dispel the gloom lingering from Noelle's disclosure last night.

~

RATHER THAN SLEEP, Erin kept him engaged in conversation as he drove. She mentioned some ideas for the series, asked him about Italy for the trip over the holiday, and changed to a new topic whenever there was a lull in conversation. They talked about anything but the ball and what happened last night.

She sat up straighter and cracked the car window as they crossed the bridge over the intercoastal waterway. Their nearness to the ocean was already working its magic based on her smile and the way she drew in a deep breath of the salt air.

When she met his gaze, a light in her eyes lifted the weight in his chest.

They stopped at one of the beach stores where he shopped for swim trunks and a pair of flip-flops. Erin picked up beach chairs and visors embroidered with Oak Island.

They ate lunch at a coffee shop near the pier. The view of the water captured Erin's attention over and over.

He made eye contact with their server after she delivered food to a nearby table. "Can I get the bill? She might dissolve like a washed-up jellyfish if I don't get her to the beach soon."

"He's not wrong," Erin laughed and finished her sandwich.

"Sure thing," the server said.

He paid, and they drove to a parking lot at one of the public beach access points with bathrooms and showers. After changing, they walked past dozens of beachgoers to find a space to set up their chairs.

"You so have a golfer's tan," Erin teased as she sprayed sunscreen on his neck and back.

"It's been two years since I've been to the beach." Memories of the whole family together at the house they'd rented on nearby Ocean Isle flooded back. The men golfing and fishing. The women spending the days on the beach and reading. A family outing playing mini golf. Everybody boogie boarding the day before a tropical storm came through. The storm kept them inside an entire day, but Jace declared it game day, and they'd played cards for hours. It had been a great vacation and their last one together.

He wasn't going to tell Erin all that. It was time for him to make new memories too. With her.

"Do you want to walk for a while before we sit?" he asked.

"Sounds good. We've been sitting all morning, and it's going to get hotter the next two hours."

They went to the water's edge, where he held her hand as they walked with Erin's bare feet in the surf. They hadn't been walking long when she stopped and raised her face to study the sky ahead, then behind them. "I hear a helicopter. I think it's military."

"If it's a Black Hawk, I'll take credit."

"Really?"

He shrugged, unable to keep a straight face.

"I see it." She pointed out over the ocean.

He picked up a large piece of a broken shell and wrote in the sand while she watched the gray dot in the sky fly closer and grow louder.

"Not a Black Hawk," she said with a sigh as it flew past.

He got to his feet. "I think it's a Marine Super Stallion."

"I'm impressed you know that."

"I've jumped from one in joint Special Ops training."

"Ah. I should have guessed that." She looked down at their initials in the sand. "You forgot something."

"What?"

She took the shell from him, crouched, and drew a heart around their initials. "It's gotta have the heart." She gave him the playful smile he loved.

"You have my heart." He used his index finger to free strands of her hair that the breeze blew across her mouth before he kissed her.

In the same way the beach breathed joy into her, her love restored joy and balance to his life. Everything they both wanted was on the horizon—unless Noelle's public accusation blew up everything like a ballistic missile.

Chapter Forty

To AVOID further encounters with the Ayers, they stayed at Erin's place again Sunday evening after coming back from the beach. Graham hoped that not hearing anything from McKittrick meant they'd miraculously kept Noelle's disclosure under wraps.

He slipped out of the condo quietly Monday morning and arrived early for the weekly briefing to get a read on the vibe from his peers. It also reduced the risk of getting ambushed by McKittrick or Pete Ayers, who walked into the room just seconds before the general and avoided eye contact with Graham. While he didn't expect a public apology for Noelle's behavior, something felt off. As Graham listened to the updates, his first cup of coffee ate at his stomach.

He relaxed a bit while giving his update from Amaya's team. Business as usual. Or a little worse, considering rebels attacked two villages last week.

McKittrick's mouth pursed, and his brows scrunched as Graham finished his report. "I thought we were about due for sit-downs between higher-ranking officers and the local tribal leaders. The recent uptick in attacks confirms that."

Adrenaline shot through Graham's body as his innate warning system triggered.

"Holmstrom, clear your schedule."

"Me?"

"You'll fly out ASAP," McKittrick kept talking as if Graham hadn't questioned the order aloud. "We'll meet to discuss your agenda after we wrap here."

Graham projected a calm demeanor as McKittrick moved on. If the general thought a week or two in Africa was warranted, that was no big deal. Except Ayers did everything short of a backflip to avoid making eye contact with Graham. That kept his nerves firing for the rest of the briefing.

When things wrapped, he followed McKittrick to his office and closed the door.

Graham kept his mouth shut rather than be the one to address the proverbial elephant in the room. It didn't matter how the general had found out. He knew.

"Pete and Noelle Ayers came to see me yesterday. They told me about an altercation between Noelle and Erin at the ball."

The Ayers told him? Seriously? He'd done what he could to try to contain it, and Noelle probably put her spin on things and threw Erin on the grenade *she* had tossed. "I wouldn't classify it as an altercation—"

"It doesn't matter what you call it." McKittrick waved a hand in dismissal. "Noelle admitted that during the exchange, she mentioned the suggestion that you marry. Except she referred to it as an order."

"She did."

"That presents a problem, as a number of your men overheard."

Graham nodded.

"Considering I didn't hear anything that night, you

managed to limit the spread." McKittrick clearly wanted to do damage control.

"For the most part."

"If your men feel you've been compromised and gave Erin access to the teams to keep your position here or in exchange for sex . . ."

"That was not the case."

"They may not see it that way." The general's mouth clamped in a tight line, and he breathed out loudly through his nose.

Now wasn't the time to mention that McKittrick signed off on Erin shadowing Bryson's team because it suited his purpose.

"What's the latest on the television series she's trying to get hired for?"

"They filmed the pilot and are waiting to see if a network picks it up."

"If it does, it could be problematic."

"How?" The uneasy sensation in Graham's gut traveled down his arms and legs.

"The men may not trust her motives. If you've lost their respect because of your romantic involvement, you'll no longer be able to lead this unit. Being away for a few weeks should give us time to evaluate the situation. I'm not sure there's any middle ground."

"What do you mean?"

"Even if you two were to get married, she'd have to cut ties with the show if you stayed here. That *could* prove to the teams that you weren't faking your relationship, and she's not using you for her purposes. If you can't commit to those things, we need to find another placement for you. And we don't have much time to make that decision."

"Nothing may come of this series"—how many times had

she stressed it was a long shot?—"but I can't ask Erin to walk away from this opportunity."

"If that's your choice, I'll be disappointed, but I'll understand. But talk to her before you decide. Life with you versus a shot at working with Hollywood—that would be temporary at best? She's a smart woman. Alternatively, there is the option for you to end things with her."

End things? No. That was *not* an option. Graham didn't doubt Erin loved him, but she wasn't ready to get married. On their first date, she'd said she couldn't see getting back with her ex since he hadn't supported her pursuing this dream. He couldn't ask her to choose.

Talk about a mission going sideways.

~

"Colonel Ayers to see you, sir," Kearns announced.

Really? Graham was not in the mood but conceded. "Send him in." He didn't bother to stand as Pete entered. He closed the door without being asked.

"I'm probably the last person you want to see—after my wife—but I need to apologize."

No. *Noelle* needed to apologize. And mean it. Not that an apology would change the circumstances. "How did Noelle even know?"

Pete shifted in his seat before returning Graham's gaze head-on. "I asked that, as well. I'm sure I got the whitewashed version, but after you started dating Erin, it came up in a conversation between Noelle and Sally. My wife had a misguided notion that I should have replaced Thomsen."

"The dinner with Maribelle?"

"I asked her what the hell that was about after you two

left that night. They'd sat together at the Gold Star brunch, and when Maribelle came back to the table after trying to catch you following your speech, you became the subject of conversation. Knowing McKittrick was on the fence about you staying for another term, Noelle thought if your relationship with Erin went south, this could be my shot at taking over 3rd Group and a step toward brigadier general. She understands now that I will never command 3rd Group, and she is never to interfere with my career again. Or yours."

Graham gave a nod. Unfortunately, the bomb had already been dropped, and there was no taking it back.

"That adage about picking your battles, I've been avoiding one I should have engaged in long before now. I was deployed so much that I didn't want to make waves at home and tolerated her behavior. I'm sleeping in the guest room for a while, and I insisted we go to a marriage counselor. Time to admit we need help because we are not operating as a team." Pete's voice broke. "I wanted Noelle to apologize to you and Erin yesterday after talking with the McKittricks, but you weren't home, and it wasn't a conversation for a phone call. I swear I didn't know he planned to ship you out. You and Erin didn't deserve this."

Pete didn't know the half of it. He was also an innocent party. Instead of helping Pete with her ploy, Noelle may have also negatively impacted his career. "I appreciate you apologizing." While Noelle owed them one, he wasn't sure if he or Erin were ready to hear it yet. "I hope you find a counselor to help you two get to a better place."

❧

ERIN LOOKED up from working on her laptop at Graham's kitchen table when he opened the side door. "You're early," she greeted him. One look at his face sent her spirits plummeting and sucked the oxygen from her lungs. "McKittrick heard what happened at the ball?"

"Yes. The Ayers went to see them yesterday."

"Great. I wonder how she spun that." That likely took things from bad to worse.

"Sounds like she did take some ownership. However, McKittrick is concerned about how the men may view our relationship in light of what Noelle said." Graham sank onto the sofa and angled to face her. "He's sending me to Africa to check on the team and meet with local leaders to let things die down and see how they shake out."

Was all the blowback on Graham? What about Noelle? Erin didn't ask. "When does he want you to leave?"

"He's already got me booked on a flight at 0700 on Wednesday."

That barely gave them any time. "How long will you be gone?"

"That's still to be determined. But it sounds like at least three weeks."

"Then what?" She could barely get the question out with her mouth so parched she couldn't even lick her lips to moisten them.

"I'm not one hundred percent certain yet. With Noelle claiming he *ordered* me to marry, McKittrick's concerned the men may feel I betrayed a code in giving you access to the teams. That we engaged in a trade for me to stay in command. He's not totally wrong."

The bad news kept coming. "This is my fault. If I hadn't engaged with Noelle—"

"This isn't your fault. I knew there were risks but figured it was worth a shot at staying here. I never anticipated we'd encounter friendly fire."

"I wouldn't exactly call it friendly." And it *was* her fault. She couldn't remember what she'd said, but she had blurted out something about spending time with Bryson's team. Now, she may have cost Graham the thing he wanted most—to stay here with his family. With Megan pregnant, he had another important reason to stay. Why had she ever agreed to this? "Is there any scenario where McKittrick will keep you here?"

"One." Graham shook his head as he said it.

"Get married?" There were worse options—like life without him in it. That thought felt like a bullet ripping through her heart. But would her girls understand?

What were the chances a hasty marriage would work out? She'd dated Phil far longer, and look how that turned out. She did not want to end up another statistic in the failed second marriages category or further hurt Graham. Her head shook of its own accord, and numbness spread through her body. "What will that mean for your career if we don't?"

"I find another assignment. It'd only be for two to three years. Or I retire."

"You aren't ready to retire."

"I wasn't planning to, but it's an option. I could go into the public sector or with a private defense contractor. An overseas assignment would mean long trips back here after Megan has the baby, and I don't know how you feel about that. Fort Lewis in Washington or maybe a base in Texas could be possibilities and would put you nearer LA or Madison. *If* you would consider going with me."

Go with him? Her heart fluttered that he'd want that, especially in light of the situation she'd contributed to putting him in. She hadn't planned past the four months she'd be at the beach since she was waiting to see what happened with the series. She squeezed his hand. "I'd need to know more and have time to think how it would work."

"I don't expect you to commit without details. While I'm away, we'll see what the options are. We may have to do long-distance commuting for a while, but we'll figure something out." He kissed her forehead and pulled her into his arms.

The disappointment in his face and tone tore at her. If only she knew if the series would get picked up. She'd begun to hope she could make it as a writer and still have a relationship with him, but what would that look like if she went overseas?

"I wanted to tell you before Jace and Megan, but I don't have much time to tell them."

She swallowed her disappointment, knowing how much they wanted Graham to stay here. "Why don't you call and invite them to a family dinner sendoff tomorrow?"

"Instead, how about we offer to pick up food from DiLorenzo's and just take it to Megan's for dinner? If we do dinner and games here, I can see that devolving into you and Megan toilet papering the Ayers' house."

"Too dangerous." But the humor helped ease the ache in her chest. "She'd likely look out the windows, and we'd get caught. We could let Reece and Jace sneak over under the cover of darkness and let the air out of her tires instead."

"Do not give them any ideas." He shook his head. "And you . . ."

"I'll stay out of trouble," she promised. "I want you back here. Soon."

"We'd talked briefly about you staying with me once your pet-sitting duties were over, but . . ."

"With you needing to keep a low profile, it's probably best if I do as well. I'll proceed with plans to go to the beach, at least until you get back." If only Erin had a fairy godmother who would have told her to leave the ball well before midnight. Too late now. They needed to ride this out and hope for the best.

Whatever that looked like.

Chapter Forty-One

When Erin pulled into Graham's driveway after her shift at the USO, the ache in her chest intensified. He'd only been gone three days, but she already missed him every bit as much as she'd expected. Knowing he wouldn't be inside now or anytime soon made their separation even more real. She didn't want him to have to leave Fayetteville permanently. With all the moves he made during his career, having his kids here made this home.

She carried in the suitcase filled with the items Graham had kept at her condo. With the cats' owners returning in two weeks, she had to clear out, and there was no point in taking his stuff to the beach with her.

After she hung his uniform and clothes in his closet, she stowed his toiletries. Did she take her things or leave them here? She'd be back here soon, right? She wanted to be strong, bold Erin, but doing so and opening her mouth to Noelle had gotten them in this jam. Actually, *Noelle* had gotten them in this jam, but Erin's comment about the sex hadn't helped the situation any.

She left her things. Packing them seemed like admitting

defeat, and she wasn't waving the white flag in surrender. There was too much on the line.

She loaded the perishables to take home and then took out his trash. After locking the door, she hauled the suitcase and bag of food to her car. A dog barked and she grumbled under her breath. Even if Noelle planned to apologize, she wasn't in the frame of mind to hear it. Erin steeled herself and turned. Seeing Sally walking her dog up Graham's driveway was a slightly better alternative.

"Erin, I'm glad to see you."

Her concerned expression appeared genuine and ignited a spark of hope that she could have some sway in her husband keeping Graham here despite their conversation at the ball. Though sending Graham to Africa certainly hampered any chance of introducing him to Piper and Madison, which Erin had told her needed to happen before a proposal. It wasn't the only obstacle, but she wouldn't help Graham's case by raising her fears about getting married again.

Sally's dog sniffed the bag of food in Erin's hand. "I'm so sorry about what Noelle said to you at the ball. When Noelle said she'd met you, I told her how happy Sean and I were for Graham. He and Bethann had such a solid marriage we were afraid he wouldn't be ready for another relationship. But circumstances being what they were with the prior commanders and then the rumor about Graham and one of the wives?" She gave a shake of her head.

Graham had never mentioned a rumor about him and one of the wives. It only took a second for Erin to know there was no truth to it.

"Well, Sean would have had no choice but to bring in someone new. I never imagined Noelle would tell you—much less a ballroom full of people—that Graham was only dating you to keep his command. And that it was an order?" Sally gave an unamused grimace. "What was she thinking? Sean may have said it could keep Graham here, but it was *not* an order."

"I'm sure no one thought it was."

"I would hope, but it's still a bad look—for Graham and Sean," Sally admitted and gave a low grumble. "Sean thought having you observe Captain Bryson's team seemed like an excellent opportunity for the men to see you and Graham as a couple. I'm sorry to say Sean didn't foresee anything coming to fruition with you writing for a television production because you are a woman and of a certain age." She paused and gave an apologetic look. "However, after what was said at the ball, he's concerned the men could think you and Graham were using each other to get what you needed."

"Graham mentioned that. However, if we—"

"Even if you eloped when he got back, it would take you cutting ties to the show to convince the men your commitment is to Graham and the unit."

Marriage and give up her dream? "Graham didn't mention that."

"He didn't?" Sally gave a nod. "*Hmm.* Sean encouraged Graham to discuss it with you. Especially since Graham said nothing may come of it."

That was a stab in the heart.

"Sean did give Graham another option. To end things—in the event this was a charade."

"He did?" Graham hadn't mentioned that either.

"Oh, my." Sally's gaze settled on the suitcase. "I—I never suspected you were faking it. That Graham would terminate your relationship, shows where his priorities are and could change things."

What? Erin had never faked her feelings for Graham. Never. And he'd accept a new post rather than end their relationship—even though it meant being separated from his children.

The realization hit her like an icy blast. Graham *did* have another option. One that made her—or them together—collateral damage. "I'm leaving town to work on the series."

"I guess you got what you needed for your writing career. I wish things had gone differently. Come on, Lulu." Sally led the dog away.

Erin didn't correct Sally's assumption as her mind reeled from the bomb that had just imploded her world.

Chapter Forty-Two

Erin fed the cats, then fixed avocado toast for breakfast. She'd barely eaten or slept last night, and the first sips of coffee hadn't worked their magic yet.

She rechecked her phone before sitting at the kitchen table to eat. Graham still hadn't responded to the message she'd sent after leaving his house yesterday.

When Sally brought up Graham saying nothing may come of her screenwriting—was that because she'd tried to keep his and her expectations low? Or did he doubt it would happen? His support certainly seemed genuine, but maybe he now saw it could be a conflict with his position.

Phil had seen dollar signs and been supportive of her screenwriting too. *Until* she wanted to spend two weeks in LA for an intensive screenwriting program. It hadn't been realistic with the girls' ages then, but he hadn't considered how they could make it work for her to attend. His support waned after five years of getting nowhere, and he wanted her to put an end date on putting any more time or money into chasing her dream. That's when she'd put together the curriculum for the class she'd taught rather than walk away entirely.

To be so close now seemed like the miracle she needed, especially after having all her and Phil's savings and investments wiped out. If she walked away from her dream and the money now, it wasn't like she'd get a second chance to join the writing team—*if* the series got picked up.

She wanted to believe Graham was willing to shift his career goals, even sacrifice staying here with his children, for her. But it was a lot to ask of him. It wasn't like she could get the studio to commit before Graham returned and had to decide about his future assignment. Even if they ordered a full season, the show could get canceled after a few episodes. Then Graham might resent her if he accepted a new posting for nothing.

Worse, she might resent *him* if she didn't take this shot. The way her marriage disintegrated had her doubting everything and questioning what it meant that she wasn't willing to walk away from this opportunity, that was far from a sure thing, for Graham. While she loved him, she had no way of knowing where things might stand between them in a year.

She rubbed her temples, wishing a solution would magically become clear. Strategic thinking was Graham's specialty, not hers. Sure, she could plot a storyline for an entire movie or television season and beyond, but that was fiction. This was real life. Not just hers, but his. And his kids. And her daughters. And the men under his command.

She groaned. Tink scampered away.

When they entered this arrangement, she certainly hadn't thought she'd fall in love—or that Graham would—so she hadn't worried about the future. Now, she wanted it all—a happy, loving relationship with a man who respected her work. Great sex. And, hopefully, a fulfilling and well-paying career as a writer.

As she ate the last bite of toast, it dawned on her. No one was telling her she couldn't have it all—except *her*. That was past Erin, listening to the lies she'd let hold her back and settle for far too long. No more.

She would not let anyone, not herself or some jealous, big-mouth military wife, steal her joy. She didn't have to settle or sacrifice what she wanted anymore. They could go wherever Graham's next assignment was, and she'd commute to California as needed. It might not be ideal, but it would give their relationship time to grow on *their* schedule, not some general's agenda.

And if the series went nowhere, she wouldn't regret not chasing her dream and giving it everything she had. Dreams didn't always work out, but she could find a new dream and purpose. She'd learned it was okay to let go of the past and not let it control and define her. Concentrate on the present, which was the only thing she could control.

It was good Graham hadn't called yet. Now she knew what she had to tell him.

❧

After Erin and Nicky finished cleaning the USO center, she headed out for the day. It'd taken a monumental effort not to spill the saga when Nicky had asked how things were with Graham. Keeping busy had helped take Erin's mind off the situation somewhat. However, every glimpse of camouflage made her think of Graham.

She pulled her phone from her back pocket before getting in her car and saw the missed call and voicemail notifications. Erin tapped on the screen to listen to the voicemail from a restricted number. Graham's voice reached out like a hug from thousands of miles away, though she nearly cried that she'd missed his call.

"I got your message. Sorry that I couldn't call earlier. We were out and had a *situation*. I'm fine. The whole team's fine. But I wasn't in a position where I could call. I haven't looked at assignment options yet, but I'll do that and call you in the next day or two. I'm going to try and get some sleep. I'm sorry I missed you. Love you."

Situation? Goosebumps broke out on her arms that he sought to reassure her he was okay. It'd been easy to ignore the dangers of his career the past few months with him here. Her storyline for the series was fiction. This was real life. The necessity of men being able to focus on the mission instead of being distracted by things at home hit her in a way she hadn't envisioned previously.

He'd called about fifteen minutes ago, probably while she'd been running the vacuum in the center. Not wanting to wait another day or two, she calculated the time difference. Near midnight. He might still be up. But would her news be a distraction from what he was dealing with there? She sighed in acceptance. She could wait.

Nearly to the condo, her phone rang. Her eyes cut to the car's display screen. Except it wasn't Graham trying again, but Ian's name and number on the display. She took a quick, deep breath and projected confidence as she greeted him.

"I hope you're sitting down. I have news."

"I'm sitting. I'm also driving. Should I pull over?" He sounded excited. However, the way her luck was running these days, she didn't want to get her hopes up.

"You should. The studio ordered a full thirteen-episode season of *Bravo Unit*."

"Oh my! Really?" She navigated onto a side street, put the

car in park, and took slow, deep breaths to keep from hyperventilating.

"Test audiences *loved* it. And it crossed a lot of demographics. Now that Chris Remington is officially a Hollywood A-lister, the studio wanted to lock him into a three-year commitment as lead. He agreed, though one of his conditions was that you are part of the writing team. He liked the depth you added to the characters."

That was flattering, considering she had only spoken to the actor for half an hour during filming.

"Once everything's official, our marketing team will reach out to the Army about doing location shoots, using equipment, and running recruitment ads. We can always use AI and CGI if they shoot us down, but getting some stock footage would be helpful."

"We won't be able to get active-duty Special Ops guys on camera. That's too dangerous for them and their families," she warned.

"This would just be background stuff, so they wouldn't need to be Special Ops. We're talking with a former Green Beret to audition for a role and as a technical advisor. You'll be an executive producer as the show's co-creator. Are you still there?"

"Yes, I'm just . . ."

"Yeah, I get it. Many try, but you grabbed the brass ring. There's one condition you need to be aware of."

"What's that?" Her racing heart braked hard.

"I know Levi said you wouldn't have to be here full time, but they will want you here for several weeks while the writing team is plotting out the rest of the season and brainstorming a series arc in anticipation of future seasons. After that, you might be able to participate via video chat for the weekly meet-ups on occasion, but for the most part, he expects you here. I hope that's not a deal breaker for you."

"I can make it work." If Graham got transferred to a base closer to LA, it could be another blessing in disguise. Or, if he were to retire, maybe she could get him involved with the series. That alternative beat taking an assignment overseas or one he wasn't excited about.

"I'll send over the contract once it's complete."

Cecilia's warning played in her mind. "I'll review it with my attorney, and we'll get it back to you."

"There is a confidentiality clause, so, until a formal announcement is made, other than the attorney, don't say a word to anyone. We're excited to have you on board."

"Do you know how long until the formal announcement will be out?"

"At least a couple of weeks for negotiations and to get contracts signed. If word leaked out before then, it could jeopardize the entire series."

"Got it."

After Ian ended the call, Erin tried to wrap her brain around the fact this was happening. The timing of his call couldn't have been better. This gave her the confidence to back her decision rather than rely on *hoping* the series would come to fruition. Could it have happened a decade ago if she'd pushed harder? Maybe not, since she couldn't have upped and moved or traveled to California weekly. But now she had the freedom, and she could have it all with Graham's continued support.

Though Ian said not to tell anyone, Graham needed to know to make his decision about a future assignment. She planned to broach the possibility of him retiring if offered a technical advisor role. He could add a whole other layer of realism to the show.

She pulled up her music app and queued Pharrell's "Happy." She couldn't care less if the drivers beside her laughed at her as she sang and jammed her way home. Her stars were finally aligning, and she was beyond happy.

Chapter Forty-Three

Erin's phone vibrated and rang loudly since she'd turned the ringtone to max volume. She dropped the bag of groceries in her right hand by the condo door to grab her phone from her purse. She was not missing another call from Graham.

Her screen read Potential Spam, giving her one more reason to hate robocalls. She unlocked the condo door and carried in the groceries. After stocking the pantry and fridge for the cats' owners' upcoming return, she started baking.

Two hours later, pans of brownies were in the oven while she mixed up icing for the cupcakes cooling on the counter. She might have gone overboard, but some would be a thank you for letting her pet sit, some would be a goodbye sendoff for the USO, and brownies might have time to get to Graham in Africa. If not, Captain Amaya's men could enjoy them.

Once she began frosting the cupcakes, she put aside a half dozen for Megan, Reece, Jace, and Alex, recognizing she'd defaulted to guilt again. It wasn't like Graham wouldn't ever see his kids or grandbaby if they left Fort Liberty. They could video chat and visit. It'd only be two or three years. Graham had referred to them all being here as an unexpected blessing, and he'd been facing a transfer before she entered the picture. This wasn't her fault. With the money she'd be making at least for the first season, and hopefully longer, they could fly here for long weekends and holidays.

While she loaded the dirty mixing bowls, her phone rang again. "Hello." She answered the restricted call with her fingers crossed.

"Hey. I'm glad I caught you this time."

"How's it going over there?" There was a slight delay in the transmission, and the connection wasn't great, but that she had Graham on the line sent a rush of energy through her.

"Not as well as I hoped." Graham already sounded tired. "You get back home and start to forget what it's like in this part of the world. The drought and food shortages. We send aid that gets waylaid and sold, putting money in the wrong pockets. It's hard to see."

"I can only imagine. Is there anything I can send you?" She eyed the brownies she'd baked for the care package.

"No, although it's already looking like I may need to be here longer than I hoped. Sorry, I don't mean to bring you down. It's just that Thomsen made promises that he wasn't around to keep. Without continuity, building trust, bringing peace, and making a lasting difference is hard. I won't put my replacement on the hook for my promises." His sigh carried across the miles.

This compassionate side was what she sought to portray in her characters. She wanted viewers to connect with the men as more than battle-hardened, alpha warriors who lived for the fight and viewed others as enemies. Sure, there was that component. However, she loved how Graham wanted to make this world a better place for others.

In that moment, her world pivoted. Loving someone often required sacrifice. It's why she'd entered a dependable career and stuck with teaching while the girls and Phil depended on her. She'd done it out of love.

She *was* free to pursue her dreams now. Graham had been right there cheering her on. Willing to sacrifice his dream of staying here at Fort Liberty with his children and the teams of men he commanded. Not because she'd asked, but because he loved her. Even when she wouldn't commit to him.

"Are you still there?" he asked.

"Yeah. Sorry, um . . ." She brushed away the tear rolling down her cheek and fought to control her voice. "What if you could stay in command of 3rd Group?"

"That's not one of my options."

"What if it were?" She sank into a kitchen chair. "I ran into Sally McKittrick while leaving your house the other day. She brought up how Sean wants you to stay and mentioned another option."

"I'm listening."

"If we weren't together anymore . . ."

"Stop right there. While he mentioned that, I didn't relay it to you because it's *not* an option."

"She thinks it is, and that we aren't together."

"What?"

"She misinterpreted what I said. I didn't correct her."

"It doesn't matter what Sally thinks."

"Maybe we should go with it." Erin couldn't believe she was about to suggest this, but in her heart, she knew it was the right thing. "Neither of us was looking for a relationship, but circumstances brought us together. And it worked out for both of us—for a while. But you owe it to Megan, Jace, and all the men under your command to do whatever you can to stay with 3rd Group, especially since Sean told you I couldn't work on *Bravo Unit*."

"There are—wait. The show has an official name now?"

"It does. Not only will I be leaving for the beach in a few days, I will be spending a lot of time in California in the coming months."

"Erin, that's wonderful. Congratulations. But that doesn't change how I feel."

"Me either." If anything, she loved him even more right now. "But you're where you need to be. Your focus needs to be your men and your mission—not distracted worrying about your next assignment and leaving your kids. With Reece and Jace under McKittrick's command, your family could end up on three different continents if he reassigned them."

"He wouldn't do that."

She wished she could be sure of that, but McKittrick had proven he'd go to great lengths to protect his career. "And I need to concentrate on my work. We need to take a step back."

"Are you saying now that the series is a go, you want to end things?"

The hurt in his voice was killing her, but she had to put it out there. "No, I don't want to end things. At least not permanently. But we need to see if this is what we both want or if the relationship has served its purpose."

"This has become something bigger and better than its original purpose. Besides, there's no guarantee McKittrick would keep me there even if we broke up."

"If he doesn't, then we admit we made a mistake. Couples break up then get back together all the time." If not for the static on the line, she would have thought the call had dropped.

"What would this break entail?"

She hadn't planned this. At all. She stared at the ceiling and forced her lungs to work. "We already won't see each other for at least a few weeks," she eased into it—for his sake and hers. "We can't communicate after this. They monitor—"

"There are ways that don't leave a trail."

Erin wiped away another tear. She knew going down without a fight wasn't in his DNA. She tried to think how to convince him. "It's too risky. If we want a shot at winning this war, we have to concede this battle. Pull back and let him think he's won. Wait it out." And pray Graham would still want to be with her if he got extended at Liberty and they had to be apart for months—or longer.

"Are you saying 'all's fair in love and war?'"

"Maybe. It may be unconventional warfare, but, at the ball, Sally said life was like war and required making sacrifices. Spending some time apart is not what I want, but I'd rather do that than rush into a commitment, whether it be marriage or where we're living, and have it not work out and be hurt or hurt you. When I married Phil, I *never* thought I'd be divorced. They say divorce is harder than losing a spouse to death because there's a lot of guilt. The guilt part's true."

"You shouldn't feel guilty."

"But I am to blame too. There are so many things I could have done differently. I do love you, Graham. More than I even thought I could. But I can't go into another marriage thinking if 'it doesn't work out, I can get divorced again.' And I'm not there yet."

She could hear him breathe in and exhale from thousands of miles away.

"I can respect that. But this doesn't mean it's over-over. When I get back, I'll make McKittrick commit, and we'll go from there. If he keeps me there, he's not likely to suddenly change his mind about us being together—especially if you're writing for a wildly popular military television show."

She laughed and sobbed at the same time as relief and

sadness battled within her. She had to focus on the long game. "When does he retire or move on?"

"That's a good question. He's got another year and a half in his current assignment. If he makes the next list for Major General, he'll move on. Possibly to someplace I'd want to be in the future. I'd prefer not to burn bridges—but sometimes, there's no going back."

Neither said the word goodbye, but after the call ended, Erin prayed she hadn't just lit the match and set fire to her chance at a future with Graham.

Chapter Forty-Four

GRAHAM STRODE toward McKittrick's office like a man on a mission—which he was. McKittrick had stretched Graham's time in Africa to five weeks. He'd visited villages and met with tribal leaders with the revised mindset that he would be in command of 3rd Group for another three years.

Until he'd seen the flaw in his strategy.

It was time to change the battle plan and end this conflict for good.

McKittrick sat at his desk reviewing intel reports from the weekend before the weekly briefing.

"Good morning, General."

"Uh, Graham." McKittrick reclined back and removed his reading glasses. "You're in early."

"I'm still on Africa time. Thought I'd see if you've looked over the reports I submitted and had any questions."

"Everything was in order. It looks like you made good inroads, and your time there was well spent."

They both knew that wasn't why he'd originally been sent, but it hadn't been wasted time, even if it had extended longer than necessary. "Any updates here I need to be aware of?" McKittrick might have already made plans to replace him.

"The training cadre is gearing up for the next round of selection. I sat down with Captain Bryson last week. Mateo *has* successfully integrated into the team, so they are on track to replace Amaya's unit as scheduled. And Mateo will come home to a new son or daughter. I'm glad things have worked out for them."

"I am too." That was a bright spot in all of this.

"More importantly, morale's been good. Somehow, we dodged a bullet with Noelle's announcement and the potential conflict of interest with Erin working for this television program. I never thought it would get off the ground."

That explained why he'd readily approved Erin shadowing the team when it suited his purpose.

"While it's still preferable that you be married, the way Bryson and his men had your back doing containment at the ball shows your men will follow your orders straight to the gates of hell. You've also made your priorities clear, and the unit would benefit from your continued leadership. I'm signing off on you staying in command."

"Actually, sir, you were right when you said I'm not the best man to continue to lead 3rd Group."

"What?" McKittrick sat up straighter.

"I was focused on keeping my command and maintaining the respect of my men and my integrity. I didn't factor in that I can't control whether Mateo or someone else fears that I would betray them with their wife. Whether I'm married, single, or in a relationship."

"True," McKittrick conceded.

"While I was away, I thought about your concerns that what Noelle said could make the men question my motives in having Erin observe Bryson's team. While it was *not* a trade for sex, I didn't envision that allowing that could result in trust issues every bit as much as those raised by Boatman and Thompson. That's a strategic planning failure on my part."

"Neither of us could anticipate Noelle publicly announcing that I *ordered* you to marry," McKittrick grumbled.

"No. But questions about my reasons could linger if I were to stay in command here. I plan to put in for command of 10th Group at Fort Carson." It was only three years, and Colorado wasn't overseas. Graham also wasn't his father. He'd still be involved in his kids' and future grandbaby's lives. They could visit here often, and Erin would be closer to Los Angeles and Madison in Austin, Texas. "I need to speak with the general there to be certain he won't have a problem with Erin's involvement in the show."

"I thought you two weren't together anymore." McKittrick studied him through the narrowed eyes of a trained interrogator.

"She and I took a break from our relationship, but I see that was a mistake. A mistake I plan to rectify as soon as I know where I'll be posted—or if I'm retiring. I've served for over twenty-seven years. What I want—is the next forty or fifty years with Erin. I will not ask her to give up her dreams for my career." When he had proposed their arrangement, he hadn't accounted for the possibility of falling so in love with her that giving up this command would be the right thing to do. "The men in 3rd Group will learn to trust whoever replaces me."

Chapter Forty-Five

When Graham arrived for the family dinner on Wednesday night, Megan barely gave him time to set the dessert on the counter before engulfing him in a hug. "We've missed you! Have you let Erin know you're back?" she launched right in, her intense gaze fixed on him.

"Not yet."

"I'm just going to say it. I freaked out thinking McKittrick could kick Reece out of 3rd Group. But I should have told Erin that you two taking a break, even a temporary one, was a horrible idea. It's causing me way more stress than a change of station for you or us. And it's not good for the baby."

"I agree. The idea of McKittrick having sway over your careers is a major reason I went along with it."

"And is McKittrick even keeping you here?" Reece looked ready to do battle.

"He offered. However, I'm not willing to go along with his conditions."

Megan pressed her hands together prayerfully and brought them to her mouth.

"I've decided to take an assignment over 10th Group at Fort Carson."

"So you can be with Erin?" Jace smiled and gave an approving nod.

"Yes. I spoke with my future commanding general today to be sure Erin's involvement with the show won't be a problem. I won't ask her to give that up. I hate to leave you all, but this is only for a few years."

"Dad, you never know how long you've got. Don't waste months or more being miserable apart. We'll be fine." Tears filled Megan's eyes.

"Agreed." He pulled his daughter into another embrace. He knew all too well that his time with someone could be cut short. "I promise we'll be here every chance we get."

"Before making promises, you need to get Erin back." She wiped away a tear. "And, considering how hard you originally worked to track her down, you can't just text or call her. You need to do something big to show her you want her in your life," she insisted.

"For sure. You should surprise her with something memorable and romantic," Alex said.

"I don't even know where she is right now. She could be at the beach in South Carolina or have to be in California now that the series is a go." Charlotte, Texas, and even Spain were possibilities.

"I'm sure her daughters would know. Do you have their phone numbers or email?"

"I don't." Another downside of not having met them in person. "But we could find them through Erin's social media account. They might have a phone number listed, or we could message them from there."

"That's a—great idea. And you would know that how?" Megan stared at him like he'd spoken another language.

Busted. "I went by the USO like you suggested when trying to find her. Except they wouldn't give me her contact information or tell me when she'd be working. However, the director mentioned that Erin was active on their social media accounts and that I could contact her that way."

"You didn't." Megan shook her head.

"It was a better option than stalking her at the USO. I set up an account and sent her a friend request—which she didn't accept right away."

"Because she thought it was a fake account! We told you —" Megan was laughing now.

"That's why I never shared that part of the story. And you're right about that, too. I had to convince her I was really me. It was pretty funny since I had no clue what I was doing. But it worked out."

"You might be the only Facebook account claiming to be a widowed military officer that's legit. Though tons of scammers impersonate generals," Alex said. "I guess it's easier to find pictures of high-ranking officers from news posts, but seriously?"

"Dad might not be scamming people, but he was trying to romance someone," Jace teased.

"Operative word being some*one*. She's the only one I contacted."

"Quit giving your dad a hard time and see if you can get in touch with her daughters," Reece ordered.

"I still can't believe you set up an account." Megan grinned as she opened the app on her phone. "I found Erin." It only took her a minute.

"Check for Piper's account." She'd be likelier to give them info on her mom than Madison, and he hadn't told his kids about the underwear video chat incident.

"Isn't Piper in Spain? With the time difference, she might be asleep."

"True."

"Other than being tagged in a friend's post, I don't see anything recent for Madison. It could be her privacy settings."

Graham gave a helpless shrug. "Is there a phone number?"

"I don't think they let you see phone numbers if you aren't friends. Let me check Piper's. No phone number, but she's been posting. I'll send them friend requests and a message to call me or you."

"Give them both numbers." Depending on how Erin's daughters felt about the break, they might contact Megan over him. Or not reply to either.

"Done." Megan set her phone on the table.

"Good. Let's eat," Jace said.

Alex smacked him in the gut with the back of her hand.

"It could be hours or days before we hear back." Jace held up an arm to fend off more strikes.

"He's right," Graham admitted. "We can't sit around and wait." And the possibility of Erin being back in his life gave him an appetite for the first time in weeks. "Ladies first." He handed plates to Megan and Alex.

"Is that ringing?" Reece looked around as the girls filled their plates.

"It's not my ringtone." Graham checked his phone anyway.

"Mine either," Megan said, but she picked up her phone too. "It's a video call from Piper!" She nearly dropped her half-filled plate to swipe the screen. "Piper! Thank you so much for calling."

Graham moved closer.

"I was about to get in bed, but your message sounded urgent. Is your dad okay? I know he was out of the country."

"I'm home now." He moved into view.

"Good." Piper gave a bashful wave, then tugged her camisole higher and tucked her hair behind her ear.

"I'm so glad you called while we're all here." Megan panned the phone screen and introduced Reece, Jace, and Alex. "How's your mom doing?"

"Honestly, she's been better."

"Same for Dad," Megan stated. "But he now admits the break was a terrible idea, no offense to your mom."

"She said the general had a problem with her work on the series and would base your dad overseas, and he might even get your husband and brother moved to other bases if they stayed together. She would not let that happen with you being pregnant."

Graham purposely hadn't told Erin that McKittrick wouldn't be on board with them staying together at Fort Liberty. How did Erin know? Sally had to have told her. That's why Erin let her think they'd ended things. And why she insisted on the break. It actually made sense now.

"There are worse things than being based overseas. Like them both being miserable without each other," Megan asserted.

"I agree. But you know about the TV series being picked up?" Piper asked.

"From her telling me she'd be in California, I deduced she'd heard good news." He'd wanted to celebrate this with Erin.

"The announcement was made in the trades Friday morning. There have been several online announcements mentioning the show. Most are about Chris Remington starring and the director, but Mom got some mentions as co-creator."

"I'm proud of her. We all are. She has to be so excited." Graham wanted Piper to know that wouldn't deter him.

"She is, though she's struggled to write the last few weeks."

Because of him. Pain knifed through his chest. It shouldn't be this way. Instead of being an asset, he was a liability. "Hopefully, I can change that. Is she out there or at the beach?"

"She's in California through sometime Friday. They wanted her there for the announcement and some promotional events."

"Do you know where she's staying?" Megan asked.

"Are you, uh, planning to go see her?" Piper gave a hopeful smile.

"Yes!" Megan answered before he could.

"I am. Break time is over."

"They put her up in some fancy hotel. I can ask which one."

"Do you know where she's staying at Kiawah?" That seemed a better option to Graham.

"I sure do. I've been there a bunch of times."

"It has to be a romantic reunion. Don't you agree?" Megan remained intent on scripting the reunion.

"What can I do to help?" Piper leaned closer to the screen.

Chapter Forty-Six

GRAHAM COULDN'T SEE the ocean, but he could smell it and faintly hear the waves crashing against the shore in the distance. His heart pounded almost as loudly as the surf as he climbed the steps to the condo building where Erin was renting. He approached the door with Megan behind him. Reece, Alex, and Jace stayed out of sight below.

"Hold on. Let me get ready to film," Megan said lowly. "Move to the left a little so I can see her face. Perfect."

He switched the bouquet of red roses to the other hand and knocked soundly on the front door. His heart raced as he waited. And waited. There was no doorbell, so he knocked again. And waited. "She's not here," he conceded. The flight Piper told him Erin would be on from California had arrived a little before midnight last night, and her car was here.

"I'm calling Piper." Megan initiated the call, though he wasn't sure how Piper could help from Spain. "We're all here at the condo. We knocked, but your mom's not answering."

"After a week in California, she probably hit the beach."

"It's not raining now, but it was on our way down here, and it's still cloudy."

"That won't stop her unless it's lightning or a hurricane. Though she could be sleeping or on a bike ride. I'll call her now and text you to confirm. I like the idea of surprising her on the beach better, anyway. Don't forget, I want a video."

"We gotcha. It might be from a distance, but Alex and I will both get this on film."

Was there a chance Erin was inside and didn't want to see him? He should have contacted her to tell her he was back and wanted to see her instead of trying to surprise her. Too late now. They were committed to seeing this through.

Piper informed them which boardwalk Erin would take to and from the condo to the beach before hanging up.

"She's walking on the beach," Megan read the text aloud a minute later. "Everyone put on your camouflage."

The girls and men pulled camouflage jackets over their shirts. Graham thought it was overkill but knew better than to buck his daughter's order. She wanted a show. While it wasn't as spectacular or involve the logistics of timing a Black Hawk to fly over pulling a banner—one of the over-the-top ideas Megan and Alex advocated for—he'd planned a meaningful way to surprise Erin.

"Erin's wearing a blue rain jacket, and she's near the Sanctuary hotel now," Megan read the text.

Reece looked at the map they'd gotten at the security gate. "Here we are, and here's the hotel. The map shows a couple of boardwalks on a street just past the hotel. We'll drop Dad at the middle boardwalk. Megan and I'll take the south position. Alex and Jace take the north boardwalk."

Jace handed one set of binoculars to Graham and another pair to Megan.

"Hurry up, people," Megan ordered. "Search and rescue time."

Though no one's life was in danger, his future depended on this mission's outcome.

"This is so fun." Alex's enthusiasm reminded Graham of Erin's excitement about spending time with Bryson's team.

Minutes later, Jace stopped at the marker for a public boardwalk between two multi-million-dollar homes. Graham bailed out and jogged down the asphalt path to the boardwalk. He stopped before hitting the sand and scanned the beach.

A layer of dark gray clouds hung over the coast to the south. Though the sky was lighter further out to sea, he only spotted a handful of people on the beach in either direction. Using the binoculars, he zeroed in on the people, not spotting anyone wearing a jacket matching Piper's description.

He strode off the boardwalk to where the tide had packed the sand, making it good for walking and writing. His first attempt at a heart turned out pathetically lopsided. Art never had been his best subject. Determining the coast was still clear, he moved closer to the water and started another to cover more territory in case she missed seeing the first.

Halfway through carving out the heart, his phone rang.

"We spotted her nearing our location now," Megan said. "She's still talking to Piper. You better hurry. We're coming your way."

He drew the other half of the heart and wrote their initials in the center before jogging back to the boardwalk. He picked a spot behind the sea oats for overwatch. Through the binoculars, he locked on the lone figure in a blue jacket, getting closer to where he'd written in the sand. He focused on Erin's face. The wind made loose strands of her hair dance wildly, but her smile as she talked on the phone made her more beautiful than ever. He'd lost one woman he loved, but he'd fight to the bitter end to keep Erin in his life.

She headed to a sandcastle that had survived the rain and tide and walked around it, then stared into the distance. *Turn around. Just come a little bit further. Where are you going?* Did she see Reece and Megan? Surely, they hadn't come out on the beach. He did a surveillance pass. There was no sign of them, but Erin headed back the way she'd come. And at a rapid pace.

He phoned Megan. "She's walking back your way."

"What? No! Why? Hold on. Piper messaged she's headed back to try and beat the storm."

He scanned the clouds moving up the beach and made out the telltale gray wall of rain. Why couldn't it hold off another half an hour?

"We're doubling back to the car and will pick you up on the street. Maybe we can make it to the boardwalk she takes to the condo before she does. I'll call Alex and give her the revised plan." Megan's ability to adapt on the fly would have made her a good operator.

She had the weather radar on her phone when Graham got in the car. "If it weren't for that sandcastle, she probably would have kept going. Piper said she couldn't risk saying anything without letting her know we're here."

Reece parked in the lot by the tall, oceanfront condo building. Thank goodness Piper had been here on vacations with Erin enough to direct them from across the ocean.

They were already on the path to the boardwalk when Jace whipped into a parking spot. He and Alex caught up to Graham and Megan while they waited for Reece to do a surveillance pass in case Erin had sprinted.

Reece motioned him to hit the beach for a second attempt to execute this mission. "She's down over half a klick. You've got two minutes. Three tops."

Chapter Forty-Seven

ERIN TRIED to answer Piper's barrage of questions about Chris Remington and what was next for the series as she hurried back toward the condo—despite her daughter continuing to simultaneously text a friend.

"The producer is good with you coming to Spain and Europe for two weeks at Christmas, right?"

"I may have to work a little, but it won't be a problem." Erin had already cleared that with Levi.

"Good. Then we need to get the trip planned."

"What would you think about going to France from Spain?"

"I thought we were going to Italy."

"If that's what you want," Erin agreed, despite the idea of going to Italy without Graham making her heart ache.

She was thrilled to see her idea make it to production and be part of the writing team, but that didn't fill the void left since persuading Graham to take a break. It'd been over five weeks with no contact. Was he back or still in Africa? Wondering if he was safe and if their relationship could survive this separation had stifled all her creative energy. He hadn't made her choose between him and her career, and she wouldn't make him choose between her and his career *and family*.

"I'll contact the travel agent Lanie recommended and have her work up an itinerary," she continued, looking down in time to stop before walking on a huge heart drawn in the sand. She stared at the initials written in the middle of the heart, unable to move or draw in a breath.

"Mom, what is it?"

Their initials. It couldn't be a cruel coincidence.

"Graham?" Erin frantically searched the beach. She spotted a man in a camouflage jacket coming off the boardwalk. "Graham!"

After a few steps, he was running. Her tears made the smile on his handsome face blur. They closed the distance until their bodies melded together like the last two pieces of a puzzle.

"You're here," she kissed him, savoring his taste, his scent, his feel. Endorphins flooded her body. She floated because gravity had no power over her in his arms.

"Mission accomplished," Piper's voice broke into Erin's fairytale reunion. "Call me later."

"Wait. You were in on this?" Erin asked as Graham set her feet back on the sand.

"I was. They needed help to find out if you were there or in California. Then you weren't at the condo.

"And you turned around right before the hearts by the sandcastle." Graham pointed down the beach. "I rushed down here hoping you wouldn't see me."

"Is that why you're wearing camouflage?" She gripped the front of his uniform top.

"That, and I know how you like a man in uniform."

"That's for sure," Piper said.

"One in particular. Thank you, honey. I'll talk to you later."

"Love you. Have Megan send Madison and me the video. Bye."

"What video?"

"The kids are here. They helped track you and are hiding in the dunes, filming our reunion. The girls said it had to be romantic and memorable. I thought about fast-roping out of a Black Hawk, but I wasn't sure I could find you, and there's the whole misappropriation of government resources." Graham winked.

She laughed. "*I* would love that, but if you had the wrong person, that might have given someone a heart attack. You'll have to do that for me another time." Piper's call, all the questions and requests for pictures of beach houses, and texting *a friend* made sense now. "I won't forget this." Before she could ask what his being here meant with their "taking a break," Megan hurried down the boardwalk, followed by Reece. Alex and Jace emerged right behind them—*all* wearing camouflage jackets.

Megan wrapped Erin in a long, tight hug. "It's so good to see you."

"I can't believe you're all here." Erin wiped away more tears.

"We couldn't send Dad alone on this search and rescue mission."

"Rescue? What do you mean?"

"From you both being miserable apart," Megan said.

"Ah. True." Except Graham was here now, gripping her hand and banishing all the doubts and fears of the past weeks.

"But we need to get off this beach, or we'll be soaked." Reece took charge and herded them toward the boardwalk.

They reached the parking lot as heavy raindrops began to

fall. Jace and Alex dashed to Graham's Lexus, but he led her to Reece's SUV. Graham opened the door and climbed into the backseat next to her.

"Hope it's okay if we bunk at your place," Graham said. "I refused to make a plan B. Failing at this mission was not an option."

"I wouldn't have it any other way." She leaned over for a kiss that reassured her this was real, not some dream. "How long are you all staying?"

"Just through Monday. I have to get back to work." Reece eyed Graham in the rear-view mirror.

"Because Dad agreed we could come down but wants alone time with you," Megan said.

"Can you blame me?" He squeezed Erin's hand.

The warmth in his eyes banished the chill of the gloomy afternoon. All she'd wanted these past weeks was to be with him. She'd missed everything about him and how he made her feel. After her divorce, she wanted to be independent and not have to answer to anyone. But Graham changed all that. Changed her. Empowered her. Their relationship had also been so different than hers with Phil.

She blended into Graham's family beautifully, as evidenced by them all coming on this mission. Piper had been involved in this reunion too. And hadn't she asked Megan to send the video to her *and Madison?*

Minutes later, they made the mad dash up to the condo through the rain, carrying what they could. Graham set a large cooler on the kitchen counter, and Erin placed a bag of groceries next to it. "The first bedroom has twin beds, and the next has a queen. Work it out without arguing."

"Yes, ma'am," Reece answered.

"You can share the master with me," she said lowly to Graham.

He raised his brows, gave her a suggestive smile, and wrapped his arms around her. "Congratulations on the series getting picked up. You never gave up despite the odds. I am so proud of you."

They moved out of the way as Megan squeezed into the small kitchen and began unloading the cooler.

Alex set more grocery bags on the raised counter and plunked down on one of the bar chairs. "I saw the interview you did with Chris Remington." She made a heart shape with her hands. "I can't believe he's going to be the lead. I would be so starstruck I wouldn't know what to say. But I'd be content to stare at him for hours."

"Thanks, babe." Jace acted insulted.

"Chris is eye-candy and down-to-earth, but he doesn't do it for me like Graham Holmstrom." Erin batted her lashes at him, and he gave that amused laugh that did things to her insides. "If you want to play the colonel in the series, they haven't cast that role yet. On second thought, scratch that. I don't want to compete with thousands of women swooning over you."

"I prefer to stay out of the spotlight."

"Does this mean McKittrick's not keeping you over 3rd Group?" As thrilled as she was to be with him, Erin had wanted Graham to have everything he wanted—especially being with his kids.

"He did want me to stay."

"But . . ."

"Sally told you that Sean has a problem with your involvement with the series, didn't she?" Graham turned serious.

"She might have brought that up," Erin confessed. She couldn't hold up under the slightest interrogation.

"A break from us is not the solution. But me taking

command of 10th Group at Fort Carson is a compromise I can live with and gets you closer to LA."

Still a long distance from Fort Liberty. At least Colorado wasn't overseas. "How do you feel about this?" Erin looked at Megan.

"We told him to go for it—with you. We don't want a sad, grumpy grandpa."

"The change won't take place for a few months, but will you go to Colorado with me?"

"Say yes," Megan urged her.

"I will."

Megan cheered. The others joined in as Erin kissed Graham. She'd go anywhere with him. These past few weeks without him made her realize a future with him was what she wanted more than a job screenwriting and any amount of money that could come with it. That he'd do all this for her to have her dream conquered her last fears.

"Since we're celebrating you, you get to decide if we go out or have dinner here," Megan said.

"We've been missing game night. I brought cards," Jace was quick to put in.

"Dinner in, then games. I can get more hugs in here." Erin draped her arms over Graham's shoulders. "I missed you."

"I missed you more."

"That's not possible." Though it still felt good to hear him say it. "I don't think we should fight about this again."

"As I recall, last time we came up with a compromise where we both won." Graham lowered his voice to the low, sexy timbre that made her body heat.

"We sure did."

"After dinner, you two," Megan said. "This baby mama is getting hungry."

"What do you need help with?" Erin asked.

"Turn on the oven, then cuddle with Dad in the family room. You weren't expecting us, and we planned accordingly. We got this."

"If you insist," Erin agreed, then they followed Megan's orders.

"I offered to rent them a place to stay so we could be alone," Graham said as they settled on the couch, "but there were only a handful of very pricey options on short notice."

"I get you all to myself soon enough. Them being here supporting you—us—means everything." There'd be some physical distance between them for a while, but Graham's relationship with his children wouldn't be negatively impacted.

Despite the rain, this was shaping up to be the perfect day: reunited with Graham and his family, and both of her daughters were on board. Maybe she had a fairy godmother after all.

Chapter Forty-Eight

"GOOD AFTERNOON, GENERAL." Kearns's voice carried into Graham's office.

"Is Colonel Holmstrom in?"

It took Graham a moment to place the voice. He quickly got to his feet. "General Miller, come on in. What can I do for you?"

Miller closed the door behind him. "I wanted to let you know I was quite impressed with your report from your recent tour in Africa. And I agree with your assessment and analysis of the situation there."

"Thank you, sir. That means a lot coming from you."

"Have you ever thought about working with Swick?"

The Special Warfare Center here at Liberty? Graham's stomach did a flip. He tried to draw a full breath. "I'd be lying if I said no."

"Good. We could use someone with your kind of astute analysis and ability to think beyond what's worked—or hasn't —in the past. You know Colonel Adams of the 2nd Special Warfare Training Group?"

"Not well, but we've played golf together a few times."

"He's just been diagnosed with cancer. Fortunately, it's in an early stage and is treatable. However, he's decided to retire and concentrate on fighting that battle. Your name came up from multiple sources to fill his position."

Was Graham being handed the golden ticket here? "Thank you, sir. I'm honored to be considered."

"There is one thing I need to clear up. Mahinis filled me in on what happened at the ball. Was McKittrick going to let you go because you're widowed?"

"He strongly suggested that I remarry for the good of the unit."

"Or?" Miller waited.

"Or I'd be reassigned to another position—at another base."

Miller gave a disbelieving grunt and shook his head. "I get the unit had some issues with past commanders. However, McKittrick shouldn't project *their* egregious behavior onto you. Though I can guess why he'd want to protect the unit—and himself."

Graham cocked his head in agreement. "I love this command, and with my kids here, I was willing to do what it took to stay. But Erin, my date you met at the ball, hasn't been divorced long, and it was important that, as much as we love each other, we not rush this relationship to meet McKittrick's timeline. He wanted me married prior to Bryson's team deploying, which was seven months from when—"

"*Seven months*? I dated Becky for over six *years*. Started my senior year of high school. We managed to make it through four years long-distance while I was at West Point. Then basic training, AIT, Airborne, and Ranger School. I proposed before she pinned my Ranger tab on me. If I hadn't, I'm pretty sure she would have pinned it through my flesh. I wouldn't be wearing two stars today if it weren't for her."

Graham couldn't ascertain if Miller meant his comment as a show of support of marriage in general or McKittrick's pushing Graham in that direction. It was what Graham wanted too.

He'd gone with Erin to Charlotte last weekend and met Madison and Connor, who were in town for the wedding Madison was a bridesmaid in. Afterward, they'd gone to Kiawah, and his kids had joined them. The gathering had gone better than he hoped. Erin had also invited him to celebrate Thanksgiving with her extended family in Ohio in a few weeks.

The trip to Italy over Christmas had grown from him and Erin going to see Piper to all the kids and spouses vacationing together. They would spend three days in Rome, take the train to Naples, and end with a few days in Positano on the Amalfi Coast, staying at a villa that Chris Remington recommended to Erin. All indications pointed to Erin being ready to commit once he and Piper met in person.

"McKittrick also wanted Erin to walk away from her opportunity to work as a screenwriter for a new television series involving a Special Ops team. If her ties to the show take me out of consideration for Adams's position, so be it. I've put in papers to transfer to Fort Collins with 10th Group." Graham decided his best strategy was to shoot it straight. He wouldn't give up Erin, even for a position at the Special Warfare Center and School.

"Would her writing and this series expose any military secrets?"

"No. I've read the first several episodes. She's done thorough research and made the action believable, but there's nothing that would jeopardize our teams or missions."

"Anything that would make the Army look bad?"

"Uh," Graham hesitated. "Not the Army per se. She may contemplate using a military wife to add some drama on the home front."

Miller nodded and chuckled. "Promise me her villain's name won't be Becky or Rebecca, and I won't have her classified as a security risk. You're the man I want for this position if you're willing to leave your current command and commit to giving me at least three years."

"That wouldn't be a problem." It was beyond tempting—on all fronts.

"I know this is out of the blue, and you have teams about to deploy, but in this role, you'll continue to lead and train not only the men assigned to 3rd Group but across all of Special Forces."

Miller drove home a good point. Graham hadn't wanted 3rd Group to undergo another change of command, but he had realized he wasn't the only man who could restore trust in the unit.

"Becky liked Erin and how she treated the men under your command. My father-in-law was career Army. He did twenty-four years enlisted, so Becky's seen things from both sides. Think it over and talk with Erin. I don't need an answer immediately. Adams will be here a few more weeks."

"I would like to talk it over with her, not that there's any reason she wouldn't be on board." Other than living next door to Noelle Ayers. Noelle had apologized to Erin and him, but it wasn't like he could envision Erin and Noelle going out to lunch together. Pete had accepted a permanent change of station to Fort Drum in New York; however, that wouldn't take place until spring. "Would accepting this position involve moving into Adams's assigned housing?"

"Typically. If you want to stay in your current billet, I'm sure we could arrange that."

"A fresh start"—in their own place and with new next-door neighbors—"would be good."

Chapter Forty-Nine

"CHRIS REMINGTON WAS RIGHT. Between yesterday's cooking class and the tour you set up today, you are making this the most amazing vacation, Tommaso," Erin complimented the chef and owner of the villa where their families were staying for the last half of their Italian Christmas vacation. "This was the best meal I've *ever* eaten,"

"Happy to be of service, Signora," Tommaso beamed at the praise and glanced at Graham.

"Tommaso is a master at arranging anything his guests need and making dreams come true," his assistant promised as she helped him clear the dinner plates.

"I'm liking the perks of my mom knowing A-list celebrities," Madison said.

"I'm going to be in a food coma." Megan patted her slightly rounded belly. "I may not leave here—ever."

"He has guests coming in after us. And you'd miss me," Reece said.

"Jace is putting in for Vincenza for his next post," Alex announced, "and we can all come here again."

"I said I'd think about it," Jace said. "I'll get the cards." He got up from the table.

"They haven't even cleared the table yet. Is he always like this?" Piper asked.

"Unable to sit still or obsessed with games?" Alex laughed.

"Both," Piper laughed too.

"Pretty much," Megan answered. "Mom used to say it would have been easier if she'd had identical twins because the two Jaces could have kept each other busy. You don't know how often I had to play games or Army man so she could fix dinner."

The two families blended better than Erin imagined they would. It didn't hurt that this trip had gone off without a hitch, thanks to Graham's planning and Chris Remington connecting them with Tommaso. They may not be celebrities, but Tommaso still treated them like royalty, and a few curious paparazzi had followed the driver taking them around Positano yesterday.

Graham laid a hand over Erin's. "Let's go check out the night view while they set up the game. And have a couple of minutes alone," he added.

Outside, she drank in the sight of moonlight reflecting off the water and illuminating the boats anchored in the bay. Lights from the homes and businesses cast a golden hue over the hillside. "It's such a beautiful view."

"I agree," he said, looking at her instead of the scenery. He always managed to say the right thing to make her feel loved and cherished.

As they stood at the railing on the veranda, Graham wrapped his arms around her from behind. The kiss he pressed to the side of her head and the warmth of his body against her warded off the December chill.

"I need to bring you here in the late spring or early summer when the bougainvillea and wisteria are in bloom."

"That sounds beautiful."

"It is. Though, the next time, I'd like to bring you here as my wife. I know you said you weren't looking for anything serious, but we crossed that line long ago."

She laughed. "We certainly did. I didn't know you when I said that. Or what life could be like with you." She turned to face him. "Are you asking me to marry you?" Even a few months ago, she couldn't have imagined being ready for such a major life change.

"I am. And I already have your daughters' blessings."

"The answer is yes."

"You don't need time to think about it?" He grinned as he stared into her eyes.

"I've already thought about it. There's nothing I want more than to spend my future with you—as your wife." She would have gone to Colorado with him, but she didn't mind the longer flights between LA and North Carolina, especially with how much Graham loved the work he'd begun with his new position in the Special Warfare training group. And, of course, he was looking forward to spending time with a grand-baby and his kids.

She'd hoped he'd propose soon after meeting Piper, even on this trip so that the entire family could celebrate the news together. The timing was perfect. And so was their kiss. Their first kiss as an engaged couple sent the same flutters through her as their very first kiss.

"How would you feel about making it a destination wedding? Here."

"I'd love that, except a spring wedding here isn't going to work with Megan about to have a baby then, and I don't want to wait over a year."

"Neither do I. How about a New Year's Eve wedding?"

"Tomorrow? You're serious?" He certainly looked serious.

"It just so happens that Tommaso is ordained to officiate weddings. We'd still have to legally marry in the States, but the family is here now."

He was right. Her extended friends and family didn't need to witness their vows. Graham had quickly won over at Thanksgiving—after they got past the initial shock that she was involved with a widowed Army colonel who'd romanced her via social media. And she didn't want to wait. Or stress about a wedding. It was the marriage she wanted. "Let's do it."

"I was hoping you'd say that." He kissed her again. A kiss filled with so much promise.

"Let's tell the kids." The goosebumps on her arms were from excitement, not the cold.

Rather than sitting around the dining table shuffling cards as she expected, the kids all lingered close to the glass doors, wearing guilty and anticipatory smiles.

"She said yes," Graham told them. "And we are getting married here tomorrow." His announcement brought smiles, cheers, and applause from everyone in the room.

Tommaso peeked in, and Graham gave him a thumbs up.

"The photographer comes at two. The wedding is at three. Then we go get pictures at the best spot for the sunset." The way Tommaso rattled off the wedding day schedule talking with his hands in his Italian accent, clearly, he and Graham had been planning this. "Then we have a wedding feast. And there will be fireworks."

"Do you have a jeweler on standby for the rings too?" Erin teased.

"I've already got those taken care of," Graham said.

"It's a good thing I said yes. You all might have flipped the script on having a shotgun wedding."

"M-4 instead of shotgun," Reece deadpanned.

Megan groaned and shook her head.

"And you're not faking it because General Miller wants you married now, right?" Reece continued.

"I never had to fake anything with Erin. Well, other than the breakup," Graham stated. "Do you realize Bryson's team deploys in two weeks? We would have met McKittrick's deadline."

"I like that this is our own decision and what *we* want. And have the support of the people who matter." She took in the faces of their about-to-be-blended family.

"Send McKittrick a wedding announcement. Maybe they'll send you a gift." Jace didn't come close to sounding sincere.

"I already got my gift." Graham hugged Erin to his side and kissed her temple. "If McKittrick hadn't threatened to transfer me, we probably wouldn't have met. Maybe I *owe* him a gift."

"Instead of announcements, I'll change my Facebook status," Erin joked. "Maybe Sally will see that before we get home and tell Sean."

"You can change your status too, Dad." Megan couldn't keep a straight face.

"Maybe I will. But the only picture I'll be putting up is of me with my *wife*."

An endorphin rush flowed through Erin at the way he said the word wife while looking at her. "I can't believe that this time tomorrow, I'll be married to an Army Special Forces Colonel who I am totally in love with. And he's the real deal. I'm glad I didn't delete that friend request."

"I am too. Just promise me you won't accept any from all

those Air Force generals who want to friend you. And no Marine generals or Navy admirals either."

She laughed. "I won't."

"Army ones, either."

"Okay. But the 'Chris Remmington *Official*' account followed me on Instagram and messaged me."

"Should I be worried?" Graham's eyes narrowed playfully.

"Nah. We're already connected on his real account. I'm sure that's how they found me. This account had two m's in Remington. And don't get me started on the grammar and capitalization errors in the message."

"Fake account," Megan said, with Alex agreeing.

"Right. I sent the faker a picture of me and the real Chris Remington together before I blocked and reported the account. Besides, Chris only plays a soldier on TV." She laid a hand on Graham's chest. "I like the real deal, Colonel Graham Holmstrom." The man who would be changing his marital status—and hers—for real.

The End

DEAR READER,

Thank you for choosing *Not Faking it with the Colonel*. I hope you enjoyed Graham and Erin's story. I truly enjoyed writing these older characters and had fun incorporating my experiences as a USO volunteer and writer trying (unsuccess-fully, so far) to get a ride in a Black Hawk and to interact with a military Special Ops team to ensure my characters don't look like sissies. Reviews and ratings are very much appreciated.

Here are links to make it easier for you to leave reviews.

Amazon

Goodreads

BookBub

I hope you enjoyed seeing John and Elizabeth from _Faking it with the Green Beret_ and _Faking it with the Bachelor's_ Nate and Cecilia again. I love revisiting my prior characters and letting readers see their love continuing to grow.

If you have not yet read the tastefully steamy (aka – there are sex scenes) Bad Karma Special Ops romantic suspense series, you can start with _Desperate Choices_, the prequel novella to the series. Then read _Deadly Aim_, _A Shot Worth Taking_, and _In the Wrong Sights_. You can also get my novel-ette, _Undercover Angel_, which is Tony and Angela's backstory FREE by subscribing to my newsletter.

Subscribe to my newsletter or social media to get updates of what's coming and when. Next is a short in the _Fake it Til We Make It Romance Collection_ with Green Beret Sebastían "Bash" Cruz.

Happy reading.

Also by Tracy Brody

Sweet with some heat romantic comedies

Faking It Series

Faking it with the Bachelor

Faking it with the Green Beret

Not Faking it with the Colonel

Tastefully steamy romantic suspense

Bad Karma Special Ops Series

Desperate Choices (Prequel Novella)

Deadly Aim

A Shot Worth Taking

In the Wrong Sights

Free Newsletter Subscriber Exclusive

Undercover Angel

Faking It Series

Sweet (with some heat) Romantic Comedies

Also by Tracy Brody
Available Now!

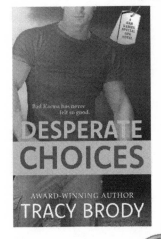

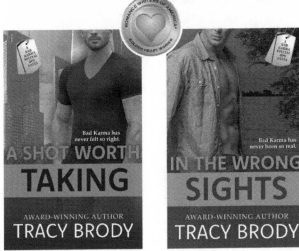

Acknowledgments

You might have picked up through this story that I am not a fan of those fakers impersonating real military officers, usually retired generals, on social media. However, they get a thank you all for the inspiration for this story. But, no, I will not send you a Friend request. Sadly, I have heard of people falling for these fakers and if this book prevents some vulnerable person from sending money to a faker, I'll be happy. If you know of someone who might be taken advantage of by those accounts, give them a copy of this book and they can have a book boyfriend instead.

Thank you to the real military personnel I've met while volunteering at the USO and offered to try and help me in my quest to get a ride in a Black Hawk helicopter or observe a Special Ops team. I haven't given up yet and you served as inspiration for this story too—even if I poke a little fun at you.

Thank you to the USO staff and volunteers for all you do to support our troops and their families. It's been a blessing to be a volunteer for the past seventeen years and counting. If any readers would like to donate to support troops and veterans through the USO, click here for a link or mail checks to: USO NC Charlotte Center, 5501 Josh Birmingham Parkway, Box 29, Charlotte, NC 28208.

As always, a shout out to MSG Dale Simpson (US Army Ret.) for continuing to answer my calls, texts, and questions about military balls and housing this go-round. I appreciate you and your sense of humor. Whatcha wearing?

To my incredible writer friends Jeanne Oates Estridge and Paula Huffman, thank you for your time and honesty and trusting that I'll put on my big girl panties and make the story better seeing things from your perspectives and making me add conflict and have my characters grow and change.

Thank you to Laura for your fabulous job with developmental insights and copy edits, especially since I have yet to score over 97% on comma usage. I'm trying!

Thank you to Sarah Paige for the lovely cover of my swoony hero and his arm porn.

Thank you to our Armed Forces and their families for serving and sacrificing. You're my inspiration and heroes. And a shout out of thanks to Gregory and Cindy Nishiyama for supporting Home for the Troops and your generosity in bidding on my contribution in the auction. It was fun working with you to develop your characters and I hope are happy with their portrayal and roles in the story.

Lastly, much thanks and love to my family for their support and patience, allowing me to do what I love.

If any of you readers are game players and want the rules for the game my family knows as Generic you can <u>get the rules sheet on my website</u> under bonus materials.

About the Author

Tracy Brody has a background in banking, retired to become a domestic engineer, and aims to supplement her husband's retirement using her overactive imagination. She began writing spec movie and TV scripts, however, when two friends gave her the same feedback on a script, saying that they'd love to see it as a book, she didn't need to be hit over the head with a literal 2" x 4" to get the message.

She's written a series of single-title romances featuring the Bad Karma Special Ops team whose love lives are as dangerous as their missions. She is currently using her sense of humor to write romantic comedies in the Faking It series and has enough ideas to keep her busy writing for decades.

Tracy and her husband live in North Carolina. She's the proud mother of a daughter and son and now a mother-in-law. She invokes her sense of humor while volunteering at the USO. You may spot her dancing in the grocery story aisles or talking to herself as she plots books and scenes while walking in her neighborhood, the park, or at the beach on retreats with friends.

Join her Private Reader Facebook Group: Tracy's SF Team!

Sign up for her newsletter at https://www.tracy brody.com/newsletter-signup if you'd like to hear more about upcoming projects. Free exclusive content including the behind closed doors scenes.

There's also *Undercover Angel*, the back story of when Tony Vincenti of the Bad Karma Special Ops team and FBI Special Agent Angela Hoffman first worked together.

Her website is: https://www.tracybrody.com/

You can find her on social media at the links below. She's mostly on Facebook which is where the majority of the fake accounts unsuccessfully attempt to engage her.

You can connect with her on:

https://www.facebook.com/tracybrodyauthor
https://www.TikTok.com/tracybrodybooks
https://www.instagram.com/tracybrodybooks/
https://www.goodreads.com/tracybrodybooks
https://www.tracybrody.com/
https://www.bookbub.com/authors/tracy-brody
https://www.amazon.com/Tracy-Brody/e/B083G9NHTL
https://twitter.com/TracyBrodyBooks